SEASIDE
Nights

Seaside Summers, Book Five

Love in Bloom Series

Melissa Foster

ISBN-13: 978-1-941480-19-9
ISBN-10: 1941480195

Cover Design: Natasha Brown

WORLD LITERARY PRESS
PRINTED IN THE UNITED STATES OF AMERICA

A Note to Readers

For those of you who have followed the Seaside Summers series, you know that Sky is our creative bohemian gal who believes in being guided by the universe and is sure that one day, love will simply find her—that is, if she can ever get out from under her overprotective brothers' thumbs. She's as tough as she is sensitive. How could I not match her up with sinfully sexy Sawyer Bass, a professional boxer waging his own emotional battle? There's no ignoring the heat between them from the moment they meet, and boy did they need to find each other! Together they discover what hope, redemption, and love really mean. I hope you enjoy their story just as much as I do.

If this is your first Love in Bloom novel, then you have many other characters to fall in love with, starting with the Snow Sisters, then moving on to the Bradens, the Remingtons, and the rest of the Seaside Summers gang. Characters from each subseries appear in future Love in Bloom novels. Each book may be enjoyed as a stand-alone novel, but for more enjoyment, read the whole series!

You can find a family tree and series checklists on the Reader Goodies page of my website, and you might find the Love in Bloom Series Guide a helpful tool in keeping track of the family and character growth through the series. http://www.melissafoster.com/reader-goodies

Be sure to sign up for my newsletter to be notified of my next Love in Bloom release, giveaways, and special events!
http://www.melissafoster.com/newsletter

Happy reading!
Melissa

Chapter One

"I CAN'T BELIEVE in a few short weeks the apartment *and* the tattoo shop will be completely renovated. Blue, you're amazing!" Sky Lacroux shoved her favorite poetry book into her patchwork purse and locked the front doors of her shop. She waited for a few people to pass before stepping back on the busy sidewalk to admire it. She still had to paint the exterior and the sign above the door and wait for the interior renovations to be done, but as she took in the narrow building she now owned, pride swelled inside her chest.

Inky Skies was located on Commercial Street, the busiest street in the artsy community of Provincetown, Massachusetts. It was sandwiched between her friend Lizzie Barber's flower shop, P-town Petals, which was painted light blue with flowers and greenery climbing up the columns out front, and the bright purple game store, Puzzle Me This. Sky planned on painting Inky Skies bright yellow, and as Blue Ryder, one of her best friends, threw his arm around her and dragged her away from the shop, she felt like she was walking on a cloud. Now, if only the universe would magically step in and find her the perfect man to share her joy with.

Yeah, right. Like that was going to happen in a primarily gay and lesbian community, especially with the way she worked all the time. *Not likely.* Her brother Hunter fell into step on her other side. *Definitely not likely with these two guarding me closer than Fort Knox.*

"Are you still planning a big grand opening, even though the shop has been open since you bought it?" Blue asked. He'd been one of Sky's best friends since she'd moved back to the Cape from New York three summers ago, to run her father's hardware store while he went into rehab to deal with an alcohol addiction. Thankfully, her father had remained sober after rehab and was back to running his store, which had enabled Sky to move out and fulfill her dream of opening her own tattoo shop. Two months earlier she'd purchased the tattoo shop where she'd been working part-time, and Blue, a specialty builder, was renovating both the shop and the apartment above it for her.

"Hell, yes, I am. It doesn't matter that it's been open during renovations. I still need to celebrate Inky Skies—my dream, my passion, my..."

Blue groaned, and Sky laughed and poked him in the side as they crossed at the corner on their way to meet their friends.

"And you're both coming," she said. "Like it or not."

"I wouldn't miss it for the world. I'm proud of you, sis." Hunter put a hand on Sky's forearm as they came to a curb and a bike whipped past.

"Hunter, I know how to stop at a curb, thank you very much." She rolled her eyes at her protective older brother.

She was used to being watched over, considering her four older brothers—and her slightly overprotective friend, Blue—had been doing it for years, but at twenty-six, with a new business and a new apartment, she was ready to spread her wings.

"Hey, just keepin' you safe." Hunter kept his dark hair shaved close to his head, and with his dark eyes and bulky muscles, he had an edge to him, but the playful grin he flashed softened all of that edginess, revealing the bighearted brother Sky adored.

"Hey, sugar!" A friendly drag queen, who went by Marcus during the day and Maxine when he performed, waved from across the street. He'd lost his lover, Howie, to cancer a couple of years ago, and as much as Sky wished he'd fall in love again, she knew from the look in Marcus's eyes when he spoke of Howie that what they'd shared was a once-in-a-lifetime type of love.

Ever since four of her friends had gotten married last summer, she longed to experience that kind of love, too.

"Hi, Marcus," Sky called. "No show tonight?" During the day, families came to shop, sightsee, and enjoy street performers, but at night, P-town turned into a colorful world of drag queens, dance clubs, and comedians.

"My night off." Marcus said something that made the man he was with laugh. Then he hollered, "I see you have your bodyguards with you again. Hey, Blue.

Hi, Hunter. When you get tired of watching over Sky, come watch over me."

Blue laughed. "You couldn't handle me, bro."

"Doesn't mean I wouldn't want to try," Marcus teased.

Blue was straight as an arrow, but Marcus loved to tease him. Sky had quickly fallen in love with the whole community when she'd begun working at the tattoo shop. It might not be conducive to meeting a guy she'd want to actually spend time getting to know in a romantic sense—it had been forever since she'd met a guy like that—but she loved the diversity of the area and the warmth of the people. Provincetown felt like home.

They weaved through throngs of people toward a crowd gathered outside of the Governor Bradford Restaurant, where Blue had handled renovations last year. At six two and six three, with linebacker shoulders and movie-star good looks, it was easy for Hunter and Blue to part the crowd as they guided Sky inside. Governor Bradford's was dimly lit, with a bar to the left, a small stage and dance floor across from the entrance, and a restaurant area to the right of the stage. The scent of fried foods and sage hung in the air.

She followed Blue around the dance floor, stopping at a table of bearded guys who had come into the shop earlier in the day for tattoos and leaned in to hug one of them. Sky got to know most of her customers while she tatted them up.

"Hey, guys. I hope you're going to sing for open mic night."

"Trust me, you don't wanna hear us sing," the burliest of them said with a laugh.

"Chicken," Sky teased as Blue took her hand and dragged her to the far side of the dance floor, where her sister-in-law, Jenna, and their friends Bella Grant and Amy Black were waiting for them.

"Finally." Jenna stood up to hug Sky. She was four foot eleven, with curves that rivaled Marilyn Monroe's, and at five months pregnant she looked even more voluptuous. "I see your bodyguards got you here safely."

Sky laughed. "I love your haircut!" Jenna had cut a few inches off of her long brown hair. It now hung just past her shoulders.

"Thanks. It's my summer cut," Jenna said, patting her hair.

Sky reached around Bella's burgeoning belly to hug her, then did the same with Amy. "You guys are like the beach-ball-belly twins. I can't believe you're both eight months pregnant—and that your hubbies are still letting you go to open mic night."

"They know we need our P-town nights. Besides, they're all out on Pete's boat with your dad." Bella looked at Hunter and Blue. "Why didn't you guys go?"

Hunter was busy ordering drinks from a raven-haired waitress.

"I worked late on Sky's renovations." Blue pulled out a chair for Sky.

"I'm sorry," Sky said, patting his back as she sat beside him. "But I do appreciate your hard work, and I even tried to get Lizzie to meet us tonight." She wiggled her brows. "I *tried* to hook you up. The way you and Duke were lusting after Lizzie at the wedding, I thought for sure you'd ask her out by now."

"She is hot," Hunter said, eyes locked on a group of

blond women across the bar.

Blue ran a hand through his thick dark hair and shrugged. "I've been busy."

"For a year?" Bella asked.

"She's come out with us several times over the past year," he said as he draped an arm across the back of Sky's chair.

"Yes. *Us.* I said *you* should ask her out." Sky shook her head, and a disconcerting thought hit her as the waitress brought their drinks. "Oh, God, Blue. Do you think we spend too much time together? Am I monopolizing you? Have I cockblocked you?"

"Whoa, sis." Hunter held a hand up to stop her from saying more.

"What? Guys can say it, but women can't?" Bella challenged Hunter. He held up his hands in surrender. Bella could be tough as nails or sweet as a summer breeze, and right now her gaze was hovering somewhere in between.

"No, you didn't cockblock me," Blue said with a laugh. "Have I...*blocked* you?"

Relieved, she said, "No. I've just decided that the next guy I date has to be someone who's really soulful and gets me, and around here, that's slim pickin's."

Blue raised his beer with a smirk. "Guys are not exactly soulful."

"No shit," Hunter said.

"Oh, come on. There are soulful people all around. It just takes some looking," Jenna began scanning the bar. "I'm on a manhunt for Sky."

"Okay, enough find-my-sister-a-man talk," Hunter said. "I looked at the sign-up sheet. They have a great lineup tonight. Comedians, karaoke, and see that guy over there?" He pointed to a guy sitting by himself at the bar with a guitar leaning against his leg. His dark T-shirt revealed sculpted biceps and strong forearms, and the fabric clung to the contours of his muscular chest. One arm rested casually on the arm of his chair, the other across his lap, his finger wrapped around the neck of a guitar. He had hair the color of night and thick scruff covering a strong jawline. His eyes were narrowed and locked on a group of people across the room, like he was studying them or deep in thought. Sky couldn't tell which.

"He played about two months ago, and he's amazing." Hunter glanced at his sister. "You'll love him, Sky."

"Holy mother of hotness." Jenna grabbed Bella's arm. "Where did that guy come from?"

"You're married," Amy reminded her.

"And preggers." Bella patted Jenna's belly. "Pete would kick his ass if he even looked at you." Sky's brother was a *little* protective of his wife.

"My interest is already piqued by that handsome creature," Sky said more to herself than the others.

"I don't want to hear that. I just thought you'd like his music." Hunter eyed the man across the room. "He looks a little rough, Sky. Not your hippie, earthy type."

Sky ignored her brother's evaluation. Yes, she had an earthy style and believed in fate and destiny and all things a little bit magical, but that didn't mean she couldn't ogle a hot guy who might not be her typical type.

While Bella, Amy, and Jenna talked about their plans for their babies and Blue and Hunter talked about work and women, Sky went back to checking out the dark-eyed man who hadn't so much as shifted his position.

The host announced the next karaoke singer, and they listened to a squeaky rendition of Madonna's "Like a Virgin." People danced and sang as they moved through several other moderately talented singers. Sky was about to pull out her poetry book, which was far more interesting than the singers, when the host called out, "Sawyer Bass," and the guy with the guitar rose and stretched, giving Sky an eyeful of just how hot he really was. Black biker boots carried him across the floor. His guitar strap was slung casually over one shoulder, as if he were carrying an old piece of lumber.

Blue bumped her with his elbow and handed her a napkin.

"What's that for?" she asked, eyes still on Sawyer Bass. *He even has a hot name.*

"Drool."

She snapped the napkin from his hands, unable to tear her eyes from Sawyer as he sank onto a stool in the middle of the stage—which looked way too small for a man of his size. He was completely relaxed, shoulders and jaw soft, eyes downcast, as if sitting in front of a roomful of people was something he did every night. He rolled his thick shoulders back and cracked his neck to either side, which for some reason amped up his sexiness.

Sawyer lifted dark eyes to the crowd, scanning everything and somehow looking as though he were seeing nothing at all. His eyes skimmed over Sky, and for a beat she held her breath, but he quickly moved on, and she couldn't help but feel disappointed.

"This guy's got serious mojo." Bella's eyes moved

around the room. "Half the women's eyes are on him. Hell, most of the guys are staring at him, too."

Sky sipped her drink and looked away from the guy who held everyone's attention. She reached into her purse and pulled out her C. J. Moon poetry book. Better to concentrate on something she enjoyed than to gawk at a guy everyone wanted. He probably wasn't laid-back anyway. He was probably playing it cool, the way guys did when they knew they were hot stuff.

"You're not really going to read, are you?" Blue put his arm across the back of her chair again and pulled her in closer.

"She's *mooning* again," Jenna teased. "Blue, take that away from her. She'll never meet a guy if she's *mooning*." Jenna always teased her about *mooning* over C. J. Moon's poems.

Blue leaned closer to Sky. "You seem a little out of sorts. Is it the renovations? They shouldn't take much longer."

Sky was renting a cottage from Amy down at the Seaside community, where Bella, Jenna, and Amy all lived. Blue had found a leak in the apartment pipes a few weeks ago, and it seemed easier for her to rent there rather than be in his way on a daily basis. She loved staying at Seaside, and she loved Blue for caring enough to ask.

"You really are a great friend, Blue. It's not that. You're doing a great job. I don't know what it is."

Sky dropped her eyes to the book and began to read her favorite poem.

A moment later, a deep, impassioned voice filled the room, bringing Sky's eyes up to the man it had come from. Sawyer sat on the stool, eyes closed, strumming his guitar and singing with an intensity that sent a shiver of seduction rippling through the room. Sky watched his fingers move confidently over the strings. His brows knitted together on the longer notes, he bowed his head as the words turned sad, and the muscles in his neck grew thicker. Passion poured out of him with every verse.

"What song is this?" Sky asked, the lyrics settling into her bones like a lonely ache. *Darkness isn't enough. Miles are too close. Nothing can erase you, wipe you clean, take away the pain you're leaving behind.*

"No idea," Blue answered.

"Never heard it before." Hunter's eyes were locked on a blonde across the room.

Sky shifted her gaze back to Sawyer. His voice was getting softer as he came to the end of the song, and it drew her in deeper with every second he held that note.

***

THE LAST NOTE lingered in Sawyer's lungs, weighing heavily on his heart and in his mind. He didn't want to stop strumming his guitar or open his eyes. He needed this release—to live in the center of this dusky bar, surrounded by people who didn't know him and who didn't know what had led him there. But when he'd sung his last note, he had no choice but to end the song and open his eyes to a loud round of applause. Still thinking of the meaning behind the words, he looked past the tables to the window across the front of the restaurant, which looked out over Commercial Street. People walked by outside, oblivious to the storm brewing inside him, like everyone else in this damn place.

He'd found himself looking for answers—more so in recent months as his father's illness progressed. And in that moment, as the crowd clapped, he conjured up the image of his father's face from his childhood, before the remnants of the war had claimed him. His lips curved up at the memory of his father's bright eyes smiling upon him—that was the part he still couldn't accept. He'd never again see his father smile. Parkinson's had stolen so much of his father's abilities to be the man he once was, it seemed unreal to Sawyer. Even though the illness had taken root several years earlier, the loss of those pieces of his father that he'd taken for granted for so long still haunted Sawyer on a daily basis. And now, looking at his father was like looking into a mirror of what his future might hold. Sawyer was running from that truth, trying to dodge it like a bullet, because it wasn't Agent Orange that might steal Sawyer's cognition like a thief in the night. Sawyer's fate wasn't being driven by the country he served. Sawyer's nemesis was the one thing that he'd lived and breathed since he was thirteen years old. It was his chosen career.

Sawyer had boxed competitively since he was eighteen. He was a formidable competitor, a monster in the ring, and boxing was the perfect outlet for his anger toward the disease that was stealing more of the man he loved each and every day. Boxing had not only been his emotional savior on too many occasions to count, but now it was going to be his parents' financial savior as well. Sawyer was challenging the current Northeast Boxing Association champion for the title, and the match carried a seven-hundred-thousand-dollar purse—enough money to pay for in-home health care for his father for the next thirty years. That goal kept Sawyer training harder than ever before and had him even more fiercely determined to win.

After a grueling training session for his upcoming title fight, he'd gone to see Dr. Malen, his physician, for his quarterly checkup. Damn doctors. They were always covering their asses, warning about worst-case scenarios. *Brains weren't meant to take beatings*, the doc had told him. He'd painted the grimmest picture— one or two more blows and Sawyer could sustain permanent brain damage. Sure, he'd had a few concussions, but didn't every fighter? They'd been giving him the same warning since he was a teenager, and he knew from his boxing buddies that they'd all received similar warnings, too. But this time the doc told him something that he'd never said before—*Think about it. This is your future. You've only got one.*

How could one sentence pack more power than an uppercut to the jaw?

Even if the doc was right, how was he supposed to decide between ensuring his father's financial future and well-being and his own?

As the applause died down, Sawyer pushed those agonizing thoughts aside. He was invincible. Too good of a fighter to end up with a head injury. He looked out at the crowd and held up a hand in gratitude as he rose to his feet. His eyes shifted to the dark-haired beauty sitting off to his left. He'd seen her looking at him from across the room earlier, and now her eyes were on him again even though the guy beside her had his arm around her. Sawyer disliked people who disrespected those who cared for them and to do it in plain sight rubbed him the wrong way. But something in the way she was looking at him made it impossible for him to look away.

The exotic-looking woman with olive skin and long, windblown dark hair intrigued him. So much so that words sailed through his mind—*languid, peaceful, wounded.* Words were as much an outlet for Sawyer as boxing was. He poured his emotions into songs, scribbling them on whatever he could get his hands on when the feeling hit. And now, as he drank in her mismatched necklaces, the word *enchanting* sounded in his mind. She had the look and presence of someone who was comfortable in her own skin, and that was something Sawyer had always been attracted to. In a few short seconds, he took in her almond-shaped eyes, the slight uptilt to her nose, and the sweet bow of her lips. He'd been watching her for only a few seconds, though it felt like several minutes had passed, and her eyes were now focused on a book, making him even more curious. Who read a book at open mic night?

Sawyer felt his muse pulling, taunting, vying for his attention, and the songwriter in him began putting a song about the woman together in his mind.

He'd come to the bar tonight because life was pressing in on him and he'd desperately needed to get out of his own head. The song he'd just played had practically exploded from his fingertips earlier in the evening, and the longer he'd played it in his house on the dunes, the worse the ache that had accompanied it had become. He'd moved outside, but even the sounds of the bay, which usually soothed the chaos in his mind, were no match for the doctor's warning and the other pressures whirling around inside him.

Being out tonight should have calmed his thoughts, but now his mind was racing again. Only this time, bits and pieces of the beautiful woman's fictional life were tumbling into verses he *had* to write.

He picked up his guitar and headed to the bar as the host announced the next act. Sawyer pulled a pen from his shirt pocket, grabbed a stack of napkins, and climbed atop a barstool to let the words flow.

Chapter Two

SKY CONCENTRATED ON tattooing the Gothic font that the girl lying on her table had chosen for the line she'd found scribbled on a piece of paper and *had* to have etched into her skin. *In your eyes I found myself.* Sky had done all sorts of tattoos over the last few years, and some of the most beautiful were the lines of text that people found lying around Provincetown, like this one. Obviously someone hadn't been careful with their poetry to continually leave pieces all over town. Customers came in with poetic lines written on napkins, crumpled receipts, and one girl even had a picture of something written in the sand. Of all the tattoos Sky had done, it was the sayings that touched her the deepest.

She thought about the song Sawyer Bass had sung last night, of the passion in his voice. Each word sounded as if it had been drawn straight from the blood in his veins. *Darkness isn't enough. Miles are too close. Nothing can erase you, wipe you clean, take away the pain you left behind.* The way he'd closed his eyes during the entire song made her wonder if he was hoping the words would wipe his memories clean or bring back whomever he was singing about. A woman, she imagined.

She'd watched his eyes before he'd left the stage. He didn't look to see who was watching him or try to catch the eyes of the prettiest girls. For a brief moment he'd looked as if he wasn't seeing anything at all. And then his eyes had shifted to her, and she'd quickly averted her gaze back to her poetry book. She wondered what he'd seen when he'd looked at her. Sky was a free spirit, and she'd learned over the years to love herself for who she was, rather than comparing herself to others. She rarely gave too much importance to what people thought about her, but something about his voice, his eyes, and the song he'd sung had spoken to her, and she wondered...Did he see what she felt? That the girl who used to be happy to go to open mic night and sing and dance with anyone who asked had taken some strange turn over the last year, seeking something more? Or did he see the girl she'd been? Or someone different altogether? She'd changed so much over the last few months—finally spreading her wings, moving out from her brothers' houses, where she was living to save money while she ran her father's shop, and finally buying her own shop. She'd also noticed other changes in herself, like a feeling of restlessness. Loneliness? She didn't think so, but maybe. Seeing her best friends fall in love, get married, and now start their families had definitely affected her.

How could someone with so many friends be

lonely?

She let that thought fall away to focus on the tattoo again, taking comfort in the hum of the tattoo gun and the beauty of each line she created. When she finished, she cleaned up the customer's newly inked area and helped the raven-haired girl off the table.

"I think I saw you the other night. Do you work at the Governor Bradford's?"

"Yeah, nights. Did I wait on you? I usually remember my customers, but I don't remember you."

"Yes, but I didn't order. My brother did—as he checked you out, of course."

"Really? Well, if he's as hot as you are pretty, maybe I'll have to look for him next time." She laughed. "Thank you so much for fitting me in for the tattoo. My name's Cree, by the way. Well, it's Lucretia, but everyone calls me Cree. I'll definitely be back." She followed Sky to the register. "Can I throw this in your trash?"

"Sure. I'm Sky, by the way."

"Sky, as in Inky Skies. Love it."

She handed Sky the paper that had the tattoo written on it. Sky set it in a basket, where she'd been keeping the tattoos that had spoken to her since she started working for the previous owner. She kept passages written on slips of papers, receipts, and napkins. She'd begun thinking of whoever had written them as the *P-town poet*. Shouldn't a poet be more careful with his or her poems? Was the poet some type of bohemian who *meant* to leave a few lines around town? They weren't ever full poems, just snippets found in odd places like restaurants, bars, and in one case, in the sand.

"That's seventy even," she said to Cree.

Sky moved her poetry book to the other side of the register as Lizzie popped her head in the front door, looking cute in a pink miniskirt and white tank top. Her hair was pinned up in a high ponytail. "Hey, Sky. Lunch?"

Sky looked up from the register. "Can't, sorry. I have some painting to do, and I want to organize the back room."

"Okay, no worries." Lizzie waved as Sky gave Cree her change.

After Cree left, Sky went to clean up her workstation, thinking about the grand opening celebration. She still had several weeks before the celebration, but she had a list of people to talk to about it. She envisioned music and balloons, a festive event.

"Excuse me?"

A shiver ran down her back at the sound of the familiar deep voice she'd heard in her dreams last night. She turned and found Sawyer Bass standing just inside the front door, wearing a pair of faded jeans and a white T-shirt and looking even more striking—*rugged, manly*—than he had last night. She tried to fit Hunter's description—*rough*—to the man, but he had a warm and friendly smile that reached his dark eyes and softened all those hard elements. No wonder his eyes had caught her interest. They were deep-set, with lashes so lush they looked lined and mysterious, and held the shiny darkness of obsidian rock. He closed the distance between them while Sky tried to find her voice.

"Hi," he said casually. Then his gorgeous eyes widened with surprise. "I saw you at Governor

Bradford's last night, right? With your boyfriend? You were reading."

Sky set down the towel she was using to wipe the table, trying to quiet the thoughts running through her mind. *You're even hotter in the daylight. Look at those abs pressing against your shirt. Wait. What did you ask me? Governor Bradford's, right.*

"Yes. No. I mean, I was there, but I wasn't with my boyfriend. I don't have a boyfriend." *Ramble much?* Her brain refused to fire properly, which was stupid, because she saw good-looking people every day in the shop. This guy shouldn't throw her off her game like this. Why did he make her feel like she had a mouth full of nails? He fidgeted with something in his hand, appearing slightly nervous himself, which made her feel a little better.

Which was also stupid.

"My mistake. The way you were sitting, I just assumed..." He glanced around the shop.

"The bane of my existence. Being overprotected." Maybe Blue and Hunter did cockblock her after all.

"I'm sorry. That's none of my business." He held her stare, and there was no mistaking the spark of interest in his eyes. "I'd like to get a tattoo."

"Sure. Come on back. What did you have in mind?" She led him to her workstation, hoping he wanted a tattoo on his forearm, because if he wanted it on any other part of his body, it would be way too hard for her to concentrate.

His eyes slid over the back of the shop. Inky Skies was small and still a little gritty while the renovations were being done. Sky had tried to liven it up, covering the scuffs in the walls with scarves and pictures, and she'd put up folding screens in the back of the room to mask the unfinished shelves that ran across the back wall. She had even draped a few of her colorful scarves over the black panels of the screens, giving the area the look of a makeshift dressing room, like they had in the Himalayan shop around the corner. She liked the comfortable look of it, even if it wasn't yet ideal.

Sawyer's gaze returned to Sky, and her pulse quickened. He handed her a slip of paper, then reached over his back and pulled his shirt off. Sky's mouth went dry at the sight of his muscular pecs, ripped abs, and those incredibly sexy muscles that made a perfect vee and disappeared down the front of his pants. She loved creating tattoos, but the idea of putting anything other than her hands or mouth on his gorgeous body made her almost as weak in the knees as the idea of putting her hands or mouth on him did.

"This is what I'd like." He handed her a slip of paper and pointed his thumb at the chair behind him. "Is that where I should sit?"

She blinked away her stupor. "Yes. Where do you want the tattoo?"

"On my back. Anywhere you can fit it is fine."

Sky dropped her eyes as she unfolded the paper to look at the design. It wasn't a design at all, but words. *Liquid to dust, shattered not broken.* What was it about this place that brought all of these random phrases into her shop? She heard him sitting in the chair and lifted her eyes. He was straddling the chair, leaning on his arms, which were crossed over the back of it. His back was covered with words, from the ridge of his shoulders to the waist of his jeans. It was the most beautiful sight she'd ever seen—such passion inked into the sculpted contours of his smooth skin. Words arched across his scapula and stretched over his flanks. Sky had tattooed all sorts of body parts, and she'd seen tattoos that ran the gamut from sweet to gruesome. To each his own had always been her motto. But this...The mixture of harsh and tender words on such a powerful man momentarily stole her ability to function.

Without any forethought, she reached out and touched his skin. It was hot and smooth. Flawless, save for the inked words. Her eyes slid slowly over the words: *Fluid like the wind, hard as stone. Unconditional. Stolen. Transparent.* What did these words mean to him? Down his spine words were strung together like a ladder, the taller letters touching the ones above, tying them together. *Lies, rage, tenderness, alone, forever, fragile—*

He looked over his shoulder, his eyes heavy, as if he were tired, and a smile on his lips, softening the sharp edge of his darkly whiskered jaw.

"Wherever you can fit it in. I'm not picky."

She looked down at the paper he'd given her and read the words again. "Where did you get this?" She had to know if he was the one leaving things like this all over Provincetown.

He shrugged and looked away again, his voice going cold. "Picked it up somewhere."

She was surprised when disappointment washed through her. After hearing him sing, seeing his back, and seeing the P-town poet's signature scrap of paper, she thought maybe she'd solved the mystery. She pulled up her stool and looked more carefully at his back, noticing the different sizes and fonts. Now that the awe had worn off a bit, she saw that there was plenty of room for her to fit these, and many more words, if he so desired.

"Do you have tattoos only on your back?" she asked.

He turned and looked at her again, his eyes darker, more sensual, sending a surprising rush of heat through her. "Only those that tread the landscape get to find that out."

Yes, please. "Oh...Sorry." She picked up her tattoo gun to give herself something to focus on besides *that* before trying to respond again, then managed, "Do you have a font in mind?"

"You pick." His thick dark brows knitted together. Then he turned away, leaned his cheek on his forearm, and closed his eyes, as if he hadn't made her hot, then flustered, then hot all over again.

She was used to clients allowing her to choose fonts and even designs, but she had so many more questions for him. She tried to tamp them down as she moved closer, spreading her legs so his hip was between them, allowing her to lean in closer with the hopes of her hand remaining steady.

"Don't you have to make a copy of the words or something, then transfer that to my back?"

"I'm a freehand artist. Unless you want me to use a guide?"

"No. Freehand's better, actually." His eyes opened and rolled down her body again. "You must be really good with your hands."

Wanna find out? Holy crap!

"I'd like to think so." She was not normally the type of girl who thought about touching and *finding out* things with guys she didn't know. Sawyer was making her mind go in ten different directions, and she needed to get a grip before her sexy thoughts came streaming from her lips.

She was thankful when he rested his hand on his arms again and closed his eyes, allowing her racing pulse to settle. She looked over his back for the right place for the tattoo, forcing her mind into artist mode. *He's a canvas. A very delicious-looking canvas.*

"Between your shoulder blades okay? With a script font? I want to soften the words, unless you want me to go the other way—blocky or Gothic?"

"Softening is good, and like I said, wherever you think you can fit them is fine."

She cleaned the area between his shoulder blades. "I haven't seen you around. Where did you have these other tats done?"

"Different places around New York, Boston, Hyannis..."

She wanted to ask if he traveled often, but she resisted the urge, not wanting to become any more distracted by him than she already was.

"I'm going to start, okay?" She watched his back lift with a long inhalation, and when he exhaled all his muscles relaxed.

"Okay," he said in a soft tone. "How long have you been tattooing?"

She concentrated on the tattoo as she answered. "Several years. I love all kinds of art. And music, actually. I really liked the song you sang last night. Did you write it?"

He didn't answer for so long that she wondered if he was going to. He finally said, "Yes."

"It was beautiful. Are you a songwriter?" *Way to keep from getting distracted.*

"No."

For a man with so many words on his back, he said very few.

She worked in silence, enjoying the feel of his taut muscles beneath her hand. She knew better than to ask why people chose certain tattoos even though she was dying to know more about his word obsession. It rivaled hers, and that made him even more appealing. After she finished the third word, she sat back and took a momentary break.

"Music has always been a calming influence in my life. Do you write songs often, like a hobby, or...?"

"When inspiration hits. What about you? Do you have any hobbies?"

She thought about that as she finished the tattoo. Reading poetry. Listening to music. Hanging out with her friends. Were those hobbies?

"I guess just about everything I do is a hobby." She didn't even know if that made sense, but it felt like the truth. "I don't really consider myself a *career* anything, so even this is kind of a hobby. I'll do it until I fall out of love with it, I guess. Although I don't see that happening for a very long time."

"That makes you even more interesting. You follow your heart. That's what I do, too."

Sky melted a little right there on the stool, sitting beside Sawyer Bass, with his smooth voice, hot bod, and wordy back. It was all she could do to remember to pick up the hand mirror to show him the tattoo. She rose to her feet and reached for his hand. She had no idea why she did it and was even more stunned when he took her hand and his lips curved up in that easy smile again as he followed her to the full-length mirror in the back of the room. He turned and assessed the tattoo in the reflection of his back in the hand mirror.

"You are good with your hands," he said with a more mischievous grin.

"I guess that makes us even, since you're good with words, Sawyer."

His brows knitted together again. "You know my name?"

"Last night. They announced your name, remember?"

"Oh, right. Well, it seems I'm at a disadvantage. I don't know your name."

"Sky. Sky Lacroux." Their eyes held, and whatever had turned her brother off last night went out the door. Everything about Sawyer Bass turned her on, from the mysterious look in his eyes to the words etched in his back—and if he was rough, as Hunter assessed, then she wanted to experience it firsthand.

"That's a beautiful name." He handed her the mirror, and their fingers brushed, sending a shiver through her.

He followed her back to where he'd left his shirt and pulled it on. Sky instantly missed the sight of his flesh. At the register he picked up her book of poetry, then met her gaze again as he pulled out his credit card.

"Are you a fan of C. J. Moon?"

She laughed as she said, "I'm in *love* with C. J. Moon."

"Really?"

"Yes," she said as he ran his credit card through

25

the machine. "My friends think I need an intervention because if I could find more information on him, I'd probably track him down like the worst kind of fangirl there is."

He cocked a brow. "Ah, so you're a stalker?"

"Of the worst kind," Blue said as he came through the door. "She's got a serious ice cream addiction, too." He held out a hand in greeting. "Sawyer Bass, right? We saw you play last night. Did she stalk you and trick you into coming here? Or are you stalking her? I only caught the *stalker* part as I came through the door."

Sky rolled her eyes.

"Nice to meet you, Blue. You're *not* the boyfriend, right?" Sawyer smiled as he shook his hand.

"I see we've already cleared up our relationship status." Blue eyed Sky with a look that clearly said, *I knew you were hot for him.* "Friends without benefits—beyond a place to crash, that is. Oh, and kitty delivery service. Merlin's upstairs."

"Thanks, Blue. You're a savior." She answered Sawyer's wrinkled brow with, "Merlin is my cat. He was at the groomer's this afternoon, and Blue picked him up for me."

"That was nice of him," Sawyer said. "If you're really interested in knowing more about C. J. Moon, I'd be happy to take you over to one of the places he wrote about. How late do you work tonight?"

Tonight?

Two of the best-looking guys in Provincetown were looking at her. One was drinking her in like she was delectable enough to eat, and the other had an I-told-you-so grin across his face. God help her, because right at that moment she wanted to hug Blue and say,

You were right! then jump into Sawyer's arms and let him see how tasty she really was. Maybe she was having some sort of hormonal episode, because she wasn't a jump-in-the-sack type of girl. She had no idea why her body felt electrified and her stomach felt like she'd swallowed a nest of wasps, other than pure, unadulterated lust.

And it had been way too long since she'd felt anything like it.

"I can take off when I'm done for the night." She flipped through her appointment book.

"You know Moon?" Blue asked.

"I have a thing for poetry," Sawyer said. "What about you? Are you a fan of his work?"

Blue held his hands up and shook his head. "No. Never read it, but I have the pleasure of watching Sky bury her nose in his books almost every day."

"If I don't get swamped," Sky interjected, "I think I can close around seven."

"Great. Why don't I swing by then?"

Sky knew she was grinning like a fool and didn't care. "Sounds great."

"Well, so much for a bonfire tonight," Blue said.

"I'm sorry, Blue," Sky said, although she wasn't at all sorry about accepting a date with Sawyer. "Is that why you came by?"

"Yeah, but no biggie. You guys have fun."

"Why don't you ask Lizzie?" she asked hopefully.

Blue shook his head. "I'll call you later." He turned his attention back to Sawyer and said, "Nice to meet you. Have fun tracking down Moon's muse, and take good care of my girl."

"*Your* girl?" Sky's jaw dropped open. Blue had

never said anything like that before.

Blue smirked. "My *friend*. You know what I mean."

"Don't worry," Sawyer said. "I wouldn't dream of letting anything happen to her."

Blue turned to leave, glancing quickly over his shoulder one last time before heading out the front door as a group of twentysomethings came in. They were laughing and talking as they looked over the sample tattoos hanging on the front walls.

"You sure there's nothing between you two?" Sawyer asked. "I don't want to come between you guys. You seem pretty close."

"Of course not. We're friends. He's just being weirdly protective." Although she had no idea why.

"I guess I'm like that with my friends' sisters. I get it."

"I'm glad, because I couldn't go out with a guy who didn't understand my relationship with Blue. He's a good friend, and I'd never want to mess that up." She smiled at the people milling about in the reception area. "Can I help you guys with something?"

"We want to get inked, but we need to decide who's getting what," said a tall blond guy wearing yellow board shorts, a tight tank, and a shoulder full of colorful ink.

"Okay, just let me know when you're ready."

Sawyer held up the paper he'd brought with him. "Trash?"

She took the paper and placed it in the basket with the others.

"You keep the tats you do?"

"Just the ones that speak to me. Besides C. J. Moon and ice cream, I guess I harbor a little word obsession of my own," she admitted.

The sensual look in his eyes had returned. "That makes you even sexier. Should I pick you up here?"

"Sure," she said, or at least she thought she did. She was having trouble thinking past his compliment.

Chapter Three

FOR A WHILE Sky had made Sawyer forget about the warning from his doctor, but when he'd arrived back home and seen the renovations he was making to accommodate his father's cane—and one day his wheelchair—the thunder rolled back in. He worked out on his heavy bag, and when that didn't calm the storm in his mind, he'd gone down to the beach to do yoga. He didn't have time for storms or doctors' warnings. He was going to win this title fight. His father's future depended on it.

The combination of working out and yoga helped. Two hours later Sawyer drove into Provincetown no longer thinking of anything but Sky. Honesty was right up there with loyalty in his book, and he hated to mislead her and her friend Blue about his knowing C. J. Moon, but his father had protected his pen name ever since he'd first published, and it wasn't Sawyer's place to reveal his true identity. *Not even for beautiful Sky Lacroux.*

He'd never dated a woman who was interested in poetry or songwriting before. Neither of which were topics that came up when he was boxing or on the rare occasion that he was out at a club—*unless you're Sky, who reads poetry in a bar on open mic night.*

He smiled as the image of Sky reading in the club sailed through his mind. She'd looked so at ease reading while everyone around her was immersed in conversation. He wanted to get to know her better, see what went on in that beautiful head of hers.

He parked at the pier and walked through town toward Sky's shop. He hadn't known that she worked at Inky Skies when he'd gone looking for a tattoo shop. He'd simply had the urge to get inked, and Inky Skies had been the closest place around. And he was damn glad he'd wandered in, after thoughts of Sky had kept him up all night penning a song. Verse after verse had formed and shifted in his mind, making his fingers twitch until he'd dragged himself from bed to the third-story room that overlooked the bay and penned more of the song he'd started writing at the bar—and was now running through his mind.

She moved like the wind. Every gust a melody. Eyes of umber, heart of gold. Who was she, but a little lost soul. And now the song had a name, "Sweet Summer Sky."

Like many of the shops on Commercial Street, the doors to Inky Skies were propped open. But while the other shops were overpowered by scents of patchouli and sage, the scent of jasmine and coconut greeted him at the entrance to Sky's shop. He'd been so surprised to see Sky that everything else he'd seen earlier was blurry. Now he took a moment to look around. The reception area was cozy, with a worn leather couch, two overstuffed chairs, and a coffee table, as if she were hosting a gathering instead of inking people's skin. The walls were covered with pictures of tattoos and a few watercolor paintings that he recognized as locations around Provincetown. He wondered if Sky had painted them. Also hanging from the walls were colorful scarves and a few necklaces with a handwritten sign above them that read, ASK SKY ABOUT ME!

He stood by the register, running his finger over Sky's poetry book, and called into the back room, "Hello?"

He walked to the edge of the reception counter and called out again, admiring the iron railing to his right—the kind that belonged on the front porch of a 1970s-style house. It might look out of place anywhere else, but there were glass beads and tiny lights wound around the railing, giving it a festive glow and somehow making it fit right in with the eclectic little shop. The walls in the work area were painted pastel peach, accented with wine-colored molding. They were faded, as if they hadn't been freshened up in decades.

He'd been so focused on not staring at Sky's full lips and alluring eyes earlier that he'd failed to notice the incredibly detailed sculpture by her work area. A sturdy steel sculpture of the moon and stars sat atop a counter, with a metal vine wrapped around the moon leading up to the stars. It was a unique sculpture that reminded him of Sky. It was ethereal and beautiful.

Hanging from the ceiling were various wind chimes made of glass and wood. He'd also somehow

33

missed the artsy screens with scarves hanging over the top in the back of the room. He wondered how many people undressed for their tattoos—which made him wonder about what body parts Sky had tattooed. The idea of her seeing guys undressed and tattooing them in private places made his gut twist.

He reached up and touched a glass chime, sending a soft serenade into the room, as hanging beads in a doorframe off to the left in the back of the store parted and Sky appeared. She flashed her gorgeous smile. She had changed from the outfit she'd had on earlier. His breath caught in his throat as he took in her oversized green shirt, which she wore open with a cream-colored shirt beneath that hugged her curves and stopped just short of her cutoffs—revealing a sliver of skin that made Sawyer's mouth water. Her chunky amber necklace matched her knee-high suede boots, and as if that outfit alone wasn't enough to send his body into a frenzy, she'd lined her seductive eyes with makeup, which gave her a dark and innocent appearance at once. It took all his efforts to resist taking her in his arms and kissing the innocence out of her right then and there.

He'd been with plenty of women, but never before had the mere sight of someone made his body simmer.

"Hi," she said as she came to his side. "Sorry. I was just locking the back door."

He leaned in and kissed her cheek. "Hi. You look stunning."

She glanced down at her outfit, wrinkling her nose adorably. "Really?"

"Stunning doesn't even come close to what I really wanted to say. But I'm pretty sure that telling you those boots make your legs look a mile long, and those skimpy little shorts bring all sorts of titillating ideas to mind wouldn't be appropriate on a first date."

Where the hell did that come from?

Her cheeks flamed, and a sweet laugh escaped her lips. "Jeez, Sawyer. Don't feel like you need to hold back or anything."

He scrubbed a hand down his face, hoping he hadn't just screwed up their date.

"I'm sorry, Sky. I never say stuff like that, and I don't know where it came from. I'm really not a pig. Honestly. I just...You're..." He shifted his eyes away, feeling like he was sixteen again and sticking his foot in his mouth at every turn. He did the only thing he could to save face. He blurted out the truth.

"Those things were true, but don't worry, I'm not going to act on them."

"Way to squash a girl's hopes." The playful look in her eyes told him she was only half kidding.

He reached for her hand. "We should go before I get any antsier and my mouth gives me away."

"I kind of like your antsy mouth," she said as they walked outside. She locked the door behind them and tucked her keys into her purse.

"I have a feeling it's going to get me in trouble if I keep hanging out with you. I'm really not the kind of guy who thinks about sex all the time."

"All guys think about sex all the time," she said casually.

He laughed. "I'm not going to touch that comment. I'm sure I'll only get myself in trouble." He laced his fingers with hers, and they walked across Commercial Street toward the pier. It felt as natural to hold her hand as it had to blurt out his inappropriate thoughts, which was how Sawyer knew that Sky Lacroux was indeed very different from any woman he'd ever dated.

He was lucky she hadn't slapped him and canceled their date on the spot.

Sky waved to a group of men and women standing at the entrance to a nightclub as they passed by.

"Hi, sugar. Have fun," a tall man with long dark hair said, and blew her a kiss.

"We will," she called over her shoulder, then turned to Sawyer. "That's my friend Marcus."

Good to know. "I could have picked you up at your place," he said as they followed a group of people around the corner, past a pizza parlor, and across the road toward the parking lot. The scents of the sea swept over the pier.

"You kind of did," she said as he unlocked the door to his old Land Rover.

"You live at the shop?" Sawyer remembered that Blue had mentioned her cat was upstairs.

"I have an apartment above the shop, but I'm renting from my friend Amy at Seaside in Wellfleet while Blue's renovating the apartment and doing a few last-minute renovations to the shop." She climbed into the truck.

He settled into the driver's seat and drove out of the parking lot. "I wouldn't have minded picking you up in Wellfleet. We'll drive right past on the way to Brewster."

"That's okay. I wasn't sure if I'd get swamped at the last minute, so this was easier. And to be honest, I only bought the shop two months ago, so it's still a thrill to be there, knowing it's mine. I'll pick up Merlin after our date and bring him back to Seaside with me."

"Ah, you own the shop."

She smiled, and pride filled her eyes. "I do."

"That's very cool. How do you like running it?"

"It's a dream come true. I know the place still needs work, but you should have seen it before I got my hot little hands on it."

He was trying not to think about her hot little hands.

"I think it looks great. Very artsy." He ran his eyes over her outfit, which was sexy yet casual. She had a unique and appealing style. "Very you."

"Thank you. I worked there for two years before buying it from Harlow Warren, the previous owner. It was pretty unloved when I took it over. But a little elbow grease goes a long way."

As Sawyer drove down Route 6 listening to Sky and watching her facial expressions go from enthusiastic to thoughtful, to pensive, then right back to excited again, the more he liked her. She was easy to be with and not at all like the women he'd dated in the past, who were so worried about every word that left their mouths their conversations felt scripted.

"Since we'll have to hurry to get to our destination before it gets dark, and it might be an hour before we make it to dinner, I thought we should get a snack first. Is that okay?"

Thinking of her ice cream addiction, he pulled into the parking lot of the Brewster Scoop.

"I'll never turn down ice cream," she said as he parked the car.

They headed into the ice cream shop and ordered

cones. The Brewster Scoop was located behind the Brewster Store, a general store where little had changed since Sawyer was young. They still sold penny candy and homemade fudge.

"What is *our destination*, anyway?" she asked as they took their cones out front and sat on the stoop.

"I could tell you, but then it wouldn't be a surprise."

"I love surprises, and so far you're full of them."

***

SAWYER EARNED BONUS points for taking the edge off Sky's nerves. She had no idea that her daisy dukes would cause her handsome date to say things that made her blush and think about all the things *she* wanted to do to *him*. As if thinking about him all afternoon hadn't been torture enough. When Jenna had called to invite her to another bonfire—this one was going to be at their beach house tomorrow night—Sky had nearly burst with excitement telling her about their impending date. Of course Jenna had squealed so loudly that Sky'd had to pull the phone away from her ear and promise to come by the bonfire *with* him tomorrow if the date went well.

"So, I'm full of surprises, huh?" Sawyer was holding his ice cream toward her with a heated look in his eyes. "Taste?"

If only he knew that she was dying for a taste...of him and that he was the most wonderful surprise of all. She never would have guessed that while she was reading her favorite poem, she'd been listening to the man she'd be spending time with the next night.

She leaned forward and licked his ice cream, and his eyes darkened.

"Thanks," she said, licking the sweetness from her lips.

He watched her mouth intently, and her pulse quickened.

"Want to taste mine?" She tilted her cone toward him.

He leaned in close and gazed into her eyes. "What is it about you that makes me feel like a schoolboy peeking through a locker room window?" He searched her eyes, and the air between them sizzled and popped.

"Probably the same thing that makes me want you to."

A devilish grin curved his lips, and they both leaned in closer. Sky was sure he was going to kiss her—and she wanted that kiss. A taste of his sensuous mouth, to know what the scrape of his thick scruff felt like against her cheeks.

But their lips didn't touch. He placed his hand over hers, holding the ice cream cone. His hand was warm and strong, and when he dragged his tongue over the creamy cap, she practically licked it right along with him.

"Sweet," he said, still holding her gaze.

Sky lifted a trembling finger and wiped a dab of ice cream from his lip. He guided her finger into his mouth, then swirled his tongue around it, sucking the ice cream off. She couldn't breathe. Couldn't think. He was still holding her hand as her ice cream dripped over her knuckles. His eyes flamed, and she knew he was thinking about licking the ice cream from there, too, but if he did...If she felt that hot mouth of his again anywhere except on her lips, she was going to lose it.

She brought her hand to her mouth and licked the ice cream off, which only made his eyes smolder even more.

An undercurrent of sexual tension wrapped around them, drawing their bodies even closer together. His breath whispered into her mouth. "Sky..."

Her mind spun. When he slid a hand to the nape of her neck, still gazing into her eyes, silently asking for her approval, she answered him with a press of her lips to his. His lips were softer than any she'd ever kissed, pillowy and inviting. The first slide of their tongues was cold and deliciously sweet, sending shivers through her even as their kiss grew hotter. Their tongues tangled together, searching, tasting, *taking*. Despite her outward calm, her insides were racing, heating, getting all too stirred up for a first date.

She forced herself to pull back, and in the space of a second their lips came together in another tender kiss. It was sweet and languid, and too incredible to stop. The ice cream fell from her hands, and without breaking the kiss, she pressed her palms to his cheeks and deepened it. His mouth was demanding, his whiskers scratchy, and his lips—*his gloriously soft lips*—slowly slipped away.

No. Come back.

He pressed a kiss to her cheek, fisted his hand in the back of her hair, and drew her in closer again.

"Sorry," he whispered against her lips. "I really didn't intend to—"

"Uh-huh." She couldn't resist pressing her lips to his again, and just as quickly, she reluctantly retreated. "My fault," she managed. She shouldn't do this. She wasn't used to moving so fast, and yet she felt powerless to resist him.

She physically scooted away, putting a few inches between them. "Space. We need...We should...Gosh, Sawyer. I never kiss like that on a first date."

He grinned and said, "Lucky me," without missing a beat.

"Yes, but..." *I want to kiss you again and again. Would three weeks be too long of a kiss?*

A car door slammed and a little boy ran up the stoop beside Sawyer. "Look, Mommy! She dropped her cone!" His mother gave an embarrassed smile as she shooed her son inside.

Sawyer and Sky both laughed as he cleaned up the discarded cone and tossed it into the trash. He reached for her hand and they walked back to the car.

Fifteen minutes—*and a car ride full of furtive glances*—later, as the sun dipped behind the trees and the temperature cooled, they arrived at Stony Brook and parked across the street from the gristmill. Sky had been to Stony Brook many times, as it was only a few minutes from where she'd grown up. It had always been one of her favorite places, with the old stone gristmill and the babbling brook. There were elaborate gardens with romantic walking paths surrounding Stony Brook Pond by the mill across the road and a wooden bridge that arched over the water. It was about as picturesque as anything could be, and with her heart still pinging around in her chest, she had to dig deep to stop thinking about their kisses and focus on why they were there.

"How do you know that C. J. Moon wrote about the brook?" Sky asked as they walked up the grassy incline on the property across the street from the mill, toward the babbling brook.

Sawyer's eyes grew serious, as if he was wrestling with his answer.

"You don't have to tell me if it's some kind of secret." She knew from her friend Kurt Remington, a bestselling thriller writer, that writers could be covetous of their privacy, and obviously C. J. Moon went to great lengths to keep his identity a secret. She was intrigued by how Sawyer knew anything more about Moon's poems than what was online, but she was even more intrigued by his apparent conflict over sharing the hows and whys of his knowledge. She had to respect a man who honored his commitments— unless he was making the whole thing up, and this was one big farce to get into her pants.

"I knew Moon a long time ago, but the man I knew is...no longer around," he finally said as they came to the crest of the hill. The brook snaked out before them, lined by pitch pines on one side and a rocky incline on the other. Grass ran between the rocks, making them look as if they were featured in the landscape.

Sky heard sadness in Sawyer's voice and immediately disregarded her thought about his making up his friendship with C. J. Moon.

"I'm sorry. At least you had a chance to know him. He was such a talented man. He was a man, wasn't he? Online they refer to the writer as a man, but I know that sometimes that isn't the case with pen names."

He nodded, and his eyes turned thoughtful as he

led her down the hill toward the brook. The sounds of the water running over the rocks and the whispering of the leaves against the evening breeze filled the silence between them.

"Yes, he was definitely a man. A good, honest, and virile man."

"I get the sense from his work that he was all those things, as well as sensitive. He wrote such lovely and powerful poems."

"He was, Sky." He took a giant step from the grass to a rock, then turned and set his hands on her hips, steadying her as he helped her down. His touch was gentle yet strong. He gazed into her eyes with a conflicted look she didn't understand.

"Sky...Are you familiar with the poem, 'Race of the Pebble'?"

"*Her current changed beneath the light of the moon.*" She'd read the poem so many times the words flowed without thought, bringing a smile to his lips. "*Lighter, darker, narrow, shallow. Dancing in her depths. Swept up in her ecstasy. Tumbling, turning, out of control...*It's one of my favorites, because it holds true to so many things."

"That's exactly what he said when he wrote it. I was with him. I was only a kid, but I remember it like it was yesterday."

"You were with him? I can't imagine how great that must have been."

Sawyer stood on a rock beside the brook, gazing at the water as it trickled by. "It meant a great deal to me. All of our time together has." He paused, and when he met her gaze again, that conflicted look was back.

"Sky, C. J. Moon is my father."

"Your father?" She watched as sadness and pride swept over his face in a look so troubled she reached for his hand. "I don't understand. You said he was no longer around. Did he pass away?"

He shook his head. "My father is very much alive, and you're the first person I have revealed his pen name to. I'm not even sure why I did, but it felt like I was lying to you, and I know this is our first date, but I didn't want to lie to you."

"Sawyer." His name came out as a whisper. She was so touched by his confession, but the sadness that lingered in his voice made her ache.

"He has Parkinson's," Sawyer explained. "It's been really difficult and heartbreaking to watch his health decline. He hasn't written since shortly after he got his diagnosis."

Wrapping her arms around Sawyer came naturally, and even though part of her worried that the comfort might embarrass such a strong man, she couldn't stop herself. They remained like that for a long moment, with the sky turning dark above them. She felt herself opening up to the sensitive man she'd only just met.

When they finally parted, his lips curved up in an appreciative smile. She didn't push for more information about his father, and when he asked her if she was from the Cape, she knew he needed to change the subject.

"Yes. I grew up in Brewster," she answered. "How about you?"

"Hyannis, actually. If you're from Brewster, then you probably know all about how the herring run from Cape Cod Bay into Paine's Creek, then into Stony

Brook, and ultimately into Stony Brook Pond."

They began walking along the rocks again, and she stumbled.

"Careful." Sawyer caught her. His fingers tightened around her waist, and it wasn't the heat wrapping around them again that brought her closer, or the way his pupils flared. It was what she felt coming off of him in waves, something longing and real, that she recognized but couldn't name.

"My father used to take us to see the herring run in the spring."

She felt herself wanting to know more about his childhood, and to share more of herself. This was too fast. Wasn't it? How could she feel so comfortable with a guy after just a few hours? She didn't know what to do, but the heat between them was melting her brain cells a handful at a time, and he was opening up to her, trusting her with his father's true identity, and that was melting her heart at the same time. Pretty soon she'd turn to liquid and trickle away with the brook.

He laced his fingers with hers and she gave in to a smile as they fell into step beside each other again.

"I think I'm just as enamored now with how the fish run upstream as I was as a kid. I have great memories of running alongside the brook, watching the fish with my older brothers, Pete, Matt, Hunter, and Grayson."

His eyes widened as he sat down on a rock, bringing her down beside him. "You have four brothers? No sisters?"

She shook her head.

"I bet you were spoiled when you were growing up, as the only girl."

"Maybe a little, but I loved keeping up with them. At least until I was about twelve, when I started really getting into painting and drawing. My dad built me this amazing art studio in the backyard. It's a shed, really, but when you're a kid and your father respects and supports your talents enough to build you your own space? Then it feels like a mansion."

He covered her hand with his. "It sounds like you have a wonderful family. Are you all still close?"

"We are. Maybe a little too close." She laughed. "My brothers are a little protective of me."

"Like Blue?"

She laughed and shook her head. "A little worse than Blue. Kind of like lions protecting their den." She squinted, thinking about how protective they were. "Yeah, like that."

"Or like older brothers protecting their only sister?" He kissed the back of her hand. She liked that he was so affectionate with her. "It's cool. I respect that. My friend Brock has two younger sisters, and I'm probably about as protective of them as Blue is with you. But Brock? It sounds like he's more like your brothers. I think it comes with sibling territory."

"Maybe. I adore them all, even if they're protective of me. But enough about me. What about you? Do you have siblings?"

"No. It's just me and my folks. I'm close with both of them, though. They're one of the few couples who have made it through thick and thin and still managed to stay happily married. I see them often, and I told you about my dad's illness, so I stick close to home. How about your parents? Are you close?"

She dropped her gaze as a familiar pang rattled

inside her. They'd gotten so far off track from talking about the poem, but it had been a long time since she talked about anything other than frivolities that she didn't want to stop. And after hearing about his father, she felt they had even more in common, and she wanted to share that with him, too.

"My mom passed away a few years ago."

"I'm sorry." He squeezed her hand. "Were you close?"

"Very. When I was away at college we talked every week, and she'd send me the funniest cards and cookies and..." She swallowed past the thickening in her throat. "Wow. I haven't talked about our relationship in ages. I had such a hard time when she passed away, but I thought I'd moved past it. I didn't realize how emotional I still was over losing her."

Most guys would probably fidget and change the subject, but Sawyer opened his arms and gathered her in close. He pressed his hand to the back of her head without saying a word, and it was exactly what she needed. She soaked in the comfort of his embrace and the thoughtfulness of his silence.

"Thank you for understanding," she said, feeling mildly self-conscious. "I'm sorry for being so emotional."

"Don't be sorry for feeling something. That's the world's great separator—those who feel and react to their feelings and those who cower from them."

"Sawyer..." She didn't know what she wanted to say, but everything he said touched her profoundly, as if he'd climbed into her head and taken notes about the way she saw things.

"Sorry. I know I have a strange view on things." He

set his hand on her leg and shifted his eyes to the brook.

She reached for his hand. "If it's strange, then I'm strange, too, because it's exactly how I see things. I just worried that I was overwhelming you. You know..." She smiled and shrugged. "TMI and all that."

"After dealing with my father's illness, I've learned that there isn't much that can overwhelm me." He held her gaze. "And certainly not anything having to do with emotions."

She sighed with relief. "I've dated a few guys who didn't really get me." She fidgeted with the edge of her shirt. "From my choice of clothing to the way I live my life."

"How's that?" he asked.

"Kind of like your father's 'Race of the Pebble' poem, I guess. *Fluid beauty rushing, rippling. Needful and overflowing.* Not the beauty part, but feeling like I'm moving through life and accepting it as it comes, just sort of soaking it all in. I don't stress over what could be or over making a ten-year plan. I live life for now, and if I'm happy with what I'm doing and the people I'm spending my time with, then life is good. If I'm not, *then* I'll reevaluate."

He touched her cheek and said, "I know exactly what you mean, *including* the beauty part."

He gazed at her for a long moment, and she felt the warmth of him flowing through her veins—and ached for another kiss.

When he gazed back at the brook, he said, "You know how the herring are thick when they run upstream and they churn the brook as they jump the concrete steps toward the pond?"

There was something so soothing about his voice that it quieted Sky's desire for that kiss, filling another part of her—a part she couldn't pinpoint and hadn't realized was also longing to be touched.

"When my father was penning that poem, he said to me, *Son*—he always calls me that, never calls me by name—*see more than others see. Be more than others are. You're too interesting to be single layered. Too many people go through life seeing only what they expect. They view life waiting to be heard, rather than listening and seeing what others do not.*" Sawyer's eyes warmed as he turned toward Sky.

"He taught me how to accept everything, from my range of emotions to differing lifestyles and opinions. He looked beyond the miraculous way the herring managed to make their way upstream and saw the pebbles below that were being tossed and turned from the herring's movements. And he spoke of the pebbles as if they were alive. I think he taught me to think of everything that way—as if it were alive."

He gazed up at the star-studded sky, and she saw his Adam's apple jump as he swallowed whatever memories made him grow silent.

"I promised you dinner. We should probably go." He pulled her in close again.

He was more than a head taller than her, and with the moonlight at his back, he looked even more handsome than he had when she'd first seen him at Governor Bradford's. Sky knew it was because he'd shared so much of himself with her that his looks moved to the background and his emotions filled the space between them. She'd never met a man who opened up so easily. She'd thought that she and Blue were as close as two friends could get, but it had taken a few weeks until they shared these types of intimate conversations—and even then they felt like they rode the surface compared to her conversation with Sawyer. She was a little overwhelmed by the sense of feeling like she knew him so well after just a few hours.

"Thank you," he said, as he tipped her chin up and gazed into her eyes.

"For?"

"For reminding me of some of the best moments in my life. I hadn't forgotten them, but I hadn't revisited them in so long that I had almost forgotten how special they were."

He drew her close again and held her. His heart beat against her cheek, and despite wanting to kiss him again and again and again, she reveled in this moment of closeness.

Chapter Four

SAWYER AND SKY ordered lobster rolls at a walk-up restaurant on the Provincetown pier and ate while sitting on the beach. The sand was cool and the breeze coming off the water was brisk, but when Sawyer touched Sky's hand, her skin was warm. They talked for a long while, and he realized that they both enjoyed similar styles of music—ranging from Top 40 to country and jazz, and they both hated sauerkraut, mustard, and mullets, which they shared a laugh over as they lay back on the beach, their sides touching, and gazed up at the stars.

"Do you ever wonder how different your life might be if just one element had been altered?" Sky asked.

"Like if I hadn't gone into boxing?"

She turned to face him, her eyes wide. "You're a *boxer*?"

"I didn't mention that?" Sawyer wasn't surprised that she didn't recognize him. Not just because she probably didn't follow boxing, but because he'd never accepted any offers for sponsorships. The idea of having his face plastered over a billboard selling boxing equipment or pushing certain clothing lines or energy drinks had always turned him off. Sponsorships were for guys whose egos needed stroking. The only stroking Sawyer's ego required was done by his own competitive nature to be the best. Winning his boxing matches was all the notoriety he needed—and if it had come without a belt, he wouldn't have cared. He'd have trained just as hard, fought just as tough, to know in his own head that he was the best damn fighter in his division. And it was that determination that would secure his father's financial future.

"No," Sky said. "I would have definitely remembered *that*."

The distaste in her tone surprised him. Usually women went crazy over his career.

"I'm sorry if I didn't mention it." He pushed up on one elbow so he could look into her beautiful, though wary, eyes.

"You actually get into a ring and punch people?" she asked. "And they punch you?"

He smiled at the simplification. "Yes, but it's really more than that."

"Enlighten me," she said, pushing up on her elbow so they were eye to eye.

"I take it you're not a fan?" He reached for her hand to see how far she was withdrawing, and thankfully, she laid her hand in his.

"I don't love the idea of fighting," she said. "But to think that you willingly do it? Let's just say I'm curious, but not a fan, no."

"When I was a kid, I was in organized sports. Pee-wee football, soccer, baseball. And as I got older I was frustrated because the bottom line of winning or losing was out of my control. I wanted something where winning or losing came down to my own skills. My own drive and determination. My dad traveled a lot when I was younger, and my mom was busy, and I went searching..."

"Searching?" It came out sounding like a question.

He met her gaze again, and something about the intense way she was looking at him, as if she were trying to see *inside* him, made the truth spill out.

"I started hanging out with these older kids. Part of me knew they were no good, but they were tough, and that was intriguing to me. Well, that lasted about ten minutes. My father came home one weekend and caught me mouthing off to our neighbor. It's embarrassing to think about now, but at thirteen, what did I know? Anyway, my father's got this way of seeing right through people, and he knew exactly what I needed. He dragged my butt down to the local fight club and handed me over to Roach."

"Roach?"

"Manny *Roach* Regan. He's been my trainer forever, but it didn't start out that way. My father took me to a fight club and told Roach to show me what it meant to be respectful, and then he walked out the door."

"He left you at the fight club?" Her eyes widened. "When you were thirteen?" Her fingers inched across the sand and covered his.

"Yeah," he said with a smile, because looking back,

he knew his father realized exactly what he was doing. "That one afternoon changed the course of my life. Roach is a no-bullshit guy. He was in his twenties, and he was massive. He had me taking out the trash, cleaning the gym, *and* working the bags."

"And you didn't hate your dad for leaving you there?" She sat up, and he could see the tension in her shoulders. "Weren't you scared?"

"Scared shitless. I thought I was tough, and then suddenly this monster of a guy is looming over me. Roach is intimidating to adults, so at thirteen..." He shook his head with the memory. "Let me tell you, I didn't feel so tough after about two minutes with the guy. But I was a quick study, and something about his toughness spoke to me. I went back the next day, and the next. And eventually I got over my frustration and anger at my father for dumping me off on Roach, because really, he was saving my life."

"And now you fight." Her eyes moved over his face, and she shook her head, as if she couldn't make sense of what she saw.

"Yes. I'm a fighter. It's who I am." He paused, thinking about that statement, and changed his mind. "Actually, it really isn't who I am, Sky. It's what I do. And Roach? He became my mentor and one of my best buddies. He taught me to respect everyone and everything, and part of respect is knowing when it's okay to fight. When two people agree to the rules and engage in a safe environment—in the ring—that's cool. Street fighting or bullying is not."

"But..." Her brows knitted together. "How can you punch some guy in the head? I don't watch boxing, obviously, but I've seen clips on television. It's so violent."

"That's how most people see it. A lot of people correlate boxing to Mike Tyson and the whole ear-biting fiasco—all that nonsense and hype that surrounded him in the years following that fight. But you've just spent hours with me. Do I seem like an aggressive media seeker to you?"

She shook her head, and a genuine smile lifted her lips as she reached up and touched his cheek. He leaned in to her touch.

"No. I can't imagine someone punching this face. In fact, it's hard to put the idea of you boxing together with the man that I've just gotten to know and the man I saw singing at open mic night. You're either really good at pretending to be someone you're not, or you've managed to divide and conquer your inner self."

"Divide and conquer my inner self? That's the perfect way to say it." Her hand slipped from his cheek. "When I was younger, all my mother wanted for me was to be true to myself. I loved music, and she signed me up for guitar and piano lessons. I'm surprised I didn't end up a boxer *and* a professional musician, quite honestly."

"Well, you do write songs and sing them in bars. How does your mom feel about your fighting?"

A breeze swept off the water, causing goose bumps to rise on Sky's arms. Sawyer pulled her in close, loving the feel of her against him.

"She won't come to my fights, but she supports me. She came to a few when I was younger, but it was too hard for her to watch her *little boy* punch and be punched."

"I can only imagine." Sky sank down to her back again.

He leaned over her and asked, "Is this too much for you?"

She shrugged like it was no big deal, but the look in her eyes and her wrinkled brow told him that it was a very big deal. "I think I'm with your mom. I don't think I could watch you fight, but I guess I won't really know unless I try at some point. When do you fight?"

"Well, right now I'm training for a title fight."

"A title fight? Is that a big deal?"

He smiled at the question. "Really big. I'm the East Coast Boxing Federation cruiserweight titleholder, and ranked number three in the Northeast Boxing Association." He couldn't keep the pride from his tone.

"Cruiserweight? Title fight? I'm sorry, I don't know the lingo."

"Cruiserweight is the weight class, usually 176 to 200 pounds. I hold steady between 198 and 200. And holding the title means you're the champion in that division. A title fight is a fight for the title, or to become the champion."

"So...you'll fight the best in the division and try to win the title from him?"

He nodded, remembering the doctor's warning, and his smile slipped away.

"Yes, that's right."

"Do you like it? Fighting, I mean?"

He lay on his back beside her again, wanting to avoid her gaze while he thought over his answer.

Sky reached for his hand. "It's okay if you don't want to tell me. Sometimes we don't know what we really feel."

He looked at her then and felt even more drawn to her than he had all evening. He didn't want to hold back, but revealing the truth would burn like an open wound, and once she realized how much he loved boxing, she might run the other way. She smiled and he realized how quickly their connection had developed. Better to find out now than after they'd spent even more time together.

"For the first few years, boxing was an outlet and obsession. I loved the adrenaline rush as much as the power of knowing I had succeeded at what I set out to do—*to win*. Then it became my passion. It was what I lived for, and then, after my father became ill, boxing took on a new meaning. In addition to being something I love, it became something I needed to succeed at to secure his future."

"I'm sorry, Sawyer. I didn't realize—"

He squeezed her hand, then pushed up on his elbow again, missing the connection he felt when he gazed into her eyes.

"He was in the Vietnam War, and like too many other veterans, he fell prey to the aftereffects of Agent Orange. Parkinson's hit him a few years ago. He's in stage three, still able to function for the most part, with deficits in speech, walking, facial expressions, and..." His chest tightened as he rattled off the parts of his father that were quickly slipping away. He inhaled a breath and felt the urge to move. Sitting still made him feel like he wasn't doing anything to help his father, and that, he realized as he stood and reached for Sky's hand, was just one of the painful realities of his father's illness. There was nothing he could do for his parents but help financially and provide emotional support.

They walked up the beach as he described what his parents' life had become—the slowness of his father's gait, his endless tremors, and his need to rely on others, which he knew his father disliked.

"I can't imagine the sense of loss your whole family must feel. My mom's death was a shock. It was unexpected and treacherous, but I can't imagine watching her deteriorate because of a disease." She squeezed his hand. "How does his health tie into how you feel about boxing?"

"I've always fought regionally because I wanted to be close by in case my parents needed me, but regional fighters don't earn as much as national fighters. And then I won my titles and finally began earning big. Big enough that four years ago I was able to purchase a house that had been in our family for generations but my parents had given up nearly fifteen years earlier because they needed money."

"That's incredibly generous, and so meaningful, to bring that family history back into your lives."

He stopped walking and looked toward Commercial Street, thinking about the last few years and how much had changed—and how much hadn't. His father's health had changed, which had taken a toll on both of his parents, and his fighting had progressed to higher levels, but he felt like he was treading the same water he'd been over many times before.

"The house was all my father talked about when I was growing up, and bringing it back into the family felt like the biggest achievement of my life. Even bigger than the titles I'd won. I'm renovating it this summer, adding wheelchair ramps and making it easier for him to get around so he can still spend time there as his disease progresses. You asked about how my father's illness fits into my boxing. The more I learned about Parkinson's, the more I realized what he'd need in terms of care as the disease progressed and how much his care would cost. The military covers a good deal of his medical expenses, but he'd never want to be put in a health-care facility full-time, despite the fact that there'll come a time when his care will be too burdensome for my mother."

Sky's eyes filled with compassion.

"He's the only man my mother has ever loved, and although she says she'll care for him..." He shook his head. "It'll be too much for her. It would be too much for anyone. I've finally made it to a point where a title fight would mean enough money to cover in-home, professional medical care for the rest of his life." *And now the doctor says another blow to my head could leave me brain damaged.* He pushed that awful thought down deep and said, "I'm going to win this title fight for him, and then I'll think about retiring."

"Sawyer." She reached for his other hand, holding both as she gazed into his eyes like she was seeing him for the first time. "You're fighting to provide for your father? That's admirable. Your parents must be very proud of you."

He couldn't confirm that as easily as he would like to, because his parents didn't know about the doctor's recent warning—if they did, he knew his father would tell him not to fight. Sawyer had one last chance to pay his father back for seeing enough in him, for believing in him enough to redirect and center him. Sawyer had had years to think about that day his father had handed him over to Roach, and there was no doubt in his mind that his father had saved him from teenage years filled with trouble. Who knew what he might have done, or where he might have ended up? His father might not have been around much, but he cared. He cared enough to risk his son being pissed off for weeks on end.

Come hell or high water, Sawyer was going to win this fight. He dropped his gaze to the sand, then shifted it to the parking lot, and watched a group of people laughing as they walked toward the lights of Commercial Street.

"He was very proud of me." He needed noise to drown out the chaos in his head and the ache in his chest that accompanied thoughts about his father and the doctor's warning.

"Was? And now?" she pushed.

Now it's like looking in a mirror, at what could happen to me if I get hit in the head again. Now I hear his slowed voice telling me to give it up and follow my heart to something else. Now I'm standing between two rivals playing Russian roulette. On one side is my father's care and quality of life. On the other is something I haven't thought about with any great significance—my own well-being.

And now the thing I never expected has happened.

Now there's you. Causing me to question my decisions in a way I never have before.

He couldn't say any of those things. Not tonight. Not on their first date.

Maybe not ever.

"Now I think we should go to a club, listen to music, and see if you're as good at dancing as you are at listening. And kissing. You're definitely good at kissing."

Chapter Five

TWO HOURS LATER Sky's and Sawyer's bodies were pressed tightly together on the crowded dance floor of a dimly lit nightclub, surrounded by a mass of people bumping and grinding to a band Sky had never heard of. The melody didn't matter. They'd been dancing since they'd arrived, and their bodies moved to a rhythm she was sure only they could hear. A private beat, fast and slow, hot and sensual. His hands splayed across her back, moving over her hips, then up her arms. Undemanding and possessive at the same time, as if she'd been his forever.

Sky didn't consider herself uptight or laden with inhibitions, but she had some level of self-control—and she'd left it behind when their bodies began their slow seduction, and her mind turned lustful and dark. It had been a long time since she'd gotten lost in someone, and that's exactly what was happening. She couldn't resist letting herself feel for the man who loved his father enough to fight for him, the man who listened and comforted her. The man who could have taken advantage of her openness, if he'd been a different type of person. The man whose soul seemed to be as deeply rooted in who he was as hers was.

Her hands traveled over the hard ridges of his chest, as their hips brushed and his arousal pressed against her, rigid and tempting. She closed her eyes, and when his mouth descended on hers in a needful, wanting kiss, she felt dizzy. Her skin prickled with anticipation of more. Her emotions whirred, and he intensified the kiss, crushing his mouth to hers at the same time he slid one hand lower and cupped her ass, brushing his thumb beneath her shorts and over the edge of her panties.

His lips slid to the corner of her mouth, then across her cheek, and he said something in a growl, but the music was too loud to make it out. She pressed in closer, craving the sound of his voice. His thumb slowly stroked her flesh, grazing her panties with each pass, making her insides smolder in flames. She wanted so much more of him. Sex was all around them. Men gyrated against men, women danced with men, and women openmouthed kissed other women in a visual orgy of sexually charged bodies, all of which heightened her arousal. When Sawyer turned her in his arms and raked his teeth over the shell of her ear, she tilted her head to the side, giving him better access. He sealed his mouth over her neck and pressed his hard length against her ass.

Somewhere in the back of her mind she was chastising herself about this being their first date, knowing she should slow down. But Sky was all about the universe pulling her in the right direction. And right here, right now, she let herself enjoy where it was taking her. Every touch, every stroke of Sawyer's tongue, made her crave *more*. She turned to him and claimed his mouth in another unrelenting kiss. He returned her efforts hungrily, until his oxygen became hers and the line between them blurred.

Sky didn't know how much time had passed before they finally left the bar, but it felt like a lifetime. A long, sensual lifetime that made her acutely aware of her sexuality and the ripe state her body had fallen into.

His arm was heavy on her shoulder, his jaw scratchy against her cheek, and she loved it all. His strength, his protectiveness. The sound of his gravelly voice.

They headed toward the shop with their bodies pressed together, their mouths connecting every few steps. She gripped his hips, clawed at his sides, touching him wherever she could. Forgetting herself—forgetting that they were on the crowded sidewalk with people walking by. She didn't care, and probably no one else did either. At night Provincetown was a plethora of sex and greed, and tonight she was lost in the thick of it. Lost in the world of Sawyer Bass.

As they rounded the dark alley beside the shop, their lips parted long enough for her to say, "I had you pegged so wrong." She was breathing hard, wishing she hadn't spoken so he'd plunder her mouth again.

"When I came in for the tattoo and could hardly keep from staring at you?" He leaned in to her and pressed her back against the cold brick wall as their mouths came together again.

"At the bar," she said. "When I heard you play the

guitar. I thought you were totally into yourself."

"I was lost in thoughts of you. I saw you reading and couldn't stop thinking about you."

"You don't need to butter me up. You're already getting kissed good night," she teased.

"If I wanted to butter you up I'd use a better line, like, *where have you been all my life*, or—"

"Cheesy!" She bumped him with her shoulder as they stumbled toward the stairs as if they were tipsy, when all they'd consumed was each other.

They ascended the narrow steps to her apartment. His hand rested at the base of her spine, searing heat right through her shirt to her skin. On the landing, Sky's pulse quickened with the need for a fast decision. She was having more fun, and felt more alive, than she had in a very long time. *Sexy fun*. If she asked him to come inside, she knew they'd likely end up in bed together, which sounded very, very good to her at the moment. But she wasn't the type of girl who slept with a man on the first date, and she was truly hoping for a second date with Sawyer—and a third and fourth.

"I had a really great time," she finally said.

He held her hips, and the surety of his grip stirred thoughts of what it would be like to be naked beneath him, to feel the weight of him bearing down on her while their hips moved in perfect sync.

"Want to come inside?" The invitation came too fast for her to stop it.

"I want to," he said, eyes dark as night, "but I think I'd better say good night here."

Worried that if she said anything at all, *Then stop thinking*, would come out, she nodded instead.

He pulled her flush against him and, *good Lord*, did he feel good. Driven by the combination of lust and something deeper that had seeded itself sometime between the ice cream and his confession about his family, she went up on her toes and pressed her lips to his.

His tongue swept over hers in a slow, intoxicating kiss. A lovers' kiss that spoke of far more history than they'd shared—and like everything else about Sawyer, it drew her in.

One hand slid beneath her hair and cupped her head, and the other crushed her to him. Sky was whirling with desire, and her hands were on a mission, traveling up his sides, over the muscles of his back, then down into the pockets of his jeans. She pressed on his firm ass, bringing them impossibly closer. The depth of her desires surprised her, and her eyes came open with the realization of just how strong the urge was. How far she was willing to go.

Their lips parted and he kissed her forehead, then pressed his hands to her cheeks and said, "I could kiss you all night long."

"Okay—" slipped out before she thought to stop it. She wasn't ready for more, despite how much she wanted it. Was she? God...did she ever want him. He smiled and pressed his lips to hers again, lighter this time, and when he drew away, her lips still tingled from their impassioned kisses.

"I like you, Sky. I like you too much after just a few hours. I don't trust myself not to do more than kiss those lovely lips of yours if we go inside."

Her knees weakened at his honesty. "I'm not sure I trust myself either."

"See how much we have in common?" He held her close, and she breathed him in, memorizing his scent to carry her through the night. "I'm training in the morning. I'd like to see you tomorrow evening. That is, if you don't mind hanging out with a boxer."

A boxer. How could she have let that get so far from her mind? Fighting went against everything she believed in, but she'd never had her beliefs tested in this way before. One look in his dark eyes drew her into his arms again.

"Honestly, I haven't had time to process how I'll deal with your career, but I know I feel more connected with you than I've felt with anyone before. And that means something to me, so I'd like to spend more time with you while we figure out the rest."

"I can't ask for more than that," he said with a smile. "Tomorrow, then?"

"Oh, wait." She winced, remembering her promise to Jenna. "I just remembered that my brother and our friends are having a bonfire tomorrow night, and I promised to go. Would you like to go with me?"

"I would love to, as long as I won't be imposing on your time with your friends."

"Not at all. It's just a few of my friends and their husbands."

"Sounds great," he said with a sexy smile. "What can I bring?"

"Me."

With his mouth a whisper away, he ran his thumb over her lower lip and said, "The second before we kiss, you get a wanting and exquisitely feminine look in your eyes, and it's the most sensual thing I've ever seen."

How was she supposed to think about anything, much less form a single word in response, after hearing that? He left her nearly salivating for a kiss and held her hand as he walked down the first step toward the alley below, then pressed a kiss to the back of it and said, "Good night, my sweet summer Sky."

She watched him disappear around the corner and finally broke from her stupor and went inside. Her apartment was dark, save for the sheen of red and yellow light streaming in the front window from the shop's sign across the street. Merlin, her two-year-old longhair Persian cat, wound between her feet. She picked him up and he purred like crazy as she nuzzled him beneath her chin.

"How's my boy?" She set her purse on the chair by the door and carried Merlin to the kitchen, the memory of Sawyer's kisses still lingering on her lips. She filled a saucer with fresh water and set Merlin down to drink. He looked up at her with his puckered face that made him appear to be in a constant state of *harrumph*.

"Yes, I'm still thinking of him. Don't look at me like that."

Merlin rubbed against her leg, reminding her of how good it had felt to lie next to Sawyer in the sand.

"Eat, sweetie. We need to drive down to Wellfleet after you've had your fill."

She heard footsteps rushing up the stairs outside her door, followed by a quick knock. One of the first things Blue had done when she'd bought the building was install a security monitor and a peephole, as well as a slew of locks and other security measures that she swore she'd never need—and he'd insisted upon. The minute her brothers had heard she balked at the idea of all those security measures, she'd landed in the middle of a text diatribe from Hunter and Grayson and a verbal lashing from Matty over the phone. Pete wasn't nearly as gentle. He'd appeared on her doorstep with a scowl and literally stood between her and Blue, keeping her from interfering with Blue's efforts. She'd lost the battle but won the war. She was out of her father's store and in her own place. That was a step in the right direction.

She glanced at the monitor hanging from the underside of her kitchen cabinets and saw Sawyer pacing on the landing, sending her heart into a frenzy.

She reached for the doorknob, hesitating for a moment to try to calm her racing pulse.

"I'm sorry," he said as she opened the door. Apologetic had never looked so hot. "I forgot to ask for your number." His cheeks were a little flushed.

"Did you run here?"

"Just from the pier." He smiled, a sweet, slightly embarrassed, smile. "I was afraid you might have already left for Wellfleet, and then I worried that if you hadn't left, I'd send the wrong message by showing up again. I..." He exhaled loudly. "I'm babbling."

"A little, but a big, bad, babbling boxer boy is supercute."

"Cute isn't exactly what a twenty-eight-year-old man hopes for." He laughed and handed her a slip of paper. "Here's my number, in case either one of us is running late tomorrow."

She held out her hand and wiggled her fingers. "Want me to put my number in your phone?"

He dug it out of his pocket and handed it to her,

his eyes warm and grateful as she added her number to his contacts, then handed the phone back to him. She stepped out onto the landing and Sawyer peered around her.

"Someone's giving me the evil eye."

"That's Merlin's adoring look." She bent and picked up her fluffy gray kitty and petted him. Sawyer lowered his face to Merlin's eye level and kissed the tip of his nose.

I have a nose that needs kissing, too.

"Hope you had a nice evening, Merlin," he said as he petted Merlin's head.

"Cute. Definitely cute. In the very best of ways," she assured him.

His eyes went dark and seductive as he wrapped his arms around her waist and said, "Thanks for your number."

She whispered, "Cute," just to see his reaction.

"I'm going to change your mind about that. You'll be calling me Hulk-like or Herculean by tomorrow at midnight."

She went up on her toes and kissed his prickly chin. "Okay, cutie pie."

"If you weren't holding your cat, I'd show you just how cute I really am."

She couldn't turn and set Merlin inside fast enough. She pulled the door closed so the kitty couldn't escape and flashed her most challenging grin, which she hoped was at least a little bit sexy, then fisted her hands in his shirt. "Show me."

"Sky." As he said her name, he stepped forward, pressing her back to the door. When he ran his hands down her hips and caressed her bare thighs, she couldn't resist leaning in to him.

"Sawyer." She loved the way his name slid off her tongue.

His rough hand cupped her cheek, his thumb brushing lightly over her jaw, heightening her anticipation. "Sweet, sweet summer Sky. What am I going to do with you?" His eyes dropped to her mouth, as his other hand slid to the curve of her ass, beneath her shorts, as he'd done when they were dancing. Shivers of heat rippled through her.

His touch, the sultry look in his eyes, and his potent masculinity swirled together and slithered over her skin. She brought her mouth closer to his.

"I'm trying to be a gentleman." He ground his impressive erection against her as he claimed her lips in a kiss that sent ecstasy spiraling through her. He held her possessively, massaging her ass with both hands, with the same insistence as every stroke of his tongue, every rock of his hips. Her thoughts spun out of control. She had no hopes of silencing the moan of pleasure that spilled from her lungs into his. He pressed her hips so tightly to his her feet left the ground, and as he lifted her, her legs circled his waist. His lips moved south, and he sealed his teeth over her neck.

Her head dropped back, and she sucked in air as sensations bowled her over. It was too much, felt too good, and when he somehow shifted her lower so his arousal pressed against her center, the friction was excruciatingly scintillating. His mouth found hers again, and his tongue thrust hard, in a powerful rhythm that matched that of his hips against her damp center. And—*holy hell*—she felt the pull of an orgasm.

Couldn't be. No way. Her hips moved harder, faster. Her belly grew tight. *Holy shit. Ohmygod.* His fingers brushed against her panties, and he groaned, a guttural, carnal sound that sent her tipping over the edge. Her head fell back and he didn't relent, pressing, stroking, and keeping her at the peak of her first fully clothed climax. And just as the full-body shudder began to ease, he pressed his fingers against her panties and brought his mouth back to her neck, taking her higher again.

"More—" The unbidden plea surprised her, but she didn't care. Everything about tonight had surprised her.

His fingers sank into her, stroking a pleasure point, and she lost all control, crying out and digging her nails into his biceps as her inner muscles clenched repeatedly in the sweetest, most intense orgasm.

She panted for air, and when she opened her eyes, bringing him back into focus, he withdrew his fingers from between her legs and wiped them over her lips, then followed the path with his tongue. Her pulse was racing so fast she couldn't think, could only suck his tongue into her mouth, seeking more.

When they finally drew apart, she opened her mouth to speak, but no words came.

His eyes narrowed as a grin curved his lips, and he dragged his tongue up the length of his glistening fingers. Sky had never known such intensity, such overwhelming passion, and as he set her on her trembling legs and gathered her in close, she was thankful for his strong arms to hold her up. He tipped up her chin with his hand and pressed a tender kiss to her lips.

"Sweet dreams, my sweet summer Sky." He held her hand as she somehow managed to walk inside the apartment, but she didn't want to let go.

It was crazy, keeping hold of him the way she was. Insane the way she tugged him through the doorframe, leaning against him as she tried to calm her breathing. She didn't know him well, and yet somehow she felt as though she'd known him a hell of a lot longer than a few hours.

"That was..." For the first time in her life, she had no words. Nothing measured up to his sensuous seduction or the longing for more that made her ache for him.

"If you say *cute*," he whispered, before kissing her forehead, each cheek, and then the corners of her mouth. "I might have to try to convince you again."

Before she could say, *Stay*, he added, "Some other time."

Disappointment washed through her, surprising her again. What was going on with her? She was like the worst kind of addict. *Give me more. No, don't. Yes, please.* It was new, and frightening, and exciting at once. She didn't understand it, and she didn't try to. She loved the way he made her feel, and laugh, and the way he spoke from his heart.

"I want to do things right with you, Sky. To date, treat you like you deserve to be treated, before we go further. I really like you, and I'm sorry if I went too far."

"No. You didn't," she said quickly. "I don't know what came over me. I pushed for more. I taunted you."

"Sky, I've wanted you since the moment our eyes met across the bar. And I'm—"

She found her voice *and* her confidence and said, "Don't you dare apologize, unless you didn't enjoy being close to me."

"Didn't enjoy it? I loved it. I want *more* of you, not less. It's taking all of my restraint to leave you tonight." He reached for her hand. "I came back for your phone number, but part of me—a big part of me—hoped for more. I wanted to touch you. To kiss you." His voice went low as he stepped in closer. "I wanted to taste you, and, Sky, your sweetness will stay on my tongue and infiltrate my dreams. But I don't want you to wake up tomorrow morning and wonder what the hell you did tonight."

"I won't." She was nervous and rattled to her core by what she'd experienced right outside her door, with a man she'd known only a short time. But still, she was sure tomorrow morning would *not* bring regret.

"Maybe not. But I'm not willing to take the chance." He kissed her softly. "You have my number. If you change your mind about tomorrow night, call me."

"I won't."

"I hope not." With that, he turned and disappeared out her door.

Sky didn't know how long she stood there, seeing his eyes in her mind when she'd opened the door and the simmering heat in them when he'd licked his fingers. Sometime later she opened the paper with his phone number on it and set it on the counter. It curled at the edge, revealing writing on the other side. She lifted it into the gleam of the sign from across the street and walked to the window, reading his note. Tall, strong letters gave life to each word.

Wanton looks, shimmering touches. Little nothings,

wild and triumphant. Into the night. Into the night. She stared at the words, feeling each intimate one as a prickle of heat beneath her skin.

She looked out the front window and saw Sawyer heading down the alley toward the parking lot. His shoulders were strikingly broad, his waist narrow. Every step was determined, unlike those walking casually on the main road. He glanced back over his shoulder, his eyes moving up the building to the window where she stood watching. Her pulse quickened again. His lips curved up, and his hand followed in the sweetest wave she'd ever seen. In that instant, Sky finally understood what her friends had felt when they'd fallen for their men in practically the blink of an eye.

And in the next second, reality sank in.

No matter how great of a kisser he was, or how she felt like they'd connected on so many levels, he was still a fighter.

A boxer.

He stepped into a ring and beat someone up. For money.

For his father? At least partially, but she knew that was a rationalization.

He was a fighter, a competitor.

She'd challenged him with her body, and he'd won her with his words—but could she win their biggest challenge? Her acceptance of his career?

Chapter Six

SAWYER RAN DOWN the beach with the sun at his back. It was just after dawn, and he was nearing the end of his six-mile run. His house came into view, sitting high atop a dune in the distance. The summer house that his parents had called a cottage had been in his family for generations. Sawyer was the only one living in the large bay-front home, and it was much larger than he needed. But the familial history was important to him—and to his parents.

In the years between when his parents had sold their summer house and when Sawyer had bought it back, his parents had lost too many good summers, during his father's strongest years. But at least it was back in the family. Sawyer's parents never asked for a damn thing from him, besides for him to be an upstanding citizen and follow his heart—but they gave him unconditional love, emotional support, and strength every day of his life. Buying back the cottage, and winning the upcoming fight, couldn't compare to what they'd given him, how they'd taught him to succeed and to believe in himself.

He sprinted the last quarter mile over the dunes. He might have run toward Wellfleet to seek out Sky at the Seaside community, but he had a feeling that if he was lucky enough to find her, his training would fall by the wayside. And that was not an option, no matter how much he enjoyed her company.

He tossed his gear into his truck and drove down to Cape Boxing in Eastham. Sawyer had trained in many clubs, but Cape Boxing had become his second home. He trained there several hours each day.

Boxing clubs weren't like the more-common fitness centers where families went to work out with plush child-care centers, lavish planters and other decorations, bars serving overpriced fruity drinks, and Top 40 music playing overhead. Fight clubs had one purpose—to provide a training ground for fighting. It was a tough, bloody sport, and there was no room for *froufrou* anything. Concrete walls and painted floors served them well. The clubs Sawyer enjoyed most were located in warehouse-style buildings with open trussed ceilings and heel-scuffed floors, like Cape Boxing. When he was training, he didn't want distractions of any kind. He needed to be highly focused—mind, body, and spirit.

Today the club environment wasn't an issue. He wondered how he would rein in his focus with thoughts of Sky lingering in his mind.

Before heading inside, he snapped a picture of himself and scrolled through his contacts to find Sky's number. He found it under *Sweet Summer Sky*, and smiled at her programming his phone with the name he'd called her.

You are my sweet summer Sky.

Their evening together made this his sweetest summer yet. He typed a text message: *See the empty space beside me? Wish you were here.* Then he attached the photo of himself and sent it off to Sky, before heading inside for his training session.

The sound of gloves hitting a heavy bag was like music to Sawyer's ears. His steps became more determined as he strode past the front desk.

"Hey, Songbird," Brock "the Beast" Garner said from behind the desk. Brock was a local fighter. He was six four, two thirty, with thick blond hair and a smile that softened him like a gentle giant. He owned the gym, worked as a trainer, and was one of Sawyer's closest friends.

"Beast," Sawyer said in return. Most of the fighters called each other by their boxing names. Songbird had been Sawyer's nickname since he first met Roach, because when he'd first started training as a kid, Roach had made him scrub down the gym, and he'd sung under his breath while he worked. Roach had coined the nickname, and it had stuck ever since.

"Can you spare some training time this week?" Brock asked. "I've got a group of adults and a group of teens dying for training. They're going into Hyannis to Eagen Boxing because I don't have the time to train."

"I'd love to make time each week, but between my own training, renovating the house, and getting over to see my folks, I'm swamped." And now he had Sky to think about spending time with, too.

"One day I'm going to kick your ass and make you commit," Brock teased.

"You know I'll do you a solid and train when I can. Right now my time's a little tight. Is Roach here yet?" Roach was one of the best-known boxing trainers on the East Coast. He trained world champion boxers and UFC fighters, and Sawyer knew how lucky he was to have him as not just his trainer, but his mentor and friend.

"In the back," Brock answered. "Hey, we're all going down to Undercover tomorrow night for a cappella night. You want to drive down with me?"

"Nah. I'll meet you guys there." Years ago, on a dare, Sawyer, Roach, and Brock had sung a cappella at the bar Brock's brother Colton owned, and they'd continued doing it every few weeks since then. It was a great stress reliever and a lot of fun. Sawyer knew that when Brock said *we're all going*, he was referring to his younger sisters, Jana and Harper. Brock's siblings had become the siblings Sawyer never had. They got together often and supported each other through bad times and good.

Sawyer walked through the club, passing the bag area, where heavy bags, double-end bags, and other training bags hung from thick metal chains. He nodded at the two guys working out there, then passed the two boxing rings off to his left and found Roach talking on his cell phone and pacing by the locker rooms. Roach nodded at him, then turned his back and continued his conversation. He was a formidable man with massive arms and a thick barrel chest. The breadth of his shoulders was twice the size of his waist. He kept his jet-black hair cropped close to his head, giving him a startlingly tough look, and like his three brothers, when Roach was working, he was about as gruff as they came.

Sawyer set his bag down and began wrapping his hands for his bag workout.

He looked across the room at the boxing ring, and his gut churned. He was sparring after the bag work, and for the first time ever, as his doctor's warning rang through his mind, the ring looked slightly menacing. He couldn't allow himself to give the warning a second thought. Second thoughts led to doubt, and doubt led to carelessness, which in turn would likely lead him to exactly what gave him the second thought in the first place—the threat of permanent brain damage.

Roach ended his call and slapped Sawyer on the back. "How's your pop, Songbird?"

"Not bad. You know. Good days, bad days," he answered as he finished wrapping his hands and reached for his gloves.

"You get a clean bill of health from the doc?" Roach shoved his phone in his pocket and looked over the bags while Sawyer mulled over his answer.

"About as clean as you'd expect." He handed his gloves to Roach, who eyed him suspiciously while he helped him put them on.

"Meaning?" Roach had eyes that could flash hot as fire or cold as ice. Either way they could elicit fear from anyone within a ten-foot radius. At the moment they were riding a fine line in between.

Sawyer had no interest in pushing him over either side, so he chose silence and took a step toward the bag.

Roach grabbed his arm. "Spit it out or you don't train."

"Roach. Let it go." Roach had been right there in the trenches with Sawyer when he'd learned of his father's diagnosis, and he'd stayed with him every step of the way as his father's disease progressed. Roach worked him hard when he needed it and gave him space to run off the pain when the ring was too confining. He was also a veteran in the industry, and Sawyer had no doubt that his savvy coach knew exactly what he was trying his best to hide.

Roach wrapped a thick arm over Sawyer's shoulder and pushed his forearm against his neck, slowly tightening like a vise grip. "Three. Two—"

"Fine." He flung Roach's arm away from his neck and muttered, "Asshole."

Roach crossed his arms over his chest and looked down his nose at Sawyer.

"One more punch to the head," Sawyer said with a piercing pain in his gut. Somehow saying it out loud made it more real. "You know the score. They try to scare the shit out of you to cover their butts."

Roach didn't say a word. His biceps twitched, and his eyes shifted to the ring.

"Say something or let's train. I've got a lot of shit to get out of my head."

"What's your plan?" Roach's dead-calm tone made Sawyer edgy.

"Train like a bastard and win the title—then I'll think about retiring."

"Goddamn it, Sawyer. You can't disregard what he said with a generalization like *he's covering his ass.*"

Sawyer stepped closer, challenging him with a narrow-eyed stare. "I'm going to fight with or without you. I'm going to win with or without you. And my father is going to have every fucking penny he needs. Now, either train me or step aside."

Roach stepped so close Sawyer could smell the anger on his breath and feel the ice in his stare. "You stubborn ass. I haven't trained you all these years to hand you over to some other trainer who will run you into the ground. If you're stupid enough and determined enough to do this, you're sure as hell not doing it without me. I actually give a shit about *you*, and no other coach is going to. It's your head and my rep on the line, so don't fuck it up." He paused, clenching his teeth repeatedly. "But you'd better think long and hard about this, because I'll be damned if I'll be the one greeting your mother in the hospital to tell her that now she not only has a husband to look after, but a son, too."

Roach walked away, leaving Sawyer to stew in his own effed-up situation.

***

AT NINE O'CLOCK Sky was still sitting on the deck of Amy and Tony's cottage, having breakfast with Jenna, Amy, and Bella. She loved mornings at Seaside, when she and the girls caught up from the night before and their husbands went jogging together. The last few years she'd come to Seaside for breakfast several times each week even though she hadn't been staying there. The girls and their husbands had welcomed her into their lives when she moved back to help her father with his store, and they'd become as close as family.

Leanna Remington came out of her cottage with

her fluffy white Labradoodle, Pepper, trotting along beside her. She held up two jars of jam as she crossed the gravel road and joined them. Her dark hair hung loose and wild over her shoulders, and her batik tank top had streaks of red jam on it. Leanna had married probably the only man on earth who could put up with her disorganized and messy ways, which was funny, because Kurt was as methodical, organized, and neat as they came. He was forever cleaning stains from her clothing, and the girls never failed to tease them about it.

"My newest creation!" Leanna set the jars of Luscious Leanna's Sweet Treats jam on the table while Pepper wound around the girls' feet and licked their bare legs, whimpering for attention, which they happily lavished on him. Leanna had started Luscious Leanna's a few summers ago, and now her jellies and jams were sold all over the Cape and used in restaurants as well.

"Wait until you try my Moon-Shine Jelly," Leanna said with a wide smile. "I'm spelling it with a hyphen between *moon* and *shine* just to give it a little something special. It tastes just like apple pie. It's made with chardonnay, apple, cinnamon, nutmeg, and sugar. It's *so* good I'm surprised I haven't gained ten pounds while perfecting the recipe."

"That sounds amazing." Jenna reached across the table for a jar.

Bella smacked her hand. "You can't have moonshine." She laid her hand over her very pregnant belly and eyed Jenna's smaller baby bump. "Your baby needs calcium, not alcohol."

Jenna's jaw was still gaping when Amy giggled and

reached for a jar. "The alcohol burns off, Bella."

"Yeah, well, I'm not taking any chances." Bella brushed her thick blond hair from her shoulder.

"Don't be silly." Leanna slathered jelly on a piece of toast and set it on her plate. "I know you're worried about what Evan and Caden will say, but I'll explain to them that it's fine." Evan was Bella's stepson. As soon as he'd found out Bella was pregnant, he and Caden, Bella's husband, had begun watching every move she made and everything she put in her mouth. They were so excited for the baby to be born that they'd decorated the entire nursery before she was even three months along.

"Evan has turned into quite the doting stepson, hasn't he?" Jenna spread jelly on her toast, then fed a piece to Pepper, who had curled up at her feet. "I can still hardly believe he's almost nineteen. Where has the time gone?"

"Speaking of time," Amy said. "I think the guys will be back from their run soon and I wanted to talk to Sky before they get here. How was your date with guitar boy?"

"Guitar boy..." Jenna raised her brows in quick succession. "I bet he knows how to strum your strings."

"I bet he's got good rhythm, too," Bella said with a smirk. "Does he like it fast and hard or soft and melodious?"

Sky couldn't stifle her laugh as she said, "That man can *strum* like nobody's business."

Jenna, Leanna, and Bella burst out laughing. Amy squealed and hugged Sky.

"You naughty, naughty girl," Bella said. "I'm so

proud of our little Sky. She's growing up to be just as dirty as all of us."

"Hey, speak for yourself," Amy teased.

Jenna tugged at her maternity top, which was stretched tight across her enormous boobs. "Sky's been strummed! And? Are you going to see him again, or was this a one-hit strummer?"

"We didn't sleep together," Sky clarified.

"So he just *strummed*?" Leanna wrinkled her brow. "Strumming is good, right? We like strumming."

"*Strumming*," Bella repeated. "His fingers took a walk on the wild side."

Sky covered her face. "Oh my God."

Leanna's cheeks flamed. "Oh. Oh! Sorry. You guys are much quicker to catch on with this stuff than me."

"Don't sweat it, Leanna. You just have a cleaner mind than we do." Jenna leaned in closer to Sky and lowered her voice. "But she gets more sex than all of us combined. You should have heard them last night."

"Jenna!" Amy snapped.

"Kurt." Jenna crossed her arms over her chest and closed her eyes. "Right...there. Oh, yeeeeeessss."

Leanna turned beet red. "Did we forget to close the window *again*?"

"Do you ever remember?" Bella patted her hand, then turned to Sky. "When are you seeing strummer boy again?"

"Tonight, at Pete and Jenna's bonfire, but don't you dare call him that." Sky dug her phone from her bag. "He's so hot. I mean, sexy hot, super-sexy hot, ultra-sexy hot. Not just hot, but...scorching freaking hot."

"We get it—he's hot," Jenna said as Sky handed

her the phone. "Jesus. He looks even better than he did at Governor Bradford's. I'd let him strum me as much as he wanted. You lucky girl." She handed the phone to Bella.

"Don't let my brother hear you say that, or he'll kick Sawyer's ass for being hot." Sky closed her eyes and tipped her face up toward the sun, thinking about how sensually and erotically she and Sawyer had danced together. Her body flamed with the memory of his hips gyrating against hers, his hands traveling over her—

"Hello? Earth to Sky." Bella's voice drew her from her reverie. "I love that he said he wished you were with him this morning. And your response was perfect."

She felt her cheeks flush. "You read my response?" She'd texted, *Maybe tomorrow we'll wake up together.*

"Our little Sky has a sexier side than we thought," Amy said as she gazed at the picture of Sawyer *and* the text. "I'm glad someone else can be the brunt of the jokes this summer instead of me."

"You can tease me all you want, but you guys know I don't sleep around."

"We know," they said in unison.

"We were plotting Operation Get Sky Laid just yesterday." Bella winked.

"He's muscular, like Tony," Leanna said as she handed the phone back to Sky.

"Yes, he is, which reminds me. He *boxes*." She knew her tone made it sound as awful as if she'd said, *He never bathes.*

"That makes him even hotter," Jenna said as she reached for another piece of toast.

Leanna turned empathetic eyes to Sky. "Are you okay with him boxing?"

Sky shrugged. "I've been compartmentalizing. I think about his romantic, poetic, warm, and sexy sides." She pointed down the hill toward the pool. "And somewhere way down there, far, far away, are thoughts about his boxing."

"Mm-hm," Bella said. "You're in denial."

"Big-time," Amy added.

"He's a good *strummer*. Give her a break," Jenna said. "We've all ignored certain things when the sex was too great to walk away from."

"We didn't have sex," Sky reminded her.

"But you want to," Jenna said with wide eyes.

"More than you can imagine, which probably makes me a slut, because we've gone out on only one very long, very fun, very revealing date."

"Well, you're definitely not a slut," Amy said. "If you were, you would have slept with Blue."

"Oh, gosh," Leanna said. "Does Blue know? He's so protective of you."

"Yeah. He met Sawyer, actually," Sky said. "He seemed to like him, but he got a little funny."

"Funny?" Bella asked.

"He called me *his girl* when he was talking to Sawyer. He said, take care of *my girl*."

"Sky," Bella said with a serious tone. "You and Blue haven't hooked up, have you? You can tell us."

"No! God, Bella. I just told you guys I got...*strummed*...after one date. I think I would tell you if Blue and I slept together after knowing him for years."

"We need to meet strummer boy and see if Blue

saw something he needs to be wary of," Jenna said. "If we think he's a keeper, then we can work on you and your aversion to sports."

"I don't have an aversion to sports," Sky said sharply. "Tony is a pro surfer, and I'm fine with that."

"But boxing?" Leanna asked. "Sky, you're all about love and kindness. No part of you is about punching someone in the face. You get mad when Bella stomps on spiders."

"Yeah, I know. That's what I'm trying *not* to think about." Her phone vibrated, and each of the girls' eyes shot to the phone.

"Is it him?" Jenna bounced in her seat.

Sky scrolled to the text. "It's him." She read the text to herself and felt her insides go warm.

"And?" Amy urged.

"Her cheeks are pink," Leanna said. "It's probably private."

Jenna elbowed her. "Did he ask you if you needed to be *strummed*?"

Sky laughed and sighed dreamily—for effect— then read the text aloud.

"*Radiant beauty. Soft as light. Dark and stormy, wild and bright. I can't wait to see my sweet summer Sky tonight.*"

"I don't care if he boxes, skydives, or steals quarters from little old ladies," Bella said. "That man just got hotter."

"That's more romantic than Petey organizing my rock collection by size." Jenna swooned. She'd been collecting rocks for years, and she had a wicked case of OCD, making what she'd suggested a supreme gift.

"Kurt's a great writer, but thrillers don't compare

to *that*," Leanna said. "Is he a poet?" Her husband, Kurt, was a bestselling thriller writer.

"He writes songs, but it's just a hobby. A seductively sexy hobby."

"No wonder Blue was jealous," Amy said. "I'm jealous."

"Blue's not jealous, but speaking of Blue..." Sky rose to her feet, and Pepper lifted his head and barked. "Sorry, Pep, but I've got to go see our friend before I open my shop. I want to check on the renovations." She glanced over the table. "Want me to carry some of this stuff inside?"

"Oh, no, thanks." Amy waved her hand. "The girls and I can handle it. How's Merlin enjoying the cottage?"

"Merlin is in heaven. He loves sleeping in the corner of your couch. I hope that's okay."

Amy smiled. "Honey, that cute little muffin can sleep anywhere he wants."

A postal truck pulled into the complex and stopped in front of Amy's house.

"Expecting a package?" Jenna asked.

Amy shook her head. "Not that I know of."

The postman, Carl, waved as he got out of the truck and flashed a bright smile that reached his sea-green eyes. "How's it going, ladies?"

"Better now," Bella mumbled under her breath.

"You definitely have a thing for guys in uniform," Jenna teased. Bella's husband was a police officer.

Carl carried a pink box under one arm as he mounted the steps. He'd been the postman for the complex for the past several years and knew each of the residents by name. "What's for breakfast?" He eyed the toast and jam. "Got any more of that Sweet Heat jam, luscious Leanna?"

Leanna's cheeks pinked up. "No...But I have Moon-Shine Jelly."

She fixed him a slice, and they all gawked as he took a bite and closed his eyes, enjoying the deliciousness.

"Mm-mm." Carl savored the flavor. "You do know how to stir things up."

"You are such a flirt," Bella said. "Who's the package for?"

"Well, first of all, not that I'm judging, but someone's going to have a fun night. This lovely package is *from* Eve's Adult Playhouse and it's *to* T. Ottoline, but it has Amy and Tony's address on it. So..." The side of his lips quirked up as he winked at Amy. "Either Amy and Tony are going incognito, or Theresa has mistakenly put the wrong address on the box." Theresa Ottoline was the property manager for the community. She was about twenty years older than the girls, far more proper, and oversaw the community rules with an iron fist.

"That is not mine!" Amy shook her head adamantly.

Sky giggled. "You sure? Maybe Tony wanted to spice things up."

"Or maybe our sweet Amy wanted to do more than ride the longboard." Jenna's head fell back with a loud laugh.

Sky caught Bella trying to stifle a laugh and had a feeling that this was one of Bella's pranks. Every summer Bella pranked Theresa, and every year Theresa's responses grew stronger. One year Bella put an old toilet on Theresa's front lawn, and rather than bitch and moan, Theresa dropped her drawers and used the damn thing, right in front of everyone. This situation reeked of a Bella prank.

Carl held one hand up. "No judgments here, Amy. Do you want me to leave it on the table?"

"No!" She pushed the box back into his hands. "March it over to Theresa's house."

"Okay..." He descended the deck, and they all burst out laughing.

"Theresa?" Leanna said in a hushed tone. "Oh my God. She's going to be mortified that she put the wrong address on the order."

That only made them laugh harder.

"Shh." Bella pointed across the gravel road, where Theresa stood in front of her house in a polo shirt and pleated shorts, her short hair layered in a 1980s style. They couldn't make out what she was saying, but her face was beet red, and she was shaking her head like she was arguing with Carl.

Carl left the box with her, and all the girls turned around so he wouldn't see that they were watching him.

"Bella, did you—"

"Shh." Bella hushed Sky. "Another summer of scheming."

"Oh my God, Bella!" Amy covered her mouth. "She is going to find out and get you back."

"On that note, I think I'm going to run," Sky said.

"Aren't you going to text Sawyer back before you leave?" Leanna asked as Sky stepped off the deck.

"You girls have had enough entertainment for one morning. Besides, I need to think of a worthy response. I don't think, *Let me show you my dark and wild side*, cuts it." *Although it's exactly what I want to do.*

Chapter Seven

SAWYER WIPED THE sweat from his brow and set the hammer down on the deck. He'd been trying to beat away his frustrations by working on the wheelchair ramp that would eventually run from the deck on the back of the house to the patio below, so his father could enjoy the views of the bay. But the more he pounded, the more he thought about Roach's comment about his mother. He sank back on his heels and shielded his eyes from the blazing sun, battling the unanswerable questions.

Was he doing the right thing?

Would he be lucky enough not to get knocked out?

Normally, Sawyer had unwavering confidence. He felt as invincible as he had his whole life—except now, when he looked at his father, he couldn't deny the what-ifs. Hell, look at Muhammad Ali. He was the best, and even the best couldn't escape the very real possibility that Sawyer denied existed every day of his life.

He pulled his knees up and crossed his arms over them. Sweat dripped down his sides as he ran through a few boxing nightmares he kept locked away for his own sanity. He'd memorized them, because even though he'd never allowed himself to lose confidence over them, he *had* to know what he was up against. In order to win, he had to be aware of the risks. *Duk-Koo Kim, died four days after a nineteen-round fight with Ray "Boom Boom" Mancini. Frankie Campbell died at the hands of Max Baer. Benny "Kid" Paret, welterweight champ, went into a coma after a twelve-round fight and died ten days later. Billy Collins Jr. lost his vision because of a cheating opponent who had removed padding from his gloves.*

Shit happened, but it wasn't going to happen to him.

He picked up his tools and headed inside to shower.

Half an hour later Sawyer drove to his parents' house in Hyannis with the radio blaring and the windows down. Anything to block out his thoughts. The workout, the renovation work, the cold shower...Nothing pushed him past what Roach had said, which was why he needed to go see his parents— to remind himself of exactly why he needed to train harder and remain focused.

He gritted his teeth against the goddamn word. *Focus.* Not only was he trying to erase what Roach had said, but he'd had a hell of a time keeping thoughts of Sky from permeating his mind when he was in the ring—and that was dangerous.

He glanced at his cell on the passenger seat. The text from Sky about waking up together tomorrow had him thrumming with the anticipation of seeing her again. He'd never met anyone like her. She was a bright, welcome light to his intense days and as ethereal as she was real, but he couldn't shake the worry about getting close to her with the fight looming over his head. He couldn't afford to be sidetracked during training or during the fight. It was all dangerous territory—but hell if he'd been able to stop thinking about her.

He tried again to push away thoughts of Sky as he pulled up in front of his childhood home. When Sawyer was growing up, the cedar-sided Cape-style home had been the most welcoming place on earth. With scents of his mother's cooking lingering and his father's books lining the walls, there was no place he'd rather be. Now, each time he pulled up to the house, his gut tightened, and he wondered how much his father's health had declined in the days since he'd last seen him. Returning after traveling for fights was the worst. While Sawyer was away, he could pretend his father was the resilient man he remembered from his youth. And it wasn't until he'd drive down the street, bracing himself for the truth after being away, that reality would puncture the bubble he'd lived in in order to keep his focus. Each time he saw his father, the pain of his declining health hit him anew.

After this many years, he should be used to the fact that his father could no longer smile, that his voice—once so filled with life he could read a passage of the most boring book and make it come alive—was now monotone, cold and emotionless.

He parked in the driveway and waved to Mrs. Petzhold, the same neighbor he'd been caught mouthing off to as a kid. She smiled and waved. Her hair had turned snow-white over the years, and her waist had thickened. After spending time with Roach and learning more about respecting others than he'd ever thought possible, he'd sought out Mrs. Petzhold and apologized—profusely.

Sawyer had been thankful for her forgiveness, and now he was glad that the neighbors his parents knew and trusted had remained on the street. His mother, Lisa Bass, was not the type to complain, but Sawyer knew that watching the man she'd loved since she was eighteen stricken with a disease that would one day render him unable to so much as embrace her was taking a toll on her. His father was a solemn man, who'd preferred his privacy to the camaraderie of friends and neighbors even when he'd been healthy, but he knew that his mother needed their emotional support.

He was happy to find his parents on the back patio, enjoying the beautiful, sunny day. Although his father was still able to handle most of his daily functions on his own, Sawyer had noticed that his gait had not only slowed but had become even more unsteady. He walked with a cane now but refused to use a walker no matter how many times Sawyer and his mother pleaded with him. Tad Bass was a stubborn man. Sawyer knew from talking with his father's doctor and researching the illness online that the progression of the disease could happen quickly and the risk of falls would increase twofold. As his father's automatic reflexes continued to slow, his ability to perform simple daily tasks would one day diminish altogether, and he'd need full-time care.

He bent to kiss his mother's cheek, and she reached up and embraced him.

"Hi, honey," she said. "What a lovely surprise." Lisa was in her late fifties, almost ten years younger than his father, although with his father's deteriorating health, they looked even further apart in age.

"Hi, Mom." He turned to hug his father, and the familiar pang of longing for the smiles his father had once shared so readily stabbed through him. Facial masking was what his father's doctor had called his father's inability to control his facial muscles. An infliction brought on by Parkinson's. His father's expression didn't change when he opened his arms to his son, but when Sawyer embraced the man who had raised him, who had preached about the importance of loyalty and keeping strong morals and ethics, the man who had taught him to throw a baseball, he felt love radiating around him. His father had responded fairly well to the medications. The tremors that had been exacerbated while his father was resting were now favorably controlled and barely noticeable, but when he embraced his father, he often felt the underlying, minimized movements.

"How's it going, Dad?"

"Fine...son," his father said. To an onlooker his father's blank expression would appear as disinterest, his quiet, raspy speech as dissonance. But it was all part of the disease his father endured for having had the courage to fight for their country. His father was dressed in a pair of sweatpants and a baggy T-shirt, which seemed to magnify how much his musculature had diminished.

"You mentioned the other day that you had some errands to run this week, Mom," Sawyer said with a smile. "You can take off while I'm here, and I'll hang out with Dad."

"Oh, how lovely. You're sure you don't mind?" His mother touched her shoulder-length dark hair. "I should freshen up before I go out."

"Take your time, Mom. I have a few hours. I don't have plans until this evening."

Curiosity lit up her hazel eyes. "You have plans this evening? A date, perhaps?"

His mother was always trying to fix him up with her friends' daughters, granddaughters, friends, or relatives. He'd let her set him up twice, and both times were disasters. The girls were less than interesting, and they'd wanted to talk about his career more than anything else. He loved his career, but he didn't necessarily want to talk about it 24-7 or pretend that he was flattered by their attention. As much as Sky's reluctance to accept his career worried him, it was also one of the things that he admired about her. She didn't fawn over him because of what he represented or the titles he'd won. She actually had her own ideas of right and wrong, and she stuck to them, and it was that independence, and so much more, that set her apart from others.

"Actually, yes, a date."

"A...date," his father said. Sawyer read past his expressionless eyes to the smirk he knew his father would inflict if he could. "Good...for...you."

"Someone special?" his mother asked with hopeful eyes.

"It's only our second date, but I really like her."

"Well, that's more than you've said about any of your other dates for a long time," his mother said. "I think I'll hang on to that shred of hope for a while."

"Mom, it's not like we're getting married and giving you grandchildren."

She leaned down and kissed his father's cheek. "A mother can hope."

"Re...lent...less," his father said.

Before going inside, his mother stood with her hand on Sawyer's shoulder for a long moment.

"What is it, Mom?"

"Hm? Just...please stay with him if he has to go inside. Your father's been a little shakier lately."

The look on his father's face might not have changed, but the energy rolling off of him sure had—it was dark and annoyed, making Sawyer's gut twist.

Sawyer watched his mother walk inside. Then he sank down to the chair beside his father, feeling his father's eyes on him.

"Why did you send your mother out?" His father's speaking abilities might have slowed, but his cognition was still very much intact.

"You picked up on that, huh?"

His father nodded.

Sawyer hated that seeing his father today brought bigger concerns—and for the first time, it wasn't just concerns over how he was going to afford his father's health care. Today it was like looking in a mirror and seeing his own future reflected back.

With Roach's comment pinging around his mind like a silver ball in a pinball machine, keeping hold of his invincibility cloak was proving harder than usual. He had thought about sharing the doctor's concerns with his father, but there was no way in hell he'd lay that on his father's shoulders.

"Dad, you know I have that title fight coming up, and the purse is a big one. Seven hundred thousand dollars."

"Yes."

Over the years he'd grown so accustomed to his father giving his two cents, whether he was asked for it or not, that his silence was unsettling, leaving too many unanswered questions for Sawyer to mull over. He wondered if his father wanted to say more but had grown frustrated with his own slowed speech and had simply stopped trying.

"Son." The word came out flat, though Sawyer knew it was a question.

He was still hung up on how much he missed hearing his father's advice. He'd give anything to go back in time and...What? He didn't know. He'd always spent a lot of time with his family, but was *a lot* ever enough? Would any amount of time ever be enough? He'd come here today to strengthen his resolve, to push away shadows of doubt put in place by his doctor, and even more doubt seemed to be mounting with the weight of lead on his shoulders. Sawyer looked away, lifted his chin, and drew back his shoulders, inhaling strength from the world around him and exhaling weakness. Practicing yoga had paid off over the years in many ways—and right now it helped him slip out of doubt and into determination.

He tightened his jaw and forced himself to speak. "If I win the fight, the winnings will cover your medical expenses, Dad. In-home care, as you wanted."

His father nodded, his expression remaining stoic,

and Sawyer felt sadness seeping in. As he'd done so many times before, he forced himself to bury it away, below the worry about whether he'd win the fight or lose his father's chance for home health care, beneath the worry about the toll it would take on his mother either way and beneath his own wretched devastation over losing his father. He fisted his hands, flexed the muscles in his legs, and readied himself for a fight to the death, if need be.

"I just wanted you to know I'm training hard, Dad." He forced a smile, and his father slowly shifted his eyes away at the same time as he reached for his son's hand.

Usually Sawyer spent time reading to his father, but today he didn't have it in him to think straight. They sat like that for a long time, and sometime later—an hour, maybe longer—his father said, "You're not going to tell me."

"Tell you what, Dad?"

"What you came for."

He heard his mother's car door shut out front, and as he mulled over his answer, holding his father's deadpan gaze, his mother came through the living room door and joined them on the deck.

"How are my two favorite men?" She kissed his father's cheek and touched the top of Sawyer's head, as she'd done when he was a boy. Her eyes moved between them.

"Everything okay?"

"Of course." Sawyer rose to his feet, feeling like a kid caught in a lie, and pulled out his wallet. "I wrote this for you last week."

His mother read the song he'd written and, as she

always did, she clutched it to her chest and then pulled him into a warm hug. "Honey, you are every bit as poetic as your father. I know you love boxing, but you should seriously consider putting your songs together and publishing them."

"Thanks, Mom, but you're my mom. You'd love anything I wrote."

"Maybe so, but your father refuses to give me any more poems. Lord knows his brain still works fine, and I can certainly write them down for him. But I've begged him, and still he refuses me." She squeezed his father's shoulder in a loving fashion. "I miss that, and maybe if you wrote with publication in mind, the competitive side of your father would come out and I'd get a few more lovely lines."

His father covered her hand with his and patted it.

Sawyer hugged her again. "I'm going to head out." He bent down to hug his father.

"You can leave"—his father's slow, determined voice sent shivers down his spine—"but whatever it is you came to say will still be there when you get home."

***

AFTER POPPING IN to talk to Lizzie about her date with Sawyer, Sky went to her apartment above the shop to check in with Blue on the renovations. But her mind wasn't on the pipes that needed fixing or the walls that needed painting. She was thinking about the text from Sawyer and the text she'd sent to him in response. What was it about him that had her offering herself up like she was? Maybe they'd wake up together the next morning. She hadn't spent the night with a guy in years, and yet, no matter how many times she tried to convince herself to feel regret over having sent the provocative text, she couldn't.

Blue scowled up at her from where he was crouched by a hole in the wall that hadn't been there last night.

"What happened?" she asked, assessing the hole.

"I dropped my hammer," he growled.

She cocked a brow. "In the wall?"

He rose to his feet and ran his eyes down her sundress. "Don't worry. I'm taking care of it. You look pretty."

Pretty? Blue never told her she looked pretty. *Hot* or *cute*, yes, but *pretty*? Never. "Thank you."

"How was your date? I came by your place around eleven, but you weren't back yet."

"You did? Oh, well, we got back late. We went to Brewster, then went dancing. We had a nice time."

Blue stepped in closer, encroaching on her personal space, which she usually didn't even notice, but this morning he was giving off a weird vibe, and she took a step back.

"What's up with you?"

"I don't know," he said with a bite of frustration. "You seemed *into* Sawyer yesterday."

"Yeah, he's a nice guy."

"I saw something more than that in the way you looked at him." Blue's eyes narrowed. "Was I misreading the heat between you two?"

She walked toward the kitchen to grab a glass of water. "Heat? I don't know." She didn't know what to make of the way he was acting, so she tried to change the subject. "What did you end up doing last night?"

"I hung out with Hunter and Grayson at the bonfire down at Cahoon Hollow. I figured if your date sucked you'd want to end your night on a better note and join us."

"Thanks, but my date didn't suck." *Well, technically, he sucked and licked and kissed in the best possible ways.*

He shoved his hands in his pockets. "You know he's a fighter, right?"

"Yes. How do *you* know that?"

Blue smiled, but it wasn't his typical easy smile. His jaw was tight and his brows were knitted together. "I'm a guy. I know sports. I didn't recognize his name at the bar the other night, but yesterday after I left I realized there probably weren't many Sawyer Basses around and put two and two together. You're dating Sawyer 'Songbird' Bass. He's a big-time boxer, Sky."

Sky leaned against the counter and sipped her water. "He told me."

Blue leaned beside her, and some of the tension seeped from his shoulders. "You're okay with that?"

She shrugged. Why couldn't everyone stop talking about Sawyer's career so she could forget about it for a little while longer?

"Sky?" His voice softened. "Do you think we missed a connection? Between us, I mean?"

"We have a great connection."

He cocked a brow.

"Oh, you mean..." *Shit. What?* "Blue, I never...We never...We're such good friends."

"I know. I'm not asking if we should try to be more." He shifted his eyes away. "I just..." He met her gaze again, and she finally saw her old friend again instead of whatever weird, stressful person had inhabited him for the last few minutes.

"When I saw how you lit up when he was talking to you, some part of me wanted to be the person you looked at like that." Before she could process what he'd said, he added, "I don't mean that either. Damn it. I don't know what I mean. I was *friend jealous*, I think. At least a little bit, which is really messed up."

"*Friend jealous*? What is that?"

"You're my best friend, Sky, and I want you to be happy. I've never thought we were anything more than that. I mean, I love you, and you're gorgeous, and funny, and I love spending time with you, but—"

"But?" But? Was he saying he didn't want more or that he wasn't really sure? She might totally regret what she was about to offer, but it seemed like it might show him what she already knew. "Do you want to kiss me and see if there's a spark?"

"What? No. That's not what I meant." Blue pushed from the counter and paced.

"Good." She sighed with relief.

He shot her another narrow-eyed stare, only this one held a hint of amusement.

"No, not *good*, like I don't want to kiss you. Wait, I *don't* want to kiss you. That's not what I meant. Wait..." She covered her mouth with her hand as his lips quirked up in a playful smile. "God, Blue. You know what I mean. I don't need to kiss you to know that I don't feel like we've missed anything. But if you feel like the only way to know for sure is to see if there's a spark, then I'll do it."

"Sky, *I* didn't ask to kiss you. *You* asked if I wanted to."

"Right. This is confusing." She paused to gather her thoughts. "With Sawyer, the second my lips touched his, I *knew* I wanted to be in his arms." She slid from the counter and reached for his hand. "I love when I'm with you, but it's a different type of love."

"I know." He gave her a quick hug. "I love our friendship, too." A moment later he ran a hand through his hair and looked at the floor, then up at her with a shy expression. "Have you ever been jealous of the girls I've dated?"

"You almost never date."

He rolled his eyes. "Sky, I'm not a saint, and you know that."

"Okay, yes. When you're out with a girl I always wonder what you're doing and if she's going to be *the one*, but not because *I* want to be the one, just because I still want to be whatever we are. BFFs."

He smiled. "Then you get it."

"Yes, I get it. I get *you*, Blue, just like you get me." She stepped in close again and squeezed his hand. "I don't know if Sawyer's the one, or if I'll date ten more guys before I find the right person. But I know that whoever I end up with will have to be able to deal with our friendship, because you're important to me. You've been a better friend to me than anyone I've ever known, except maybe the girls."

He laughed a little. "I rank right up there with the girls. That's awesome."

She swatted his arm. "It is."

"I know! I meant it. It really is awesome. I'm sorry I was an ass when you came in. I saw how he watched you the other night at the bar, and yesterday there was an energy between you two that was so thick I felt like I'd stepped onto an island where I didn't belong, and it was weird."

She turned away so he wouldn't see her cheeks flame up. "You always belong, but I'm not going to deny that whatever's between me and Sawyer is pretty intense."

"Intense is good, Sky. As long as he treats you well. But I do worry about him being a fighter and you being a butterfly." He touched her shoulders, and she reached up and covered his hands with hers. "In all fairness I should tell you that I had Duke check him out." Duke was Blue's eldest brother. He owned a number of hotels and had connections in every industry known to man.

She turned to face him. "You spied on him? Behind my back?"

"No. I checked him out to make sure he wasn't a freak with skeletons and abused girlfriends in his closet."

"Okay, first of all, don't *ever* do that again. That's kind of creepy." Although, she had to admit that she liked knowing he cared enough to do it, despite the fact that it bothered her. She still needed to draw this line.

"We don't know him from Adam, and you looked at him like you wanted to jump his bones—"

"So what? That's my prerogative, Blue. You don't get to decide who I go out with or whose bones I jump. I don't check out your girlfriends." Anger simmered inside her. "Have you done this before? Checked out guys I dated?"

"No, of course not. He's big, Sky. He's strong. He's a fighter." His jaw clenched. "I wasn't *deciding* who you go out with. I was just making sure you were safe."

He reached for her, and she held her palms up to stop him. "Fine. No, it's not fine, but since you did it out of some warped protective intent, I guess I should say thank you. But next time ask me, okay? That should be my choice. And without telling me anything personal about him, because I really think he should be the *only* one who decides what he shares with me...Did Duke find any skeletons?"

He shook his head. "Nothing. The guy's never done a damn thing wrong."

She sank down to a chair. "I wouldn't expect you to find anything bad about him. But I have to admit, even though he makes my head spin in the best possible way, I can't wrap my head around his fighting."

"Because that's not your world." He crouched beside her, and his eyes warmed. "He seems like a nice guy, despite the fact that I had him checked out, and from what you've just said, you really like him."

"So now you're *pro* Sawyer after you were the one who checked him out *because* he was a fighter?"

"I checked him out because...I don't know. Tons of fighters have issues and bad reps, run-ins with the law, and I've never seen you look at a guy like that before. I wanted to be sure you were safe. We've already established that it was a bad move."

She sighed. "It wasn't a bad move. I appreciate that you care, but I don't appreciate that you ran to Duke without telling me first. Shouldn't you have clued me in that you were worried?"

"You would have rolled your eyes at me."

"True," she said with a smile, because he was

right. Short of finding out something horrific about Sawyer, nothing would have stopped her from going out with him. "If he was a freak, I could have been killed last night and the information wouldn't have mattered."

Blue smiled. "Yeah, I sort of thought of that this morning, too. Not my brightest idea, but I am glad I did it. Even if it pissed you off. Now I don't have to worry when you're out with him."

"Guys are so weird." She looked around the apartment, thinking about saying good night to Sawyer last night and how much she'd wanted him to stay.

"Are we still cool, or do you want to give me hell for overstepping my bounds?"

"How can I give you hell? If you didn't do it, then one of my neurotic brothers would have the second they found out."

"Yeah, well...Hunter and Grayson weren't thrilled about this."

"See?" She threw her hands up in the air. "Why'd you even tell them?"

Blue shrugged. "I don't know. We were shooting the shit and they were surprised I showed up without you. Anyway, even if you didn't want the info, now at least you know Sawyer's an okay guy."

She shrugged, noncommittally. "Well, he's still a fighter, and I need to figure out if I can deal with that."

"Fighting is what he does, Sky. It's not who he is."

"That's weird, because he said, *I'm a fighter. It's who I am.*"

"He was probably just trying to be tough and impress you."

111

"I'm pretty sure he wasn't, although he did revise the statement afterward and tell me exactly what you did. That fighting is what he does, not who he is, so maybe he's confused by it, too. Or maybe he was trying to impress me by changing it, because he knows I'm not on board with fighting." She didn't get the impression that he was trying to impress her either way, and the more she thought about their conversation by the brook, the more she wondered if he really wasn't sure. She was still having trouble putting the hard and soft pieces of Sawyer together.

"Maybe you should go watch him fight so you can get a feel for it."

"I can't watch him get hit." The thought made her stomach queasy.

"No, I didn't think you'd agree to. But you could watch him train. I'll go with you. I'd love to watch him do his thing."

Not for the first time, she silently thanked the universe for sending her Blue. She had visions of watching Sawyer in the ring, totally losing it, and running from the fight club in tears. "Thanks, Blue, but what if it's better that I just pretend he doesn't fight and keep dating him? What if I can't handle it?"

"Sky?"

She lifted her eyes to his.

"What if you can?"

Chapter Eight

BONFIRES WERE THE go-to summer activity on the Cape, and for the first time since Sky returned to the Cape, a bonfire didn't sound appealing—at least not as appealing as going someplace to be alone with Sawyer. Sky wanted nothing more than to turn around and drive away, and spend the night with Sawyer, getting to know each other better. Emotionally and physically. Well, maybe physically and *then* emotionally.

They'd exchanged flirty texts all afternoon, and by the time they'd seen each other, she'd practically jumped into his arms and devoured him. They'd kissed so many times since he'd picked her up for their date that she'd lost count—and each kiss made her want to kiss him again. And the things he said to her? The man strung words together like jewelers strung pearls, and she tucked each and every romantic nugget away.

And now, as he gathered her in his arms at the top of the bluff by Pete and Jenna's house, with a cool bay breeze blowing her long skirt and his heated gaze warming her from the inside out, she felt selfish, wanting to whisk him away when she knew her brothers and friends wanted to meet him. It was an unfamiliar feeling, and she knew she should feel bad about it, but as he held her in his arms, she couldn't muster that type of negative energy.

Sawyer touched his forehead to hers. "How is it possible," he said in a tender tone, "that I missed you so much after only knowing you for one day?"

"I've been asking myself that all day." She pressed her lips to his, thinking about how much she loved being with him.

"Then maybe we shouldn't question it, and we should just go with it. You look happy, like you had a nice day. Did you?" he asked.

"My days are always great, but they're even better when I get to see you." She smiled up at him. "I did have something exciting happen."

"I can see it in your eyes. Tell me."

I love that. "I'm having a grand opening celebration for Inky Skies in a few weeks, and there's this artist I really wanted to come. His name is Duffy, and he does caricatures. I thought it would be fun if he did them for customers. And he's agreed to come by for a while. I'm really excited."

"When is the grand opening?"

"The eighteenth. It's going to be really laid-back and fun. A few of the street performers said they'd spend an hour out front drawing in the crowd. I have a lot to do between now and then, but I'd love it if you'd come by for a while. Maybe, if we're still together, you could bring your guitar and sing for a while?"

"*If* we're still together?" He smiled down at her.

"Are my days numbered?"

"Not if I can help it," she answered honestly.

"How about this. How about if I bring my guitar and spend the afternoon with you? I'll serenade you, or read some of my dad's poetry to you while you tattoo big, hairy men."

She laughed at the *big, hairy men* reference. If he only knew how many guys shaved practically their entire bodies these days just to show off their tattoos. "You would spend the afternoon at my grand opening? You might be terribly bored."

He kissed her softly and tucked a lock of hair behind her ear. "Sweetheart, if we're together, there's no chance of that."

A breeze carried music up from the beach, but Sky's pulse was already beating to *songs of Sawyer*. She tried to rein in her desire to press her body to his and kiss him again, but when his arms tightened around her shoulders, she couldn't resist going up on her toes and kissing him. Their mouths connected urgently, as if they both knew that in a few minutes they'd be barraged by friends and family.

"We should go before they come looking for us," she said against his lips.

"We should."

He pressed his lips to hers again.

At the sound of barking, Sky reluctantly forced the lust from her brain and focused on getting down to the bonfire. The sooner they made an appearance, the sooner they could be alone again.

"Want to bring your guitar down?" she asked, patting down her long yellow skirt as it lifted with the wind.

"Maybe next time. I can't hold you if I'm strumming my guitar."

She felt her cheeks flush at the reference to *strumming*.

Pete and Jenna's golden retriever, Joey, bounded over the rocks and made a beeline for them. Sawyer dropped to his knees and ruffled her fur.

"Aren't you a fluffy pup," he said as Joey licked his face.

"That's Joey. She's Pete and Jenna's." Sky crouched to love up Joey, and as Sky and Sawyer reached for each other's hands, Jenna and Amy came over the dune and waved, looking adorable in their maternity sundresses. Sky was excited to introduce Sawyer to her friends. Even though this was only their second date, she felt like she'd been dating him forever.

"The shorter one is Jenna, my sister-in-law," she filled him in quickly as she waved to her friends. "She's five months pregnant. You'll love her. And the other *very* pregnant woman is Amy, Tony Black's wife."

"The professional surfer?" Sawyer asked.

"Yup. Tony's a great guy. I know you'll love him and all my friends, and hopefully my brothers, too. Amy's just about the sweetest person on earth."

He pulled her against him. "I doubt that. *You're* about the sweetest person on earth."

Jenna and Amy greeted them with open arms. After hugging Sky, Jenna put her hands on her hips and smiled at Sawyer. "You must be Sawyer the strum...guitar-playing boxer."

Sky's and Amy's eyes widened with surprise at her slipup.

"And you must be Jenna, Joey's mom," Sawyer

said, petting Joey's head.

Jenna spread a hand on her baby bump as Pete and Hunter came over the dunes behind them. "And soon-to-be a human baby's mom, too. It's nice to meet you, Sawyer."

Amy walked right up to Sawyer and hugged him, shifting her belly slightly to the side. Her hair was pulled up in a high ponytail, and Sky knew that Jenna had picked out Amy's yellow bracelets to match her dress, because Jenna was the queen of making sure the girls' outfits were perfectly coordinated.

"Hi. I'm Amy. Soon-to-be mom to a little surfer girl or boy. It's nice to meet you, Sawyer." Amy hugged Sky and whispered, "He's even cuter up close!"

He sure is. "Where are the others?" Sky asked.

"Bella was tired, so she and Caden stayed home. Leanna got a huge jam order, so she stayed home to work, and Jessica and Jamie called to say they wouldn't be able to make the trip yet because something came up at Jamie's office." Jamie and Jessica were married last summer. Jamie had developed one of the world's largest search engines, and Jessica was a cellist with the Boston Symphony Orchestra. They lived in Boston full-time and summered at the Cape with Jamie's grandmother, Vera, who raised him after his parents were accidentally killed while on safari.

Pete put an arm around Jenna and extended a hand to Sawyer. Like Sawyer, he was over six feet tall, making Jenna look even more petite. "Hi. I'm Pete. Sky's oldest brother."

"Nice to meet you, Pete."

"*Songbird* Bass. Hunter filled me in." Pete nodded to their brother.

Hunter shook Sawyer's hand. "I'm another one of Sky's older brothers. I saw you play the other night. You were great."

"Thanks. I remember seeing you at the table with Sky," Sawyer said.

A motorcycle roared down the street.

"Here's Blue," Jenna said.

They turned as Blue stepped from his bike and hung his helmet on the back.

"Do you guys get together often?" Sawyer asked.

"We get together pretty often over the summers," Pete explained.

"Hey, guys." Blue reached out to touch Sky's arm, then shoved his hand in his pocket.

For a brief second Sky held her breath. She realized that she'd never brought a guy with her to one of their bonfires before. This was going to take some getting used to—for both her and Blue.

"Good to see you again, Blue." Sawyer nodded to him as Blue knelt to pet Joey.

"Come on. We'll introduce you to Grayson, our other brother, and Tony," Pete said to Sawyer.

Sawyer turned to Sky. "Okay?"

She loved that he thought to check with her instead of barreling off with the men. "Of course, just don't listen to any of their stories about me. They're lies, all lies."

"Would we do that?" Pete said sarcastically.

"Now I'm curious." Sawyer kissed her cheek, then followed the guys down the beach.

"Look at our men," Jenna said with a sigh. "Hot, hot, hot."

"You can say that again," Sky said. She could watch

Sawyer all day long.

"Did you see how Blue almost reached for you?" Jenna laughed, and when Sky didn't, her tone went serious. "Uh-oh. What happened?"

They walked over the dunes and down to the beach as they talked. "Blue called Duke and had Sawyer checked out."

"Oh, that." Jenna waved a dismissive hand. "Of course he did."

"How can you say that? It feels like a violation of my privacy."

"Sky, he was with Hunter and Grayson, and you know Gray...He was all hot under the collar about you dating a boxer. He said he wasn't going to let his sister date Mike Tyson. Hunter told Pete all about it, and Pete told me about it."

"So it *wasn't* all Blue's doing?" Blue was taking the heat for her brother? Now that sounded more like Blue, trying to keep the peace between siblings.

"From what Pete said, Blue was a little funny about the whole thing, but more because you guys are so close than anything else. But when Grayson said he was going to pay Sawyer a visit, Blue stepped in and offered to call Duke." She looped one arm into Sky's and the other into Amy's as they neared the bonfire.

"I think it's sweet," Amy said. "Even Grayson's whole protective older brother thing."

"You wouldn't if you grew up with every guy you ever dated being given the third degree."

"They only did it because they love you, Sky," Amy said sweetly.

She glanced at Sawyer, standing with Tony, Blue, and her brothers. Seeing him with the people she loved most made her stomach flutter. He was laughing and looked totally at ease, and when he turned and their eyes met, his smile widened.

"Someone can't stand to be away from you," Jenna said.

"I feel the same way. Jenna, it's so fast."

"Fast is so much better than slow. Trust me," Jenna said. "I loved Pete for years before we finally got together. It was torture."

"Hey, I waited more than a decade for my man," Amy said, reminding Sky that Amy hadn't even slept with another man after her teenage love affair with Tony. "And it was worth every second."

They joined the others, and Sawyer reached for Sky and pulled her in close. She loved that he didn't hesitate to be affectionate in front of her family.

"Are they playing nice or trying to scare you off?" she asked.

"No one could ever scare me off." Sawyer pressed his lips to hers.

"Hey, sis," Grayson said.

"I have a bone to pick with you." She turned to Sawyer as she grabbed Grayson's arm. "Excuse me for a minute." She dragged Grayson away from the others.

"I guess you heard about us checking out Sawyer?" Grayson was the youngest of Sky's brothers, and at two years older than Sky, the closest to her age. He'd always had a chip on his shoulder, and at the moment, Sky didn't know, or care, why.

"Yes," she said, folding her arms over her chest and raising her chin to meet his eyes. "And I'm not happy about it."

"I can tell." He draped an arm over her shoulder

and she shrugged out from under it with a groan.

"You can't just play nice and pretend you didn't spy behind my back, Grayson. Why'd you do it? And did you know Blue took the blame?"

Grayson shook his head. He had a mop of dark hair, with big brown eyes that softened his imposing, thickly muscled stature. Grayson and Hunter owned Grunters Ironworks, and in addition to their main raw materials business, they also created elaborate sculptures and unique hibachis that were sold all over the Cape.

"No, I didn't know that, but it doesn't surprise me," he said. "Look, Sky. After what we went through with Dad, I didn't want you to find yourself in a bad situation."

"Grayson..." She could hardly remain angry with that kind of reasoning. Beneath the gigantic chip on his shoulder was a heart of gold. "He's not an alcoholic, and he's not an abuser. He's just a guy who sings and fights." She had no idea how she could say that so easily, when she didn't feel at all at ease with his fighting, but she felt the urge to protect Sawyer just the same.

"But you wouldn't have been sure of that if we hadn't checked him out. And by the way, it was either us checking him out, or your other big, bad protector camping out on your doorstep."

She knew he meant Blue. Annoyance coiled like an asp inside her. She wasn't a child, and she didn't need an army of protectors.

"Okay, you know what? Here's a news flash. I'm an adult. I can handle picking out my own dates and keeping myself safe. I don't need you or Blue or anyone else taking care of me. Got it?" Once she'd found her footing again after they'd lost her mother, it had taken forever for her to convince Pete to back down from watching her every move. But once he and Jenna got married, he'd backed off. Now she had to deal with Grayson?

He arched a brow at her eye roll and draped his powerful arm around her shoulder again. When his lips curved up in a smile, his dimples became more prominent, reminding Sky of all the years when they'd come home from school to homemade cookies. He'd flash that smile, those dimples would appear, and she could practically see her mother's heart melt every time.

"Sis, there's not a chance in hell that we're going to stop caring about you."

"God, you're a pain." She laughed because the whole situation was ridiculous. She knew they'd never back off, and part of her probably didn't really want them to, but she definitely needed a little breathing room. "I don't want you not to care. I want you to let me make my own mistakes."

"We did. You stopped living and stayed in bed for two weeks, remember? You didn't answer the phone. You didn't answer our texts. It was like you died, too."

"Our mother had just died! And do you think I'll ever forget? I felt guilty as hell for Pete putting his life on hold to help me deal with losing Mom. It might have taken me two weeks, but I got out from under that grief and not only pulled myself together, but I've created an amazing life for myself. Besides, is two weeks really too much time to mourn the woman who was there every day of our lives?" The last few words fell off her tongue like an accusation, taking her heart with them. She'd never said it out loud, but she *did* feel guilty, and she hadn't fallen apart forever, damn it. She'd gotten her shit together, regardless of missing her mother every day of her life.

Grayson folded her into his arms. "Sky, I didn't say it wasn't for a good reason. But it was a wake-up call for all of us. You're our sister. We love you. We're going to be there even when you don't want us to be."

She shrugged him off. "Then don't tell me about it. And don't let Blue take the heat for your craziness. I got mad at *him* because of *you*."

Grayson held his hands up in surrender. "I'm sorry about Blue, but I never asked him to take the heat. And I'm only *slightly* sorry about checking out Sawyer, because at least now I know that he's not going to go into a steroid rage and kill my sister."

The love in his eyes softened her resolve. "Grayson..."

Grayson shrugged. "You may not know this, but when you were hiding in your bed after Mom died, I was hanging on by a limb. The thought of you falling apart after losing Mom? That was just about as bad as actually losing her."

Grayson had always kept his emotions close to his chest. She heard the sincerity in his voice and saw the honesty in his eyes. The fact that he was opening up to her touched her deeply, but knowing she'd caused him pain cut her to her core.

"I'm sorry, Grayson. I had no idea."

"I know you didn't. So if I'm a little overprotective, bear with me, okay? I'll work on taming it. And I'll definitely talk to Blue about taking the heat for my shit."

He opened his arms, and she walked into his warm embrace, feeling like she was just getting to really know him for the first time in their lives. "No, don't say anything to Blue. Just let it drop."

"I love you, sis."

"I love you, too."

They headed back to join the others around the bonfire. Pete sat with his arms around Jenna, and Tony sat beside Amy, one hand on her belly, his lips pressed against her cheek. As Sawyer reached for Sky's hand, she thought about his father. And she realized that there were far worse things in the world than being loved too much.

***

WATCHING SKY WITH her family and friends might just be Sawyer's new favorite pastime. She was positively glowing under their taunts about bringing him to the bonfire and wondering what kind of tattoo she'd get next. He'd noticed ink on her shoulder, but he'd been so caught up in her that he hadn't been able to slow his thoughts long enough to wonder about it. Sky taunted them right back, teasing Tony about a tattoo of a kitten she'd given him last summer, and *wouldn't they like to know* about her next tattoo. She was definitely not a pushover, and he liked seeing that side of her. Hell, he liked everything about her.

Pete was busy making Jenna marshmallows, which was an event all to itself, as she apparently liked them golden brown. Not golden, not brown, but perfectly golden brown. Sawyer never knew there was a science to making the perfect marshmallow, but apparently everyone in this close-knit circle did, because when Pete produced the perfect marshmallow and Jenna popped it into her mouth, they all cheered, and then Pete pulled a plastic tiara from a bag and placed it on Jenna's head.

"She's the marshmallow princess," Sky explained.

"What are you the princess of?" he asked.

She got a wicked glint in her eyes as she scooted closer and pressed her cheek to his. "I'm still waiting to figure that out."

"Why does everything you say make me want to kiss you?" He pressed his lips to hers again, knowing he could kiss her a million more times and he'd never tire of it.

"Hey!" Jenna snapped her fingers. "You two."

"What?" Sky said with feigned annoyance.

"No making out around the fire." She held her hands up beside her mouth as if she were telling a secret and said, "Your brothers will see you!"

"Too late," Hunter said. "She's a big girl. She can kiss whoever she wants." Hunter nodded at Sky like he'd done her a big favor—and to Sawyer, he had.

Sky blushed, and it made him want to kiss her again.

It was obvious how much her brothers cared about and protected her. They'd given him the third degree while she and Grayson had been talking. Sawyer hadn't taken offense by their inquisition, because if he had a sister, he might do the same thing. He was glad she had people who loved her enough to look out for her. But he could also see that Sky was a little uncomfortable. He shifted, giving her a little more space. She furrowed her brow and scooted closer to him.

"Don't let them scare you off," she said, touching his leg.

"I was just giving you space. I thought I was making you uncomfortable."

She shook her head and smiled. "Never. I like to be close to you."

She didn't need to tell him twice. He pulled her against his side and kissed her cheek, feeling the eyes of her brothers and Blue on him, despite what they'd said.

"Sawyer." Blue's voice cut through the heat simmering between them.

"We were trying to figure out what song you were playing the other night," Blue said.

Sky rested her hand on his thigh, making it hard for him to concentrate.

"That was just something I'd thrown together," Sawyer said modestly.

"Thrown together?" Jenna smiled. "If you can throw together a song like that, you should be a professional songwriter in addition to being a boxer."

"Thank you, but they're just words strewn together." He'd been told the same thing a number of times over the years, and like all those times, he shrugged off the compliment. His father was the wordsmith in their family. But even as he denied it, he knew that his songs were so much more than just simple words strewn together. They were some of his most intimate emotions, torn from his soul and sung aloud as a way to keep them from dragging him under. And even now, as he sat with Sky and her friends, verses were forming in his mind.

"We have an announcement." Amy smoothed her dress over her belly and waited for everyone to look over. "Tony and I have decided to sell our second cottage."

"Really?" Sky's eyes widened.

"Yup." Amy smiled at Tony.

"We thought we'd see if you or Blue wanted to buy it, and if not, then we'll hold on to it for a while," Tony explained. "We're not in a hurry to get rid of it, but with the baby coming, we were thinking of getting something bigger, maybe on the water. And we aren't interested in selling it outside of the families of the current owners, so we thought we'd offer it up."

"Is that the cottage you're renting?" Sawyer asked Sky.

She nodded. "Bella, Jenna, and Amy, along with our other friends, Leanna and Jamie, all own cottages at Seaside, and they grew up spending summers together there. The cottages were passed down through their families."

"Since Tony and I got married, we have an extra one." Amy rested her head on Tony's shoulder. "Maybe we should hold on to the cottage for a while after all. It came in handy this summer for Sky. Right, honey?"

"Right, kitten," Tony answered before pressing his lips to hers.

"I would *love* to buy it, but since I just opened the shop, I think I'd better hang on to the little savings I have," Sky said.

Blue ran a hand through his hair. "I just got a call this afternoon about that lighthouse deal that fell through last summer. I'm considering sinking my cash into that."

"Well, we just wanted you guys to know. Leanna's brothers or sister might be interested, too," Amy said. A breeze swept up from the bay, and she shivered against Tony. "It's getting late *and* cold. I think I'm ready to call it a night."

Sawyer touched Sky's cheek. "Are you chilly?"

"You know what? I think I'm ready to call it a night, too."

She licked her lips, and the look in her eyes told him everything he needed to know, and so much more.

Chapter Nine

THE LAND ROVER idled at the end of Pete's dark, tree-lined road, where Sawyer had one foot pressed on the brake and his arms wrapped around Sky, as his tongue explored her mouth.

"You taste so sweet," he said between kisses.

"Marshmallows," she said quickly, crashing her lips to his again.

Her hand slid over his thigh, pulling a groan from his lungs.

"We should go." He reluctantly pulled back, then pressed his lips to hers again. "Jesus, Sky. I can't stop kissing you." He buried his hands in her hair and held her still as they claimed each other's mouths. He wanted to lay her down and feel her luscious curves beneath him right there in the truck.

Headlights illuminated the interior of the truck from behind, and he forced himself to tear his lips from hers again. They both looked behind them, then laughed as Sky moved back into her seat and buckled up.

"Your brothers are going to hate me," he said as he turned onto the main road.

"That's Tony's truck, and it's about time my brothers realize I'm a woman, not a little girl." Her tone was thick with defiance, and it did all sorts of things to his already heated body.

"Would I be taking advantage of that statement if I asked you to come back to my place?"

"I'd be disappointed if you didn't," she answered with a seductive smile.

"Take advantage, or ask you back to my place?"

"Both."

The word hung between them, suspended by silent promises that he couldn't wait to keep.

Fifteen minutes later he drove up the windy narrow road to the seashell driveway that led to his three-story house overlooking the bay. He didn't need four bedrooms or an acre of dunes, but the family lineage made the large house feel like a home.

He helped Sky from the truck. Her hair was disheveled from their make-out session, and tendrils framed her face as she gazed up at him. Her beauty was subtle and overwhelming at once, and the tantalizing combination of innocence and rebellion dancing in her eyes drew him right in.

"Want to go inside and talk?" he offered, because he'd already said inappropriate things on their first date, and telling her that his body was vibrating with the need to taste more of her was probably too forthright for a second date. "There's so much I want to know about you."

She hooked her finger in the waist of his jeans.

"Me too."

Her voice was breathy, her eyes heavily lidded and seductive, and when he lowered his mouth to hers, she made a soft sound of surrender the second before their tongues touched. He savored the feel of her warm and yielding skin against him. The floral scent of her shampoo mixed with the salty sea air as it whipped around them, and when she pressed her delicate hands to his sides, keeping him close, it sent a tingling down his spine. He succumbed to the electrifying need burning inside him and pulled her tightly against him. The breadth of his hands covered the width of her back as he pressed his thick thigh between her legs. She moaned into his mouth, and it ricocheted through him. His body throbbed as she rode his thigh, his hard length pressed against her hip. The sounds of the sea faded into their heavy breathing. He had to feel her skin against him. He lowered his hand to the curve of her ass and gathered her long skirt in his fist, then drew back and searched her eyes, making sure they were on the same page.

"Sawyer," she murmured.

Hearing the desire in her voice sent heat coursing through him as their mouths crashed together again in reckless abandon. She clutched his hips, pressing against his thigh and driving him out of his blessed mind. Fervently kissing her, he unfurled his fist, sending her skirt sailing over his open hand as he clutched her sweet ass through her lacy panties. Her head tipped back, and her lips parted with another sexy, needful sigh. Her hips gyrated against his thigh with precise, determined moves. He sealed his mouth over her neck, sucking and stroking her silky skin, loving the quickening in her breathing, the tightening of her fingers. He wanted to be so much closer to her, to know everything there was to know about her, but his body was on fire, and she was clinging to him like he was her anchor—and damn did he want to be her anchor.

His hands trembled with restraint, and when she rocked her hips against him again, his impatient fingers slid to the center of her damp panties.

"Oh God," she whispered.

His hand stilled, wanting desperately to sink into her, to feel her warmth surround him, but he wanted so much more of Sky than this. He pressed his cheek to hers and whispered, "I want you, Sky, so very much of you."

"Yes, Sawyer. I want you, too," she answered.

His chest tightened with her confession. "Not here. I want you naked in my bed, where I can pleasure you over and over again," he rasped against her ear, before taking her in another demanding kiss. Kissing Sky was hell on his self-control. It took all he had to keep from stripping her down and taking his fill right there in the sand.

With his pulse racing in his chest, he pulled back, forcing himself to withdraw from between her legs, and he touched his forehead to hers. "Still with me?"

"God, yes—"

"Sky..." Emotions blurred his thoughts. He wanted to take her inside, needed to take her away from the cool air and the dense sand. Desperate to make her *his* and utterly powerless to find the resolve to pull away, he sealed his lips over hers again. His tongue searched, his hands claimed, and his mind spiraled into someplace hot and dark. Her fingers fisted in his hair as he slid his hand behind her knee and lifted it to his hip, pressing his throbbing erection against her.

"More. I need more," she pleaded.

A low growl rolled up his chest. There was nothing romantic about the way their mouths came together. It was a hard, toothy, wet kiss, filled with unstoppable desire. Rough hands lifted her skirt and tore down her panties as he furtively sought the spot he knew would make her cry out his name. She clawed at his shoulders. Her hands slipped to his biceps, nails digging into his skin, pulling downward as he dropped to his knees and spread her thighs, then brought his mouth to her.

"Oh...God...Sawyer."

Words streamed from her lips as he licked and nipped and finally—Lord, finally—sank his fingers inside her tight heat. She grabbed his head and held his mouth against her as he skillfully lapped and teased. She went up on her toes, and he felt her whole body shudder as the climax gripped her and she came against his mouth.

"Ohgodohgod...Sawyer...Ah...So good."

He didn't relent, pressing a third finger inside her as he pleasured her, taking her up, up, up, until she shattered against him again. With his fingers still inside her, he rose and claimed her mouth in another passionate kiss. He wanted to touch all of her, to taste every inch of her flesh, to see her luscious mouth around his hard length, but he wasn't about to do anything more out here.

He swept her, weightless, into his arms.

"Can't wait," he said, nipping at her swollen lips.

"Hurry," she urged, spurring his powerful legs into a sprint. With one hand holding her up, he dug into his pocket for his keys and unlocked the door.

He kicked the door closed behind him and carried her up the stairs to his bedroom, where he stood stock-still, unsure where he wanted her first. Now that they were in his bedroom, he didn't want to rush this moment. He'd thought about making love to her since he'd first seen her in the bar, wondered what she'd feel like, sound like, taste like—and now that he knew her, he wanted to make her feel better than she ever had. He wanted to cherish her. He lowered her to her feet, and she melted against him. Her eyes were soft, her lids heavy as her trembling hands pressed against his chest.

***

SAWYER LOWERED HIS lips to hers in a tender, sensual kiss, lacking the urgency of moments ago. Sky didn't know if he sensed how nervous she was or if he'd calmed just knowing she was there in his bedroom. His for the taking. She'd been so lost in sensation outside that she hadn't been thinking at all, and now she was having trouble forming coherent thoughts.

Standing in the center of his bedroom, with moonlight glistening off the bay just beyond the picture windows and his king-sized bed, her mind reeled. It had been a long time since she'd been with a man. Almost a year. That was a *long* damn time. What if she was too out of practice to do things right?

His hands traveled up her sides. His touch was

confident, strong, as his thumbs brushed the undersides of her breasts. Pleasure radiated through her and she closed her eyes, letting go of her worries. She inhaled a sharp breath as she lifted his shirt, fumbling to push it over his broad chest, wanting desperately to feel his skin against hers. He tugged it over his head and tossed it to the floor. His gaze was hot, his body hard and tight, but when he caressed her cheek with his rough fingers, her scent lingering on them, his touch was gentle.

"You okay?" His thick dark brows knitted together.

She dropped her eyes to her fingers trembling against his chest and splayed them flat, unable to calm her buzzing nerves.

"It's been a long time," she admitted.

"For me, too."

She heard the honesty in his voice.

"Do you want to wait?"

"Maybe?" She trapped her lower lip in her teeth, and when he brushed his thumb over it and said, "Okay," she breathed a sigh of relief.

He gathered her in close and pressed his hand to the back of her head. "I'm sorry, Sky. I got lost in you."

She closed her eyes and breathed him in. "*I'm* sorry. I didn't realize how nervous I was."

He tipped up her chin and pressed his lips to hers. "Never apologize for following your heart. When we come together, I want to know it's what you want with your head as much as your heart."

"Thank you."

He kissed the top of her head and held her. She didn't know how long they stood there, his strong arms wrapped around her, her breathing calming, but it felt like a long time. She seemed to lose all track of time when they were together, which had never happened with anyone else—and she liked it. Sawyer didn't rush her, or try to move her toward the bed. He didn't do anything more than *be* with her, which was exactly what she needed. The same way that when he'd been touching her outside, it had been exactly what she'd needed *then*. What they'd needed.

How did he know?

"Come with me, sweetheart." He led her out the bedroom door and down a wide hallway to a spiral staircase. She followed him up to a room with a glass, open truss ceiling. There were enormous pillows on colorful rugs over glistening hardwood floors. Overstuffed chairs were set at odd angles, and a plush sectional sofa, larger than any she'd ever seen, was near the far wall. The walls were constructed of alternating panels of glass and stone, providing views in all directions.

"This is amazing." She gazed up at the rafters surrounding the glass in the ceiling. The mixture of textures—glass and old, scarred wood—and colors—forest green, yellows, reds, browns, and blues—called out to her, instantly making her feel at home. She could live in this room, with views of the dunes and the bay and the stars gazing down on them like eyes in the night.

"This was my family's cottage, the one I told you about that my parents had to give up. My great-grandfather built this room. We call it the skycap. He carved his and my great-grandmother's initials in a heart on the third rafter from the left."

"Really? Is it still there?" She looked up, trying to find their initials.

"Yes. The people who bought the place from my parents never did anything with the ceiling, as you can see. So it's still there. And my father carved my parents' initials in the farthest rafter from the right." He smiled at Sky. "Family tradition."

"I love that. It's so romantic. You must have been young when they sold, then?"

"I was, but I remember spending summers here. My parents and I would go clamming at low tide, and we had this little boat. It wasn't anything fancy, but it was a sailboat big enough for the three of us, and we used to go out and have dinner on the water. Sometimes we'd spend the night on it."

"That sounds wonderful. My dad and Pete are boat fanatics. I bet Pete would let us borrow his boat one night to stay out on the water."

He ran his knuckle down her cheek. "You would do that?"

"I would love to do that with *you*." She would do anything with him. "I'll ask Pete if we can borrow the boat. I'm sure he won't mind."

He took her hand, and as they sank down to a pile of thick green pillows, she realized that she was no longer nervous.

"This is where I write my songs. Well, when I'm at home and writing. The night you saw me sing, I wrote a song about you. I wrote most of it at the bar, but then I came home, and in the middle of the night I came up here and finished writing it."

"About me? But we didn't even speak to each other."

He stretched out on his side, looking relaxed and not at all annoyed by her stopping them before he'd had a chance to find his own release. She relaxed beside him, resting her cheek on her arm.

"I didn't need to hear your voice to feel your energy."

She lifted up on her elbow, matching his position, and smiled. "If my friends heard you say that they'd think we were cut from the same cloth."

"I'm not so sure we aren't."

She fell silent at that, hearing something deep and longing in his voice.

"I'd love to hear what you wrote," she said, curious to know what he'd thought of her at first sight.

"Soon," he promised.

He stretched out on his back and tucked her in close beside him as they gazed out the ceiling at the dark, starry sky.

"Do you believe in wishing upon stars?"

"I used to," she admitted. Her mind turned to her mother, and the familiar ache that accompanied thoughts of her moved in.

"Me too." He brushed her hair from her cheek. "Why don't you anymore?"

She sighed and told him the truth. "Because when my mom died, I knew that all the wishes in the world couldn't bring her back."

He tightened his arms around her, and they lay in silence for a long while, gazing up at the stars, each lost in their own thoughts.

"If you could say one thing to your mom now," he said with a thoughtful tone. "Anything at all. What would it be?"

She rifled through the first few thoughts that sailed through her mind. "There are so many things I want to tell her. *I miss you. I love you. I wish you were still here.*" She swallowed against the lump forming in her throat. "But if I could tell her only one thing, I would tell her I was sorry."

Tears welled in her eyes with the confession that struggled to finally be set free. He turned on his side and pressed his lips to her forehead without pushing for an explanation, and that made her want to open up to him even more.

"When she died, I sort of fell apart." She gazed into his empathetic eyes and was drawn into them. "Actually, I fell apart. There was no *sort of* about it."

"That's understandable. You'd lost your mother."

"That's what I told myself as I stopped living my life and allowed myself to lie in bed and wallow in the ache of missing her. It's understandable to be sad, to grieve. It's even understandable to go through weeks of crying, making deals with the devil to bring her back. At least, in my opinion it is. Don't we all want to bargain our pain away? But to allow myself to get so mired down in the darkness of losing her that I couldn't function? She didn't raise me like that." A tear slipped from her eye, and he tenderly brushed it away. "She raised me to be strong and decisive. To face issues head-on."

"*Issues*, not *losses*, Sky. There's a difference."

She nodded. "Yes, I know that. But...I found out last night from Grayson that when I fell apart, he took it really hard. I never knew."

"It's obvious how much your family loves you." He kissed a tear away. "You're lucky, Sky. Love is the foundation of strength in a family. It's obvious that Grayson's love for you only got stronger."

"Yes, but at what cost? How much worry did I cause him when I was hiding in my bed?" She couldn't stop the truth from flowing. "Pete got so worried about me, he put his life on hold and moved in with me for a while, until we both knew I wasn't going to go down the rabbit hole again."

"He sounds like a good brother, a good man."

"He is. All of my brothers are, but it was selfish of me, wasn't it? To allow myself to become so out of it? Obviously that's why they're all so protective of me now, but it caused them to lie to me, and I hate knowing that."

Confusion riddled his brow. "How?"

She'd never told anyone outside of her closest circle of friends about her father's drinking. And now, somehow, Sawyer had stepped inside that circle and she wanted to share it with him, too.

"My father began drinking after my mother died. For two years he was a functioning alcoholic. He was able to run his hardware store, but at night he drowned his sorrows in alcohol, and I never knew. I was living in New York at the time, and my brothers kept it from me. When I came home to visit, they made sure that I was away from him every evening. Meanwhile, Pete was taking care of him, getting him into bed at night, making sure he didn't choke on his own puke." She turned away, embarrassed.

"Hey." He turned her face gently toward his again. "That's not your fault. That has nothing to do with you falling apart."

"But it does. They didn't think I could handle it,

and maybe they were right. That makes me a loser *and* a burden. Pete didn't need to come after me when he was caring for our father. He already had so much on his plate. Grayson was worried sick because I was weak, and...If my mom was looking down on me, she would have been mortified."

Sawyer gathered her in his arms and held her close. "You know what I think?"

"That you wish you'd never come into my shop for a tattoo?"

"No." He kissed her forehead again. "That we are made from the same cloth after all. You lead with your heart, Sky. I lead with mine."

"But my brothers—"

"They love you, Sky. I saw it in the way they teased you and watched my every move. Blue, too. They're all proud and protective of you."

"Because I'm weak," she said in a deflated voice.

"Because you're strong enough to be weak when you need to. That's a blessing. Most people are so hardened to their feelings that they mask them. I see it every day in the ring. Hell, Sky, I do it every day of my life."

"What do you mean? You seem to be in touch with your feelings. At least around me."

He smiled. "I can't escape my feelings for you, can I?"

She felt her cheeks flush, and when he lowered his lips to hers and took her in his arms, everything felt right, and good, and *safe*.

"Do you hide your feelings from everyone else?" she asked.

"I'm a fighter, Sky. I can't bring sadness or worry,

fear, or even happiness into the ring with me. Fighting takes total focus and dedication. Everything else gets buried down deep. I think everyone does that on some level just to get through each day. It's why I write songs, because the passion, the anger, the love, it's all too much sometimes. I have to get it out."

"Like your tattoos."

His lips curved into an easy smile. "Yeah, like my tattoos. Only those are things I want to keep hold of, too. Those are feelings that will always be a part of me. They represent times in my life that I don't ever want to lose. Good and bad."

She gazed into his eyes as he leaned over her, and she wondered what stars had to align to bring them together—and what greater force saw past his fighting and past her dislike of the sport to something bigger than both of them?

He brushed her hair from her cheek. His eyes roved over her face, lingering on her eyes, and she swore she could see his emotions radiating from them.

"I see so much when I look at you," she said softly.

"Tell me what you see." His voice was silky smooth, like water flowing over her.

Sky had always seen emotions in colors, as she was now. The sensations had always fascinated her, but she was sure it was exactly what the universe wanted her to see. "I see shades of the color blue, and I feel..." She hesitated. The things she felt were so personal, so intense, that she was afraid to say them aloud.

He brushed his thumb over her cheek. "Tell me, sweetheart. What do you see?"

"I see devotion. Deep-seated. And honesty." As she

said the words they bloomed bigger, fuller, more meaningful and real. She reached up and ran her finger along his jaw. "And a lot of passion, which feels red to me. I get the sense of stability beneath it, but it's not really stable. Like you're standing in the middle of a plain and just beneath the surface the earth is shaking. And..." She traced the ridge of his cheekbone. "Lots and lots of orange and yellow." She smiled, and curiosity filled his dark eyes.

"What do those colors mean?"

"That you're powerful, creative, and emotional. Very emotional." She pressed both hands to his cheeks. She'd been dying to really touch his face. To feel his energy. "I see other stuff, but it's not colorful. Inner peace that's tethered by something dark. Truth. And love, Sawyer. I feel like your entire being is so full of love, which makes sense since you're fighting for your father. And when I close my eyes"—she closed her eyes and breathed deeply—"I see you searching for balance, like you're walking on a tightrope."

Her eyes came open, and pain was etched in merciless lines across his forehead, underscoring the longing in his eyes.

"How can you see all of that in me?" His voice was full of wonder, as his body shifted closer.

She raised her shoulders in response. She didn't have the answers. She'd never seen or felt so much radiating from a person before, and her heart was racing with the magnificence, and intensity, of it.

"What do you see when you look at me?" she asked.

"A future."

He lowered his mouth to hers, and Sky didn't try

143

to rein in her desires or to figure out if she was ready as his hands moved over her skin. His lips were soft and warm, his body safe and strong. As his mouth trailed along her shoulder in a sweep of slow, shivery kisses, heat spread from the tip of her head to the ends of her toes.

They kissed for what felt like hours, with the stars shining down on them, and the bay ebbing and flowing just beyond the dunes. And when he lifted her top over her head and unclasped her bra with his thick fingers, she wasn't nervous. She wasn't caught up in need and out of her mind with desire. She was blissfully, happily swept up in *them*.

Being with Sawyer felt too right to be wrong.

"You're beautiful, Sky. Inside here." He pressed a kiss above her heart. "And in here." He kissed her forehead.

His hands slid up her arms, light as a feather, leaving a trail of goose bumps. He brought her fingertips to his lips and kissed each one.

"I want to cherish you." He dragged his tongue along her wrist, spreading an erotic rush of heat through her.

He lifted her arm above her head and kissed the sensitive crease of her elbow, working his way up to her neck, then along the curve of her shoulder again. He dragged his tongue along the ridge, and then followed the line with his finger, and when he stopped, she knew he'd noticed her tattoo.

"May I see?"

She rolled onto her stomach, and he gathered her hair to one side, then traced the lines of her tattoo with his finger.

"Roots," he said. "They run deep."

"Family," she whispered.

She closed her eyes as he traced the roots across her shoulder blade, then down the center of her spine. His finger trailed up the trunk of the tree. Then he pressed his lips to the center of her back.

He moved his hands down, and he traced the word *Blessed* that was tattooed at the base of her spine.

"After I lost my mom, when I got back on my feet, I had that done. Her name was Bea, which means blessed."

He pressed his lips to each of her vertebrae. "Why are there only two limbs on the tree?"

She rolled onto her back. His eyes were so dark, so serious, that she felt herself falling into them again—falling into him. "When I designed it, I didn't know what my future would look like, so I left it blank. After my father got out of rehab, I added two limbs to symbolize his growth and mine."

"Same cloth, Sky. You weathered your mother's death and your father's alcoholism. I've endured the slow loss of my own father. Every word on my back symbolizes a piece of me or a piece of him. A piece of my family being chipped away. The twisted, awful pain, and the incredibly wonderful memories. You and I wear the scars of our lives in words and symbols."

She didn't wait for him to lower his lips to hers. She arched up to press her mouth to his, opening up to him in ways she never had to anyone else. The way he spoke, as if every word came directly from his soul, drew her further into him and made her want to know more about him, to feel the emotions inside him.

His arms circled her. She'd already become accustomed to the way he held her so close, like he couldn't get close enough, and she felt it, too. Her emotions swelled when they were together, and her desires spiraled through her, vying for more—more of him, more of his time, more of his truths.

Their kiss spoke of their intense connection, without pretenses, without fear or a frantic pace. He deepened the kiss, and she didn't want to hold back anymore. She didn't care that this was only their second date, or that she'd once said she'd wait to have sex if she felt herself falling for a man. She didn't want to wait until she fell head over heels in love—she wanted to feel their bodies join together, to feel herself tumbling down that magical slope.

Her fingers moved over the hard planes of his chest, to the grooves between his abs, and finally came to rest on the button of his jeans.

He covered her hand with his. "Sky." He searched her eyes again, and she wanted to thank him for being so patient and for caring enough to ask again just to be sure. But all she could do was get lost in the emotions in his eyes.

"You're sure?"

"Very," was all she could manage before wrapping her arm around his neck and pulling him into another kiss.

She fumbled with his zipper, wanting to be closer. To feel his skin on hers, his weight pressing down on her. Without breaking their kiss, he worked the zipper of his jeans, then rose up above her as he dragged the zipper down. Her mouth went dry at the sight of the wide crown of his erection.

"Protection," she said hastily, reaching for the hips of his jeans and tugging them downward. He was on his knees, and his jeans stopped at the bulk of his massive thighs as he dug into his back pocket and withdrew a condom from his wallet.

He rose to his feet and moved his hips in a sexy striptease as he stripped bare, revealing the thick girth of his arousal. He brought the condom packet to his teeth, and Sky couldn't resist going up on her knees and slicking her tongue up the length of his eager erection.

He hissed out a noise, his eyes pinned on her, as she licked him base to tip again, then wrapped her fingers around him, stroking him as she swirled her tongue over the tip. His moan of pleasure vibrated through him as she took him into her mouth and gripped his hips, sliding him in and out slowly as she stared into his eyes.

"Sky..." A warning.

She felt him swell in her mouth, and she slowed her efforts, releasing his hips and gripping his shaft. Her eyes still on his, she dragged her tongue over the tip again. She'd never felt so confident, so in control as she did right then. She'd always been a little hesitant sexually, a little unsure. But the way he touched her, the way he looked at her, like she was the only woman he ever wanted, made her confidence soar. And the way he made her feel when he touched her made her want to pleasure him, to give back with the same intensity he gave to her.

His hands were shaking as he reached for her, but she wasn't ready to relinquish control just yet. Wanting to give him the same thrill he'd given her, she rose to her feet, hips swaying as she stripped off her skirt, then shimmied from her lacy panties and dragged them across his chest.

"Sky," he groaned as he gripped her hips. "You're killing me."

She rocked her hips against him, earning herself another heady groan. His chin fell to his chest, eyes blazing with desire. She brought his fingers to her mouth and swirled her tongue around them, feeling a rush of satisfaction by the hunger in his eyes. She pressed his fingers between her legs and sank onto them as she curled her hand around the nape of his neck, drawing him into a fierce, possessive kiss. He stroked and thrust, kissed and nipped, as they moaned into each other's mouths. Then his mouth was on her neck, his fingers still stroking her, taking her higher and higher, and his mouth—his hot, gloriously talented mouth—came down upon her breast, circling the tight bud with his tongue. He sucked her nipple, applying exquisite pressure that seared straight to her core. She cried out his name, gripping his arms and gasping for breath as she succumbed to the intensity of their passion. Her body throbbed and pulsed, desperate for more of him, as he lowered her to her back and perched between her legs. Her lust-filled brain brought him in and out of focus as he sheathed his shaft and lowered himself down upon her.

His thick crown pressed against her, taunting, teasing as he gyrated his hips, pushing into her one torturous fraction of an inch at a time. Stretching her, nudging her thighs open with his knees as she arched to take him in.

"So big...So good." She pressed on the back of his

hips, urging him deeper, craving all of him faster even as he took her slowly.

"You're so tight. I don't want to hurt you."

"You won't." She wrapped her legs around his thick waist.

He gripped her hips and pressed them back down to the pillows. "It's been a long time for me, Sky. If I move too fast, this is going to be over before we really get started."

She couldn't suppress her smile. "You mean you're not out there porking all your fangirls?"

"Porking my...? No." He half laughed as he pressed his lips to hers and his hands slid from her hips.

She arched up and slid down, burying him inside her with one swift move.

A groan rumbled through his chest. He ground out her name as their bodies began moving in perfect sync. "Sky...Shit...Slower..."

She clung to his biceps. "Can't. Feels too good." She rocked her hips, loving the feel of being so full of him. His chest pressed against hers, and she felt his thundering heart, but it was the look in his eyes that once again made her insides melt. Two days was all it took—two days, a handful of kisses, and his warm and open heart—to make her his.

He slid his hands beneath her ass and held on tight as he drove into her faster, harder, so deep she knew she'd be the best kind of sore tomorrow.

"Sky—"

He sealed his lips over hers. Pleasure radiated down her chest and spread through her limbs, rousing more and more passion inside her. His raw power rivaled the sensuality of his languid kisses, filling her with anticipation. Her breaths came in long, needful gasps.

"Oh God...Sawyer." She clung to him, her thighs tight, her pulse racing, as he moved with perfect precision, stroking her into a frenetic rush of bucks and cries. She had no idea what words streamed from her lungs as his teeth grazed over her shoulder and lights exploded behind her closed lids.

"Not...Gonna...Last." He buried his face in her neck as he surrendered to his own intense release. "So...Good."

Her inner muscles pulsed around his thick length, and she felt every shudder of his release vibrate through him, until they collapsed on the pillows, spent and sated. Moonlight streamed over their glistening bodies, as he rolled to the side, rid himself of the condom, and gathered her against him.

"Lay your head on my shoulder. Your heart next to mine," he whispered. "I'll take it all. Hear it through." He pressed a kiss to her temple. "I'll wrestle your demons, to remain beside you."

She wondered at his words, but as she closed her eyes she was lulled to sleep by the beat of his heart.

Chapter Ten

THE NEXT MORNING Sky awoke early to an empty room, with the early-morning sun peering down on her through the glass ceiling of the rooftop room in Sawyer's house. She rolled over and found a handwritten note on the pillow beside her, and like the one he'd given her the other night with his phone number, it was written on a torn scrap of paper. Lying beside it was a single pink Knock Out rose. She smiled as she lifted the rose and inhaled its sweet aroma, then read the note.

Crying out in your movements. Graceful, longing, hanging by a thread. The longing I see. Set it free, lovely. Come to me.

She marveled again at his words, wondering if he was the P-town poet. Turning the paper over, she found another note, written less hastily, every letter carefully formed.

You were sleeping so soundly I couldn't bear to wake you. There's coffee on the counter and clean towels in the bathroom. I'm sure by the time you wake up I'll be inside, but if not, join me? S.

She walked naked to the windows overlooking the water and noticed a few pencils and pens and a scrap of paper against the wall. He'd said this was where he wrote songs, and she imagined him sitting by the window, overlooking the sunset as he scrawled verse after verse. She gazed out the window and caught sight of Sawyer down on the beach. His shoulders were rounded forward, his hands fisted, as he punched the air. He bounced on the balls of his feet, the way she'd seen fighters do on television. He was shirtless, and from her vantage point, the words on his back blurred together, shadows of darkness inked into his skin.

She watched him with interest as he fought an invisible contender. She pressed the note to her chest. She hadn't ever woken up alone in a man's house before, and strangely, she didn't feel as though she'd been abandoned. Sawyer intrigued her. There were so many layers to him. He'd cherished every inch of her body last night with tenderness and had taken her equally as roughly and possessively in the wee hours of the morning, somehow knowing exactly when or what she'd needed and wanted with every touch.

She gazed out the window as Sawyer turned toward the house. Even from so far away she could tell he was smiling as he lifted his hand in a similar wave to the one he'd given her outside her window in P-town. She felt a pang of excitement race through her and then realized she was standing there naked. A shiver of embarrassment slid over her and just as quickly melted away.

After a moment he went back to fighting the invisible opponent.

He was a fighter.

But boy did he know how to love a woman.

Twenty minutes later she'd showered and used his toothpaste on her finger as a toothbrush as best she could. She dressed in her clothes from the night before and headed out to greet the day and find the man who had set her head spinning. As she descended the stairs she realized that there were substantial railings on both sides that she hadn't noticed last night. For his father, she assumed, and she wondered if he could still navigate the stairs.

How had she missed the enormous gaping hole that was cordoned off in the center of the house between the living room and the kitchen? And what on earth was it for? Outside, she realized just how consumed by their passion she must have been, because she also hadn't noticed the wheelchair ramp beside the steps, or the heavy railings on the steps there, either. She walked around the back of the house and found more recently installed ramps, one leading to the patio doors, another to the first level of the deck, and it looked as though another unfinished ramp ran between the first and second levels of the deck. Sawyer had obviously been hard at work to prepare the house for his father, and that touched her even deeper.

She headed over the dunes. The sand held the chill of early morning beneath her bare feet. The sounds of the waves met her as she walked over the top of the dune and Sawyer came into focus. He faced the water, one powerful leg planted in the sand, his other foot rested against his inner thigh. From the rear she could see his elbows and knew his hands were pressed together. She had done yoga for many years, but was surprised to see a man as big and strong as Sawyer—a fighter—practicing something so passive. In her mind, she pictured fighters in constant motion, spirals of tension wound tightly together and bound by anger. Sawyer was proving her wrong at every turn.

In an effort not to distract him, she walked a little closer, then sank silently down to the sand and watched him. Sky was as taken with a hot male body as the next woman, but she was even more drawn to who a person was inside, and she liked who Sawyer was. When he'd said that it took strength to allow herself to be weak, it had resonated with her in a way that she hadn't fully realized until later, when he'd slept soundly behind her, holding her in his arms. She'd felt feminine and protected. She'd always enjoyed her femininity, but all around her society sent messages that women were supposed to be strong.

As she watched Sawyer standing as stable as a mountain in front of her, the memory of his touch lingered on her skin.

She guessed she wanted to have her cake and eat it, too, because she wanted her own business and to know that she was building a future doing the things she enjoyed. She wanted to be respected and treated as the smart, creative person she was—but she also reveled in the feeling of being soft and feminine in Sawyer's arms. Cared for and protected. The fact that she was getting tired of being protected by her brothers wasn't lost on her. Maybe this was what happened when younger sisters began spreading their wings.

Sky wasn't sure, but for now she had other things on her mind. Wanting to be protected was a world away from knowing the guy she spent the night with walked willingly into a boxing ring to punch and be punched. Her stomach knotted with the thought. She had been pushing away thoughts of his career for two days. Before they'd slept together she was able to separate what he did from who he was. She realized, as she sat there watching him with a gentle breeze sweeping off the bay and seabirds pecking at the sand, that she'd probably handled things backward. She should have given his career serious thought *before* she'd opened her body, and her heart, to him.

Now her thoughts were blurred by the memory of his touch, the sweet things he whispered in her ear, the look of want and need, appreciation and lust, that filled his eyes when they were making love—and the other parts of her that he'd already filled.

***

SAWYER SENSED SKY'S presence before he heard the sweet little sigh that followed her deep inhalation. He hadn't wanted to leave her alone this morning, but he'd been too revved up to lie beside her. He'd already kept her up half the night, and he knew she probably had things she had to do today. If he had lain beside her for one minute more, he wouldn't have been able to resist taking her in his arms and making love to her again. And after his run, when he'd seen her standing naked in the window, his body had reacted even more strongly. He'd had to rely on yoga just to center himself and calm down.

He lowered his foot to the sand and turned to find her gorgeous eyes trained on him, spurring a rush of memories of her sweet sounds and the way she'd writhed beneath him, arching her back, angling her hips so she could take him deeper. He crossed his arms and ran his fingers over the crescent-shaped scars from her fingernails on the backs of his biceps.

"Good morning," he said as he leaned in to kiss her. He'd loved waking up with her in his arms and seeing her smiling face now. And the way she was looking at him, like she felt the same pull he did, made his chest feel as though it might burst.

"Hi," she said in a breathy, soft voice.

He knew he'd always think of that voice as her morning voice. She spoke with the tone of a satisfied lover and the shiver of a new one full of hope.

"Thank you for the rose and the note."

He draped an arm over her shoulder, and it felt natural when she rested her head against him. "I'm glad you liked them, because, Sky, I *really* like you."

"I really like you, too," she said, meeting his gaze. "Can I ask you something?"

"Anything."

She turned to face him, and she looked so beautiful that he had to press his mouth to hers again.

"Sorry," he said as he brushed her hair over her shoulder. "You looked so beautiful, and you smell so good...and I've thought about kissing you all morning."

Her lips curved into a smile that sparkled in her eyes. "You're apologizing for kissing me? More, please." She leaned forward with a sultry look in her eyes.

He could kiss her for hours, get lost in her taste, her warmth, and the sexy little sounds of appreciation that slipped from her lips. When they finally parted, it took a moment for her to come back into focus, and he could tell by her heavy lids that she was still hovering in a lustful cloud, too.

He pressed his hand to her cheek. "How can your kisses transport me so far away?" He tipped her chin up and kissed her again, softer this time. "What did you want to ask me?"

"Ask you?" she whispered, making him smile.

"You said you had something to ask me."

"Oh. Right." Her cheeks flushed. "Um...The note you left for me and what you said last night when you held me. Are you...? I mean, is it you...?" She drew in a breath and exhaled slowly before meeting his gaze again. "Are you the P-town poet?"

"I don't know what I was expecting you to ask, but it wasn't that." He gazed out at the water, wondering what in the heck she was talking about. "I don't know anything about a P-town poet, but I'm pretty sure I'm not him."

She narrowed her eyes. "Are you sure? Because there are so many similarities, that I just thought..."

"I think I would know if I were a poet. It's kind of cool to know that you think my songwriting is poetic, though."

"Sorry. It's just that your words are so powerful. You're like this incredible mix of strength and tenderness."

He pulled her in closer and kissed her again. "I'm a man. I should be hard, rough, and callous."

She laughed. "Oh, you're hard, all right." She

dropped her eyes to his lap with a mischievous grin.

"You are a clever girl, aren't you?" He kissed her again, lowering her back to the sand as she laughed.

"I speak the truth," she challenged.

"And I'm proud of it." He pressed his hips against her thigh.

Her eyes widened with feigned innocence. "Oh, my, you big strong man." She batted her thick lashes. "Maybe you should show me *how* proud you are." She wound her arms around his neck, and he showered her lips, jaw, and neck with kisses, inciting another heart-tugging giggle.

They made out like teenagers, kissing and necking on the beach until a family came walking over the dunes down a ways from them, but close enough to see them. Two towheaded boys ran toward the water laughing excitedly.

Sawyer helped Sky up from the sand. Her cheeks were pink from his whiskers. He rubbed his jaw. "I should probably shave this off, huh?"

"I love your scruff." She touched his cheek, and he closed his eyes, soaking it in.

"I don't want to scratch up your beautiful face."

She went up on her toes and said, "Scratch me up, baby."

He tugged her in close again. "What are your plans today?"

She shrugged. "Let's see...Go home and feed Merlin, change into clean clothes, do some painting at the shop, and look for more chimes and maybe a new chair for the shop. I live a *very* exciting life."

"Trust me, *exciting* is overrated. *Happy* is much better."

She pressed her lips to his chest. "Everything you say is poetic."

He draped an arm over her shoulder as they walked toward the house.

"That's not poetic. It's just the truth."

"It's also poetic."

"You like me, so you hear more than the words I say."

She gazed up at him with confusion in her eyes. His hand slid down her arm, and he laced their fingers together.

"You listen with your heart, Sky. *You're* a true romantic."

"Maybe," she said. "But I don't know how to listen any other way, and even *that* was poetic. I've never met anyone like you, Sawyer. You make me feel things I never felt before, and..."

"And?"

She lowered her voice and said, "And do things that I don't usually do with a guy after knowing him for such a short time."

"Sky, you can't possibly know how much it means to me that you trust me enough to be an intimate part of your life. You should know that I'm not a guy who hooks up with every woman I come across."

"I didn't mean that—"

"I know. But I want you to know this. I'm a pretty private guy. I like my solitude, and..." He paused, trying to figure out how much he should reveal. One look in her trusting eyes and he knew he couldn't hold anything back. "I'm not a saint, but I haven't been the kind of guy that sleeps around for a very long time, and I think I've pretty well sowed any wild oats I might have had."

She searched his eyes, and he hoped she saw the sincerity in them.

"I knew you were nervous when I first carried you upstairs, and I realize that was presumptuous of me. I'm sorry if you felt at all rushed. I was so caught up in you—"

She shook her head, and her lips curved into the sweet smile that he already couldn't imagine living without. "I think I rushed *myself*, but by the time we came together last night, everything felt perfect."

Relief washed through him. "For me, too, and I'm sorry that I was outside when you woke up, but if I had stayed beside you, I wouldn't have been able to keep my hands off of you."

"That's about the best reason I can imagine to be left alone. Actually, it was better. You gave me a chance to breathe. We skipped the whole awkward morning-after thing, and I got to see how clean you keep your bathroom." She arched a brow. "Impressive."

"If a clean bathroom is impressive to you, wait until you see how spotless my gym is." He expected her to laugh, but as her smile faltered and her eyes skipped away from his, he knew he'd struck a nerve.

"You don't like clean gyms?" he said to lighten the mood, knowing she was still wrestling with his career. She didn't respond, and that worried him. "Sky, talk to me. If you can't handle what I do for a living, please tell me."

When she looked up at him, he saw how conflicted she was and felt it like a kick to the gut. "Why did you sleep with me if you're unsure?"

"Because I *really* like you, Sawyer, and I guess I just pushed the whole fighting thing away. It doesn't even feel real to me."

"Oh, it's real all right, Sky. It's very real."

"I get that, and I'm sorry. It's just that I've seen you play your guitar, and I've spent time hanging out with you. Heck, I saw you do *yoga* on the beach, and that's about as passive as it gets."

"Yoga centers me." He hated how frustrated he sounded, but he'd opened his heart for the first time *ever*. Sky was intelligent and sweet. She was creative and thoughtful, and she obviously put family first, just as he did. He'd never felt this strong of a connection before. She saw the world through the same lens he did—except with regard to his career—and he didn't want to think about losing her because of his career.

"Yoga is a way to come down from the high of my workout. Before you woke up, I did a hundred push-ups, two hundred sit-ups, a weight workout, and I went for an eight-mile run."

"And you punched the air," she added wistfully.

He looked at her in confusion.

"I saw you on the beach. You were punching the air."

He pulled her in close and kissed her again, despite the string of doubt hanging between them. "You're so damn cute, Sky. Shadowboxing. It's a way to warm up, or in this morning's case, to release energy."

She pressed her forehead to his chest, and he wrapped his arms around her. He held her, memorizing the feel of her. If he took her home and she decided that this was all they'd have, he wanted to remember the feel of her against him. How the hell she'd had such a big impact on him so fast, he had no idea. But he wasn't about to pick it apart to figure it out. He soaked in her scent, the feel of her soft curves against his hard body, and he hoped—*holy hell did he hope*—that she'd come around and give him a chance.

Chapter Eleven

SKY FILLED MERLIN'S bowls with fresh food and water and crouched beside the kitchen counter to love him up. He purred as he rubbed against her. Sawyer had dropped her off a few minutes ago, and her head was still spinning from their conversation.

"I *know* that he told me he was a boxer before we slept together, but that's not the point," she said to Merlin, who stared at her like she was talking to him about the virtues of cat food.

"Ha!" Jenna said as she came through the screen door. "I told you she slept with him."

Bella and Amy followed her in, each of them wearing sundresses over their bathing suits, their go-to summer outfits.

"Did the fact that I didn't come home last night clue you in?" Sky asked with a laugh.

Jenna bent down and petted Merlin. "Hello, baby boy. Did Mama give you all the details on her hot sex god of a boyfriend?"

Bella snagged a pretzel from the jar on the counter and pointed it at Sky. "You have that freshly fucked look, but it's rough around the edges, like maybe he wasn't as good as we hoped he would be?"

"I didn't know we were hoping for good sex." Sky flopped down on the couch with a loud sigh. "To answer your curiosity, he was a-ma-zing in bed, thank you very much."

Bella tapped her chin. "I remember a certain someone who said that when she fell for a guy, she was going to wait to have sex."

Am I falling for him? "I *tried* to wait, but..."

"He was too big and strong and enticing?" Jenna suggested as she sat down beside Sky.

"He was too tasty of a morsel?" Amy asked with a wiggle of her brows.

"No, you guys. This is Sky. Our earthy girl. I think it has more to do with who he is as a person than any of those things." Bella narrowed her eyes. "We know he says really sweet things, so I can only imagine what came out of his mouth when you guys were all hot and heavy."

Sky rested her head back on the couch and sighed dreamily. "He's...God, you guys. I think romantic things just flow directly from his soul. Bella's right. It's *who* he is." She couldn't suppress her smile. "And all those other things you guys said, too."

"So why did you have the long face a minute ago?" Amy asked as she sank down beside her on the couch.

"Because I finally meet a guy who isn't an asshole or dumb as a doorknob, and he's a *boxer*. A *fighter*. He takes pleasure in beating the hell out of other people."

"Five bucks." Jenna held out her hand to Bella.

Bella took it and set it on top of her little baby bump with a sly smile.

"My own sister-in-law bet on me? Did you bet on me having sex or on me freaking out about him being a fighter?"

Jenna pointed at Bella. "She said you wouldn't sleep with him *because* he was a boxer, so I said you would because the way he looked at you last night was like you were the only person on the entire beach."

"And everyone knows we women melt when we're looked at like that," Amy added. "She really meant it in the best way."

"I'm sure she did. You guys, what am I going to do?"

Merlin pawed at Sky's leg, and she lifted him into her lap. He purred as he settled his chin over her leg and closed his eyes.

Sky sighed and said, "Why can't he be like Merlin, just—"

"Furry with a motor you can turn on and off?" Bella asked. "That pretty much describes every man I know."

"Caden isn't very furry," Amy said as she rubbed her belly. "He's got hardly any chest hair at all. Like *my* man. The perfect amount of fur and a motor that revs up with a kiss."

"Okay." Sky set Merlin on Amy's lap and rose to her feet. "You guys are totally not helping, and I need to go get some work done at my shop before it gets any later."

"Wait." Amy pulled her back down beside her. "You can't just leave us in limbo like this. So how did you leave things with Mr. A-ma-zing?"

"I don't know. I told him that I needed to think about everything, and then I kissed him."

"And now you can't see straight." Amy threw her hands around Sky's neck and hugged her. "It's okay, Sky. You're supposed to feel all dizzy and not be able to think straight when you're falling for a guy."

"I'm *not* falling." She pushed to her feet, hating her indecision and annoyed with herself for not thinking through Sawyer's boxing before she allowed herself to get closer to him. His voice was already ingrained in her mind, his touch still lingered on her skin—and she needed to get the heck out of there before her friends saw it written all over her face.

An hour later Sky was standing on a stool outside her shop, painting a coat of bright yellow on the columns between the windows, when her cell phone rang. She pulled it from her pocket and saw her brother Matt's handsome face. She'd wondered when the news of Sawyer would reach him.

"Hey, Matty," she said.

"Hi, sis. How's everything going?" Matt's tone was patient, whereas her other brothers always seemed in a bit of a rush.

"I'm sure you already know the answer to that." She smiled when he laughed. "So tell me what you really want to know, and you might as well butter me up with a promise to be at my grand opening."

"You know I wouldn't miss it for the world, Sky."

She saw Matt so rarely that when they spoke it made her miss him even more. "Thank you."

"Don't thank me. Just tell me everything's cool with you and this boxer guy I'm hearing about. Is he treating you well?"

She rolled her eyes and smiled. "Yes, of course."

"And are you happy?"

"Do I sound happy?" she asked.

"You always sound happy, but are you happy inside? I'm too far away to know."

"Yes, Matty. Very happy. If you'd move back here you'd see just how happy." Matt was a professor at Princeton, and most summers he took on summer courses, leaving him little time to visit or take vacations.

He was silent for a beat, and Sky wondered if she'd annoyed him. She asked him to move back practically every time they spoke.

"Maybe I'll consider that," he finally said. "Hold on. Someone's here." She heard him open a door, and a female voice rang out. There was a heated exchange, and Matt got back on the phone and said, "Sis, I've got to run. I love you. Call me if you need anything or want to talk."

"Love you too, Matty." She hung up the phone, wondering what that was all about, but as she glanced down the street at all the people and the town she loved, she let that worry fall away.

She watched a mother carry a young boy into Puzzle Me This, and just beyond, a couple was kissing in front of Shop Therapy. She loved the graffiti-style paintings that ran from the roof to the sidewalk and brought Shop Therapy to life. She turned and looked over her shoulder at the Little Shop, a small cottage-style shop painted bright red, and her eyes were drawn to the bright yellow café, Blondies & Burgers, beside it. Commercial Street was so vibrant and alive. A gentle breeze carried the paint fumes away, and every so often the scents of baked goods wafted up from the Portuguese bakery.

This was where she belonged. She hadn't realized how much she'd wanted—needed—to put down roots after she'd lost her mother, but she already felt more grounded than she had in years. And as laughter and commotion filled the air from passersby, she grew even more excited about her impending grand opening. She imagined Sawyer sitting on the stoop by the front door playing his guitar, and her smile faltered a little. Why couldn't coming to grips with his fighting be as easy as knowing she'd put up her shop in the right place?

"Hi, sweetie!" Lizzie shaded her eyes from the sun and smiled up at Sky. "I just got these in and wanted to bring you some." She held up a vase full of colorful flowers.

"Thanks, Lizzie. Those are beautiful." Sky climbed down the ladder and followed Lizzie inside to set the flowers on the coffee table.

"We've got spray roses, daisies, button spray chrysanthemums, Monte Cassino asters, and of course, Limonium. Always Limonium." Lizzie sighed as she glanced around the shop and set her hands on her hips. Limonium was used in many bouquets, and Lizzie always said if there was ever a flower she could tire of, it was that one. Sky thought it was pretty. "Look at this place. It's really coming along."

"I know. I'm so excited. I'm hoping to do some shopping later and pick up a few more chimes and maybe a chair. Want a soda from the back?"

"No, thanks. I can't stay. The store has been crazy busy, but I wanted to drop those off to brighten your day—and see how things with Sawyer are going, of course." Her eyes widened with curiosity.

"He's amazing," Sky said as they walked back out front. "He's coming to the grand opening and he agreed to play his guitar. I really like him, Lizzie."

"That's awesome. I Googled him. Sky, he's totally hot." Lizzie peeked into her store.

"Do you need to go?" Sky picked up the paintbrush again.

"In a sec. There aren't any customers. Everyone seems to like Sawyer."

Sky climbed the ladder and began painting again. "Everyone?"

"I saw Blue when he was working on your shop earlier and he said your brothers met him and that everyone thought he was a good guy—and crazy about you!"

"What else did he say? Did he tell you he had him checked out?"

Lizzie laughed. "No, but it doesn't surprise me, the way he hovers around you."

Sky rolled her eyes.

"Sorry, but he does. Anyway, he said Sawyer didn't shy away from their inquisition, which I wouldn't imagine was a *whole* lot of fun for him."

"Inquisition? Sawyer never said anything to me about them questioning him."

"They're just watching out for you." Lizzie gazed with interest at a group of hot guys walking by.

"I can take care of myself," Sky said with frustration. "I've always paid my own way and I make my own living. I don't need to be *taken care* of."

"Oh, Sky. Everyone needs taking care of."

Why was it that when Lizzie said something like that it felt real and important? And, she realized, for all her fighting about her brothers being overprotective, it validated what she felt when she was with Sawyer.

"Most important," Lizzie said. "What do you really think of him? Beyond the surface stuff."

"I like him a lot. He's smart and kind, and he's so good to me. He seems to really love his family, and you know that's important to me."

Lizzie smiled at a family as they passed. Then she crossed her arms and her voice turned serious. "Sky, it takes a certain type of person to step into a ring and fight."

Sky's pulse quickened with the urge to defend Sawyer—even though she wasn't sold on his fighting either.

"And? What's your take on it, Liz?"

Lizzie shrugged and said, "That you're a big girl and you'll figure it out."

"That's your advice?"

"You just finished telling me that you can take care of yourself, and I have faith in your ability to make sound decisions. You always have before."

"Not after Mom died."

"Oh, Sky. Yes, you did. You didn't go out and get blitzed or turn to drugs or anything like that. You curled up for a while in your safe little nest."

"And needed Pete to rescue me."

"No, Sky. You didn't *need* rescuing. You needed someone to be there for you so you could find your way past the loss of your mother. The more I get to know Pete, the more I think that he needed to take care of you. That was part of *his* grieving. You said that

170

you two have always had a give-and-take relationship like that. He protected you, and you gave him reasons to. But I've noticed that since your dad got out of rehab Pete no longer takes on that role with you."

He had eased up—that was for sure. It wasn't Pete who had wanted to check up on Sawyer, but Grayson. Did that mean that Grayson hadn't moved past their mother's death?

"You've both grown," Lizzie pointed out. "You've shown him that you can handle difficult situations, and he's left behind the need to be everyone's savior. He has Jenna to take care of now."

"And what about Grayson? He's gotten *more* protective of me."

"Gray? He's been protective of you for as long as I've known you guys. But he's also been eclipsed by Pete's big shadow."

"Is life really that complicated, Lizzie?"

Lizzie laughed softly, put her hands in the pockets of her cutoffs, and said, "It's that complicated and that simple."

When Lizzie went back to her shop, Sky wondered if she was making life more complicated than it had to be. She put away her paints and was washing out her brushes when Blue came downstairs from the apartment.

"Hey, Sky. I've got that hole all patched up."

"Thanks. I'm leaving for a while. I'll hang the *Closed for the Morning* sign out front."

"Is everything okay? Do you need more paint? Because I can run down to the hardware store and grab it if you don't want to break your stride."

She dried her hands on a towel and said, "Actually,

I think I'm going to stop by the fight club and watch Sawyer train."

"Really? You okay, or do you want me to go with you?"

She drew in a deep breath, thinking of what Lizzie had said and wondering about the roles that everyone played in her life—her brothers, her father, her friends, Blue—and the role she played in theirs. "I'm okay, but thanks, Blue. I appreciate the offer."

"Hey, Sky?"

"Yeah?"

"I just want you to know that you looked really happy with Sawyer last night, and I'm happy for you."

Maybe life really was that complicated, and that simple.

***

STEP INTO THE ring strong and step out stronger. That was what Roach had taught Sawyer since the first day he'd begun training him. Roach didn't believe in saving strength or strategizing the best time for a fighter to give his all. He'd made it clear to Sawyer and anyone else who would listen that they were either in it to win the whole way through or they were in it to lose. Period.

Sawyer was never in *anything* to lose.

"You're a powerhouse today, Songbird." Roach paced beside the ring, eyes stern, arms crossed.

Adrenaline coursed through Sawyer's veins. He'd been so wound up after Sky's confession he'd come straight to the gym. He'd gone eight rounds on the heavy bag, four rounds on the double-end bag, five rounds of skipping rope, and by the time Roach came in, he was geared up and ready to spar. He was on his fifth round sparring Tanner Delroy, a professional sparring partner, and he had no desire to slow down.

"Come on, Delroy," Roach hollered. "Get back in there and give him hell."

Sawyer sneered around his mouth guard at Roach as he stepped into the ring. Roach was responding to the belligerent attitude Sawyer couldn't seem to shake, and it only made Sawyer's blood boil more intensely as he finished the round.

Sawyer was a master at staying grounded in the ring. He wasn't a bouncer, like amateurs who fidgeted and moved all over the ring like scared mice. He was a powerful fighter who kept his center of gravity, stayed low, and had a core made of brick. He was fast and relentless, with match-stopping jabs that his competitors had said *looked like they came from every direction*—skills that had driven him to the top. Tanner Delroy was a strong competitor. As a professional sparring partner, he took a beating, but it was his chosen career—and he handled it well.

Tunnel vision brought Sawyer in close, taking advantage of the slightest opening with body shots and one final jab that sent Delroy flying off-balance and into the ropes.

"Ho! Hold up!" Roach stepped between Sawyer and Delroy, giving Sawyer a serious *and* proud stare.

"You got me good," Delroy said to Sawyer. A welt the size of an orange was spreading near his Adam's apple.

"Sorry, Delroy. You'll feel that one later."

Delroy grinned and wiped blood from his lower

lip with his forearm. "That's what I'm here for, man. It's all good."

Sawyer paced the ring, itching to go again. Roach stepped up close, and Sawyer was sure he was going to give him hell for going after Delroy so hard.

"You paying attention to your body? Any numbness in your fingers? Blurred vision?"

Sawyer gritted his teeth, holding Roach's dark gaze. "A warning doesn't suddenly fuck me up, Roach. Back off. I'm fighting." Guilt clawed at his shoulders. Roach had been with him since the start, and Sawyer loved him like a brother, but he wasn't going to let him come between him and winning that title fight for his father. "I've got this, and no, no signs of any of that horseshit."

Roach nodded. "Stubborn ass." Roach glanced over his shoulder at the front of the gym and asked, "You expecting company?"

Sawyer looked over Roach's shoulder and saw Sky, wide-eyed and holding on to the registration desk as if she needed to in order to remain standing.

He removed his gloves and climbed from the ring. "Give me a sec."

"Sky." Up close, nervousness radiated from her entire being, like a wounded bird with a cat hovering above.

As if she'd noticed this slight reveal, she pulled her shoulders back and lifted her chin. He leaned in and kissed her cheek, hoping to ease the shock of seeing him fight, but she remained rigid beneath his touch.

"I didn't know you were coming by." He glanced at Brock, standing behind the counter, and Brock respectfully turned away.

"Neither did I." She looked past him at Delroy. "Is that guy okay? You punched him in the neck."

"Delroy?" He glanced back at his sparring partner, who was engaged in a serious conversation with Roach. He reminded himself that what he saw and what Sky saw were probably two very different things. "He's my sparring partner. He's paid to fight."

"But *look* at his neck."

"It's not as bad as it looks." He reached for her hand, and although she didn't readily grasp it, she also didn't pull away. He was so thankful that he nearly said it aloud as he guided her away from the reception desk. The gym didn't have sofas or chairs or a cozy nook in which to talk, but the other men in the gym were respectful enough to turn away.

"I...I should go. I don't want to interrupt your training."

"Sky." He stepped in closer, and the wounded look in her eyes softened, although they were still bouncing between him and the back of the gym. He laced his fingers with hers, and when she accepted them, truly embraced his hand, a relieved sigh slipped from his lungs.

"I know this is probably hard for you to understand, but boxing is more than just two guys beating the hell out of each other."

"How? I just don't understand it, Sawyer. I came here thinking that maybe I was overthinking your fighting. That maybe we weren't so far apart in our beliefs, since we're so close in every other way. But..."

"Don't say *but*, Sky. Not yet. Boxing is just another art form. Like tattooing or singing, or playing the drums, or dancing."

She scoffed. "You're not serious."

"Totally serious." He wasn't used to defending his career. Most people thought it was cool and exciting that he fought—but he didn't give a damn about most people. He gave a damn about Sky. "Sky, I've worked for years to perfect my techniques and conquer my weight class. I've put years of study, years of practice into figuring out what worked, and honed my skills so I could beat everyone else. It's not a game, or a way to just let loose and hurt someone. Boxing takes finesse as well as power." The forcefulness of his tone surprised him, but he didn't want to take a chance that she'd walk out that door without at least trying to understand. "I've gone through years of grueling workouts and given up significant parts of my life for months at a time. Fighting is a part of me, Sky. It's what I've done since I was thirteen."

Her lips parted as if she was going to say something, but no words came.

Acutely aware of Roach's and Delroy's time, he glanced over his shoulder and found them both watching him impatiently.

He turned back to Sky, trying to figure out how to squeeze a day's worth of explanation into the next three minutes. "Where are you headed?"

"Work, I think. I...Work." She nodded, and he could see she was even more conflicted than she'd been when he'd dropped her off at the cottage earlier that morning.

"Can I come by and see you later?"

She dropped her eyes to the floor, taking his stomach with them.

"Sky." Her name slipped from his lips on a

whisper. He lifted her chin and gazed into her eyes, needing her to see *him* and not only what he did for a living.

He ran his hands down her arms, gently bringing her closer and wanting to bring her closer still. "Sky, I'm the same guy I was last night. The same guy you were with this morning on the beach. The same guy who gets crazier about you every second we're together—and twice as head over heels when we're apart."

"I know." Her voice was thin, tethered.

"Then give me a chance? I've got one more fight to win, Sky, and nothing will keep me from it. I hope you can understand that. This one's for my father." He wanted to bend down and press his lips to hers. To remind her of the man he was, separate from boxing, but he respected her too much to do that. He knew this decision had to be made with her heart. Not based on their sexual chemistry.

She surprised him then and placed her hands around his waist and nodded.

He touched his forehead to hers. "My sweet, sweet summer Sky. Thank you."

Roach cleared his throat as he approached, bringing Sawyer back to the world he'd stepped away from only moments earlier. Sky had once again transported him away from everything else around them. How did she do that?

"I should go." Her eyes darted to Roach, who'd stopped by the desk to talk with Brock.

"How late do you work?"

A tentative smile *finally* lifted her lips and reached her eyes. "How late do you want me to work?"

He shook his head and smiled, feeling like he'd just been given a gift. "Damn, Sky. You're going to drive me batty. I thought I'd lost you just now."

She pressed her finger to the center of his chest and said, "I'm not going to lie and say I'm okay with..." She shifted her eyes to the ring, then met his gaze again with the familiar warmth that made his pulse go crazy. "All of this. But I really like spending time with you. I like who you are, and I like how you think. And I like who I am and how I feel when I'm with you."

"But, Sky, I can't change this part of me."

"I know," she said softly.

"This isn't the place to discuss it. Can we talk more later? I need to get some work done at the house this afternoon. The company that's installing the interior ramp is coming by for another preinstallation something or other. Can I come by the shop and see you around six? You said you had some shopping to do. Want to do that together?"

"Interior ramp?" Without giving him a chance to explain, she added, "I'd love that, and six is perfect." She lowered her voice to a whisper and said, "I think I'd better go. That guy looks like he's ready to blow his top."

"The ramp is for my dad. It'll allow him to go up to the skycap again. I can build the smaller ramps, but the interior one was a major renovation. And that guy over there you asked about? That's my trainer, Roach. The guy he's talking to is Brock. Roach always looks like that, but he's a good guy. Hey, why don't I introduce you?"

"Um." Her forehead wrinkled with indecision.

"It would mean a lot to me if you could meet the

guy who helped me get where I am. He's a good friend. He just looks like a Rottweiler—he's really more like a German shepherd."

"Is that supposed to make me feel better?" She reached for his hand as Brock looked over at them.

Sawyer ran his eyes down her white tank top to her emerald-green miniskirt, which he hadn't had a second to appreciate, and a spear of jealousy shot through him. The leather and silver bangles settled around her wrist as he lifted her hand, and the anklet she wore had a starfish ornament hanging from a chain that went down the center of her foot—all very *Sky*. What was he thinking? He might as well have put her on a silver platter for Brock and Roach to ogle. What man wouldn't want to gobble her up?

"Trust me?" he asked, wishing he'd just walked her out to her car instead.

She nodded, and the way she looked at him, like he was the only man she wanted, despite his fighting, plucked the claws of jealousy out of his neck.

Sawyer was around the guys so often that he forgot how imposing they probably looked to her. Sky tightened her grip on his hand, and in an effort to make her more comfortable, and because he adored holding her, he draped an arm over her shoulder and proudly introduced her to his buddies.

"Sky, this is Brock 'the Beast' Garner, the owner of the club."

Brock smiled, softening the Beast and charming a smile out of Sky.

"It's nice to meet you, Sky."

"Thank you. Nice to meet you, too."

"I'm Manny Regan, but most people call me

Roach." Roach held a hand out and Sky shook it.

Sawyer was relieved to feel the tension ease from her shoulders.

"Do you guys fight, too?" she asked.

"We all fight, but it's not as bad as it looks." Roach looked over at Delroy, who was hitting the heavy bag. "See? He's no worse for wear."

"I can't even imagine getting hit by one of you." Sky looked up at Sawyer, then back at the others.

"You're with Songbird, so you'll never have to worry about being hit by anyone. He's a monster in the ring and a pup out of it." Roach winked at Sawyer. "You should put gloves on her sometime and show her how to protect herself."

"Oh, no," Sky said, taking a step closer to Sawyer. "Thank you, but I really don't think—"

"That's the best way to see what it's really like," Brock added. "You'd be surprised at how empowered you feel. My sister fights. She's a tiny little thing, but she packs a powerful punch."

"Okay, enough of the hard sell. I'm going to walk Sky out to her car. I'll be back in a few minutes." Sawyer guided her toward the front door. "I'm really sorry. I didn't think they'd push like that."

"That's okay. I mean, I probably do the same thing when people judge tattoos. I always tell them that maybe if they tried a henna tattoo for a week they might like it." She held his hand as they walked across the parking lot.

A group of kids standing by Sawyer's truck ran toward him when he came out the door.

"Songbird, can we train today?" The request came from a tall, skinny, dark-haired teenager.

Sawyer smiled at the eager boys. They showed up a few times a week, and when he had time, he showed them a few moves. "I'll squeeze in a few minutes when I'm done training. But you guys have got to focus. No playing around today. I'm on a short timeline."

"Cool!" the tall kid said and gave his friend a high five. "We'll focus."

"I'm gonna text my mom to bring over my gear," another teen said as he pulled his phone from his pocket.

"Come on," a third boy yelled as he ran toward three bikes that were lying in the grass beside the parking lot. "Let's go get our stuff!"

Sawyer shook his head and turned back to Sky. "Sorry."

"Don't be. I love that they're so excited, but don't you worry about teaching them to hit each other?"

He shrugged. "Kids are going to fight whether you teach them how to do it right or not. They're trying to learn from watching YouTube videos, and YouTube doesn't teach the finesse they need to be safe—or give them the guidelines of the important things, like being respectful of others, fighters or not, respectful of property that's not their own, following the rules, caring for their gear."

A smile curved her lips. "You really care, don't you?"

"More than you can imagine. Just because I box for a living doesn't mean I'm an animal. I'd better get back inside, but I'm glad you came by." Sawyer pulled her into his arms and she smiled up at him. "Is this okay? Holding you like this?"

"Yes," she said with a smile.

"I know you're wrestling with my boxing, so I don't want to overstep my bounds."

"See? That's one of the things that makes me want to get closer to you. You don't push yourself on me or ignore the things that make me uncomfortable." She went up on her toes and pressed her lips to his chin. "You say that I'm driving you batty, but, Sawyer—*Songbird*—how do you think it feels to hear you say sweet things and then to know that you can turn all that goodness off and clock some guy in the neck?"

He put on a serious face. "I don't turn off my good side to fight, Sky."

"Well, you have to do something with it. There's nothing nice about hitting someone." She tilted her head and shaded her eyes from the sun as she blinked innocently up at him through thick lashes.

"It's not like that. I don't go into a ring thinking about how I'm going to beat the crap out of someone. It's about winning a match. It's about finesse and talent, not just who's bigger or who can inflict the most damage." As he tried to explain, she looked even more confused.

"I know my career isn't something you necessarily like or understand, but that's only one part of me, Sky. And I'm hoping that as you get to know me better, you'll come to like *all* of me and maybe even accept my career."

"You're not upset with me about this?"

"Upset? Sky, I've dated plenty of fans, and the truth is, I'd much rather you like who I am and accept what I do for a living than like me *for* my career. Speaking of which, I'd better get back inside before Tanner takes off, but I'll see you at six at Inky Skies?"

182

"Yes, and, Sawyer, I'm sorry if I took up too much of your training time. Please apologize to Roach and your sparring partner, too."

That was another thing he admired about her. Even though she was obviously having a hard time with what he did for a living, she was still considerate of him and the others.

"I will, but you can have as much of my time as you want."

He pressed his lips to hers, and as he drew back, *she* deepened the kiss. She was a walking contradiction, and he couldn't get enough of her. He tugged her in closer and kissed her with all the passion he'd been holding back. When they finally drew apart, she was breathless—and he was aroused.

Her eyes grew openly amused as she looked down at his tented shorts and said, "Oops."

"Oops, my ass," he teased, and swatted her butt as she climbed into the car.

"Now I feel bad. You can't go inside like that."

He leaned down and kissed her again. "I don't have much of a choice, do I?"

She giggled, and he kissed her again. Damn, he needed to stop kissing her if he had any chance of regaining control, but she was too delicious to stop. Through the window, Sky wound her arms around his neck and kissed him again.

"Sky," he warned.

"I can't help it," she answered. "You're standing there in nothing but a silky pair of shorts and your body's so hard—no pun intended."

He clenched his jaw to stifle his smile. "This is totally fun for you, isn't it?"

She flashed a cheesy grin that made him laugh.

"You're the one who keeps kissing *me*," she said as she gripped the steering wheel.

"I'm the...Okay, you little tease. Get your cute little butt out of here before Roach comes looking for me and finds me like this." He kissed her again through the window, then watched her drive away, turning his thoughts to his father's looming medical expenses and the renovations he was working on—anything to lessen the heat soaring through him.

Chapter Twelve

"WELL, IF IT isn't the queen of ink! You look cute as hell up there on that ladder, giving the world a Skyful of your ass."

Sky laughed as she turned to greet the only person on earth who would come up with a *Skyful* of her ass other than Bella.

"I see we're Maxine tonight?" She climbed down the ladder and hugged Marcus, who was in full makeup and dressed in a skintight green dress that was open nearly to his navel, revealing thick chest hair. His black high heels were higher than Sky could wear without falling. His hair was styled even more beautifully than half the women in Provincetown, making Marcus the perfect drag queen.

"Honey, I've got a show to put on." Marcus hugged her and air-kissed her cheeks, then gazed up at the sign she'd been painting on the front window. "I love how you painted *Inky Skies*. It's so fresh and so you!"

"Thanks. Do you think the design is okay, or *too*

me?"

He stepped in closer and lowered his voice. "Honey, if there's one thing I know about this world, it's that all we've got is who we are. So don't you ever stop being *too* you."

All we've got is who we are. Her mind shifted to Sawyer, and even with conflicting thoughts about his fighting and the rest of who he was, thinking of him brought a smile to her face. "Yeah, you know what? I think you're right."

"You stick with Maxine. I'll never lead you astray." He gazed up at the sign Sky had painted. "I think Howie would have loved the swooping birds and the clouds you painted around *Inky Skies*."

"Are you missing him more lately?" She reached for his hand, and Marcus blinked several times, then drew in a sharp breath.

"Not a day passes that I don't miss that big pain in my..." He smiled and winked. "No pun intended."

Sky laughed as she gathered her paints. "I have a date in a few minutes."

"By any chance is it with a strappingly handsome, wide-shouldered man with the darkest eyes I've ever seen and a mouth I'd like to see around my—"

"Hey!" Sky bumped Marcus's shoulder. "That's enough, playboy." She followed his gaze to Sawyer walking toward them in a pair of jeans and a white linen shirt. Excitement skittered through her chest. "God, Marcus...Sorry, Maxine. How did I get so lucky?"

"Sugar, he's the lucky one. You're one hell of a catch."

Sawyer's smile widened as he came to Sky's side and bent to kiss her cheek. "Hi. The building looks great." He extended a hand to Marcus. "Hi, I'm Sawyer."

Marcus laid his hand gently in Sawyer's, as if he expected Sawyer to kiss it. Without missing a beat, Sawyer did.

"Oh, sugar. He *is* a keeper," Marcus said to Sky, then to Sawyer, "I'm Maxine. It's a pleasure to meet you."

"Nice to meet you, too, Maxine." Sawyer glanced up at the bright yellow paint and the intricately painted sign above. "This looks great, Sky. Did you just do this?"

"Yeah. I've been working on it all afternoon."

"I'll let you kids have your fun," Marcus said. "Sky, baby, come by if you can to see my show later, and bring your hunka hunka burnin' love with you." He winked at Sawyer and sashayed into the crowd.

"Sorry," Sky said as she picked up a paint can.

Sawyer took the can from her. "Why? She was nice. Where's her show?"

"The Crown and Anchor. He...she's there all summer. Marcus by day, Maxine by night." Sky and Sawyer gathered the painting supplies.

"I can't get over that sign," Sawyer said as he gazed up at it again. "It looks like a decal it's so perfectly painted. So you paint as well as tattoo?"

"I mess around, like you and your songs. The paintings in the shop are mine, too."

He picked up the ladder and followed her inside with an armful of supplies, pausing in the reception area to look over the paintings. "Sky, you're incredibly talented. You should sell your artwork."

She set the paintbrushes in the sink and put her

drop cloth over a chair. "And you should sell your songs." She gave him a quick kiss when he smirked. "Besides, I do sell my artwork. I just etch it in people's skin." She wrapped her arms around his waist and gazed up at him. "Maybe we should sell your songs alongside my artwork here at the store. Everyone self-publishes these days. We could make a little book of them and sell it."

"You have a lot of faith after hearing only one of my songs. How do you know the rest don't suck?" He smiled down at her, his eyes as warm as his embrace.

"Because nothing that comes out of your mouth sucks, so I'm sure your songs are all wonderful."

He lowered his lips to hers. "You never fail to surprise me, Sky."

"I could say the same about you. Let me clean the paintbrushes, and then we can head out before another customer comes in. How was your afternoon? Did everything go okay with the ramp guys?"

"It went great. They're starting on the installation in a few days. It'll be nice for my dad to be able to go up to the skycap again."

"I bet. He must be excited about the renovations you're doing."

"I think he is."

"Before I forget, I talked to Pete this morning. He thinks it's fine if we borrow his boat for a night. I was thinking about one night next weekend. Does that sound okay?"

He gathered her in close and kissed her. "Okay? It sounds amazing. I'll let Roach know I need two days off."

"He'll hate me."

"No, he'll just bust my ass harder the other days."

They spent the next few hours walking through the shops in Provincetown and enjoying the warm summer evening.

They had just rounded the corner of Commercial Street and Standish when Sawyer pointed in the window of Recovering Hearts, the local bookstore, and said, "Sky, how about here?"

Recovering Hearts was a cedar cottage-style shop with purple trim and a bright red awning over the front door. There were rainbow flags, colorful stained-glass hearts, and peace signs hanging in the front windows.

"I love that store, but I haven't had a chance to go in since I bought my shop."

Sawyer pointed to a sign in the window and said, "This made me think it's a shop you might like." The sign read, GIFTS FROM THE HEART. GIFTS FOR THE HEART. "And those sold me on going in." He pointed to the back of the store, where dozens of different types of wind chimes—glass, ceramic, metal—hung from the ceiling.

"I think I'm in heaven." She pulled him into the eclectic store and was immediately enveloped by warm scents she couldn't name. Sky hadn't been in the shop since the beginning of the summer, and they'd added new items, like patchwork bags and hoodies, books, and wooden plaques with cute sayings about life and love.

"I want to work my way from the front of the store to the back so I don't miss anything," Sky said as she looked over a display of candles.

Sawyer walked across the store, and a minute

later he tapped her on the shoulder. She turned and found him holding up a wooden sign that read, HAPPILY EVER AFTER STARTS HERE. His eyes were pleading like a sad puppy's.

Her emotions soared as she closed the distance between them and said, "I think I have to buy that sign."

"I was hoping you'd say that."

They picked out an incense burner and a pack of coconut incense for Sky's shop and one for Sawyer's home—*to remind me of you.* And then they went back to look through the wind chimes.

"This one has stars, so it might go with your sculpture." Sawyer reached up and brushed his fingers along the dangling metal stars.

"You noticed that? My brother Grayson made it for me the summer after we lost my mom." She looked up at the ceiling, touching one chime after another, and sending delightful sounds through the store.

"It's a beautiful sculpture, and it was obvious that he put a lot of love into making it."

She watched Sawyer as he moved through the store, picking up fragile knickknacks and delicate faux floral arrangements. He was a broad-shouldered, thickly muscled man, and when she'd seen him in the ring, it had seemed like every muscle, every brain cell, was attuned to his fight. He looked aggressive and precisely focused. And yet by the time he'd come to the front of the gym, all that tension had eased from his body and he'd been awash with concern for her. She didn't understand how he shifted so easily between the two personas.

Did it bring him a feeling of freedom to be able to

achieve such opposite parts of his personality? Were they really opposite? Or were they two parts of the same? Was his aggression in the ring like her focus and skill when crafting a tattoo or painting? Could he have been right about that? In Sky's mind, it was like comparing apples and oranges, but when she was with Sawyer, there was no part of him that felt aggressive. The things he said and the way he moved, everything seemed natural and easy, not overly planned. And when she'd seen him in the ring for that brief time, she had to admit that even though he'd harnessed all that power and used it to knock his competitor to the ropes, he wasn't swinging wildly or chasing the guy down. He moved like a panther on the prowl, slow, controlled, and when he struck, it was one fast punch, whereas the guy he was fighting was throwing a number of punches that Sawyer had easily blocked.

He was leaning over a glass case now, his eyes focused on something, his body relaxed, and when he turned and caught her looking at him, his smile shot straight through her.

They meandered through a few more shops and ate dinner at a café overlooking Commercial Street. After dinner they headed back toward her shop. The crowds had thinned, and the lights of the shops illuminated faces of a younger crowd. Music filtered out of bars, and drag queens stood out front of playhouses and bars handing out postcards with information on their shows. A guy playing a guitar sat on the steps of the library, surrounded by people listening to his music.

"I love it here," Sky said as they stopped to watch the guitarist play. "I love the energy of the people and the music, the colorful shops. And the pier. God, I love the pier so much, and the smell of the water at night, when the temperature dips and the fishy smell turns to something crispier, more alive. Everything about this town makes me feel good."

"I've always liked the diversity of Provincetown, but it's been ages since I've spent any time walking around here. Spending time with you reminds me of the things I've been putting on the back burner, like enjoying an evening out. It seems like I've been training hard and working on the renovations to the cottage forever. Before the addition of the handicapped ramps, I worked on other projects, like raising the floors to eliminate the step down to the living room, and before that there was the renovation of the bathrooms to make them handicap accessible."

"Wow, you have been busy. I didn't realize you'd done so much."

"It's all worth it. That house means a lot to our family, but, Sky, spending time with you is better than anything else in my life. When I'm with you it doesn't matter what we're doing. You make everything special. You make me feel alive in ways I haven't for a long time."

"We make each other feel that way, Sawyer. I've never been happier than when I'm with you."

"Even though I'm a boxer?"

She reached up and touched his cheek, then answered him with a smile. "Even though you're a boxer."

"You can't imagine how much that means to me. This is my last fight, and I know I'm going at it hard, but I *have* to win. It's one fight. Then I'll retire, and you won't have to worry about my fighting anymore."

"One fight. I think we can weather that storm. Just don't get hurt."

"I'll try not to get hurt. I want time with you, Sky. The last thing I want is to be injured. But you don't have to worry. I'm an animal in the ring. I'll kil—" He stopped himself, as if he didn't want to use the word *kill* around her. "I've got this. I'll win this fight."

Sawyer had a new, even more confident bounce in his step as they walked down the street toward her shop and the music faded behind them. People chatted on the steps of Puzzle Me This, and a man sat with his black Labrador retriever on the stoop of Shop Therapy. The thick scent of sage hovered in the air like marijuana at a concert. Sky leaned her head on Sawyer's shoulder as they walked, feeling relaxed and comfortable.

When they reached the shop, they both admired the freshly painted sign. *Inky Skies* was painted in a font that looked like a tattoo, with parts of each letter thickly painted and other lines so thin they were barely visible. Each letter was perfectly scripted. Teardrops appeared to be dripping from the bottom of the *k* in *Skies*. Clouds were painted above the words, fading as they sank halfway down behind the letters. Flecks of black spewed from the top of the *k* in *Inky*, fanning out into a flock of colorful birds, and in the bottom swell of the script *I* in *Inky*, Sky had painted a golden half-moon.

"I can't get over the sign, but why didn't you name it Inky *Sky*?"

She dug her keys from her bag and unlocked the front door before answering. He followed her into the dark shop, and she sensed him all around her—in the pulsing air, in the coiling heat in her belly, in her swelling heart—as if he'd already become a part of her. As she put her keys and bag on the counter and reached for her poetry book, she felt his father's presence, too. She didn't even know the man, but she somehow felt like she did from reading his poetry. Her friends thought she was *mooning* over C. J. Moon, but it was his words that spoke to her. The emotions he'd put down on paper that wound around her insides and tied themselves into a little knot of hope. And now his son—his wonderful, romantic, caring son was standing behind her as she lifted herself up on the counter and sat facing him.

Gazing into Sawyer's intensely dark eyes as he moved between her legs and placed his hands on her hips, she knew his father had poured all of those emotions into him. Of course Sawyer was made of warmth and strength and loyal fiber. Of course he was thoughtful, loving, and romantic. Sawyer Bass was placed here on earth just for her.

Her pulse quickened with the thought. It was one of those thoughts that her friends might roll their eyes at and her brothers might scoff at, but Sky didn't care about any of that. Everything he said spoke to her. Every touch, every glance, every whisper when she was in his arms, drew her further in. She already knew she'd never get enough of him. A tiny pulsing nag in the back of her mind ticked off the word *fighter*, and she rolled it over in her mind. Why would the universe drop a fighter in her lap? Someone who did something so far afield from the things she believed in?

His words sailed through her mind.

Because you're strong enough to be weak when you need to. That's a blessing. Most people are so hardened to their feelings that they mask them. I see it every day in the ring. Hell, Sky, I do it every day of my life.

The answer was easy.

Because you needed me, too.

"I didn't name the shop after myself," she explained. "I know everyone thinks I did, but I didn't." She flipped through the poetry book and began reading. "*Sun drifts, moon breaches, cool air whispers into the night. Tears fall, arms comfort, birds in the distance take flight. Waning crescent, smother my cries, take me up to the inky skies.*"

She gazed up at him with solemn eyes. "It's one of my favorite poems."

"It's my father's." His voice was thick with emotion.

"It's destiny," she whispered.

Chapter Thirteen

SAWYER AWOKE THE following morning to soft paws stepping onto his chest. He opened his eyes and found Merlin's scrunched-up furry face staring down at him accusingly, as if he'd taken his spot on the bed. Sawyer shifted his eyes to Sky, fast asleep beside him. Her head was nestled against his chest, one thigh rested over his, and her arm was draped possessively over his stomach. Her long dark hair fell over her shoulder, covering her bare breast, save for a small patch of ivory skin. He never knew it was possible to feel so much for someone so quickly, but every ounce of his soul was wrapped around Sky Lacroux. He'd never met someone whose essence was so similar to his own.

Merlin stretched his paws straight up the center of Sawyer's chest, then sank to his belly and closed his eyes. A second later Sawyer felt the gentle vibration of his contented purr. Sawyer closed his eyes and draped one arm across Sky, and with the other he stroked

Merlin's back. Life didn't get much sweeter than this.

He thought about the day ahead and the sparring he'd undergo during training. The doctor's warning came rushing back, and his thoughts turned to his father. He'd call him later that morning and see how he was doing.

Sky sighed in her sleep, and he pressed a kiss to her head. She was such a nurturing and loving person, and so sensual, open, and trusting, that it made him want to do everything he could to make her happy. As he lay there beside her, beneath her precious kitty, with the sun peeking through the curtains and the scent of their lovemaking lingering around them, he knew he needed to get a grip on the emotions she'd awakened in him. He knew that the second he stepped into the ring, thoughts of her would be right there with him, reminding him that it was no longer just *his* head, just *his* body—if he wanted Sky, he owed it to her to remain in one piece, wholly functional and cognitively capable.

That meant that he needed to practice even harder, hone his every move even more effectively. Remain completely focused.

Sky's hand moved up his stomach to Merlin's back. "Mm. We have company. Sorry." Merlin purred louder.

He loved her hazy morning voice. "Don't be. Merlin and I have an agreement. I get to sleep beside you in the bed, and he gets to use me as a mattress. It seems pretty fair to me."

She lifted her head and looked up at him with sleepy eyes and a contented smile. "I like that deal, too."

Merlin stirred with her movement and lifted his

head, as if he were deciding whether he should close his eyes and try to sleep or if his snuggle time was over. A second later he walked leisurely off Sawyer's chest and leapt from the bed.

Sky laughed softly. "Think he knew I wanted to get closer to you?"

Sawyer rolled over her, gently lowering her to her back as his chest rose above hers. He loved the feel of her beneath him, soft and warm. He brushed her hair from her forehead and looked beneath her sweeping lashes to her sleepy eyes.

"You've lured me in to you, Sky."

Her lips were faintly pink, lighter than after they kissed, after their passion turned them dark and well loved. The urge to kiss her was strong, but not as strong as the desire to tell her exactly how he felt, to reveal to her the way his thoughts turned to her at every move.

"I'm totally falling for you," he admitted. "If we keep spending time together, I know I'm only going to fall deeper into your depths."

Her fingers trailed up his side as she swallowed hard, her eyes never wavering from his, turning mildly serious. He felt her pulse quicken, and he knew she felt his speed up, too.

"Should I be worried?" she asked in a whisper.

He smiled at her response. She never said what he anticipated, and it made her even more appealing.

"Only if you're going to have second thoughts about us. I've never given away my heart before, Sky, and honestly, it's a little scary." He fought fierce competitors, willingly opened himself up to a physical beating every damn day. But nothing—*nothing*—

compared to what Sky could do to him if she walked away, even after a few short days. He could only imagine how his feelings for her would grow after another week, a month, a year.

"I think I'm done with second thoughts," she answered. "I can't fight what's between us. It's too big."

"I want to fall into you, Sky, and never find my way out."

She pressed her hands flat to his back and whispered against his lips, "Fall, Sawyer. I'll be right there with you."

***

LATER THAT MORNING, on her way to work, Sky stopped at a yard sale and found the perfect chair for the shop. The paisley fabric was a mix of blues, wines, creams, and yellows. It had an old-fashioned look to it, though it was obviously much newer and in perfect shape, save for the comfortably used look of the cushion. The guy who sold it to her loaded it into her car, and once her busy afternoon was over, she'd have Blue help her carry it inside.

She spent the first hour at the shop researching Parkinson's. She read about the progression of the disease, the symptoms and eventualities that Sawyer and his family were facing. She wanted to know as much as she could, to better support Sawyer, and the more she read, the more she connected dots between her father's alcoholism and his father's disease. They weren't the same, of course, because her father's deterioration into alcoholism was voluntary and

Sawyer's father's disease didn't have a remedy waiting behind the doors of a medical facility, the way her father's had. But her father had dealt with a disease that was stronger than him, the same way Sawyer's father was. The same way her mother's life was stolen from her. She wondered what it felt like to be a man, the pillar of strength for a family, and to feel that strength slipping away. For her father, she thought perhaps he readily gave it up in order to keep his sanity after losing his wife. He probably saw it as a reprieve from the pain and loneliness—and she knew just how lucky they were that he'd done well in rehab and had remained sober ever since.

Sawyer's father didn't have that option, and even without having met the man, he had her love and her respect. And she already knew she'd do whatever it took to help his family.

She spent the rest of the day moving between painting the final touches on the sign out front and tattooing customers. She'd barely had a chance to breathe. She didn't even have time to slow down and fill Lizzie in about her and Sawyer when she popped in at lunchtime. Her mind had been drenched in thoughts of him ever since she'd left his arms that morning, when he'd said he had a surprise for her tonight. He wanted her to get to know all sides of him.

She was pondering how many more sides he could have when Cree breezed through the front doors waving something above her head.

"I *love* your new sign," she said as she slapped a napkin on the counter. "And the yellow really livens up the place." She knelt to lace up her worn black boots, then tugged on the bottom of her tank top, pulling it over the hips of her black miniskirt.

"Thanks. I painted it yesterday. I didn't expect you back so soon." She wondered if she was just killing time before her shift started at Governor Bradford's.

"I didn't expect to be back, but I forgot I had this, and I really wanted to get it done."

"Great." Sky read the writing on the napkin. *I'll take it all. Hear it through. Wrestle your demons to remain beside you.* She lifted her eyes to Cree, wondering if this was some type of trick Sawyer had put her up to. Those were the exact words he'd said to her after they'd made love the first time.

"Where did you say you got this?"

"Some guy left it on the bar a few nights ago. Why?" Cree was way too casual for this to be a trick.

"I think my friend wrote it. I just wonder why he'd leave it there."

Cree shrugged. "I guess he didn't like it. His loss is my gain. I have to get to work early tonight. Do you have time to tat me up?"

"Sure, of course." Sky took her into the back, and for the next forty-five minutes she permanently inked the words Sawyer had said to her after they'd made love onto Cree's body. The words had seemed so heartfelt and sincere and had touched her so deeply that now jealousy snaked through her. She didn't like tattooing Sawyer's lovely words onto Cree, like they were hers for the taking.

A steady stream of customers kept Sky busy all afternoon, which was a good distraction from the tattoo that had her mind spinning. Blue arrived sometime earlier to work on the renovations, and as Sky finished up a tattoo that had taken two hours on a guy's calf, Blue finished applying a final coat of paint on the back wall.

After the customer left, Sky closed up the shop and headed into the back to join him. She plopped onto a chair with a loud sigh, thinking about Cree's tattoo.

"What a day. I swear someone must be out there singing the virtues of tattoos or something." She rubbed her stiff fingers.

"That's a good thing. It would suck if you had no customers." Blue set the toolbox and painting supplies on the table next to Sky. "I'm just about done with the painting. I have some spackling and painting to get done upstairs, I want to build the shelves for your supplies behind your screens over there, and I think I can make a great row of built-ins upstairs. Then the place is all yours. Good as new."

"You're the best, Blue. Thank you." Not for the first time, she thanked her lucky stars for Blue's friendship.

"Paybacks are hell. You're going to give me free tattoos for life *and* get me into Sawyer's next fight, right?" He shoved his hands in his jeans pockets and cocked a smile.

"Free tats? You've never let me put a lick of ink on you, but if you ever do, absolutely. And as far as Sawyer's fight goes, I don't think I'm going to go to it, but I'll ask him for a ticket for you."

"Was it that bad watching him train?"

Sky fidgeted with her bracelets. "It was like what I imagine it would be like to watch Merlin mangle a mouse." She met Blue's gaze. "The same way I can't imagine my sweet kitty hurting anything, I don't want to envision Sawyer hitting someone. But I saw it, so I know it's real, unlike Merlin, who I can still pretend doesn't ever kill mice."

She got up and paced. "You should have seen the two of them. Even *I* could tell that the other guy had no business being in the ring with him. He was smaller, and none of his punches connected with Sawyer, but Sawyer's punches?" Her eyes widened with the memory. "Blue, he hit the guy *hard*."

"He's supposed to. That's what training is all about—perfecting his technique."

"Well, he sure perfected it. The other guy had a huge welt on his neck." Sky stopped pacing and leaned on the counter beside Blue. "I've never been in this situation before, Blue. I *really* like him. I like who he is and I like everything about him—except the fighting."

"Well, that's a big thing, but it doesn't have to be a *make it or break it* thing, does it? What if he were a lawyer who defended criminals or a stripper or—"

"A stripper? Really? I would never date a stripper."

"Wow, you are uptight." He laughed with the tease.

"I'm being serious. He's fighting for a noble reason—to earn money to pay for his dad's future medical care—but still...I don't think I can watch him fight again."

Blue shrugged. "I don't see the problem. So don't go to the fight."

"His mom won't go to his fights either. Oh, let me show you something else." She headed up to the front and grabbed the basket of tattoos she'd collected. She fished out the one Sawyer brought with him and the two Cree had brought in and handed them to Blue.

"Same handwriting, right?"

"I guess. Close anyway," he said as he looked them over.

"Well, I think Sawyer is the P-town poet." She crossed her arms and tapped her foot.

"And?"

"I asked him if he was and he said no." She grabbed the napkins and papers and read them again before setting them back in the basket. "And that one on the napkin?" She pointed to the napkin on top of the pile. "That's what he said to me the other night. Those exact same words."

"What are you worried about, Sky? That he's hiding that he likes to write poetry?"

"No. It's just...Why would he hide something like this?"

"This is why I don't date. Weird shit comes up and then everything falls apart over notes in a basket." Blue reached for his tools. "He doesn't seem like he's the kind of guy who's hiding anything. Show him the papers and ask him about them. It seems like a simple thing."

"I'm going to, but I asked him already."

"I don't know, Sky, but if you're having trouble with his fighting *and* you don't trust him—"

"I totally trust him!" She grabbed the basket again, knowing she wasn't making any sense, but she had to know if the man she was falling for was the same man who wrote all the beautiful sayings she'd been saving for two years.

"Then why are you questioning this? If he said he's not the guy, he's not the guy." He reached for the back door. "I have to run. Lizzie asked me to come by and fix a leak in her roof."

"She did? Good. Go." She shooed him toward the door.

"Don't get any ideas. It's a leaky roof, that's it."

"Yeah, and I'm going to walk away from Sawyer," she said sarcastically.

"So you *are* really into him!"

"God, Blue. Guys are so slow sometimes. *Of course* I'm totally into him. I told you I *really* liked him. Otherwise why would I care if he told me the truth about being the P-town poet or not? Now, go see Lizzie, and tell her I said hi."

"You're bossy when you've got a boyfriend."

She blew him a kiss, closed the door, and leaned her back against it. The basket sat on the counter, taunting her with the little slips of paper and crumpled napkins. She snagged it and headed out to her car.

An hour later, freshly showered and wrapped in a towel, Sky stood in the cottage with Bella, Amy, and Jenna, staring into her closet.

"Everything is long and flowing," Bella said as she flicked one of Sky's skirts.

"That's what I like to wear." Sky took a skirt from the rack and held it up against her. "The miniskirt I wore today isn't long or flowing. I could wear that."

"But it doesn't say *Tell me all your secrets*, does it?" Jenna asked. "Why don't you wear this?" She held up a black silk tank top.

"I love that. And what skirt?" Sky asked.

"Just the shirt!" Jenna said, holding it up against her pregnant belly. "Look, it comes to my thighs. We want answers, and the best way to do that is by being ultrasexy so he can't think about what he's saying."

Sky held the shirt up in front of herself. "It comes to your thighs because you're four foot eleven. I'm not. This would barely cover my coochie."

"Even better," Jenna teased.

"No. No way. I'm not going to get answers by flashing my naughty bits."

"At least you're not wearing Hello Kitty shirts," Amy said. "They had a field day with my clothes when Tony and I finally got together, remember? Luckily, he likes me best with no clothes on." She leaned in close and whispered, "Saves on clothing expenditures, too."

Sky grabbed a black miniskirt. "This will work, with a few long necklaces and my bangles, don't you think?"

Jenna rolled an assessing eye over the dark outfit. "I like it. It's sexy, but with your accessories it'll be understated enough that he won't feel like he's under attack."

"Says the girl who wanted me to go with no bottoms," Sky said.

"Oh, he'll be under attack, all right," Bella said. "Didn't you hear Sky say that every time she kisses him she can't stop?"

"I was too focused on the basketful of romance to hear that part." Jenna rummaged through the back of Sky's closet. "Don't you have any scarves? It might be chilly tonight."

"I think I left them all in the apartment." Sky opened a dresser drawer. "I'll take a sweater."

Amy pushed the drawer shut. "Bad idea. You can't get cold if you wear a sweater. Jenna taught me that. Jenna, can't you lend her a scarf?"

"I'm on it!" Jenna headed out the front door.

"You guys have dating down to a science. It's kind of scary." Sky smiled at her friends.

"You're lucky, Sky." Bella sat on the bed with a hand on her burgeoning belly and pulled Sky down beside her. "None of us was very good at the whole dating thing. We learned as we went along. Sweaters keep you warm. Scarves leave room for a chill. You want the chill so you can snuggle up to your man. See? You get to benefit from our mistakes." She sucked in a breath, eyes wide. "Oh my God. Feel this." She grabbed Amy's and Sky's hands and placed them on her belly.

"Oh my God! Is she kicking?" Sky asked. "Or is that a knee? Or an elbow?"

"I'm not sure, but I wish she'd come out already." Bella sat on the bed and leaned back on her palms. "It's hard to breathe with her in there sometimes, and when she kicks my bladder, you better make room for me to dart to the bathroom."

"I know what you mean," Amy said. "I swear I have to pee every five minutes. Speaking of..." She headed for the bathroom just as Jenna came in the door with an armful of scarves and dumped them on the bed.

"Wow, thanks, Jenna." Sky began sifting through them.

"You can't pick out a scarf until we pick out your shoes. They have to match. Flip-flops, sandals, or..." Jenna picked up Sky's favorite ankle boots. "Fuck-me boots?"

"Let's go with sandals, please. I don't even know where he's taking me, but just in case, I think I better not look like a hooker." Sky took the boots from Jenna and tossed them in the back of the closet.

"You never look like a hooker." Jenna scrambled to pick them up, despite her burgeoning belly. "You can't just toss your boots." She set them up beside Sky's other shoes and sandals, then began lining them up so the toes of each pair aligned.

"Jenna," Sky said. "You know I'll just mess them up tomorrow when I grab something to wear."

"Then I'll come back and line them up again," Jenna said with a smile.

Merlin sauntered into the closet and rubbed against Jenna's leg. "Merlin will be my watch cat. He'll claw at you if you mess them up."

"Good luck with that. Merlin's more likely to lick me to death." She picked up her kitty and kissed him, then set him down and began getting dressed.

Amy came out of the bathroom with a bottle of perfume. "This is so yummy, Sky. You should wear it."

"Okay." She held out her wrist and Amy sprayed it. Sky waved her hand in the mist. Then she pulled her tank top over her head and put on several bracelets and two long necklaces. "What do you think?" She spun around, and all the girls smiled.

"Stunning," Amy said.

"You always look hot," Jenna said.

"Is it too much?" Sky hated the idea of looking like she'd tried too hard.

"No! You look comfortably sexy," Bella said.

Jenna sifted through the scarves and draped a pale blue one around Sky's neck and wiggled her brows. "Scarves are so handy. Feel free to *play*, if you know what I mean."

"Oh my God." Amy grabbed Jenna's arm. "Have you gone all *Fifty Shades* on us?"

Jenna laughed and turned beet red. "No. Not *all Fifty Shades*. Besides, Bella has fuzzy handcuffs. What's wrong with scarves?"

"And don't you try to look innocent, Amy." Bella narrowed her eyes. "You told us all about your little hands-behind-your-back escapade with your sexy surfer husband."

"Hey, I never heard about that," Sky said. "Where was I?"

"That was the night you and Sawyer were learning the ins and outs of each other," Jenna said with a loud laugh.

"I thought we told you about Amy's sexy romp," Bella added.

"I think I'd remember Kitten getting tied up," Sky teased.

There was a knock at the door, and they all gasped.

Amy peeked out the bedroom window. "He's here, and *ooh la la*, he looks yummy."

They stumbled over one another to fit through the bedroom door.

"I feel like I'm in high school." When Sky opened the door, her heart nearly stopped. She was vaguely aware of sounds of appreciation coming from behind her. She'd seen Sawyer wearing jeans, shorts, and completely naked, all of which were enough to make her go a little crazy, but she'd never seen him look like this. His broad shoulders were even more powerful in a black dress shirt tucked neatly into a pair of dark slacks, opened at the top to reveal a smattering of chest hair.

His eyes took a slow drag down her body, making

her feel hot and electric at once. He touched her hand as he kissed her. The scent of his cologne embraced her, and when he spoke, it was like she was hearing his voice for the first time, sending her stomach into flurries.

"You look gorgeous," he said with an easy smile. "You ladies look gorgeous, too," he said.

"Thank you," they said in unison.

Sky glanced over her shoulder at the girls and caught sight of the basket sitting on the table. Somehow it didn't seem as pressing now as it had earlier. She didn't want to get into a serious conversation about poems right now. Did it really matter if he was the P-town poet? Not enough to sidetrack what was sure to be a lovely evening.

"They were just leaving," Sky said.

"Right," Bella said, but she made no move to leave. "What's the plan? Can't you clue us in on your secret date?"

Sky shooed them toward the door. "Come on, my married *and* preggers friends. Stop drooling over my man and prying him for information."

The girls wished them a fun evening and filed out the door in a gaggle of whispers.

"Sorry. I think when we all get together we turn into teenagers."

"I wish I'd known you as a teenager," he said in a voice that could melt butter. "Then we'd have had even more time together."

Chapter Fourteen

SAWYER PARKED IN front of Undercover, a bar overlooking the beach in Truro. Sky had never been there before. Sawyer helped her from the truck and said, "Okay, sweet summer Sky, it's time for you to get to know another side of Sawyer Bass."

"Should I be worried?"

"Maybe so," he teased as he held the door open for her. They stepped inside the dimly lit bar. "You don't mind meeting a few of my friends, do you?"

"I would love to, as long as I don't have to watch them fight."

With a hand on her lower back, he led her past booths and tables that were filled to the brim with happy customers. They crossed the crowded dance floor to a booth by the bar.

"Songbird!" a guy with white-blond hair yelled from behind the bar.

"Hey, Colton." Sawyer waved and slid into the booth beside Sky.

"I guess you come here often?" she asked, glancing at the guy behind the bar, who ran a hand through his hair, flashing a number of tattoos on his left arm.

"That's Brock's younger brother," Sawyer said. "He owns the place."

She studied Colton's face a little more closely. His cheeks were chiseled and much narrower than Brock's, and while Brock's eyes had been intense, Colton's were a soft blue, with a gentler look to them.

Sawyer draped an arm over her shoulder and pulled her in closer. "I know I should probably wine and dine you to make up for my lack of a more acceptable career, but—"

"Hey." She could tell by the lightness of his tone that he was kidding, but she still felt compelled to clarify. "I didn't mean that your career wasn't acceptable to *anyone.*"

He pressed his lips to hers. "I know. I just want you to get to know all of me, including the people I hang out with."

"All of you?"

"When you think of me, you see a guy who fights in the ring, and there's a lot more to me than that, Sky. There's more to my friends than that, too, and *that* is what tonight is about."

Colton came around the bar to their table. "Hey, Songbird." He lifted his baby blues to Sky. "Hi. I'm Colton." The year *2012* was inked on the inside of his left forearm, and the sleeve of his T-shirt revealed sharp lines of another tattoo.

"Hi, I'm Sky. I like your ink."

"Thanks, Sky." He looked down at his tattoos. "Everyone's got a story, I guess. It's nice to meet you, too. What can I get y'all?" he asked.

"Sky?" Sawyer asked.

"A sea breeze, please. Thanks."

Sky followed Sawyer's gaze toward the front door as he asked for a beer and was surprised to see his trainer and Brock heading toward them, with two tall blond women in tow.

"Cool. Sibs are here." Colton waved at Brock and the others. "I'll be right back with your drinks."

"You brought your coach? Am I in for a lecture?" She fidgeted with her necklaces nervously. The taller of the two girls wore a white crinkled cotton skirt and a black and green tie-dyed tank top with lace circling the bottom. The other girl had on a pair of cutoffs and a flowing pink and blue blouse that hung off of one tanned shoulder. Her long blond hair hung halfway down her back, and she wore a cute leather headband across her forehead. Like Sky, both women wore a number of bracelets.

"No lectures. I promise. Tonight I brought my *friend* Roach. He left the coach side of himself at home. And those are Brock's sisters, Harper and Jana." He rose and shook Roach's hand, embraced Brock with a brotherly slap on the back, and then hugged each of the girls before sitting back down beside Sky.

Brock leaned down and hugged Sky. "Nice to see you again, Sky. These are my sisters, Harper and Jana."

Roach moved in for a hug next, barely giving Sky time to catch her breath. "Glad you're here."

"Hi," she said as Roach sat down beside Sawyer.

Harper and Jana sat down across from Sky, and Brock slid into the booth beside them.

"How's our *other* brother?" Jana asked.

"Doing great." Sawyer leaned closer to Sky and said, "Harper's a screenplay writer, and—"

"And television writer now, too," Harper interrupted, smiling at Sky. "I just got hired to work on a sitcom."

Jana bumped Harper with her shoulder. "Show-off. Hi, Sky. I'm Jana, *not* a screenplay writer."

"Hi," Sky said, immediately liking the girls' energy. Sawyer reached for her hand.

"Jana's a dancer," Brock said, then added with a proud smile, "and a fighter. The girl packs a mean right hook."

Sky thought they were kidding. Jana was graceful and lithe, not muscled or harsh-looking like Sky pictured female fighters. "Really?"

Harper patted her sister on the back. "She really is. Strange, I know. But when you grow up with brothers like Brock and Colton..." She shrugged.

"Do *you* fight, too?" Sky asked Harper.

Jana laughed. "Her? No way. She wouldn't hurt a bee if it stung her."

That made Sky a little more comfortable. At least she wasn't the only girl who didn't like fighting. "What kind of fighting do you do, Jana?"

Jana gathered her hair over one shoulder and twirled a lock around her finger. "Brock's been training me to box for the last two years. I haven't won anything big yet, but I will." Determination filled her eyes. "You should come by and watch sometime. Brock could show you a thing or two if Sawyer hasn't already."

"Sky isn't really into fighting." Sawyer squeezed her hand.

"Then she can watch," Jana suggested. "It's fun to watch, too."

"Thanks. I'll think about it." She still couldn't imagine the pretty blonde fighting. "What about dance? What type do you do?"

"Everything from ballet to tap and hip-hop. I perform with all the local theaters."

"I did a ton of theater with local groups in New York when I was in college." Sky smiled at Sawyer. "We should go watch her dance sometime."

"I've been watching Jana dance since she was a kid. Sounds good to me."

They talked a little about Jana's dancing and Harper's script writing, which Brock teased her about, saying she was writing porn, because the sitcom she was writing was for cable and apparently very racy.

"I don't even want to hear *Harper* and *porn* in the same sentence, please," Sawyer said with a grimace.

Harper rolled her eyes.

"Did you put our name up?" Brock asked Sawyer.

"No. We just got here," Sawyer answered.

"Name up?" Sky asked as Brock headed up to the stage.

"You'll see," Sawyer said.

"Ooooh! We're being secretive tonight. I like that," Jana said. "How long have you two been dating?"

"Just a few days," Sky answered, feeling like it had been much longer. "I heard him play the guitar, and the next day he came in for a tattoo."

Harper, who had been busy eyeing a guy across the dance floor, turned serious eyes to Sawyer. "Another tattoo, Sawyer? Is your father doing okay?"

"Yeah, he's doing pretty well."

Worry filled Harper's gaze, and Sky noticed Sawyer shifting his eyes away.

Colton brought their drinks and set a pitcher of beer down on the table.

Roach filled the glasses and pushed one to Harper and another to Jana and Brock. His dark eyes weren't filled with fire the way they had been in the gym, and his shoulders weren't riding just beneath his ears, as if he held all the world's tension in them. He could have just as easily been a bouncer or a weight lifter as a boxer.

"Surprised to see us tonight?" Roach asked.

"Sort of," Sky admitted. "But it's nice to see you again. And to meet Harper and Jana."

"A toast." Sawyer held up his glass, his eyes trained on Sky. "To the mystery of the moment."

"God, Songbird." Roach shook his head. "Don't you ever say anything normal?"

"You're just jealous because everything he says sounds like it's spun from gold." Jana tapped the table in front of Sky. "You're a lucky woman, Sky."

"Yeah," she said in a breathy voice that took her by surprise. "I am."

Sawyer slid his hand to the nape of her neck and pressed his lips to hers.

"Get a room," Roach teased.

"Jealous?" Sawyer growled as he pressed his lips to Sky's again.

Sky loved the way the guys teased each other. It reminded her of the guys at Seaside and made her feel even more comfortable.

Colton walked by the table again on his way to the dance floor, grabbed a microphone from the stage and tapped it, gaining the attention of the customers.

"Welcome to Undercover. We've got a fun night planned for y'all tonight."

"Damn right you do," Brock hollered.

Jana laughed. "My brother, the shy one."

"For those of you who are new here, welcome to a cappella night. Let's welcome the A Cappella Boys to the stage." Colton fanned a hand across the stage toward the table where Sky was sitting.

"See you in a minute, sweet girl." Sawyer pressed a quick kiss to her lips, and before she had a chance to ask what was going on, he, Roach, and Brock were heading up to the stage.

"It's so fun to watch them." Jana came around to Sawyer's seat beside Sky. "You're gonna love this."

Harper and Jana clapped and whistled. Sky watched with interest as Sawyer, Roach, and Brock stood shoulder to shoulder, dwarfing everything around them. Powerful arms arched out from their sides, their thick legs rooting them in place like tree trunks, and Sawyer's warm gaze found Sky, making her stomach flutter.

"He's looking right at you," Jana whispered. "I've never seen him look at anyone like that."

Sky could barely register anything *but* that look. The crowd silenced as Roach brought the microphone closer to his mouth. He closed his eyes and began singing "Love Story" by Taylor Swift. He sang about being young and seeing a lover for the first time. His voice was perfectly pitched, his face a mask of longing. His eyes flew open as he sang of begging someone not to leave and sank to one knee in front of Brock, serenading him while Sawyer swayed to the nonexistent music.

"They're so serious," Sky whispered to Jana.

Jana giggled. "Their group started as a joke, but they had fun with it. They try really hard to be serious and do a good job, but by the end they have a hard time holding it together."

As Roach's voice faded to a whisper, Brock's rolled out, deep and melodic. He sang about wanting to be taken away and of a prince and a princess. There was so much emotion in his voice as Roach rose to his feet between Sawyer and Brock and their enormous bodies moved to the music of their voices. Everyone in the bar was mesmerized, including her.

Their voices silenced, and Sawyer stepped forward, his eyes still locked on Sky, as he sang about being tired of waiting around for a lover to appear. His eyes narrowed and his voice lowered as he sang about wanting to be saved—then dropped to his knees with a dramatic sweep of his hand and pretended to pull out a ring and hold it up to Roach. How they kept from laughing, Sky had no idea, because she, Harper, and Jana couldn't stifle theirs. She couldn't tear her eyes from Sawyer as he sang with the others. The passion he put into the song rivaled the passion she'd witnessed when he was training. The emotions in his voice spoke directly to her heart, and when their voices went soft again, eventually silencing altogether as the song came to an end, she finally exhaled. She hadn't even realized she was holding her breath.

Their broad shoulders rounded forward and they took a bow.

Sky and the crowd clapped as the burly boxers swatted one another on the back and Brock and Roach headed back to the table laughing.

"That was the greatest thing I've ever seen," Sky said, anxiously waiting for Sawyer, who was still up on the stage. He pointed right to her, and she pressed her hand to her chest and mouthed, *Me?* He nodded and motioned for her to come up to the stage.

"Go. Go." Jana gave her a gentle nudge.

Sawyer was moving toward her, one hand outstretched. She'd been onstage many times with theater groups, but somehow this felt different. *She* wasn't the one entertaining, and she had no idea what to expect as Sawyer took her hand, led her to the center of the stage, and began singing about how something had to change and how much he needed her. She felt the eyes of the crowd boring through her, but it wasn't the weight of their stares that had her rooted to the floor. It was Sawyer's husky voice and his penetrating gaze, as the words fell from his lips directly to her ears.

He circled her like a lion stalking its prey as he brushed his chest against her back, crooning about being unable to pinpoint exactly what he needed but knowing she was it. His voice vibrated through her until the song she recognized as One Direction's, "One Thing," fell away, too, and all she felt was the simmering heat of him as he moved around her to the silent beat, his breath whispering along her neck. Her pulse quickened, and she wanted to sing right back, to answer his needs, but she stood stock-still, held prisoner by the emotion in his gaze as he poured his heart into the song.

She startled and blushed a red streak when Roach and Brock ran up behind her and sang about getting out of his head. Then Sawyer reached for her hand and everything else fell away. There was only her and Sawyer and the intensely passionate look in his eyes while he unabashedly professed that she was the *one thing* he needed. Sawyer's voice faded to silence and the crowd went crazy again, giving him a standing ovation.

Sawyer didn't seem to notice or care. He was totally focused on Sky as he drew her into his arms and spoke in a gravelly voice that slithered inside her and warmed her from the inside out. "I want to be your one thing, sweet girl."

She drew back to meet his gaze and said, "You're already so much more than my *one* thing."

Chapter Fifteen

IT WAS AFTER midnight when they arrived back at Seaside. The community was dark, and as they walked around to the back door of Sky's cottage, the leaves above them swooshed in the breeze. After spending the evening sharing stories with Sky about the first time he sang and the first time he fought, the first time she was in a play and the feelings she went through when she went away to college, he felt closer to her than ever. Every time they were together he felt the earth shift beneath them, but seeing Sky laughing and joking with his friends made everything about their relationship feel bigger, more real.

They climbed the stairs to the landing and before reaching for her keys, Sky slipped her fingers into his back pockets and gazed up at him. All night he'd felt her eyes searching for answers—in his eyes, around the bar, from his friends. He wondered if she'd found the answers and if she felt as close to him as he felt to her.

He slid his hand beneath her hair, brushing over the baby-fine hairs on the back of her neck.

"You okay?" he asked.

"More than okay. I don't want the night to end," she said as she stepped closer.

He lowered his mouth to hers, hovering a breath away, reveling in the closeness, the electricity sizzling between them. Her breath slid over his lips, and when she pressed her hands against his ass, pulling their bodies in tight, their lips grazed and her fingers tightened against him. Their mouths finally came together in a blistering-hot kiss that sucked him under. Every slick of their tongues, every press of her hips, sent shocks of lust coursing through him. Sounds of pleasure slipped from her lips, driving him farther away from the edge of reason. His hands tangled in her hair, his mouth slid over her jaw and down her neck, and then he took her earlobe in his mouth. She moaned loud and lustful into the night. Her hands traveled up his back, down his sides, clawing for purchase as she arched into him.

"You taste so good," he said against her neck before sealing his teeth over her silky skin and laving it with his tongue, earning another heady moan. "Sky..."

"Yes—" A heated whisper full of desire.

He knew he needed to respond, needed to let her know how he felt more whole than he ever had, how when he'd been singing to her, he'd meant every word he'd said, but he wasn't able to force another word from his lungs. Their mouths crashed together in another savage kiss. He couldn't resist pulling her roughly to him.

"Feel what you do to me."

"More," she challenged.

A groan rumbled through his chest as he lifted her to the railing, hiking her skirt up her thighs as he took her in another rough kiss. He felt himself losing control, handling her too roughly, kissing her too deeply.

"Oh God...Yes." She dug her nails into his skin, sending shocks of pain and pleasure rippling through him.

"Inside." He reached for her purse, and she fished for her keys with one hand, holding on to his shirt with the other so she didn't tumble off the railing. She withdrew the keys, and he lifted her down to the landing, unable to resist kissing her again, alighting more sparks between them. He forced himself to pull away long enough to unlock the door and push it open, then swept her in beside him. The sharpness of her breathing raked over him like a heady invitation. The silence of the cottage magnified the intensity of the heat pulsing between them. His hands found hers, lacing their fingers together as he lifted them beside her head, pressing his body to hers against the door. Thigh to thigh, chest to chest, he licked the shell of her ear and whispered, "I will never get enough of you."

He sucked her earlobe into his mouth, feeling her chest fill as she held her breath.

"I want to taste every inch of you," he whispered. "To feel your naked body against mine."

He moved her hands above the center of her head and gripped both wrists in one of his powerful hands. She blinked up at him, so open, so trusting, her eyes darkening with desire as she rocked her hips, pressing into him again. He sealed his lips over hers, taking her in another kiss, heat thrumming through him. He drew back with a tormented groan, needing to regain control, to slow himself down.

His head bowed between his shoulders, breathing fast and hard. Sky clamped her teeth over his nipple—*hard*—sending an excruciating mix of pain and pleasure searing through him. His head tipped back with a hiss, and he released her hands.

She gasped, eyes wide. "Did I hurt you?"

"Only in the very best way." He searched her eyes, needing answers to questions he didn't want to ask. But every ounce of his being was racing, burning, aching for her. Only for her. "Sky..."

She blinked up at him, looking innocent and seductive, making it even harder for him to figure her out.

"Sky, what you did to me...Do you like it rough?"

Her brows drew together and her lips pressed into a firm line. He feared he'd crossed a line, embarrassed her, hurt her feelings. He gathered her in his arms and held her close.

"I'm sorry. I shouldn't have asked."

"I do," she whispered.

His eyes came open. "Do?"

"Like it like that."

He drew back and searched her eyes again. They were full of emotions, bigger than want, more powerful than rampant desire.

"I think," she said as his lips curved up.

"Oh, sweet girl. Don't say it because you think I like it. I only want to pleasure you—in every way possible."

226

He slicked his tongue over her lower lip, then sucked it between his teeth and gave her plump lip a gentle tug.

"*That*. I like that," she said. "I don't know exactly what I like. I haven't really explored beyond...well, beyond normal stuff."

He led her into the bedroom and unwound the scarf from her neck, setting it on the bedside table, then lifted her necklaces off, set them carefully beside it, and kissed her softly.

"We'll find out everything you like." He kissed her again, deeper, more intensely, and moved his lips over her jaw to the sensitive skin just below her earlobe, grazing it with his teeth, and she sucked in a jagged breath.

"And that. *God*, I like that."

"That's my girl. Tell me everything you like." He kissed her again, then lifted off her shirt and set it on a chair by the window. "You're so beautiful, Sky." She fumbled with the buttons on his shirt, and he pressed his hand to hers.

"Let me." He quickly removed his shirt and toed off his shoes, then went back to undressing Sky, taking off her skirt, then her bra, pausing to love her breasts with his hands and mouth. And finally he slid her panties down her legs and set them on the chair, too.

She tugged at his pants, and he took those off, too, leaving them both naked in the dark bedroom. He pulled her against him, reveling in the feel of her soft curves, her heated skin sending currents of need through him. He laid her on the bed and followed her down. He wanted her so badly, needed to feel her heat wrapped around his hard length, but first he wanted—

needed—to let his sweet girl explore. To give her the courage, and the safety, to delve into the darker part of herself and share it with him.

He sealed his lips over hers and laced their fingers together again, applying no pressure, giving her free range of movement. She slid her arms above her head and tightened her fingers around his. He searched her eyes to be certain he understood what she wanted.

Her lips curved up as she whispered, "I like this."

He pressed her hands into the mattress and felt her hips rise to meet his as their mouths came together in a hungrier kiss, a kiss that begged for more, a deeper connection. He drew back and searched her eyes again.

"More," she whispered, and pushed her hands together.

He gripped them both in one of his. "Okay?"

She nodded and arched against his hips again. He kissed her lips, then slid a hand along the underside of her arm, to the side of her breast. He lowered his mouth and circled her taut, rosy nipple with his tongue. Sky whimpered, arching against him.

"Too much?"

She shook her head. "So good. More."

He took her breast in his mouth, teasing and taunting her nipple with his tongue, then grazed his teeth over the tip. She arched against his mouth.

"God, that's good."

He laved her nipple with his tongue, caressing her breast as he kissed a path across her breastbone to love her other breast, brushing over the first nipple with his thumb.

"Sawyer," she pleaded.

He loved hearing her say his name and feeling her flesh heat up against him. He rolled one nipple between his finger and thumb and sucked the other into his mouth, loving, teasing, as she moaned and whimpered and rocked her hips against his eager length. He brought his mouth to hers again, kissing her hungrily and feeling the greediness of her response.

"More," she said, more demanding this time.

He shifted his hips over hers, settling between her legs, and released her hands.

"I liked that," she said with a hint of disappointment that did funny things to his stomach.

"I need to touch you, Sky. I need to feel you in my hands, against my mouth, wrapped around me."

"You could..." She shifted her eyes to the scarf lying on the bedside table.

"Have you ever been tied up before?"

She shook her head, her eyes trusting, wanting.

He touched her cheek. "Sweet girl, having you tied up, willing and wanting, is a fantasy come true, but not until I have your total and complete trust. Not until I know that you have no lingering doubts about us, about me, about boxing."

"But—"

He sealed his lips over hers, swallowing whatever she was going to say. It was hard enough denying something he knew they'd both enjoy, but the closer they became, the more he realized that he didn't want to leave any room for doubt, *or regret*. He didn't want her to wake up tomorrow worried about what they'd done.

He brought her hand to his mouth and kissed each finger, then laid it on her stomach and did the same with the other hand. Then he took them both in one of his and kissed her again.

"Okay?"

She nodded.

"God, you're incredible. Keep your hands there? No ties, just willpower. I have to taste you." He felt her shudder beneath him as he lowered his chest to hers and kissed her again, exploring the dips and curves of her mouth, feeling her body hum with anticipation. He moved down her body, loving her breasts, teasing her as he nipped and kissed along her waist and hips. She reached for him and he pressed a hand over hers.

"Can you keep your hands there?"

She nodded, closed her eyes, and rested her head back. She looked so unguarded, like she was totally free. Freer than he'd ever seen her, and that realization sent his body moving against her again. She needed his touch as much as he needed to touch her. He'd seen it in her eyes the first night across the crowded bar. The longing hidden inside her, longing that he wasn't sure she even knew existed.

He ran his hands over her breast, barely brushing her skin, leaving a trail of goose bumps in his wake. She bit her lower lip, pressed her hands into the soft curve of her belly, as his fingers trailed over her hips, to the tops of her thighs, and farther still, to the taut arches of her calves, then back up the front of her legs, to the juncture of her thighs. She was breathing harder, her breasts rising with each fast inhalation. He brought his mouth to her thigh, placing openmouthed kisses along first one, then the other, feeling anticipation in the tightening of her muscles.

She spread her hands on her lower belly as he

kissed around her damp curls, along the sensitive skin of her inner thigh, over her pubic bone, causing her to writhe and rock, begging for more. He spread his hands over her thighs, opening her legs wider. Her scent was intoxicating, drawing him in, but he wanted to eke out every bit of pleasure for Sky. He wanted her to come on his mouth, his hand, his body, until she could barely breathe, and then, when she was ready, really ready for all of him, he'd take them both over the edge.

He sealed his mouth over her inner thigh and brushed his thumb along her wet center. She moaned, digging her fingers into her stomach and arching up against his hand. He was careful, teasing, brushing so lightly he felt her dampen even more.

"More, Sawyer. Please." She spread her legs wider, and he dragged his tongue along her swollen sex.

"Lord, you're sweet." Her taste was almost too much, too tempting for him to hold back. He used his fingers to pleasure her, teasing her wet, sensitive flesh, circling her clit with his thumb, but her lure was too strong. She moved too sensually. Her noises were too alluring, too damn sexy for him to resist, and he sank his fingers into her.

"Ohyesyesyes." She arched her back, rocking her hips in time to his efforts.

He brought his mouth to her again, licking and teasing as he probed and stroked over the spot that made her whole body hot and her insides clamp down around his fingers.

"Oh God, Sawyer!" Her hips bucked off the mattress. He pressed her back down, holding her there as she rode out her climax, one mind-blowing pulse after another. She fisted her hands in the sheets, panting, digging her heels into the mattress as he drew out her pleasure, until he felt the last of her release ripple through her. She lowered her legs to the mattress, and he brought one hand up, squeezing her nipple as he loved her with his mouth again.

"Oh God! Yes!" She clenched her teeth as he squeezed harder. "Ohmygod. Sawyer."

He was lost in her. In the feel of her hips bucking against his mouth as his tongue probed and taunted, his fingers stroked, and she succumbed to another intense release. He clutched her hips, holding her still as she came. A loud moan of pleasure escaped her lips as she pressed her hands into the mattress.

"That was..." She gasped a breath. "It was like..."

He moved up her body and laved his tongue over her nipple, earning another sexy moan. Her lips curved up as she reached for him, fisting her hands in his hair and meeting him in a greedy kiss.

"More," she begged. "Please more."

He lowered his arousal against her center, slicking his full, hard length along her but not entering her. It was pure, unadulterated torture to not bury himself deep inside her, but he wanted her to know what her body was capable of, to enjoy everything, which would make it that much sweeter when they finally came together.

She gripped his hips. "I want you inside me."

"Not yet." He kissed her again, feeling her need in the intensity of her kiss.

"This is torture. Please, just...please."

"Not yet. I want to see you, all of you." He wrapped her in his arms and rolled beneath her. "Sit up, baby."

He positioned his erection flat along his body, and she straddled him, sliding along his shaft. He gripped her hips, fanning his fingers over her ass. When she clutched his shoulders and found her rhythm, he rose and took her breast in his mouth.

"Oh God. You're gonna make me come again." She dug her nails into him as her hips moved frantically over the length of his throbbing erection.

He let her control their rhythm, moving one hand to her nipple, rolling it between his finger and thumb as his other hand slid between her legs, stroking the swollen, needy bundle of nerves that he knew would take her over the edge.

"You're stunning." Her breathing quickened with his words, so he gave her more. "Your whole body is flushed. So sexy. So hot."

She whimpered and dug her nails deeper into him. "More. Tell me more."

"Your lips are pink from our kisses, and when you inhale those sexy little breaths, it makes me want to come." He slid a finger inside her, and seconds later she arched back, gripping his wrists and holding his hands in place—one on her breast, the other between her legs. She rode his hand and his raging erection. He clenched his teeth against the need to give in to his own release, and as the last of her climax rolled through her, she collapsed on top of him. Her body bucked every few seconds as he gathered her in his arms and rolled her beneath him again, blanketing her body with his.

He pressed his lips to hers. "Still with me?"

"Oh God, yes," she whispered. "I never knew I could come so hard without you inside me."

He held her for a long moment, trying to regain enough control to reach for a condom.

"It was intense for me, too," he admitted. "Watching you let go, feeling you come apart against me. Sky...There's nothing more beautiful than your trust."

She closed her eyes, and her lips curved up in a sweet smile. He kissed her again and reached for his pants, fishing out a condom with shaky hands. After rolling it on, he came down over her, searching her eyes. If she was too tired, he would wait, despite how desperately he wanted her, needed her. Despite the longing he'd be left with. What he cared about most was that she felt safe and felt good about the two of them.

She must have seen his concern, because she reached up, touched his cheek, and said, "I want you, Sawyer. All of you."

He gave in to the emotions building inside him, and as their bodies joined together there was only Sky and the feel of their bodies moving as one. He gazed into her eyes, feeling every emotion as they washed through them. Every breath she took, every lift of her hips, every sweet sound that slipped from her lungs dragged him deeper into her, and deeper still, until it was hard to remember that they were two separate people.

Their mouths came together with the same eagerness of their bodies, moving, rocking, searching for more. She dug her heels into the mattress, angling her hips. He moved with her until her eyes fluttered closed with every stroke, and her jaw went tight, and he knew, felt, that she was quickly climbing up, up, up and nearing the edge again. He sealed his mouth over her neck the way he knew she loved, licking and stroking, and finally sinking his teeth into her shoulder at the same time as he slid his hands beneath her hips, lifting her higher so he could take her deeper. Heat rushed to the base of his spine. He laced his hands with hers, holding them tightly beside her head, wanting to lose himself in her.

"Sky—"

"Sawyer!"

Their mouths crashed together as her hips rose off the mattress. Her inner muscles pulsed around him, pulling the come right out of him. A thousand lights exploded behind Sawyer's lids as he called out her name, riding the wave of their passion, the peak of their ecstasy, until they both collapsed to the mattress, their damp bodies tangled together as he gathered her in even closer, never wanting to let her go.

"I like...*that*," she whispered.

He couldn't keep his heart from tumbling out. "Ecstasy rolls like thunder, rippling through my sweet summer Sky." He rubbed his thumb over her jaw. "She weeps, she whimpers, she gasps, she roars." He pressed his lips to hers. "She stills my heart and steals my breath."

Sky sighed, her eyes full of emotions too big, too powerful for him to name.

Sawyer kissed her again. "She came in like a whisper and claimed pieces of me as if they were stars, taking them as her own like a pixie in the night." He closed his eyes and lay back, holding Sky against him. Emotions exploded inside of him. He waited for them to ebb and flow like the tide, but the surge continued, growing bigger, stronger than anything he'd ever felt, and he knew he wasn't far from falling over the edge.

"Sawyer," Sky whispered. "That's beautiful."

"That's you, my sweet girl. Only you."

Chapter Sixteen

THE MORNING SUN beat down on the basket in the center of the table, illuminating the slips of papers and napkins, giving weight and importance to the snippets of words that had spoken to Sky's heart so perfectly that she was sure each one was meant just for her. Her mind was still reveling in the aftermath of making love to Sawyer, and she couldn't help but wonder once more if he'd written them. He'd spent the night again and had gone running an hour ago. She missed him already. She'd thought about asking him about the papers in the basket before he left for his run, but they'd had such a wonderful evening and morning that she didn't want to take a chance of ruining it.

She pushed the basket farther away and turned her attention back to her poetry book, but her eyes refused to remain on the page and shifted to the basket again. She pulled it closer, staring at the darn thing like it was going to do something. She almost wished it would, instead of feeling like a giant question mark.

The worst part was that it wasn't just the stupid basket that had her tied in knots. Last night, when she'd opened herself up to Sawyer and he'd held back, wanting her to feel safe and wanting to know that she had no qualms about them before he did anything to restrain her—she'd felt her feelings for him bloom so large she'd nearly said she loved him. *Loved him!* She'd never been in love before. Could she fall in love and still need answers about something like a silly basket of notes? And was it fair of her not to want to watch him fight when he gave so much of himself so freely?

Sky heard Jenna laughing and looked across the quad, glad for the distraction from her thoughts.

Bella and Amy were shaking their heads as Jenna tugged at the hem of her dress, which even from a distance Sky could see was way too tight. Bella grabbed Amy's arm and pulled her toward Sky's cottage. They both waved. Jenna trailed behind them, still tugging at her dress. The way the bright morning sun was shining down on them, they really did look as though they each had a pregnancy glow. Their cheeks were fuller, their eyes brighter. Sky wasn't ready for babies, but she couldn't deny that seeing her friends so happily in love brought her thoughts to places she hadn't considered before.

"She's reading again," Bella said as she stepped onto the deck and sat beside Sky.

"She's *mooning*," Jenna said as she wiggled her hips. "Sky, what do you think of this dress? Does it still work for me? Bella says it's too small, but I think it's kind of sexy."

Amy placed her hand on Sky's shoulder and

squeezed as Sky tried to figure out how to tell Jenna that her spaghetti-strap dress was too tight across her boobs *and* her hips and made her look a little like a bowling pin.

"Jenna, how does it feel?" Sky asked, hoping Jenna would say something like, *A little tight*, giving her an opening to agree.

Jenna ran her hands down her hips and wiggled. How the hell she managed to look sexy in that dress was beyond Sky, but when she swayed her hips from side to side, she did.

"Hot. *Sizzling* hot." Jenna raised her brows, her blue eyes wide with delight.

Amy pulled Jenna into a chair. "Sit your hot bod down before you set the place on fire."

"Wait. I want Sky's opinion. Sky?" Jenna pushed.

"I think you always look hot," Sky said honestly. "It's a little tight, but if you feel good in it..."

Bella rolled her eyes. "He's not even here. He and Caden went out on the boat for the morning."

"A little tight?" Jenna frowned. "I was kind of hoping you'd say that these two preggos were wrong. They want me to go maternity clothes shopping, and I want to look sexy for Pete. I don't think I'll be my hot and sexy self in maternity clothes." She fluttered her lashes like she was teasing, but Sky knew Jenna probably did worry about those things.

"Pete would think you were sexy wearing a muumuu," Sky assured her. "He adores you."

Bella pulled a few pieces of paper from the basket and silently read one after another, and Sky's stomach knotted with each one. She shouldn't have brought the basket home. She didn't know what it meant that

Sawyer said he wasn't the P-town poet, but the more she tried to let it go, the more she wanted answers to how his words had ended up in Cree's hands.

"Petey does, doesn't he?" Jenna said happily. "I guess it's time to go maternity clothes shopping after all."

"Why do you listen to Sky and not to us?" Amy asked.

"Because you and Bella just want to go buy more clothes and drag me along. Sky has no vested interest in shopping for maternity clothes."

"You're so weird. We'd never lead you astray." Amy leaned across the table and put her face close to Jenna's. "We love you, you goofnut. We want you to look great, too. You're just not used to having a belly." Amy sat back and patted her stomach. "I *love* being pregnant. I can't wait to meet our little one."

"Enough baby talk. We have a single friend who looks freshly sexed-up, and she's got a basket full of love notes," Bella said. "So, Sky, did Sawyer stay up all night writing you these love notes and *then* give you that freshly effed glow, or did the writing come after the superfab sex session?" Bella read from a slip of paper, "*Fire in my belly, you in my soul.*"

Freshly sexed-up? She could say that again. Just thinking about the way Sawyer touched her and the weight of his body on hers brought a rush of heat to her cheeks. She thought about how sexy he looked when he came out of the bathroom wrapped in a towel before his run, his hair wet and adorably tousled from his shower. He kept a gym bag in his car, and when he'd changed into his running shorts, memories of how aroused he'd been the other morning in a similar pair of shorts had swept through her, making her want him all over again. She'd had to fight the urge to beg him to come back to bed—and his scorching-hot goodbye kiss hadn't made it any easier.

"Sky?" Bella nudged her.

Sky tore her eyes from the basket and pushed her book aside.

"Sorry. I spaced out." She exhaled a sigh that sounded overly swoony and a little embarrassing.

"Sex first *and* last," Jenna said.

"Definitely." Amy patted Sky's hand. "You're so cute when you blush."

Sky rolled her eyes and smiled. "I don't know if he wrote those. My suspicion is that he did, and I'm going to ask him when he gets back from his run."

Amy pressed her hand to her belly. "Ohmygod. Baby surfer is kicking."

"Baby surfer?" Bella laughed. "We really need to pick names."

"We already know our baby's name," Jenna said proudly. "Bea for Pete's mom or Neil for his dad."

"You're..." Sky swallowed past the lump that instantly filled her throat. "You're thinking of using our mom's name?"

"Oh, Sky." Jenna's brows knitted together. "We just talked about it last night. We should have asked you first. I don't want to take your baby names."

"I've never thought about baby names, but, Jenna..." She looked away, blinking tears from her eyes. "I love that you guys thought of our mom. If you have a girl, it would mean a lot if you named your baby after her."

"Really?" Jenna asked. "But you're tearing up."

Sky fanned her eyes to dry them. "I just miss her. Sometimes it hits me. I wish she were still here. I think it's Sawyer. If she were here, I could tell her all the things I was feeling and she'd put it all into perspective."

Amy wrapped Sky in her arms. "Honey, there's no perspective when it comes to matters of the heart. If anyone knows that, I do."

"But I'm so confused about everything, and I'm sure you guys were never this confused." She wiped her eyes and watched her friends exchange looks like she'd said something crazy.

"We were all confused," Bella said. "I drove back home and almost didn't come back to the Cape, but in the end I couldn't imagine life without Caden and Evan."

"Why are you confused?" Jenna asked. "Did something bad happen last night?"

"No, something wonderful. Really wonderful. The whole night was like a dream come true, but that's the problem."

"Sky, that's what love is all about. It's full of hopes and dreams and makes you feel like you're walking among the clouds one minute and drowning the next." Amy reached for her again, holding her tight. She stroked Sky's back and said, "Tell us what's wrong. We're not your mom, but we care, and we can help."

Sky tried to gain control of her rampant emotions, thankful for the women who had opened their hearts to her at a time when she was hurting—when she'd first returned to the Cape and found out about her father's drinking—and welcomed her into their lives without question. These were the sisters she'd never had, and she knew they'd do all they could to fill the gap her mother had left behind.

She drew in a steadying breath and tried to put words to what was whirling around in her mind.

"Well, for starters, love? I don't know if this is love." *Is it?* "That's part of the problem. When I'm with him I *feel* so much, but this is like a bullet train. I haven't really ever dated anyone seriously, and almost overnight I'm head over heels for Sawyer. Last night he and his boxing buddies sang at this bar. Get this. They're the *A Cappella Boys*. It was really funny, but do you know what it was like watching these powerful men sing to each other like lovers?"

"Maybe they are," Jenna said with an arched brow.

"No, they're not," Sky responded with a soft laugh. "They're so different from when they're at the gym. When I met his friends in the gym, they were intimidating. All sharp edges and bruiser-like. And then they smiled, and the harshness softened, but the underlying power and some kind of darkness was still there. Like...like coffee brewing, when the steam lifts and lowers the lid of the pot. You know what I mean?"

"Oh yeah. I know what that looks like," Jenna said. "Have you ever seen Grayson and Pete get into it over something? They don't do it often, but sometimes they push each other's buttons and I have to walk away."

"Right. Same thing. Anyway, away from the gym and the testosterone that must fill their lungs in that place, they were just these guys who laughed and sang like they'd never lift a hand to hurt a soul."

"So this all wraps back to Sawyer and his fighting?" Bella asked.

"No, I don't think so. I think this has to do with *me*

and my selfishness—and that damned basket. Sawyer is doing this huge title fight to win money to take care of his dad's medical bills, and it doesn't get more chivalrous than that, right? He sank his savings into buying a beach house that had been in his family for generations but his parents had to sell a long time ago. I mean, it's obvious that Sawyer has the biggest heart on the planet. He's got the fight of his life coming up, and all I can think about is how hard it would be to watch him and how I don't want to go. And that kind of makes me a bitch, right?" Before they could answer she added, "I met his friend Brock's sisters, and one of them fights, too. A girl! Fighting! She can *fight* and I can't even watch? What is that about?" She still couldn't picture Jana's cute little figure in a boxing ring.

"Well, first of all, lots of girls fight," Bella said. "You really have lived a sheltered life. How do you not know about sports? You grew up in a house full of guys."

"Because she was always outside in her art studio," Jenna said. "I totally get it. Was she all muscles or feminine?"

"Cute as a button. I loved her, and her sister, and their brothers. I loved them all, and Jana and Harper, Brock's sisters, and I exchanged numbers. Jana offered to help me learn self-defense, but I don't know."

"I wanna go," Bella said. "That would be awesome, learning to defend ourselves."

Amy dropped her eyes to Bella's belly. "You cannot fight with baby handcuffs inside you."

"Baby handcuffs?" Jenna laughed.

"Well, Caden *is* a police officer," Amy explained.

"I don't want to fight now," Bella said. "But I think

there's definitely something cool about being able to defend yourself."

Amy waved a dismissive hand. "Our men will defend us."

"See?" Sky said. "That's another thing that I'm confused about. I really love being taken care of by Sawyer."

"Every woman loves to be taken care of," Jenna agreed.

"I don't think so. It annoys the hell out of me lately when my brothers do it."

"Of course it does." Amy rubbed her belly and smiled. "They're your brothers, not your lovers. They're keeping men at bay from their baby sister. Sawyer's protecting his woman."

"It all goes back to the Neanderthal days," Bella said.

"No way. I'm not some weak woman who wants to be dragged around by my hair and taken from behind by a grunting animal killer." As she said it, the idea of being *taken from behind* by Sawyer sent a prickle of excitement up her limbs. "God, you guys. This is *another* thing. With Sawyer, I'm..." She lowered her voice, and they all leaned in toward the center of the table. "I'm so sexual. Like I can't get enough of him."

"Primal." Bella nodded adamantly. She tucked her hair behind her ear and said, "You can say you don't want all that, but that's bullshit. Every woman likes to be taken by their man. Not by any man, but by the one special man who makes your body turn to liquid heat and your mind go all mushy."

Sky rested her head back on the chair and closed her eyes. "You're telling me it's *normal*? Because it feels foreign."

"Good foreign or bad foreign?" Amy asked.

Sky's chin tipped forward, and she leveled a serious stare on Amy. "The sinfully good type. The kind that makes me feel like a slut—and *like* it. The kind that makes me want to try out Bella's fluffy pink handcuffs and practically had me begging Sawyer to *play* with Jenna's scarf last night."

"Ha! Yes! You go, girl!" Jenna gave her a high five.

"That's the most delicious kind of carnal desires," Bella said. "And he's poetic? Sky. I think you might have found your ideal man."

"Except if that's true, then why can't I convince myself to watch him fight? I feel like I'm not being supportive, and I see it in his eyes, his worry over my thoughts about his fighting," Sky explained.

"Well, you're not a bitch, that's for sure, but I do think you should try to watch him fight," Jenna said. "It's not like he's out on the street beating the crap out of strangers. It's his career, and one he's apparently really good at, from what Petey says. We could go with you."

"Or you could go see Jana fight first. Is that her name?" Amy asked. "Maybe if you see a girl doing it you'll feel different?"

"Maybe," Sky relented.

She eyed the basket. "And that stupid basket? I don't know if he wrote all that stuff or not, but I have to find out. It's like an itch that won't go away."

Tony and Sawyer came into view, jogging around the bend down by the pool. Sawyer's broad shoulders and shredded abs glistened with sweat. His powerful thighs bulged with every step. How was she supposed to think clearly now? His eyes lifted and immediately found hers, and a smile spread across his handsome face.

The universe had served up a creative, smart, caring, and emotional man who made her head spin, and the more time she spent with him, the harder she fell. But how could she expect him to feel for her what she felt for him if she didn't give him the same unconditional support he gave her?

As he stepped onto the deck and reached for her hand, surrounded by the people she loved most, she knew what she had to do. She had to watch him fight.

***

SAWYER'S HEART HAMMERED against his chest as he and Tony joined the girls on the deck, but it wasn't their run that had every ounce of his body aflame. It was his sweet summer Sky and the emotions radiating from her smiling eyes.

She laced her fingers with his and said, "I'm glad you found a running mate."

As he leaned in for a kiss, Amy and Jenna said, "*Aww.*"

"She's hard to resist," he said honestly. "I caught up with Tony across Route 6."

"It was nice to get to know your new beau, Sky," Tony said as he rubbed Amy's belly, then bent to kiss her. "We ran down to the bay and stopped by Kurt and Leanna's. Leanna's business has really taken off. She's hiring more summer help, and she can't really come back to Seaside until she's got that under control. They aren't sure when they'll be back."

Sky rose to her feet. "Sawyer, why don't you sit down and I'll sit on your lap."

He did, and stole a kiss while he was at it.

"You guys are so cute," Amy said, then looked up at Tony. "Was Leanna doing okay?"

"I think she's working too hard," Tony answered. "She looked exhausted, and I know she misses you guys. She said she wished she could move Seaside to the bay so she could walk outside and see everyone."

"That would be amazing, wouldn't it?" Amy said. "The more Tony and I have thought about it, the more we're leaning toward buying on the bay. Then we could live there over the colder months and here in the spring and summer."

Sawyer gathered Sky's hair over one shoulder and said, "I can see why she misses you. You're like one big family—without the fighting."

"You are supercute," Jenna said. "Really, look at you playing with her hair."

Sawyer laughed. "She's supercute. I'm just lusting after her." He wrapped an arm around Sky's waist. "I had no idea that you knew Kurt Remington. I've read all of his books."

"You like thrillers?" Sky asked. "I learn something new about you every day."

"I like lots of books. Thrillers, poetry, even cookbooks. I make a killer soufflé."

Tony winced. "Dude, you shouldn't admit that."

"Looks like someone's got mail." Sawyer pointed down the street to the mail truck pulling up in front of Amy and Tony's cottage.

"Again?" Amy looked up at Tony. "Did you order anything?"

Tony shook his head. "I'll go see what's up."

Everyone except Bella watched the mailman pull a hand truck loaded with pink boxes up the center of the gravel road. Sky couldn't hear what they were saying, but Tony pointed to Theresa's house and then joined them on the deck again.

"He must have had seven boxes from Eve's Adult Playhouse for Theresa with our address," Tony said with a wrinkled brow. "What's up with that?"

They all looked at Bella, who held up her hands in surrender. "What?" She pushed to her feet and hurried from the deck toward the quad.

"Wait for us!" Jenna hollered as she and Amy went after her.

"Christ, this can't be good." Tony went after them.

"Where are they going?" Sawyer asked.

"Every summer Bella pranks Theresa, the property manager. Last summer she changed all the pictures in Theresa's house to pictures of Bradley Cooper and had one of Caden's police officer friends pretend that they'd had a complaint about stalking."

"Are you serious?" Sawyer laughed.

"Yes. Then Theresa *brought* Bradley Cooper—the *real* Bradley Cooper—to their wedding! It's really funny, but I'm sure at some point Theresa's not going to be so cool about it."

"Do you want to go with them?" Sawyer asked.

She wrapped her arms around his neck and pressed her lips to his. "Nope. I'd rather stay right here. How about you? Do you need to leave for the club?"

"I told Roach last night I'd be late. We're meeting at ten." He eyed the basket on the table. "Were you thinking of getting another tattoo?"

Sky's smile faltered. "Actually, I wanted to show you these." She pulled the basket closer, and she rose to her feet and moved toward the chair beside him.

He touched her hips and said, "Stay with me. I'm already going to miss you when we're apart today. Let me feel you close for a little while longer."

She sank down to his lap. "Okay." She tucked her hair behind her ear and began taking the papers out of the basket. "I wanted you to see these."

"The tattoos you've done?" He sat up and looked over the papers she was laying out before them. His gut clenched as he read each one. *Fire in my belly, you in my soul. Wandering through life, wanting, waiting, reaching for more.* Every word made the hair on the back of his neck prickle.

"Where did you say you got these?" The accusatory sound of his voice surprised him and was obviously not lost on Sky, who furrowed her brow.

"From customers."

"Because they touched you," he said more to himself than to her, remembering her words.

"Yes. Exactly. Why do you sound upset?" She searched his eyes, and he wondered if she could see the anger he felt simmering inside him.

"Because, Sky. These are *my* words. All of them." He unfurled a napkin and read a passage. *How can I move forward when you're slipping away?*

"Then you *are* the P-town poet? But you said you weren't."

"P-town poet? Is this what you meant? These?" He lifted her to her feet and paced the deck. "I don't understand how you could have gotten those."

"*I* didn't get them." She looked at the papers littering the table. "Sawyer, I told you. Customers came in with these—these papers and napkins and pieces of receipts—and asked me to tattoo this stuff for them. I still don't understand. If you're the P-town poet, why are you denying it? These are lovely. They're really heartfelt and—"

"Sky, I don't know anything about a P-town poet. These are *my* words from *my* songs. This is my handwriting." He picked up a handful of papers and sifted through them. "You're telling me that there are people walking around with verses of my songs tattooed on them?"

"One for each paper you see there, yes." She sank down to a chair. "You know the night we first saw each other at the Governor Bradford's?"

"Of course." He sat beside her, feeling like he was in the *Twilight Zone*.

She picked up a napkin and handed it to him. "One of the waitresses brought this in yesterday."

He read the words. "I must have left it behind. After I saw you I began writing the song at the bar. All I had to write on was a stack of napkins. I guess I do that a lot, write on scraps of paper and napkins. I never think twice about leaving a crumpled-up napkin with the trash from my meal. That night, I wrote and rewrote the verses until they felt right, and I thought I took all of the napkins with me when I left, but obviously not." The idea that other people had seen his writing made him feel exposed, violated. He'd have to be more careful.

She placed her hand over his and smiled warmly. "Maybe when you're writing songs, you get so caught up that you lose track of some of your notes?"

"Yeah, I guess. I can't believe someone would pick up my stuff. I mean, it was on a *napkin*. Who would do that?"

"Someone who recognized the beauty of your words." She opened the napkin and read the passage aloud. *"I'll take it all. Hear it through. Wrestle your demons to remain beside you.* Those are the words you said to me after we made love the first time. You said, *Lay your head on my shoulder, your heart next to mine."*

Anger curled up inside him. "Even though I choose to occasionally sing the songs I write, that's *my* choice. I don't like knowing that strangers find my notes and hang on to them." He looked at Sky, and it sank in that she'd been keeping his words, his songs, and that tugged at all of him, pushing the anger to the side, making room for love.

"Come here, sweetheart." He pulled her onto his lap again and pressed his lips to hers. "That's part of the song I wrote for you the first night I saw you."

He sang to her in a soft voice, every word laden with emotion.

"I saw it in your eyes.
Wounded, hiding, somewhere deep.
Tell me, lovely, do you cry when you sleep?"

Her lips drew down, and a lock of hair fell in front of her eyes. He tucked it behind her ear and began singing again.

"Crying out in your movements.
Graceful, longing, hanging by a thread.

The longing I see.
Set it free, lovely. Come to me.

Lay your head on my shoulder.
Your heart next to mine.

I'll take it all.
Hear it through.
Wrestle your demons
To remain beside you."

"Sawyer," she whispered, her eyes warm.

"I have been drawn to you since the very first time I saw you, Sky. With an intensity that I've never felt before."

Her brow wrinkled with confusion. "But...the *longing* you see? You saw that in such a brief time?"

"You have the most expressive eyes I've ever seen, but it wasn't just your eyes, Sky. You had this aura around you. Everything about you spoke to me. I can't explain it."

"I *was* longing for something." She lowered her eyes and seemed to be thinking. "I was longing for this closeness. I must have been waiting for you all along."

Chapter Seventeen

LATER THAT MORNING, Sawyer's eyes burned from salty droplets of sweat dripping into them. Sweat slid down his body, spraying off his arms with every punch. Each breath brought a heated grunt, stoking the fire that flamed within him. His mind ran through quick calculations, looking for an opening, watching, waiting, then making his move and slamming into Delroy's willing body. They were on their ninth round, and Sawyer was laser focused, measuring Delroy's breaths, watching his cadence as he moved around the ring, anticipating his punches and skillfully avoiding every strike. Roach called out from the side of the ring, but today even that wasn't making it past the rush of blood in Sawyer's ears. He was training to win, his father's health care the driving force behind each hit.

When the match was over, he paced the ring, adrenaline coursing through him, his mind racing. *How can I improve my power? I gotta move faster. Hit harder. Need to train to conquer tougher opponents. No one can touch me. I've got this.*

He climbed from the ring and set his gloves and mouthpiece with his gear.

"That was awesome." Delroy wiped his face with a towel, still breathing hard. "You're hitting harder. I can feel it."

"Or you're getting soft," Sawyer said with a friendly shove.

"You're both getting long in the tooth," Roach teased. "Sawyer, give me fifteen minutes of rope work, one hundred abs, and stretch."

"You got it, Roach." He went to grab a jump rope.

Roach followed him over. "How's Sky?"

Sawyer couldn't temper his smile. "Man, I've never met anyone like her. I think I'm going to introduce her to my folks."

"Seriously? That's a big step. It signals a future to women." Roach grinned.

"No shit, Coach? Teach me something else." He grabbed a rope and began skipping.

"I saw it the other night, you know. When you were singing to her." Roach crossed his arms and lowered his chin. Sawyer knew he was analyzing his skipping, his steps, his quickness, his hand movements. Roach was always analyzing. It's what made him a superior coach. "You wiped your heart all over that stage."

"So what?"

"Don't let it fuck you up in here."

Sawyer smiled. "Has it fucked me up yet?" He knew he was too focused, too strong, for Roach to see a detriment.

Roach shook his head, then rubbed his chin.

"Worried about what the doc said?"

"They've been telling me that shit since I was nineteen." He knew Roach was just feeling him out. Making sure he was solid, and as he assured him, he realized he was also assuring himself. "No one can touch me, man. I've got this."

***

SKY AND AMY carried food for a spur-of-the-moment barbecue over to Bella's cottage, while the guys set up tables and chairs in the quad and began making a fire in the fire pit. The sun was setting, promising a cool evening for their gathering.

"I still can't believe the renovations on my apartment will be done soon and in a few weeks I can move in. I'm going to miss living here," Sky said to Amy.

"You're welcome to stay as long as you want," Amy said.

"Thanks. I'll have to really think about it. There are benefits to living above the shop, but there's no chunky-dunking." She laughed. Chunky-dunking was what Sky and her friends called skinny-dipping, which they did in the pool at Seaside when they could get away with it.

"Where's Jenna? I didn't see her car when I drove in."

"She and Pete went to get something from their beach house. They'll be back before dinner." Amy stopped walking and pressed her hand to her belly. "Sorry. Baby wants out." She blew out a breath. "Okay, I'm good."

Sky held the gate to the deck open for Amy to walk through. "Your baby looks like it has dropped. Are you sure about the due date?"

Amy rubbed her belly. "As sure as I can be. The doctor seems to think I have another few weeks. But I have no idea how they really know. We were going at it like rabbits, making up for lost time." She stopped talking as Caden walked out the door.

"Hey, girls. Let me take that." Caden smiled as he took the groceries and they followed him inside, where Bella was busy seasoning chicken and steak. Evan hovered over Bella, watching her every move.

"Don't touch the raw chicken. It'll get you sick." Evan's voice had deepened over the last two years, and he'd filled out since he'd begun college. At almost nineteen, he no longer looked like a teenage boy, but a young man.

"Ev, I've been cooking longer than you've been alive," Bella said.

Evan patted her head as if she were a child. "But you weren't carrying my baby sister or brother."

"Evan, come over here and give Auntie Amy a hug hello." Amy opened her arms. "Let's give your stepmom a break from all the nagging."

Evan laughed. "Auntie Amy?" He embraced her, then hugged Sky. "Gotta love a woman *without* a baby in her belly. How are you, Sky?"

"I'm doing well, but when did you turn into a *man*? Gotta love a woman...?"

"College does that to a guy," Evan said. He'd completed his first year at Harborside University, which was about an hour away from the Cape.

"I take it you're enjoying college life," Sky said.

"Why are you home? I thought you were working down there this summer."

"I am. I've made a bunch of friends and I'm working at Endless Summer Surf Shop. It's owned by this supercool guy, Brent Steele. You should see the place. There are tons of hot girls there *all summer long*." He smiled at his father, who shook his head. "I came home to grab a few things from the house, but I'm heading out now. I'll be back when Bella has the baby."

"In other words, he came to make sure I wasn't doing anything I shouldn't be while carrying his sibling." Bella patted Evan on the back, then kissed his cheek. "You're going to be a great big brother." She leaned toward Sky and teased, "I hope we don't have a girl."

"Can you imagine Evan around a baby sister?" Sky teased. "He'll be as protective as all of my brothers wrapped into one."

"She'll be one lucky sister," Bella said. "At least we'll always know she's cared for."

"You can count on it." Evan picked up his keys from the counter. "I'll teach him or her to surf, like Tony taught me." He hugged Caden and Bella, and with one hand on the door said, "And if it's a boy, I'll teach him how to get laid." He took off out the door, laughing.

"God." Bella laughed. "Are all nineteen-year-old boys like that?"

Caden kissed her with a wide grin. "All teenage boys think about is sex. But I think he's all talk."

They heard Evan's car pull away as Caden walked out the door with the food.

"He *hopes* he's all talk," Amy said.

"We're going chunky-dunking tonight," Bella said quietly. "You in, Sky?"

"I'm hoping that Sawyer is going to stay over, so..." She wasn't about to leave him to go skinny-dipping.

"We figured," Amy said. "That's why we're going after all the men are asleep. How long after you...you know...does he fall asleep?"

Sky giggled. "I don't know. It's not like I time him."

"Jenna does," Amy said with a smile. "She said Pete's out in seven minutes or less."

"God, really? Seven minutes?" Sky thought about Sawyer and wondered how long it *did* take him to fall asleep. "I just assumed he fell asleep at the same time as me. What about Leanna? Is she staying over and going, too? Oh gosh, and what about Theresa? She's home tonight. I saw her car—and about a dozen pink boxes on her porch, thanks to you, Bella. She must be pissed."

"I'm not sure if Leanna is going to stay or not, and I've been watching Theresa. She's had her lights out by nine thirty every night so far this summer. We'll be quiet. It'll be fine." Bella touched her belly. "Another kick," she said with a smile. Then she said to Amy, "It's not my fault Theresa likes adult toys." She handed Sky a head of lettuce with a hint of a smile on her lips. "Can you chop?"

Amy smirked. "Like you're not the one sending her the stuff? You run over to see her face with every delivery."

"That's because I want her to know that *we all know* what she's ordering."

Amy washed two tomatoes and began slicing

them for the salad. "I don't know why you keep pranking her after the whole Bradley Cooper fiasco."

Bella put condiments on a tray and settled one hand on her hip. "If I give up, she wins. You know me better than that."

"Aha!" Amy laughed. "As if I didn't know it was you sending the sex paraphernalia."

"You had your doubts." Bella picked up the tray and looked at Sky again. "You're in for chunky-dunking, right?"

"If he falls asleep, yes, but you may have to go without me. We're—"

"Screwing like monkeys. We know," Bella teased. "You're in that honeymoon stage, where you can't get enough of each other." She smiled at Amy. "The rest of us are still in that stage, too, but we *know* to wear our men out early on chunky-dunking nights. So we expect you to retire to your bedroom early so you can come out and play with us."

"Oh, the pressure," Sky teased. "What if I don't want to leave him?"

Bella got as close to Sky as her belly would allow and narrowed her eyes. "You are not allowed to turn into one of those women who ignores her girlfriends for a guy. That hot hunk will still be in your bed after you come out and have fun with us, but who knows when the next time is that we'll have a chance to skinny-dip without worrying about waking our babies."

"Good point. My bad." Sky secretly loved that Bella was so pushy. Growing up without sisters made her treasure her kinship with the Seaside girls even more.

"I'll bring the cookie dough," Amy sang out.

***

SAWYER SAT BY the bonfire with Tony, Pete, Caden, Grayson, Kurt, and Blue after dinner, watching Sky and her girlfriends giggling and whispering on the other side of the fire pit. Jenna's head tipped back with a hearty, loud laugh, the kind of contagious laugh that made the others join in. Bella's laugh was husky, and Leanna's and Amy's were nearly silent. But Sky's laugh had a feminine ring to it. Sawyer tuned everything else out and listened to her laughter. It seemed to float from her lungs and radiate outward from her chest, ending in a quick inhalation. And her smile—*Christ, her beautiful smile*—did funny things to his stomach every time he saw it.

"Welcome to Seaside," Pete said. "Are you surviving your indoctrination?"

Sawyer laughed. "Seems to me like you guys are really lucky to have each other. Thanks again for letting us use your boat overnight, Pete. I'm looking forward to being out on the water again. It's been ages."

"No problem," Pete said. "I'm psyched that Sky's dating a guy who enjoys boating. You'll fit right in with the rest of us. I heard that you're coming to Sky's grand opening. You'll finally get to meet our brother Matt."

"Yeah, I'm looking forward to it. And I hope to meet your father, too." Sawyer had heard so much about their father that he was looking forward to meeting the man who had built Sky her own art studio and had loved his wife so much that her death had sent his world off-kilter—and loved his family enough to right his ways.

"He wouldn't miss Sky's opening for the world," Pete said, then took a swig of his beer.

Tony pointed to Amy and smiled. Each of the girls had a hand pressed to her stomach. "It doesn't get much better than this. It's gonna be a trip when all our babies are born. I think the girls will be sad when Sky moves up to Provincetown."

"She's pretty happy about the renovations almost being done, but we haven't talked much about when she's going to move." Sawyer imagined she would go through a wide range of emotions when she moved, and he hoped he could help when she did. He turned to Blue. "Thanks for taking care of Sky's renovations, Blue. I know she really appreciates all that you do for her."

"No worries. She's a good friend." Blue took a swig of his beer. "And she seems happier than she's ever been."

"Thanks. That means a lot to me, knowing how much you two mean to each other." Sawyer noticed Sky watching him and smiled. She blew him a kiss.

"Okay, enough sappy shit," Grayson interrupted. "Let's get to the good stuff before my sister monopolizes you again."

"Good stuff?" Sawyer asked.

"Your fighting," Tony explained.

"We were wondering if you'd mind if we came by the club to watch you train," Grayson said with hopeful eyes. "We'd love to check it out sometime."

"Would I mind? I'd welcome it. Do you want to come down one day next week? My coach is bringing in a heavyweight for me to spar with to get ready for my title fight. I'll let you know when."

"Definitely. Whaddaya say, Blue?" Grayson asked.

"Hey, I'm there," Blue said. "Maybe we can even get Sky to go. If we're all there, she might be willing to give it another try."

"Maybe, but I don't want to push her. It's okay if she doesn't want to watch. I get it," Sawyer said.

"Sky would go if Jenna and the girls went," Pete said.

"Bella wants to see your friend's sister fight," Caden added. "I'm sure she can talk the girls into going."

"I still can't believe you're dating my sister," Grayson said. "She hates fighting, and here she is, dating a champ."

"I'm one lucky bastard. Lucky she's willing to look *past* my career." Sawyer watched Sky as she turned toward him again. The embers of the fire cast an orange glow on her legs as she circled the fire with a seductive look in her eyes.

"I'd also like to hear the songs you've written," Kurt said.

"I'm playing at Sky's grand opening. Will you be there?" He reached for Sky's hand, wondering if her brother and friends could feel the emotions pouring off of her and see the look of wanting in her eyes.

"As long as Leanna's feeling okay, we will," Kurt said, his eyes trained on his wife.

"Is Leanna okay?" Sky asked Kurt. "She doesn't seem like her perky self tonight."

Kurt's brows drew together. "She's been feeling a little off lately. I think she's working too hard. In fact, I'd better see if she wants to call it a night and head back to our other house. She's working early tomorrow to fill those big orders that came in." He rose and held a hand out to Sawyer. "We'll see you at your sparring match."

Sawyer shook his hand. "Absolutely."

"Sparring match?" Sky asked.

"They want to watch me train, so I invited them to watch me spar. You're welcome to come, but don't feel any pressure to. I know you don't like to watch me fight."

"Actually, I was just telling the girls that I want to watch you train again."

"Sky, you don't have to do that," he assured her.

"I want to support you. It might take me a few baby steps before your big fight, but I want to cheer you on, and I think Bella talked me into at least letting Jana show me a few self-defense moves later in the fall after Bella's baby is born. She seems to think it'll help me understand what you do." She stepped in closer. "No promises, but I'm willing to try."

His heart swelled. "Sky..." He pulled her against him and closed his eyes, unable to believe she would make such a big concession for him. "Thank you."

"Hey, gang, I'm calling it a night," Caden said. Pete followed him over toward the grill.

"Come on, Blue, let's give them some privacy." Grayson pulled Blue up to his feet. "If we leave now, we might get lucky at the Beachcomber."

"Ugh. Grayson," Sky chided him. "I don't want to hear about you trying to get lucky."

Grayson laughed. "Then don't listen. Besides, Hunter's been there for hours. He's probably already scared all the hot girls away." He swatted Sawyer on the back. "We'll see you at your sparring match, if not before. Take care of my sister."

"Hey, you smack him on the back, but you don't hug me or anything?" Sky pulled Grayson into a hug, then reached for Blue and did the same. "I miss hanging out with you. Don't let my brother turn you into a manwhore."

"I miss you, too, and Grayson's not a manwhore," Blue said with a smile. "He just believes in sharing the love."

Grayson flashed a devilish grin. "And the lust, and the—"

Sky held her hand up and silenced him. "Don't say another word. TMI!"

Sawyer laughed, and when her brother and Blue moved away to say good night to the others, he pulled her in close again. "Did you have fun tonight?"

"I always do." She slid her hands into his back pockets. "But now I'm ready for a little Sawyer fun."

Her voice was soft and sensual and sent a ripple of awareness through him.

"I should help them put all the chairs away, then..." He pressed her in tighter against him. "Then I'm going to..." He felt himself getting aroused and decided to keep his thoughts to himself.

"Going to?" She pressed her lips to his chest. "Tell me what you're going to do to me, Sawyer." She grabbed his butt and rocked her hips against his, taunting him as she dragged her tongue along her lower lip.

Powerless to stop the words from spilling from his mouth, he said in a near growl, "I'm going to start with those luscious lips of yours and kiss you agonizingly slowly to pay you back for this. I'm going to kiss your neck and every inch of your beautiful breasts, loving them the way you like it. I'm going to drag my tongue over every inch of your body." He pressed his hand to her back, holding her against him, feeling her breathing go shallow. "I'm going to taste your inner thighs, then lick you until you're so turned on that you can't remember your name."

Her hands fisted in his shirt, eyes dark with desire. "And then?" Her voice was shaky, hardly audible.

"Oh, my sweet summer Sky, you are a sensual girl."

She tightened her grip on his shirt and pressed her body unbearably closer. "Tell me," she urged.

"And then I'm going to bury myself deep inside you and make love to you until you come so hard you can't move." *So much for not getting aroused.* He was hard as steel, and she was barely breathing.

"Hurry," she urged.

Chapter Eighteen

SKY THOUGHT SHE was dreaming, that the harsh whispers were tangled voices of her subconscious. Sawyer had kept his promises and had made love to her until they both lay on the mattress boneless and sated, and she'd fallen right to sleep...until now.

"Sky!"

"It's time!"

Her eyes took a minute to adjust to the dark, and her brain took another moment to register that the voices coming through her open bedroom window belonged to Bella and Amy. She slid quietly off the bed, surprised her legs could hold her up, and peeked behind the curtains.

"God! We've been calling you for ten minutes!" Bella snapped. She, Amy, and Jenna were each wrapped in a towel, with their hair pinned up messily with clips. Even in the dark Sky could see that Jenna's red towel matched her hair clip, which matched her flip-flops, *of course.*

"Hold on. Give me one sec to wash up and grab a towel." She dropped the curtain and tiptoed into the bathroom, where she soaped up a washcloth, rinsed the scent of sex from her body, and donned a towel and a hair clip of her own.

She slid the glass doors open quietly and stepped out onto the deck.

"I forgot my flip-flops." She reached for the door again.

"Shh." Bella grabbed her arm, pulled her toward the grass, and headed for the pool. "Too bad," she whispered. "It's already two in the morning, and Caden has to be up at four for his shift. He got a call at midnight and had to run out, and he just got back a little while ago. I want to get in the water before he wakes up and notices I'm gone."

"Pete went out around then, too. He said Grayson's motorcycle broke down and he had to give him a ride." Jenna handed the pool key to Bella. "I can't see a darn thing. Amy, why didn't you leave the lights on by your deck?"

"I thought I did." Amy grabbed Sky's arm. "Sorry, Jenna. At least I remembered the eggless cookie dough from the health food store!"

"It's the little things," Sky teased.

The heavy metal chain clanked against the gate, and they all shushed Bella.

"I'm trying," Bella snapped. "The lock is being fussy. Hold the chain so it doesn't wake up Theresa. She's got supersonic hearing." The pool was closed after eight o'clock, and Theresa took her job as the property manager seriously. She was a stickler for rules.

"How long did it take strummer boy to fall asleep?" Jenna whispered to Sky.

"I don't know! I was too nervous to pay attention. I kept thinking that you guys were going to show up at the window right in the middle of...you know. And then I got too into it to care."

The lock clicked open and they scrambled through the gate.

"I didn't think Caden was ever going to fall asleep," Bella said, closing the gate quietly behind them.

Jenna dropped her towel and ran naked across the pool deck toward the steps at the far end.

"I swear I'm going to tie your towel around your body so you stop doing that," Amy said. "You need to either tweak your OCD so you can keep your towel on until you get to the steps, or climb in at the far side. You're like a rebellious, naked, pregnant teenager, and I'm always worried you're going to fall."

"I'll never change!" Jenna giggled as she stepped into the water. "Brr. Hurry up and get in. It's freezing."

"I still don't understand why you run across the deck naked," Sky said as she draped her towel over a chair and walked into the chilly water.

"Because!" Jenna rolled her eyes like it was the stupidest question on earth and sank down so her shoulders were beneath the surface. "I did that the very first time we ever went chunky-dunking. I can't change it now."

"That would drive me crazy," Sky said to Jenna. Bella and Amy walked hand in hand down the steps and sank under the water. "Your bellies really do make you even more beautiful."

"Hey, what about me?" Jenna splashed Sky.

"You, too, of course. But your belly is still little. Look at them. Pregnant nudity really is attractive." Sky swam to the side of the pool, grabbed four foam noodles, and gave one to each of the girls.

"All I know is that being pregnant is awesome," Bella said. "I can eat as much as I want and not worry that it'll show." She hung her arms over the noodle, and they all came together in a tight circle, kicking their feet to stay afloat.

"I can't believe we're going to have babies. We'll have to ask our hubbies to be on baby duty so we can chunky-dunk," Amy said as she reached for Jenna's hand. "Do you think it'll take the fun out of it?"

"No," Bella answered. "As long as they don't tell Theresa, we'll still have fun."

"I'm around to babysit," Sky offered.

"Babysit? You'll be chunky-dunking with us," Amy reminded her.

"Not after I move," she said sadly. She'd miss being so close to her friends when she moved, having breakfast with them and spur-of-the-moment barbecues.

"We'll text you to come down and give you enough warning that you can join us." Jenna shook Sky's noodle.

"Yeah, like the sound of a car won't wake Theresa? You can park on the road and walk into the complex." Bella kicked away from the group. "I'm hungry."

"We just got down here," Jenna said.

"Well, the baby has to eat when the baby has to eat." Bella swam to the stairs and climbed out of the pool, shivering. She grabbed the cookie dough and hurried back into the water, holding it above her head.

"That baby is going to weigh ten pounds," Amy teased.

"So what?" Bella tore open the cookie dough, and each of the girls held her hand out. "See? You guys wanted it just as badly as I did." She bit off a hunk and handed the package to Amy. "Sky, is this the weekend you're going out on Pete's boat with Sawyer?"

Sky smiled. "Yup. My brother came through for us. He's letting us take the boat out overnight, and Sawyer said he can take two days off of training, which surprised me."

"I told you love makes people do all sorts of things." Amy floated onto her back with her big belly protruding out of the water.

"Love," Sky said dreamily. She shifted onto her back and floated, gazing up at the starry sky.

"Love?" Amy swam over to Sky. "Love?"

"Sky's in love!" Jenna threw her noodle in the air.

Bella caught Jenna's noodle and shushed her.

Sky held on to the noodle and dropped her feet back under the water. "I didn't *say* I was in love. Although Sawyer is *everything* I could want in a man. Seriously, he's a great listener, and he really gets me. And he loves his family, and he's hands down the best lover I've ever had, and—"

"Oh my God. You *are* in love. Our little Sky is in love!" Bella said so loudly that all the other girls shushed her.

"Stop it." Sky laughed. "I've never been in love. I'm trying it on for size."

"Okay, so you're not in love yet," Jenna said with an emphasis on *yet*. "Would you be if he wasn't a fighter?"

She shrugged. "It's not his fighting. This is his last fight, and he's fighting for his dad, so I have to be okay with it, right? I've just never been in love before, and it's such a big feeling. Sometimes I feel like my heart is going to jump out of my chest, or I want to huddle away with him for hours. Isn't that weird?"

The girls exchanged a look that told her they knew everything there was to know about love and she was the only one left in the dark.

"Honey," Amy said softly, "can you imagine a future without him?"

Could she? Would she want to? She was already used to falling asleep next to him and waking up in his arms, even though it had been only a few days. She looked forward to his flirty and poetic texts, and every single time she saw him, her heart went crazy and she wanted him to stay right there with her.

"Not willingly," she finally admitted.

Jenna and Amy smiled, and Bella said, "You're definitely falling. Ten bucks says you marry the guy."

"I'm *not* betting on my future." Sky laughed, but inside she was shivering with delight just thinking about a lifetime with Sawyer. "Lizzie says life is *that easy and that complicated*. I think I'm sitting in the center of easy and complicated and I don't know where I'll end up—but it sure feels like I'm in the right place regardless of if it's easy or complicated."

"That's because you're falling in love. That's how it happens, so you'll tip over right in the middle where easy and complicated intersect," Amy said.

"And Sawyer will catch you," Jenna added.

"With a poem at the ready." Bella reached for Sky's hand. "Take it from the girl who never thought she'd find the right guy. The *only* man who is right for you is the one you don't want to live without."

All this talk about forever and Sawyer was getting Sky hot and excited all over again. She dunked under the water to cool off. When she broke the surface, she said, "Wow, my heart is going a mile a minute. You guys...I *love* love! And I think I love Sawyer, too!"

The girls squealed and immediately shushed one another and laughed.

Sky snagged the cookie dough from Bella and bit a hunk off. "Did I tell you that he *is* the P-town poet? He just had no idea that there was a *real* P-town poet."

"That's because there's not. You made him up, remember?" Amy pointed out.

Sky looked up at the stars and exhaled loudly. "What a night. I feel so much for Sawyer that I swear I almost told him that I loved him the other night, and I didn't. Thanks for making me feel like I'm not moving too fast. That it's normal to fall this hard this fast." She floated on her back again and rested the tube of cookie dough on her stomach as she gazed up at the stars, feeling like she'd cleared the fog from her head.

Jenna floated on her back, too, and Amy said, "I can't lie on my back again. My baby will squash me."

They all laughed.

"I was looking forward to our boat trip before, but now? I feel even more excited now, like it's okay to feel so much after such a short period of time—and I'm going to enjoy it."

"Two days alone with Sawyer? You'll be so deeply in love when you return you'll be in the ring fighting *for* him." Jenna reached for the cookie dough.

Bella turned her head from side to side. "Shh. Do

you hear that? What is that noise?"

"What?" Amy lifted her chin, listening.

"Shh!" Bella snapped. "It sounds like...cicadas?"

"I hear it," Jenna said, whipping her head from right to left.

"It doesn't sound like cicadas to me," Sky said, tipping her ear toward the sound. "It's coming from all around us. And it sounds different, not like bugs at all."

Bella shushed them again, and they all swam toward the edge of the pool.

"I can't see a damn thing—can you guys?" Bella asked.

"No." Amy walked between Bella and Jenna, holding on to them both.

Bella motioned for Sky to hurry up. Sky swam to Bella and linked arms with her.

"What is it?"

"It sounds familiar." Jenna gasped, pointed at the fence, and shouted, "There's something moving against the fence."

"Shh!" the three others chided her.

"Do you want Theresa running out here?" Bella squinted into the darkness. "What is th—"

Suddenly a string of holiday lights lit up around the pool, illuminating a plethora of vibrating sex toys, handcuffs, and other sex paraphernalia hanging on the fence. Vibrant yellow, bright pink, and shimmering blue vibrators shivered and shook. Some flashed, and others remained like steady beacons in the night.

"Oh my God!" Jenna yelled, then cackled loudly, hanging on to Bella so tight she nearly pulled her under the water.

Amy and Sky burst out laughing, while Bella's face

was a mask of shock—eyes wide, mouth agape.

"Look!" Jenna pointed to the gate, where Theresa stood with her arms crossed and a smirk on her lips.

"Oh, I will get her back for this," Bella promised as laughter finally burst from her lips. "I will get her back so good!"

Jenna crossed her arms over her boobs and sank under the water up to her chin. "Get down!"

They all sank under the water up to their chins, laughing and holding on to one another.

"The cookie dough!" Amy yelled, which only made them laugh harder.

"Can we keep the toys?" Jenna hollered between laughs.

Sky roared with laughter and lost her balance, falling beneath the water. When she broke through the surface, her finger shot toward the sky, and she yelled, "I call the blue one!"

"Hear that, Sawyer?" Tony's deep voice cut through their laughter. Pete and Caden rose to their feet from beach chairs they'd set out on the lawn and clapped and whistled. Sawyer stood off to the side with a hand over his mouth, and Sky knew he was stuck between wanting to laugh and not knowing if he should.

"Ohmygod," Amy said. "Did our men *help* her?"

"They are so dead," Jenna said, stomping toward the stairs.

All three girls dove after her, holding her in the pool.

"You're naked!" Bella yelled.

"Pete is dead meat," Jenna said with a scowl. "Naked or not, he's a traitor and he's gonna pay." She squinted in the direction of a pair of fuzzy green handcuffs hanging on the fence. "I just need those handcuffs!"

***

WHEN TONY CAME by Sky's cottage and woke Sawyer up, telling him, *Time for your initiation*, he had no idea what to expect—and he was shocked to find that he was alone in Sky's bed. He heard the girls giggling as soon as he and the others snuck down by the pool, but still they hadn't filled him in on what was going on. Now, as the girls hollered for the men to turn around and Theresa walked toward her house snickering, he could barely contain his laughter. But as he stood with his back to the pool, giving Sky and the girls privacy to cover themselves up, it was what he'd heard while sitting in the dark that was replaying in his head like a rerun—Sky's voice, filled with happiness: *I* love *love! And I think I love Sawyer, too!*

He'd spent his entire adult life training for fights, but nothing could have prepared him for the way his heart nearly exploded inside his chest at hearing Sky say those words, even if only to her friends.

"Hey," Sky said as she came to his side, shivering in a towel. Her hair was wet and her cheeks pink, and she had an adorable smile on her lips.

He wrapped her in his arms and pulled her in close, while a few feet away Bella and Jenna gave Caden and Pete hell for helping Theresa.

"What happens now?" he asked.

She shrugged with a soft laugh. "According to Bella, Theresa just upped the ante. I guess next summer will bring a whole new level of pranking."

Amy and Tony talked quietly as they walked past Sawyer and Sky.

Tony lifted his chin to Sawyer. His smile reached his eyes, and as Amy gazed up at her man, her smile was just as broad. "Welcome to Seaside."

Sawyer looked down at Sky and said, "I can't think of anyplace I'd rather be."

Chapter Nineteen

SAWYER TRAINED HARDER than he ever had for the next week. He decreased his running, increased sparring times, and Roach brought in incrementally harder sparring partners, all leading up to next week's heavyweight sparring match, which Sky's friends were coming to watch.

Sawyer had been spending nights at Sky's cottage since the night of the sex-toy prank, which her friends were still laughing over—and Bella was still stewing over. The more time he spent with Sky and her friends, the more he felt like part of their group. He and the guys had gone for several morning runs together, and he'd gotten to know Tony, Pete, and Caden well. They were all so in love with their wives that they talked about them even while they ran. That had made Sawyer feel even more at ease, as Sky was always on his mind, and it would have been hell trying to cover that up.

He'd come back to his house this afternoon to

oversee the final painting of the interior and to pack for their overnight on Pete's boat. The ramp to the skycap had finally been installed. He assessed the wheelchair ramp that ran up the center of the house. The ramp led up to a landing on the second floor, where there was enough room to turn a wheelchair around safely, and then continued up to the skycap. The painters had left an hour ago, and once the paint dried, the house would be presentable before his father's return after Sawyer's title fight—to celebrate Sawyer's win. He had no doubt that he'd win his title fight. He was ready.

Sawyer went up to the bedroom and packed a duffel bag with enough clothes for the week, knowing that he and Sky would rather spend time at Seaside than here, and there was no longer a question of *if* they would stay together. Their coupledom was a given, and that was something he'd not only never had before, but he'd never imagined wanting. And now he couldn't imagine a life without Sky.

He set his duffel bag out in the hall and went up to the skycap one last time before heading over to pick up Sky. It was a clear afternoon, and from the third-floor room he had a clear view of Provincetown curling out to sea, like a protective arm around the bay. He remembered the stories his father had told him about the walks he'd taken along the shore with Sawyer's great-grandfather and the bike paths they'd ridden on, and how they would always return to the skycap and drink iced tea as they admired the distance they'd gone. Sawyer had taken numerous walks with his father before they'd sold the house. As he looked out over the land his family had called their own for so many generations, he thought about one day taking those walks with his own son or daughter. He chewed on that thought for a few minutes, having never gone there before. It had always been just Sawyer, and then his thoughts had become about him and caring for his father, and in turn, caring for his mother's emotional well-being, too.

Now there was Sky.

Now there was *us*.

He glanced back at the pillows on the floor where he and Sky had first made love in the room his great-grandfather built, and he realized that she was the first and only woman he'd ever made love to in that house. He glanced up at the rafters, smiling as his parents' initials came into view, and when he crossed the floor and found his grandparents' initials, a whole new warmth filled him. He wanted that permanence. He wanted to look back thirty years from now and see his and Sky's initials and remember the very first time they made love.

He pulled his cell phone from his pocket and read a text from Sky he must have missed earlier. *Can't wait until tonight!*

They still hadn't said the three sacred words that felt like they'd been kept behind bars since the night at the pool, when he'd heard her admit that she thought she loved him. He was waiting for the right moment to tell Sky how he felt.

He typed in a response. *Every second we're apart feels like a lifetime. Having 48 hours together will feel like an eternity. One I never want to end. Xox.* He sent it off, then sank down to the pillows on the floor, thinking about the text he'd just sent.

A lifetime with Sky was exactly what he wanted, but that wasn't the only thought heavy on his mind as he sat in the skycap of his family home thinking about the future. The completion of the ramp loosened all the things he'd been keeping tied down in the back of his mind. How many years did his father have ahead of him bound to a walker or a wheelchair, with slowed speech and tremors? Had his father ever imagined such a future for himself? When he was fighting in the war, praying every moment to make it out alive, did he ever dream that living out his years with this horrible disease would be his fate? Sawyer's chest tightened with the painful thoughts.

What hopes and dreams had his parents made that they were missing out on? Sawyer had another few weeks until he could retire, and then he would have forever with Sky, or so he hoped. But hadn't his parents counted on the same thing?

Words began to sail into his mind—*moonlight, sunlight, cloudy days*—shifting quickly from light to dark. *Fissures of love. Struggle and stretch.* He tried to ignore the persistence of them, but they kept coming, one after another. *Bonds fraying, years ending.* Like the night he met Sky, he knew these weren't passing thoughts and there was a song in there somewhere. He grabbed a pen from the floor, and at a loss for paper, he scrawled the words on his forearm.

Silence. Pleas.
Strength. Forgiveness.
More. Always more.
Tenuous days. Harsh endings.

He sucked in air, swallowing past the tightness in his throat. He rose to his feet and paced the hardwood floor, fighting against the song he didn't want to write. It was one thing to keep himself so focused on winning the fight that he separated his father's illness from the truth of where it was headed. But now it was staring him in the face—and all the fighting in the world couldn't shelter him from it. He let out a tortured groan as more words coursed through his mind.

Like the wind in the night, shifting, stealing, paving the way. There will come a day, come a day.

The pen fell from his hands.

Sawyer lifted his eyes to the window, thinking about history and family and all the things that mattered. Love and honor, trust and commitment. Those were things that could never be taken away, no matter how much of his father was stolen by the disease. *Memories.* His father would never have a chance to create the same kinds of memories with Sawyer's children as Sawyer had of his grandfather, but that didn't mean that Sawyer and his father couldn't create other types of memories that could be carried forward and shared for generations to come.

With his hands fisting at his sides and his chest swelling with every inhalation, he pushed past the urge to ignore the future of his father's disease and grasped at the *now*.

He pulled out his phone and called his parents.

"Hi, honey." His mother answered on the second ring, and he could hear the smile in her voice. "I didn't think I'd hear from you. Don't you and Sky leave today?"

"Hi, Mom. Yeah, we're leaving shortly. I wanted to check on you and Dad before we take off." He hadn't gotten down to see them this week, with the ramp renovations taking precedence, and even though he'd called twice, he felt a little guilty.

"We're fine, honey. You go and enjoy your time off. Maybe when you come back you can bring Sky to meet us?"

The hope in her voice made him smile. "I will. I know she'd like that. She's one of Dad's biggest fans. Actually, I wanted to talk to him about something. Is he around?"

"He's right here. Hold on."

He heard his mother try to hand the phone to his father.

"Hold on, honey," his mother said into the phone again. "I'm going to put you on speakerphone and hold it up so it's easier for your father."

"Okay," Sawyer answered, hoping she couldn't hear the tug of his heartstrings as loudly as he felt them.

"Son," his father said in his slow drawl.

"Hi, Dad. Guess where I am?" The silence stretched so long that Sawyer wondered if his father had heard him. He was used to long stretches of silence, but this one felt interminable—he realized that it probably felt that way because he was bursting at the seams to get his thoughts out.

"The...gym?" his father finally answered.

"No, Dad. The skycap. The ramp is done. It's beautiful, and I can't wait to bring you up here to look out over the water. I was thinking about the times you brought me up here and told me about the walks you took with your father and grandfather."

"Good...times."

Sawyer smiled. "Yes, they were." His throat

swelled with the reality that one day these phone calls might be impossible, too. "Dad, I'm sitting here looking out over the bay, and I'm thinking about the future—and the past. I want to do something with you, Dad. Something of our own."

"Anything...son."

He pinched the bridge of his nose, squeezing his eyes tightly shut against the tears that threatened. "Thank you, Dad." His voice was so thick with emotion he didn't recognize it. He cleared his throat to try to regain control of his emotions and said, "I want to write with you, Dad. I know you haven't written in years, and I know you don't want to write and that I'm not as good with words as you are. But, Dad, I want to bring our voices together in a poem, or a song, or both. Whatever you're willing to do, I want to do this together. I want something that we can have forever, that I can share with my children, and..." He realized he was rambling and paused again to regain control. "Dad, it would mean the world to me if you would consider doing this with me. *For* me."

His father was quiet for so long he wondered if he'd pissed him off. A full minute or two later he heard the speakerphone click off, and his mother's emotional voice came on the line.

"Honey?"

"Mom, did I push him too hard? Is he upset with me?"

"No, honey. He's just too overcome with emotion to talk."

Sawyer closed his eyes against new tears vying for release.

"Sawyer?"

"Yes, Mom?"

She lowered her voice and said, "Thank you. Thank you so very much."

Chapter Twenty

AS THE SUN kissed the horizon, the last of its warm peach rays rippling across the dark sea, Sky wrapped her arms around Sawyer's waist and leaned her head on his chest. The brisk evening air whipped against her legs as they sailed toward Monomoy Island.

"Two whole days alone, Sawyer. No customers, no painting, no building ramps, no tattoo guns, no sparring." They decided to anchor at Monomoy for the night so they wouldn't have to worry about other boat traffic.

He tipped up her chin and the wind whipped her hair across her cheek. They both laughed as he pressed his lips to hers right through the whipping strands. "No flashing vibrators, no sneaking out to go chunky-dunking."

"Who needs vibrators when I have you?" She zipped up her hoodie.

"Just what I wanted to hear." He kissed her again, moaning a little in pleasure as he tugged her in closer.

"I still can't believe I have you all to myself for two days. Whatever will I do with you?"

She raised her brows in quick succession. "Considering that nothing is going to come between me and my man, I'd say anything you want." Sky liked the way *my man* felt as it slid from her tongue. He was the man she thought about when she woke up in the morning and the man she fantasized about when they were apart. He was the man who had shared her bed every night for days on end and the only man she hoped to wake up to from that day forward.

Sawyer's eyes warmed. "I like the sound of that."

She watched him steer the boat closer to the island. His movements were graceful and determined at once, swift and virile. His biceps flexed deliciously as he set the anchor and brought down the sails. The boat rocked with the current, a gentle, comforting motion that produced soothing sounds of water slapping against the sides of the boat as the rim of the sun dipped beneath the horizon, giving way to the hazy glow of night.

"I always forget how dark it gets at sea," Sky said as her eyes adjusted.

"Not to worry, sweetheart. The moonlight will be enough." He sat on the cushioned bench and pulled Sky down onto his lap. As he tucked her hair behind her ear, his eyes rolled over her face with a tender gaze.

"I can't believe you're really going to write with your dad. I'm so excited to see what my favorite poet and my favorite person come up with."

"Your favorite person?" A serious look hovered in his eyes.

"Yes, of course." She pressed her lips to his, and he smiled. "I thought you didn't want to do anything more with your songs than use them as a hobby and that your father was done writing. What changed your mind? What changed his?"

"Sky, I haven't slowed down much over the years to think about anything other than fighting. My life has been a circle of *train, fight, win.*" He paused and brushed his thumb over her cheek. "And then came you."

"Did I throw you off your game?"

He laughed under his breath. "That's one of the things I love about you. You have so much going on, between your shop renovations, your apartment, the grand opening, and still you worry about if you threw me off my game. No, Sky, you showed me that I was playing the wrong game. You opened my eyes."

Sky's heartbeat quickened.

"When I was at the house this afternoon, everything sort of hit me at once. Seeing the ramp drove home my father's fate, which further validated the need for me to win the title fight. But it also made me realize that while we're busy making it through today and planning for tomorrow, some higher power, or whatever, could already be planning its own actions, which negate ours."

"You lost me. What do you mean?"

"What I mean is that I don't want to live my whole life hoping for a day when life will slow down enough, or the time feels right enough, to move forward and start my life. I love you, Sky, and I don't want to wait another second to tell you. I don't care that it's fast. I've felt connected to you from the moment I saw you across the room. I love being with you, talking with you, making love with you. I don't want to miss out on a single second with you, Sky. I don't want to do what my dad did and work his whole life looking forward to retirement when he and my mom could have more time together—and then have something go wrong."

"Sawy—" Her voice hitched in her throat.

He pressed his finger to her lips. "Let me finish," he whispered. "I'm not saying we should get married, but I'm hoping that someday we'll be ready to. Sky, I want to carve our initials in the rafters. I want to stand in that skycap and look out at the land below with you right there by my side—and one day with our children, if you're willing—and create our own history. I want to wake up with you in my arms and know that at the end of the day, you're right there with me, sharing our headaches and celebrating the best times in our lives. I want to grow old with you and watch you do tattoos and paint in your long flowing skirts with your windblown hair and that sparkle in your eyes, while I play the guitar and sing songs that I write for you and our family."

"Oh, Sawyer." Sky could hardly speak past the tightening in her throat. She wrapped her arms around him and pressed her lips to his. "I love you, too. I want all those things, too."

He exhaled a long sigh of contentment. "This is my last fight, Sky. Once I win, my parents' financial future will be secure, and then I'm going to retire. No more fighting. I'll become a trainer so you won't have to worry."

"I don't want you to give up fighting for me. I'm okay with it now, and I don't want you to resent me."

She could hardly believe how much her feelings had grown for him, and part of that growth meant accepting his career.

"I could never resent you. Fighting has risks, and that might not have mattered before, but now that we have *us*? I don't want to leave our future to chance."

"You would do that for us?" Sky's eyes dampened. "Sawyer..."

"Sky, I would do anything for you, and in turn, for us."

Sky felt their worlds twining together, without hesitation or doubt, and when he drew her closer and whispered his love for her, she sealed her lips over his, cutting him off midsentence, wanting to feel his words as they moved through her body and settled into her soul.

"You've turned my world around, Sky," he said as he laid her down on the cushions. "I want everything with you. I want to make all your dreams come true, and I still don't even know what they are. What do you want from life?"

She leaned up and pressed her lips to his. "I don't have big wants, Sawyer. I want you, and I want to be happy. I want to get to know your family and have you get to know mine. I want to have a simple life where if we want to shut away the world for an afternoon, we can do so without the rest of our world falling apart. I want to love you and be loved by you."

***

THERE WERE NO words for the emotions coursing through Sawyer. Love, happiness, and desire were all there, but they were wrapped in something more important, something bigger. They were wrapped in anticipation for a future with the woman he loved.

He gazed into Sky's eyes and could feel her love for him. "I will always love you. I will cherish you, and I will spend the rest of my life making sure that you feel safe enough to be strong, or weepy, or silly, or whatever you want or need to be. Because I love you for *you*, Sky, and I want all of you."

Their mouths came together in a kiss full of promise and hope as his hands explored the soft lines of her waist, her hips, her ribs. He unzipped her hoodie and helped her out of it, tossing it to the deck, then lifted her shirt off and set it aside, too. Her nipples firmed instantly under his touch, and a soft sigh escaped her lips as he brought his mouth to her breast.

"Sawyer, you make me feel too good."

He drew his shirt over his head and tossed it to the deck. "I have to feel your skin against mine."

His hands slid over her, and he felt her heart beating fast as he lowered his mouth to hers again.

"Touch me," she whispered against his lips. "I want to feel your love everywhere."

He caressed her breasts, kissing, sucking, loving her nipples the way she liked, and moved down her body, tasting every inch of her warm flesh.

"You have no idea what you're doing to me," he said as he unbuttoned her shorts and worked the zipper south. "When you tell me what you want, it makes my whole body hot."

"Then I'll tell you more often," she said with a teasing smile.

He hooked his fingers in the waist of her shorts and pulled them down, stripping her bare. Then he rose to his feet, shed the rest of his clothes, and came down over her again. Their mouths came together hard, tongues thrusting, searching, taking, as their hips ground together.

"Sky," he growled against her mouth. "I want you so badly."

He moved straight down her body, unable to wait a second longer, and pressed her thighs to the cushion. He lowered his mouth to her hot center and dragged his tongue along her wetness.

"So sweet," he said against her skin. He licked and teased and rubbed his thumb over her clit as he thrust two fingers inside her.

"Oh, good Lord." Her hips shot off the cushion as she dug her fingers beneath his hair. "Oh yes. Like that...Yes...Sawyer..."

Every word made him harder, more eager to feel her come apart against him. He licked and loved and took her sensitive, swollen clit between his teeth.

"Yes. Oh God...Ohmygod." Her back arched off the cushions as the climax claimed her. "Sawyer!"

Desire mounted inside him at every sweet word that left her lips, every frantic thrust of her hips. He moved back up her body, using his hand to continue pleasuring her as he took her in a greedy kiss, breathing air into her lungs as she gasped her way through the final rush of her release.

She reached between them and stroked his eager length. "Let me...taste you."

He nearly came apart at the demanding tone of her voice and the hungry look in her eyes. Before he could move, she pushed him onto his back and took his throbbing erection in her mouth.

"Holy hell, Sky." He gritted his teeth, and she teased the tip and then sucked all of him into her hot, wet mouth, shattering his remaining brain cells. His head tipped back against the cushion as she slowed her efforts, licking him base to tip, then teasing him over and over again. He fisted his hands, resisting the urge to come.

"Let go," she said in a seductive voice that brought his eyes to hers. "I want to taste you like you taste me."

"Sky, I want to make love to you."

Without a word, she wrapped her fingers around his hard length and stroked as she ran her tongue along the tip, pulling a moan from deep within him.

"Sky," he warned.

She stroked and sucked, faster, squeezing tighter, until he was dizzy and every muscle pulsed with heat. Ice shot down his spine, and he grabbed her shoulders—a warning she did not heed. She took more of his shaft into her mouth, and an electric shock scorched through his body as he hurtled past the point of no return, his eyes shut and his body racked with shocks. His thoughts fragmented as her hands and mouth continued their hungry devouring.

When the last shudder ripped through his body, she lay over him and kissed him roughly. Their mouths parted, and she gazed down at him with a savage inner fire burning in her eyes.

"I've never done that before," she whispered.

He stroked her cheek. "You don't have to do that with me, Sky."

"I wanted to be as close as we can be. I'm yours,

Sawyer. All of me, and I wanted all of you."

He gathered her in close and kissed her again, ignoring the taste of himself still lingering in her mouth and savoring the closeness of their bodies, the bonding of their love, as their breathing calmed and they gave in to their exhaustion and dozed off beneath the starry sky.

Chapter Twenty-One

AFTER A MORNING of skinny-dipping, making love, and teasing each other about being eaten by sharks while naked, Sawyer and Sky showered in the cabin, then took a leisurely sail to Nantucket. It was a sunny morning, and there was a nice breeze as they crossed the harbor.

"I still can't believe that neither of us has been to Nantucket," Sawyer said as he docked the boat at the marina.

"I think that's because we grew up here," Sky said. "When I was growing up, my dad was running the store on the weekends and my brothers were in sports. There wasn't much free time for us to go away for a whole afternoon."

He tied off the boat and stepped onto the dock. He turned back and helped Sky out of the boat. "My dad is such a private person. He traveled for book signings, but he wasn't really into exploring new places. When I was young, we spent afternoons on the beach, or at the cottage, but once they sold the cottage, we pretty much stuck close to home. And then I got into boxing, and nothing else mattered."

He rolled an assessing gaze over the marina. "It looks like home."

Sky wrapped her arms around his waist and said, "Only better. We have a whole day together before we need to return Pete's boat."

They walked along the marina hand in hand. Sky felt like she'd had new life breathed into her. The air felt lighter. *She* felt lighter. It wasn't the sweet scent of flowers as they passed a little floral shop in the parking lot, or the summery dress she was wearing. It wasn't the way the sun highlighted the happy glint in Sawyer's eyes or the strength of his hand, holding hers. It was love. Pure, unadulterated love that had seeped inside her and made her feel rejuvenated. She couldn't imagine being happier than she was right at that second.

"Hey," Sawyer said, stopping in the middle of the street to gaze into her eyes. "I love you."

She smiled and went up on her toes to kiss him. "I love you, too."

"It feels so good to tell you that. I have a feeling I'm going to say it way too much, but I can't help it." He pulled her closer and kissed her. "I love your sweet little nose"—he kissed her nose—"and your beautiful lips"—he kissed her lips—"and the way you wrinkle your brow when you're thinking." He kissed her forehead. "I love the way your hand feels in mine, and"—he lowered his voice to a whisper—"that seductive look you get in your eyes right before our lips come together."

He kissed her again, and she melted against him, reveling in his words, his touch, his love. She was still busy swooning when he took her hand and pulled her toward a cedar-sided building with scooters for rent parked out front.

"Come on," he said. "Let's go have some fun."

They rented a double-seated scooter and tooled around town wearing their spiffy blue helmets. They window-shopped and ate in a café overlooking the water. The area reminded Sky of many small towns on the Cape, with cottage-type shops and old-fashioned light posts. Bikes were parked along the brick-paved sidewalks, giving the town an even quainter feel. There were flags and plants adorning many of the shops, with colorful blooms filling flower boxes beneath big picture windows.

One of the shop owners told them about a music festival taking place in the late afternoon and evening. They picked up a picnic dinner from a diner on the way and rode the scooter across the island to the festival grounds. As they were walking across the crowded lawn, already full of families sitting on blankets and children running around playing, Sawyer's cell phone rang.

He pulled it from his pocket and glanced at the screen. "It's my parents."

Worry riddled his forehead as he answered the call.

"Hello?" He paused to listen and stopped walking. "When?" He squeezed Sky's hand—hard. "I'm on my way." When he ended the call, he headed back toward the parking lot. "My father's fallen. We have to go back."

Chapter Twenty-Two

SAWYER BURST THROUGH the emergency room entrance, making a beeline for the registration desk. They'd used the motor and powered through the harbor to get there as fast as they could, and even though his mother had assured him that his father was okay, he feared the worst. The idea of his father falling on the way to the bathroom slayed him.

After what felt like an hour, but in reality was only a few minutes, he and Sky were allowed into the room with his parents. His mother rose from a chair beside his father's bed and embraced Sawyer.

"He's okay, Sawyer. They did X-rays and he's okay. Nothing's broken."

"Mom, are you okay?" His eyes locked on his father even as he embraced his mother again, to reassure her as much as to reassure himself.

"Yes. I'm shaken up, but fine."

Sawyer glanced at Sky, and she motioned for him to go to his father and not worry about her. Even so, he was thankful she was with him. His father lay on the stark white sheets, looking frail and nonplussed. *Goddamn Parkinson's.* What Sawyer wouldn't give to see his father's smirk and hear him grumble about how a little fall wasn't going to keep him down. His father's facial expression didn't change when Sawyer went to his bedside. Sawyer touched his arm and felt the underlying tremor, saw the purplish bruise on the side of his cheek, and nearly crumpled to his knees.

"Dad." He couldn't ask if he was okay—of course he wasn't fucking okay. He'd never be okay again. He was vaguely aware of his mother greeting Sky, but he was too focused on his father to take it in.

"Son." His father held his gaze.

Sawyer wanted to climb inside his father's head and find his voice. He wanted to know exactly what his father was thinking, what he was feeling. He missed that part of him so damn much that it burned in his gut.

"What can I do? What did the doctors say? Are they keeping you overnight?" Sawyer looked at his mother, who was talking quietly with Sky. Only then did he notice the look of sorrow on Sky's face and realize that she and his mother were holding hands, comforting each other.

"They're waiting for the doctor to sign off on the discharge papers," his mother said.

Sky went to his side and placed a hand on his back as his mother reached for his father's hand. His father's stoic gaze shifted to Sky. Sawyer didn't know if his father would be upset by having someone he didn't know in the room with them. He kicked himself for not thinking about that sooner, but Sky was part of him now, and it wouldn't have felt right not to have her by his side.

When Sky smiled kindly at his father, he felt the fissure in his heart heal up.

"Hi, Mr. Bass. I'm Sky, and I'm so sorry that you got hurt and that it took us so long to get here." She reached for his father's hand as if it were the most natural thing in the world and held it gently. She didn't look away from him, and she didn't seem bothered by his stoic gaze. "I'm glad they're releasing you soon."

His eyes shifted to Sawyer, then back to Sky. "Thank...you...for..." He paused, and Sawyer held his breath, hoping Sky would understand that he had more to say. Sky waited patiently. She didn't rush his father or seem irritated by having to wait for him to speak, and that meant more to him than anything ever could.

When his father spoke again, Sawyer heard a crack in his voice, despite the slowness with which he spoke. "Showing my son there's more to life than fighting."

Sky smiled at Sawyer. "I think we've both learned a lot about life."

He kissed Sky's cheek and whispered, "Are you okay for a second while I talk to my mom?"

She nodded, and he led his mother to the other side of the room.

"Honey, she's lovely," his mother said.

"I know. I'm a lucky guy." He glanced at Sky and saw that she was talking with his father again. "Mom, there's still a month before I fight, and then it takes time to get the money. I have some savings. I want to hire a nurse to help you out."

"Sawyer, you need money to live on. We'll be fine." She glanced at his father, and worry filled her eyes. "I won't leave him alone again. You know how stubborn he is. I heard him get up while I was doing dishes and told him I was just going to dry my hands and I'd be right out. Seconds later I heard him fall." Tears filled her eyes.

Sawyer folded her into his arms. "It's okay, Mom. Dad's okay. It's not your fault, but he needs full-time care. It's time." *And I'm going to train twice as hard to make sure I win.*

"I'm going to ask Mrs. Petzhold and a few of the neighbors to help me out until we figure things out. We can also draw more from our retirement funds. We'll be okay. I'll keep a closer eye on him." She drew in a breath and touched his cheek. "Honey, I'm sorry to call you away from your romantic weekend with Sky."

"Don't worry about that," he assured her. "I'm sorry it took us so long to get here."

He glanced across the room, Sky was sitting on the edge of the bed, holding his father's hand and reciting one of his father's poems. Her gaze was soft, her voice laden with emotion, and in that moment, his love for his family and his love for Sky coalesced.

Before crossing the room to be by Sky's side, he stood with his mother by the door and said quietly, "I'm going to marry her one day, Mom."

His mother reached for his hand. "Don't wait, Sawyer. Life's too short for *one days*."

Chapter Twenty-Three

AFTER HIS FATHER was discharged from the hospital, Sawyer and Sky went to his parents' house to help them get settled. By the time Sawyer and his mother had gotten his father comfortably into bed, it was well after midnight, and Sawyer and Sky were both exhausted. They decided to spend the night and leave in the morning instead of driving back out to return the boat that late at night.

Sawyer assured Sky that sleeping in his childhood bedroom together wasn't an issue, even though he also admitted that he'd never brought a woman to his parents' home for the night before. That both pleased and worried her. She didn't want his parents to think poorly of her. But his mother had been gracious and kind the evening before, setting clean towels in the bathroom and offering her and Sawyer an extra pillow. She didn't seem to mind that they'd spent the night in the same bedroom.

Sky got up extra early and took a quick shower,

then went to the kitchen in search of caffeine.

"Good morning, Sky." Sawyer's mother was standing in her bathrobe, putting coffee in the coffeemaker. "You're up early. It's only six thirty."

"Good morning. I thought I'd get up early to see if there was anything I could help with."

"Thank you." She pointed to a cabinet as she turned on the coffee machine. "You can grab a few mugs."

"Sure. You're up early, too." Sky set four cups on the counter and took a moment to look around. From the moment she'd arrived last night at the hospital, she'd felt welcome. She knew from dealing with her father's alcoholism that the one thing she could do to help Sawyer was to act normal. If she'd freaked out over his father's fall, or his awful bruises, it would have only made Sawyer more upset. The strange thing was, there was something in his father's eyes that was also comforting—at a time when she knew he needed it the most.

"I'm not taking any chances," his mother said. "Tad is still asleep, but he's awake by seven every day. I thought I'd get the coffee started, and then I'll go get ready and read in the bedroom until he wakes." She touched her dark hair and smiled at Sky. "Between last night and this morning, I must look a wreck."

"You look beautiful," Sky assured her.

"I'm sorry we met under such stressful circumstances, but I'm glad to finally meet you."

"Thank you. So am I," Sky said. "I've heard a lot about you both from Sawyer."

"He's a good boy. Man," she corrected herself with a smile. She pulled out an address book and began flipping through it. "I need to start calling a few friends and neighbors to line up some coverage for the next few weeks."

"Coverage?" Sky asked.

"People to stay with Tad when I have to go to the grocery store or pick up his medicines."

"Oh, I see." Sky tried to figure out how she could help. "Would you like me to cook breakfast for you and Mr. Bass?"

"Oh, honey, Lisa and Tad, please." She tightened the belt on her robe, then lowered her voice. "Was Sawyer okay after he went up to bed? I worry about him so."

Sawyer had been terribly upset and had spent a long while talking with Roach on the phone about amping up his training and trying to figure out how he was going to fit in extra training while trying to also spend more time with his parents. And then he'd stewed over their date being cut short, but of course she'd reassured him a million times that she wasn't at all bothered by it. It should be the last thing on his mind at a time like this—and yet he had such a big heart that he wanted to please everyone.

They'd talked half the night—Sawyer planning his training and Sky listening to the grief in his voice and wishing she could help him in some way. They'd eventually fallen asleep in each other's arms, and when Sky awoke this morning, Sawyer had held tightly to her, trying to get her to stay in bed. As much as she'd wanted to lie in his arms, she thought his mother might need some help or comfort, too. Sky wasn't about to tell his mother any of that. She didn't need to worry more than she already was.

"He was okay, just tired. Why don't I finish making coffee and take care of breakfast while you shower, so you don't have to worry about being ready when Mr— Tad wakes up?"

"Thank you, Sky. That's awfully kind of you."

"She's an amazingly kind woman," Sawyer said as he came into the kitchen wearing his jeans from the night before and no shirt. He hugged his mother and kissed the top of her head. "Morning, Ma. Dad up yet?"

"I'm just going to check on him."

Sawyer leaned in and kissed Sky. "Morning, beautiful."

"Good morning. I was just going to make breakfast. Are you hungry?" Sky was mentally ticking off her day to see how else she could help his parents. She had to work, and with the grand opening coming up, she didn't have much time off, but she *was* off work today, so maybe she could help now and then help out later as she was able.

Sawyer drew her into his arms and held her close as his mother went to shower. "Hungry for you," he said. "I'm sorry about our date, Sky."

"Would you stop? It's fine. I was actually thinking that you could go return the boat to Pete and I'd stay here and help your mom for a few hours."

"You want to stay and help?" His eyes narrowed.

"Yes. Your mom needs the help, and she can probably use the company. We were just going to make googly eyes at each other all day, so why not? Besides, she has phone calls to make, and I can get to know your dad a little better."

"Sky, are you sure?"

She touched his cheek, and he leaned in to her

310

palm. God, she loved this man. "More than sure. I would offer to return the boat so you could spend time with your parents, but I have no idea how to sail it back to Wellfleet."

He kissed her again. "What did I do to deserve you?"

"Everything."

Chapter Twenty-Four

IT HAD BEEN three days since Sawyer's father's fall, three days since Sky had met his parents, and three days since he'd had a good night's sleep. His parents' neighbors had rallied around them, and that helped tremendously. Despite his mother's arguments, Sawyer hired a part-time nurse to help during the day, and she was working out well. That put his mind mildly at ease, but all of it—his father's fall, the devastation of reality knocking on their door—increased the pressure for him to win the title fight.

Today Sky and all of her friends were coming to watch him spar the heavyweight Roach had lined up.

Sky. Sweet, beautiful Sky, full of dusky pleasures, confidence, and tenderness. The woman who had stayed with his parents without having been asked. The woman who had just told him that she'd researched his father's disease after knowing him only a few days, so she could help him and his family. The woman he was going to ask to marry him after he won his last fight. Now wasn't the time, with the fight and his father's fate hanging over his head, but soon...She'd become his whole world, and his parents had both told him how much they adored her. Not that he needed their blessing, but he was still damn glad to have it.

He watched her put her favorite C. J. Moon poetry book into her patchwork bag and slip her delicate feet into her sandals as she got ready to go to the tattoo shop for a while before his sparring match. Blue had finished the shelves in the back of the shop, and she wanted to check them out and put a few finishing touches on her work area where Blue had created cubbies for her supplies. But he knew Sky well enough to understand that she needed to keep her mind busy rather than sticking around the cottage and thinking about what he was doing later that afternoon. She'd done a 180-degree turn, supporting his career the way she was, and he truly appreciated and loved her even more for it. But he knew it wasn't easy for her.

Her flowing white skirt swept over her feet as she crossed the living room, straightening the basket containing pieces of his poems as she passed. She wore a skintight light pink tank top that hugged her curves and did nothing to hide her pert nipples, and as she usually did, an armful of bangles and gold swoopy earrings that sparkled in the light against her chestnut hair. She looked gorgeous. He reached for her and pulled her down onto his lap.

"It's weird seeing you leave before me." He nuzzled against her neck. "Christ, you smell good enough to eat."

She leaned back, giving him better access to her neck. "I think you had enough of me this morning."

"I'll never get enough of you," he said honestly.

"You better win your sparring match today, or you won't get any more yummy Sky tonight."

He laughed. "Oh, I won't, will I?" He cupped her breast and dragged his tongue along her collarbone, knowing just how much she loved it and earning himself a lustful moan.

"All my friends are going to be there today, and I want them to see my Herculean boyfriend." Her eyes danced with the tease.

"At least you didn't say your *cute* boyfriend."

She kissed his chest and then pressed her lips to his as she wiggled her ass against his erection. "Cute went out the window a long time ago, Mr. Big, Strong, Alpha, Sexy Boxer Boy."

He growled and swept her onto her back, holding her hands above her head as she giggled and squirmed beneath him. He nipped at her lower lip, then rubbed his scruff along her cheek, earning himself another sexy moan.

"You know I love that," she said in a heady voice.

"I want you to think about me all day, so by the time we come back together tonight, you can barely wait."

"Oh my, you are demanding." She leaned up to kiss him, and he pulled away so she couldn't reach him. "Tease!"

"Self-preservation. I'm already in a bad state." He pressed his hard-on to her leg. "Any more and you're not going to work."

"Promises, promises."

He sealed his lips over hers and slid a hand beneath her skirt, stroking her through her panties.

She was damp in seconds, and when she moaned, "Sawyer," against his lips, he couldn't resist slipping a finger beneath that damp material into her velvety heat.

"Sky," he whispered. "I crave you every minute of the day. I can't get close enough to you, and I'll never, ever get enough of loving you. You better leave, or..."

"Love me, Sawyer. Love me now. Taste me so I stay."

He moved her panties to the side and brought his mouth to her sweetness.

"Oh, God..." She fisted her hand in his hair and held him to her, rocking her hips to meet his efforts. "Don't stop. Oh God. I'm gonna need another shower."

He lifted his head. "Want me to stop?"

"No, no, no." She pushed his head back down, and he took her right up to the edge, feeling like he was going to come just from pleasuring her.

He scooped her into his arms, sealing his lips over hers as he carried her into the bedroom.

"Hurry up," she said with a giggle as she slipped out of her panties and skirt and grabbed a condom from beside the bed.

He kicked off his pants and watched as she rolled the condom on, getting even harder with the way she was licking her lips as she stroked him. He lifted her into his arms, guided her legs around him, and lowered her onto his throbbing erection. They both groaned at the intensity of their love.

"Sky, I'm ready to explode. God, what you do to me. Do you want quick or—"

"Quick and hard," she said as she kissed him. "Later we'll celebrate your win and make love all evening long."

He spread his hands over her hips, lifting her up and down over his hard length with quick, determined movements as she clawed at his shoulders. He wore her marks proudly.

Her thighs tightened around him as their mouths crashed together, and moments later they spiraled over the edge together.

***

"I'M TELLING YOU, I've turned into a sex maniac," Sky said as she, Bella, Jenna, Leanna, and Amy walked across the parking lot of the gym to watch Sawyer fight. "I didn't even go into the shop this morning because we couldn't keep our hands off each other."

"And your problem is?" Bella teased. "Look at my man up there, all police-officer hotness with handcuffs at his waist. I still can't keep my hands off of him."

"I'm right there with you. Look at Kurt." Leanna smiled at her handsome husband as he held the doors to the gym open for them. He leaned down and kissed her, then swatted her butt as they walked inside.

They gathered around the registration desk with their husbands, waiting for Brock, who was walking toward them from the back of the gym where Sawyer and Roach were huddled in a corner and another massive boxer and two other guys were huddled on the opposite side of the floor.

"I missed work," Sky whispered. "For sex!"

Pete turned angry eyes toward her, then hissed out, "I seriously don't want to hear this."

"Ohmygod." Sky felt her cheeks flame, and they all

burst into laughter.

Brock smiled as he approached. "Hey, Sky. You guys, you must be here to watch Sawyer. It's gonna be a mean sparring match." He put his hands on his hips, and his eyes turned serious. "Here's the deal. You can watch, but you stand behind the black lines that are on the floor. No profanity, no nasty slurs. This is a friendly fight."

"Okay," they said in unison.

"Sky, Jana's here," Brock said. "She's getting changed from practice, but she's excited to see you again."

"Who is Jana?" Hunter said as he draped an arm over Sky's shoulder.

"She's Brock's sister. Hands off," Sky said as Blue and Grayson walked through the front door.

"Brock, you may want to tell Jana not to come out of the locker room," Sky teased.

Brock narrowed his eyes and laid a dark stare on Hunter. Then his lips curved into a wide smile. "She'll kick both y'all's asses. Follow me."

Sky's brothers got a nice laugh out of that. They followed Brock through the gym to the ring where Sawyer and his opponent were readying to fight.

"Your posse is here," Brock said.

Sawyer's gaze found Sky's in a hot second, and while he smiled and thanked everyone for coming, it was Sky he made a beeline to.

"You sure you want to be here?" he asked quietly.

"Yes. I love you, and I want to support you."

Blue came to her side. "We'll take care of her, Sawyer. You just show us how to win a fighting match."

"Thanks, Blue." He kissed Sky. "I love you, sweetheart."

"Ooh, sweetheart," Jana said in a singsong voice as she came up behind them. She threw her arms around Sawyer. "Go get 'em!" She turned to Sky with a wide smile and embraced her, too. "I'm glad you're here. You'll see, it's not that bad."

"I hope so. I have an army of support if I want to run screaming from the gym," Sky said, only half kidding.

Jana laughed, and her eyes moved over Sky's shoulder. "No way. Oh, no. Tell me you don't know that guy." She pointed to Hunter.

"That's my brother Hunter," Sky said, worried about the annoyed look in Jana's eyes.

Hunter turned, and when his eyes connected with Jana's, they nearly bugged out of his head. "Holy shit." He ran a hand down his face.

"You know him?" Of course she knew him. Hunter looked like he'd been caught with his pants down, and Sky imagined that wasn't far from the truth.

"Let's just say we've met." She smirked at Hunter.

"Should I worry?" Sky asked.

"Nah. Too much tequila a long time ago," Jana said.

Hunter mouthed, *Sorry*, and Jana turned away.

Brock walked in front of the ring and held his hands up to get everyone's attention. "Sawyer, Crane, you guys ready?"

Sawyer and his opponent, Crane, both nodded and went to opposite corners of the ring.

Sky's heart was already going a mile a minute. She reached for Blue's hand and squeezed it. Amy and the girls moved closer to her.

"You okay?" Amy whispered.

"For now," Sky said. She pressed her hand to Amy's belly. "Let me have some baby love. That'll calm me down."

"Baby surfer is sleeping today. Riding on my bladder."

Brock climbed into the ring and went over the rules with Sawyer and Crane.

"He's easily thirty pounds heavier than Sawyer," Grayson said to Pete.

"Sawyer's got this," Jana said. "He's smooth as butter. This guy's big, but slow." She lowered her voice. "He's also a first-class asshole. A real nasty loser."

The fight started, and Sky gripped Blue's hand tighter, thankful when she felt Grayson's hand land on her shoulder.

Crane moved in fast, throwing one unsuccessful punch after another. Sawyer deflected each one with fluid movements, barely breaking a sweat. Crane's feet moved forward and back, his massive shoulders rounded forward. Each punch drew a sharp inhalation from the guys and caused Sky to close her eyes. She didn't mean to, but how was she supposed to watch? What if his fist connected with Sawyer's handsome face? She opened her eyes, needing to watch and make sure he was okay.

Sawyer moved fast as lightning, smooth as water, throwing multiple body punches, a right to the jaw, and another punch from beneath that put Crane on his back. All the guys cheered, but as Crane pushed up with his thunderous knees, he sneered at them through the ropes, silencing them all with an angry growl.

Sky held her breath as one round ended and the next began. Each round brought more tension, and by the fourth round she felt like her whole body was one big knot. Meanwhile, the guys were cheering, and Jana, Bella, Leanna, and Jenna were hollering, too. Amy clung to Sky's hand, while Blue moved up closer to the ring with the other men.

Sweat dripped from the boxers. Crane was breathing hard, tiring. Every punch packed power and fatigue as his massive fists were intercepted time and time again by Sawyer. Crane's face grew tighter, his eyes narrower with each block. If smoke could come from a person's ears, it would be streaming from his. At the end of the round, Brock announced that the next was the final round, and Sky felt relief wash over her. During the next round, Brock stepped between Sawyer and Crane three times to say something to Crane that Sky couldn't hear, but each time the sneer on Crane's face made the hair on the back of Sky's neck stand on end.

Sawyer moved in swiftly, landing one punch after another and clocking Crane from the underside of his chin. Sweat spewed over the ropes as Crane flew backward, his broad shoulders landing against the ropes. He sprang right back up, swinging and missing, time and time again, making tortured, violent sounds that made Sky's blood curl.

She closed her eyes and squeezed Amy's hand.

"It's almost over," Amy assured her.

Sky couldn't respond. She couldn't move. She forced her eyes open, remembering her promise to herself to support Sawyer. Crane scared the shit out of her. She'd never seen someone so angry, and all that anger was bottled up inside the largest, most muscular man she'd ever seen. But it was the way he looked at Sawyer that frightened her most, like he wanted to kill him, not just win the fight. She wondered how anyone could watch this sport without having a heart attack. She felt like hers was going to explode. Her stomach was so tight she thought she might be sick, but she kept reminding herself that Sawyer was fighting for his father, and that was enough to keep her rooted in place, silently praying that the match would end without anyone getting hurt.

When Brock called the end of the final round and held up both fighters' hands, Sky finally exhaled. Sawyer's eyes found her, full of pride and full of love. He took a step toward her, and Amy placed a hand on Sky's back, urging her toward the ring, just as Crane spun around and clocked Sawyer in the side of his skull.

"No!" Sky screamed as Sawyer's eyes rolled back in his head and he fell, lifeless, to the floor.

Chapter Twenty-Five

SKY HELD SAWYER'S hand, silently begging the powers that be to let him be okay. She couldn't stop shaking, even though Sawyer had already come to, but according to the doctor, it had taken longer than he would have liked. It had also taken Sawyer several minutes to relay basic information such as what he'd had for breakfast and what he'd done the day before. Sky didn't know much about being knocked out, but she knew from everything the doctor had said and the worried look in his eyes that this was not normal and far from a good sign. They were running all sorts of tests and waiting for results. Roach stood beside her with one hand on her shoulder, a steadying force in a sea of fear, handing her dry tissues every few minutes. The doctors wouldn't let any of the others in the room, and she knew they were probably going crazy with worry, but there was no way she was going to leave Sawyer's side.

The right side of Sawyer's head was swollen and

already bruising.

"Sky," he rasped. "I'm okay. Don't cry."

"Don't cry? You got knocked out, and the doctor was worried that you weren't going to wake up." She swiped at her eyes and leaned over him, kissing the side of his face that wasn't stricken, his forehead, his mouth, everywhere she could. "You scared me so badly, Sawyer. I was wrong. I can't watch you fight again. I can't do it."

Sawyer wrapped his arms around her. "Okay. It's okay. I only have one more fight, and you don't have to watch."

The doctor came back into the room. He was a tall, older man with salt-and-pepper hair and serious eyes behind wire frames.

"I just got off the phone with your doctor." He shifted his eyes to Sawyer. "He says he's already told you not to fight."

Told you not to fight?

Sawyer's dark eyes held the doctor's gaze. "Dr. Malen gave me the same warning every doctor gives every fighter."

"Sawyer," Roach said in a husky voice.

Sky looked up at him as Sawyer released her. His eyes narrowed. "This is *my* fight, Roach."

Sky had never heard his voice so cold before.

"Perhaps there was some miscommunication," the doctor suggested. He folded his hands in front of him and said, "Although I know Dr. Malen well, and he's meticulously precise."

Sawyer's jaw clenched.

"Can he fight or not?" Roach asked.

Can he fight?

"Is he physically able? Yes," the doctor said. "Is it advisable? No. I would not send my own son into a ring after being concussed as Sawyer was. Nor would I have let him into the ring after having endured so many concussions prior to this one." He turned stern eyes to Sawyer. "It took you too long to come out of it, Sawyer. You got lucky. You're playing with fire. As Dr. Malen told you, you've had numerous concussions, and the next one could leave you permanently brain damaged or worse."

"Wait. What?" Sky looked at Sawyer. "You've had numerous concussions? Your doctor told you that already and you still fought?"

"Sky, all fighters get concussed. It's not as bad as it sounds. They've said that for as long as I can remember."

Her heart lodged in her throat, and it took all of her focus not to yell as she turned to the doctor and asked as calmly as she was able—which wasn't calmly at all—"Are you saying that his doctor *already* told him that he could get brain damaged, or worse, if he got knocked out again?"

"No," the doctor replied.

Sky let out a relieved breath.

"I'm saying that, according to Dr. Malen, he's told Sawyer that he could suffer brain damage or worse *without* losing consciousness. A simple blow to the head could be enough."

A simple blow to the head. *Simple* blow. What the hell did that even mean? Her legs went weak, and she held on to the side of the bed, her whole body trembling, her mind reeling.

"Sky?" Sawyer's voice was muted through the rush

of blood in her ears.

"Doctor, can you please give us a minute?" Sawyer sat up and swung his legs off the bed.

The doctor put a hand on his shoulder. "Do not get up. Try not to get riled up. I'll be back in a few minutes."

The doctor walked out the door, and Sawyer shifted his eyes to Roach. "Do you mind, Roach?"

"Remember what I told you, Sawyer. I'm not making that phone call to your mother." Roach laid a supportive hand on Sky's shoulder before turning and walking out of the room, leaving them alone.

"Sky." He reached for her, but her body was too shaky, her mind too chaotic, to be touched. She turned away.

***

SAWYER'S HEAD WAS pounding and his body ached from slamming into the floor when he fell, but nothing hurt as badly as the devastated look in Sky's eyes.

"Sky, listen to me. I have to fight. I have to do this for my father. He's not doing well. I don't have much time."

Tears streamed down her cheeks. "If you fight, you might be more right than you know, Sawyer, about not having much time. How can you even think about going back in a ring after what the doctor just said?"

He steeled himself against her words, as he'd done with Roach so many times in the past. "My parents need this win, Sky."

Her voice trembled as she reached for his hand.

"And I need you. We've just found each other, Sawyer. You could have been injured for life today, and what's worse is that you knew this was a risk. Why didn't you tell me?"

"Because it's the same crap they've been saying for years, Sky. They say it to everyone."

"It sure didn't seem that way, Sawyer." Her voice escalated. "Even Roach doesn't want you to fight. I can see it in his eyes."

"I'm fighting, Sky."

"Don't you care about us at all? Don't you care about your family? What about all that talk about a future? Was that *all* bullshit? You just decided to write with your father so you would have something with him for the future. The *future*, Sawyer. Remember how much you wanted that?" She pushed away from the bed and paced, her arms crossed over her chest as tears fell from her eyes.

"Of course I want a future with you. But I'm a fighter, Sky. It's who I am."

She stopped pacing and leveled him with a cold, teary-eyed stare. "You told me that fighting was what you did, not who you are."

"I was wrong. I have one thing to give to my parents. And this is it."

"Then you need to make a choice, Sawyer, because I love you too much to sit back and watch you suffer brain damage because of some asshole who hits you upside the head on your way out of the ring—or worse, to watch you die."

"How can you ask me to choose between loving you and my father's well-being? My parents' entire future?" Anger brewed in his gut, for the brutality of the illness his father faced and the unfairness of the battle he and Sky were having.

"I'm not asking you to choose between me and your father. I'm asking you to love yourself enough to *want* to live a whole life, with all of your cognitive functions intact." She sucked in a breath through her tears. "And to have faith that together we'll find another way to make ends meet for your father's medical bills."

"Sky, you gave up your life to help your father get through rehab. You gave up your friends, your job, your apartment, and you moved back here to run his business. How can you not understand this?"

"It's different! I couldn't have died helping him." She was trembling so badly that he wanted to wrap her in his arms and make the pain go away—make the decisions go away. He wanted to reverse time to before he got hit in the head and pretend everything was just fine and that the doctor's warning didn't exist.

He'd pretended so well for so long.

"Sky." His voice was a thin thread as he tried to rein in his anger.

"No. No more *Skys*, Sawyer. I love you too much for this. I lost my mother to something she had *no* control over. You're losing your father to a fate that's out of his hands. *Your* fate—*our* fate—is in your hands. You once said that you didn't want to leave our future to chance. Well, Sawyer, that's what you're doing. If you don't love yourself, or us, enough to do what it takes to save yourself, then we have nothing left to talk about." She spun on her heel and walked out the door.

"Sky!" he called after her as he rose to his feet to

go after her, but the room spun around him. He gripped the edge of the bed for stability, trying to make sense of what had just happened. He lifted his eyes to the door, and the room continued to spin. One step sent him off-balance, and he fell to his knees on the cold floor. His head and chest ached like never before. The ache of a broken heart, it turned out, was all consuming and ten times as bad as any punch could ever be.

Chapter Twenty-Six

"SKY, IT'S BEEN two days. You have to do something," Bella urged. "Call him. Go see him. At least talk to him."

She and the girls were sitting on Bella's deck having breakfast, as they'd been doing for weeks— only it no longer felt as wonderful as it had just a few days ago, when Sky knew that any moment Sawyer would come jogging around the bend with Tony, Pete, or Caden. Over the last two days Sawyer had called her a number of times, asking to see her, but when she'd asked if he was still going to fight, he'd said he had to. They were at a standstill. She refused to see him and had even put her phone away, because if she had to see his picture on the screen when he called, or look into his eyes and see his love for her, the love she knew he had in his heart, she'd give in. And giving in meant opening a door to his getting hurt irreparably— and she couldn't do that to him or to herself.

"I can't," Sky said softly. "I've thought about it, and it's not fair of me to come between him and his parents' future. Sawyer was right about that, but damn it..." She swallowed past the thickening in her throat, which seemed ever-present since she'd stormed out of the hospital. "He said he wanted a future with me, but he's not willing to protect that future. I just can't. I don't know what to do."

Amy leaned over and hugged her. "Honey, you're sure about what the doctor said?"

Sky leveled a narrow-eyed stare on Amy. They'd asked her the same question a hundred times. She wasn't an idiot. She'd heard the doctor loud and clear. "The problem isn't what I heard the doctor say, Amy. The problem is what Sawyer *didn't* say."

"You are truly between a rock and a hard place." Jenna held up her palm, as if she were weighing something. "Over here is his need to win that fight for his dad." She held up her other palm. "And over here is your relationship. How can he choose? Could you choose?"

Sky pushed away from the table. "I don't know, okay? The only thing I know is that I love him. I love him with every ounce of my soul—and when you love someone that much, you don't do something that might tear you away from them. And he's doing just that, which means he doesn't love me the same way I love him."

"Sky." Bella's voice turned serious. "Aren't you doing the same thing by walking away?"

She wiped tears from her eyes. "Whose side are you on?"

"I'm just saying that there's no right answer. That's his *father*. He loves him, and he loves you. How can the guy choose?"

"I. Don't. Know! I realize it makes me selfish to ask him to protect himself in this instance. I get that. I'm a selfish bitch, fine, whatever. I love him, Bella, and my heart tells me that something else can be done to get that money. There has to be another way. He wouldn't even consider the possibility of other options. There *are* other options. There has to be. Loans, other jobs, whatever." She stormed off the deck.

"I'm sorry. I'm a mess and not at all rational right now. I don't mean to yell at you guys, so I'm going to leave and go to work, where I can take out my frustrations on cleaning, or painting, or bury my heart in a tattoo."

"Why don't you take the day off?" Amy suggested. "We can hang out at the pool and relax."

Sky glanced down at the pool, and the memories of making love with Sawyer before going skinny-dipping with the girls came rushing back.

"I think I need to be alone, but thanks for the offer."

By midafternoon Sky had rearranged her shop, given three customers tattoos, and thought about Sawyer every single damn second. She couldn't shake the feeling that Bella was right. By walking away, she had done the same thing he was doing. She'd walked out on them. Ended their relationship. Torn them apart. But was that her fault? Did she have any other choice? Maybe she should wait it out. Pretend he wasn't fighting that one last fight and then go see him when it was over.

If he wasn't brain damaged—or worse.

She couldn't go a minute without thinking about him. How could she pretend he wasn't risking his life in a fight? And why should she have to? Shouldn't he love her—himself, his family—enough to want to remain healthy and cognitively aware?

He does love his family. That's why he's fighting.

Even her own brain was making her crazy. She walked outside and inhaled the fresh air, hoping to clear her head. People of all ages walked through the streets laughing and talking, carrying shopping bags, eating ice cream, and holding hands. A month ago she'd have been just fine chatting with people as they passed by the shop, but now? Now she wanted to cry just watching people enjoy what she'd never have with Sawyer.

She tried to distract herself from the pain by tallying what she still had.

I finally own my own tattoo shop.

I have a great apartment.

Great friends.

A wonderful, loving family.

She glanced in the window of Lizzie's store and saw her talking with Blue. She'd been hoping they'd start dating, but now she almost wished they wouldn't. She didn't want either of them to ever go through the pain she was going through.

"How is my favorite tatty girl?"

Sky turned at the sound of Marcus's happy voice. He was dressed as Marcus today, in a pair of dark cargo shorts and a yellow tank top, his hair brushed away from his face and not a speck of makeup on his clean-shaven face. His eyes rolled over her face, and his smile turned to a grim line.

"Oh, my, sugar." He opened his arms and pulled her into a hug. "You look like someone stole your tattoo guns. Let Marcus make it all better." He patted her back, and when he drew away and searched her eyes, it was all she could do to keep from crying. "Come." He pulled her down to the stoop in front of the shop and sat with one arm around her, the other holding her hand in his. "Tell me all about it."

"I'm fine," she lied.

"You are *fine*, as in hot, but this." He used his index finger and drew circles in front of her face. "This is not fine. This is *I've given up on even trying to look fine*. I smell trouble with Mr. Sawyer."

Sky exhaled and dropped her eyes. She couldn't talk about Sawyer, because if she did, those tears she'd been holding back would break free, and that was the last thing she needed.

"Marcus, can I ask you a really unfair question?"

He narrowed his eyes and tilted his head. "Doesn't everyone?"

She knew that Marcus and many of the drag queens around Provincetown were asked tactless questions by inquisitive tourists.

"This is *really* unfair, and you don't have to answer me, but I don't know how else to figure this out." She met his gaze and took another shaky breath before asking, "If Howie had opted not to get treatment for his cancer, how would that have made you feel?"

Marcus shifted his eyes away, and now it was his turn to take a deep breath. "You don't pull any punches, do you, sugar?"

"I'm sorry. You don't have to answer."

"It's okay. If it'll help you, I'll tell you. Howie and I actually talked about this a lot. When we were in the thick of his illness, I couldn't imagine him not getting treatment. We fought over that, because he had done his research, and he knew that even with treatment, his life wasn't going to be a life at all. It was going to be time between treatments, most of which was spent sleeping, or fighting skin infections due to radiation, or bouts of nausea." Marcus swallowed hard. "I know he went through the treatments because I *needed* him to."

"Do you regret asking him to?" she asked, trying to figure out her own feelings.

"Those treatments gave me Howie for another two years, and even if those years weren't the best years of our lives, it was two solid years of holding him. Kissing him. Caring for him. Loving him while he was still here with me."

"But? I hear a *but.*"

"But I knew from the start that he didn't really want to go out of this world that way, and I still live with the guilt of that decision." His eyes dampened, and he rested his head on Sky's shoulder. "Maybe it would have been better, or kinder, to have let him die on his own terms. To leave me sooner. I just loved him too much to honor what he really wanted. I'm not sure there's a right answer. Either way I lost the only man I've ever loved, but I do know this. Whether he had died after a month or two years, I did everything within my power to treasure every second of the time we had. And I'm glad I did, because I've known love, Sky, by the most remarkable man who has ever lived. He showed me enough love in those days to fill my soul for a lifetime. I was just gluttonous. I wanted more."

He lifted his head from her shoulder and looked at

her. "What is this all about, Sky?"

She shook her head, unable to answer. Did she love Sawyer too much? Should she be happy for whatever time they had together and not worry about the future? She knew the ache of losing someone she loved. Her mother had left a hole so vast she thought she'd be navigating around it her whole life. She lifted her eyes to the alley across the street, remembering the first night she and Sawyer had gone out and the way he'd waved and run back to get her phone number. That was when things had begun to change—the ache of losing her mother had started to subside. Sawyer had begun filling that great abyss.

What about the immense hole *he'd* leave behind?

Could she survive losing Sawyer?

Reality hit her a moment later.

I'm already losing him.

Chapter Twenty-Seven

SKY PRESSED SAWYER'S speed-dial number for the third time as she drove down Route 6 toward his house with her heart thundering in her chest. His voicemail picked up again, and she left another message.

"It's me. I'm sorry for walking out and not taking your calls. I want to talk. Call me?" She ended the call and set the phone on the passenger seat. Sawyer had left her five messages apologizing and asking her to please return his calls. The sixth message had cut Sky to her core. *Sky, how am I supposed to just walk away from us? I no longer know how to be me without you.*

She drove off the exit in Truro and navigated the narrow streets to the private sandy road that led to his house on the dunes. The house came into view over the treetops, and her pulse sped up. She didn't know if what she was doing was right or wrong. She only knew that two days without Sawyer had been hell, and the idea of not being with him ever again was incomprehensible. She needed to see him, to talk to him when he wasn't lying in a hospital bed having just been knocked out. When she wasn't still on the verge of a breakdown from thinking she'd lost him forever. They'd communicated so well with each other until now. Their hearts were made of words and love and all things in between. They had to be able to figure this out together.

She pulled into his empty driveway and her stomach sank at the sight of a "For Sale" sign in the center of the front yard. Her jaw dropped open as she stared at the sign. He was moving? After two days? Tears sprang to her eyes as she slammed on the gas and backed out of the driveway. She had to find him. She had to talk to him and find out what was going on. She sped down the road and headed to the one place she knew she'd find him—the club.

Out on Route 6 she tried his number again and left another hasty message. "You're moving? Where are you going? Don't move, Sawyer. Call me back, please?" Her finger hovered over the End button, and she added, "I love you. Please call me." She put the phone in the cup holder in the center console, hoping he'd call back.

Her phone rang a few seconds later, and she fumbled for it, blinking away tears. Amy's name flashed on the screen. She put the phone back down. She couldn't talk to Amy or anyone else until she spoke to Sawyer. She sped down the road, confused, upset, and feeling like her heart was being torn to shreds. Had she already lost him for good?

Ten minutes later she pulled into the club parking lot—and Sawyer's truck wasn't there. She slammed on the brakes, staring at the building. *They have to know where he is.* She parked out front and ran inside. Brock looked up from behind the registration desk with wide eyes, which turned serious as she hurried to the desk.

"Hi, Sky." His eyes traveled over her face.

She knew she looked a wreck, but she didn't care. She had to find and talk to Sawyer. "Do you know where I can find Sawyer?" She was breathing so hard, she felt like she'd just run a mile.

Brock dropped his eyes. The muscle in his jaw flexed. "Haven't seen him since the fight. He met with Roach last night, but I haven't seen Roach either."

"Was he okay?" She started to wonder if his concussion had been worse than the doctor thought.

Brock shrugged. "If I see him I'll let him know you came by. Are you okay?"

"I honestly don't know anymore." She hurried from the gym out to her car and started the engine. Where was she going? She had no idea where to look next. He could have gone to his parents, but she wasn't about to show up there looking like this. She glanced at her phone. She'd missed another call from Amy—and none from Sawyer.

Clutching the steering wheel so tightly her knuckles turned white, she gave in to the tears streaming down her cheeks. Sobs began in her chest, bubbling up and coming out loud and tortured. She'd fucked everything up. He'd fucked everything up.

She drove back to Seaside, completely drained and confused. She drove by the pool and saw the girls lying in the sun. Maybe she needed to disappear into them for a while after all. She definitely couldn't weather this storm alone.

***

SAWYER HEARD TIRES on gravel before he spotted Sky's car driving up the road. He tightened his grip on the leather notebook he'd brought with him, silently hoping his unhappiness wouldn't keep him from making sense when he spoke to her.

He knew she needed time and they needed space to figure this out. They needed to talk with clear heads, but clear heads went out the window when she stepped from the car with tears streaming down her cheeks and a look of dismay on her beautiful face. Her T-shirt and shorts were wrinkled, and she had no bangles on her wrists or necklaces hanging around her neck. Her hair was tousled, and her nose was pink. Sawyer rose to his feet and closed the distance between them.

"Sky." He opened his arms, and for a beat she just stared at him, slack-jawed, and then the edges of her lips curved up as sobs sprang from her lungs—confusing him and killing him in equal measure as he gathered her in his arms.

"I'm so sorry, Sky." He'd felt so empty without her for the past two days that having her in his arms brought tears to his eyes. "I was in denial about the doctor's warning. I wasn't trying to keep it from you. I was keeping it from myself. It's just that you were a part of me, so you got caught in the crossfire. I'm so sorry."

She drew back and opened her mouth, but her voice was silenced by sobs. He swallowed hard against the ache in his heart and held her close again, until they both calmed enough to look at each other without breaking down. She took a step back and crossed her arms, creating a barrier he wanted to burst through. But he knew there was no bursting. They were still straddling a great divide, and they needed to talk.

"What are you doing here?" she asked as she wiped her tears. "You're selling your house."

"Yes, I am. How do you know that?"

"I drove by looking for you." Fresh tears slid down her cheeks. "God, Sawyer, don't you ever check your phone?"

Given how many of his calls to her had gone unanswered, he could have responded with, *Don't you?* But what good would that do? "My phone is in my car over by the laundry building."

She looked across the quad at the building.

"Sky, I have no right to ask anything of you, but if there's one thing I've learned from our relationship, it's that following my heart has always been the right thing to do." He stepped closer and handed her the notebook he'd brought with him. She stared down at it without accepting it.

"I don't have much left. And no matter where we go from here, I want you to have this." He set the notebook in her hands. "These are my songs. All of them, including yours. You believed in me, and in them, and I want you to have them."

"Sawyer—"

"They're yours. I have all I need right here." He touched his chest over his heart. "I'm no longer the man who walked into your shop asking for a tattoo. I have no career, and my house is under contract, which means I'm homeless, at least at the moment. Where I'll go from here is up in the air. I can train with Brock, write with my father, or move away and start over."

Her lower lip trembled as fresh tears spilled down her cheeks.

"I don't have much to offer you, but if you'll give this broken-down ex-boxer another chance at doing things right, I promise I'll never let you down."

"You..." Her hands dropped limply to her sides. "You're no longer a boxer? I don't understand."

"I quit. I'm not fighting anymore. I want to be in one piece for us, Sky. I want a future with you. A family. A life."

"But your dad?" She reached for his hand, and he was so thankful for her touch that his eyes filled with tears again, too.

"The sale of the house will cover his medical expenses forever. Who knew that over the last few years bay-front property had doubled in value?"

"But it's your family's legacy." Her voice was fraying as she stepped closer to him.

"Yes. That was their legacy. But it's not mine. It won't mean anything without you by my side. I can never look at that house again without seeing you standing in the skycap or lying beneath me on the pillows. Or laughing with me on the dunes. I know I have nothing to offer you, and you could find a guy who's got a job, and a house, and so much more than what I have to offer." The truth hurt like a bullet through his chest.

"But you're wrong, Sawyer. I loved you *despite* your job, not for it. You have the only thing I want— your heart."

"Do you mean that? You'd take me back even though I'm homeless—"

"I have an apartment." She stepped closer, bringing their thighs together.

"Jobless?"

"I have a job." She wound her arms around his neck, and his heart skipped a beat.

"An idiot for taking two days to figure it out?" He folded her into his arms, and she answered in a whisper against his lips, "You're my idiot."

"Sky," was all he could manage as he was bowled over with emotions.

"Kiss me, Sawyer."

She didn't need to ask twice. Their tears mixed and mingled on their cheeks, and when she whispered, "Carry me inside. If I'm going to be your sugar mama, I plan on using my power for all sorts of sexual favors," he was sure he'd found heaven.

Epilogue

Six weeks later...

SKY GLANCED UP from the tattoo she was creating on Cree's shoulder at her brother Matt and her father as they looked over her artwork. She'd missed seeing them both and was glad they'd come for the grand opening. Matt picked up her poetry book and sat down to read it. It didn't surprise her that he'd ignore the music and the people milling about and bury his nose in a book. Sky was about to call him over when Lizzie and a dark-haired girl came into the shop. Lizzie hugged Sky's father, and the girl she was with struck up a conversation with Matt.

She looked back down at the tattoo she was doing and then took a second to glance up at Sawyer, who was sitting on the front stoop beside Marcus, Lizzie, Amy, and Tony, while he sang one of the songs he'd written since they'd moved in together in the apartment above the shop. What Sawyer hadn't told Sky the night he'd come to see her after the hospital visit was that Tony and Amy had been the ones to put an offer down on his beach house. He'd come to Seaside looking for her that morning after meeting with the real estate agent, and the agent had called him later with the offer. Apparently he hadn't wanted to mention it was Tony and Amy because he didn't want her to feel pressured by the connection. Sky was happy for Tony and Amy, and she knew they'd start their own family traditions in the lovely home. Sawyer had made enough money from the sale to provide for his father's future and also to buy a little cottage somewhere. But neither Sky nor Sawyer was in a hurry to move out of their cozy apartment. They'd toyed with buying Amy and Tony's extra cottage, and they might one day do that, but for now they wanted to enjoy being settled in their own place for a while.

Sawyer was working as a trainer at the club with Brock, and he and his father had begun writing together. His father's editor was so stoked about the collaboration that he'd already made them a six-figure offer. This was Sky's third clue that the universe was stepping in this summer to help guide her and Sawyer. The first clue, of course, was that they'd met in the first place, and the second was that they'd found their way back to each other.

Sky turned her attention back to putting the finishing touches on Cree's tattoo as Sawyer's parents came into the shop, accompanied by the private nurse Sawyer had hired for them. Mira was in her midtwenties, and she and Sky had already become close. Mira pushed Sawyer's father's wheelchair across the floor with ease and waved to Sky. Sky smiled and said, "I'm glad you're here. I'll be done in a minute," then finished up the tattoo.

"I haven't found any more of those poems around lately," Cree said.

"The P-town poet must be busy these days." She glanced at Sawyer again as he set his guitar aside and reached for Hannah, Amy and Tony's two-week-old baby girl. Bella had given birth the day before yesterday to baby Summer and had to miss the grand opening.

Sawyer met Sky's gaze and smiled. Lifting the baby, he mouthed, *Want one?* She laughed and mouthed back, *Not yet.* They were having way too much fun practicing making babies to settle down and have one yet.

Grayson walked into the shop with Kurt and Jamie. Jamie and Jessica and Jamie's grandmother, Vera, had finally arrived last week. The Seaside gang had celebrated with a barbecue and ended up celebrating far more than Jamie, Jessica, and Vera's return to the Cape. Both Jessica and Leanna had announced their pregnancies that evening. Apparently they'd both thought they were just exhausted from working too much, but their doctors had confirmed that they were both pregnant. The universe had stepped in once again, in the summer that Sky would forever remember as the summer of miracles.

Matt rose and embraced each of the guys, then said something to Lizzie and her friend and walked out the front door with the girls. Grayson and the guys walked through the shop toward Sky.

"Matt's going to check out something over at Lizzie's with some hot chick," Grayson said.

"I'm sure she has a name," Sky teased.

Cree rose off the seat, and Grayson's eyes took a slow stroll down her body. Sky nudged him with a *tsk!* on her way to the cash register.

"Hi, Kurt. Hi, Jamie. Are you guys having fun?" she asked as she rang up Cree's tattoo and saw Grayson elbow Hunter, who was busy checking out Jana and Harper. Sky never did follow up on what had happened between the two of them, but there was no doubt something had gone on, because every time Hunter caught Jana's eye, she sneered at him. Better to leave *that* up to the universe, too.

"Yes," Jamie said. "This has been fun. It's so good to finally be back at the Cape. Vera, Jess, and Leanna went window-shopping."

349

"Probably for baby clothes," Sky said. Then she hugged Cree goodbye and turned to Kurt. "Ready for a new tat?"

Kurt held his palms up. "I've got enough, thanks."

Sky hugged Sawyer's parents and Mira as Sawyer joined them and drew Sky into his arms.

"Do you have time to do one more tattoo?" Sawyer asked.

"What did you have in mind?" She loved how close they'd become. She'd thought they were close before moving in together, but living in a five-hundred-square-foot apartment brought *close* to a whole new level. Sawyer had created all sorts of pillow beds for Merlin in the corners of the apartment, and he'd chosen the balcony above the shop as his new writing spot. Sometimes after Sky fell asleep, she knew he went out there to pen a song. In the morning she'd wake up and find slips of paper in the basket by the bed—verses of songs Sawyer had written just for her.

He handed her a piece of paper on which he'd written, *S.B. + S.L.*

Her heart squeezed. "What is this?"

"My ancestors carved their initials into rafters, but houses come and go and skin is forever."

"Sawyer," she said as she went up on her toes and kissed him. "I want this tattooed on me, too."

"We can make those initials S.B + S.B. if you'll marry me."

Sky searched his eyes, her pulse racing, unsure if she'd heard him right, or if he was kidding. He dropped to one knee in front of her family, friends, and a handful of customers milling around the shop and smiled up at her with love in his eyes.

"You are my wind, I am your rain. You are my sun, I am your earth. I wrestled your demons, sweet summer Sky, and you slayed my truths and showed me the way to our future. We're no longer two wild hearts drifting on a cloud. Let's become one, tethered and bound. Marry me, Sky, and I promise to always be whatever you need."

Sky's legs turned to Jell-O as she sank to her knees and did the only thing she could manage—she nodded.

Sawyer pulled a ring from his pocket and held her trembling hand as he slid it onto her left ring finger. "This was my grandmother's ring. She once told me that when I felt lost, to look to the sky and I'd find my way. I think she knew you were out there waiting for me."

And as their lips came together and her friends *aww*ed and clapped, Sky closed her eyes and sent a silent thank-you to the universe—for coming through for them yet again. Maybe life really was that easy, and that complicated.

—The End—

Hunter, Grayson, and Matt Lacroux will each be getting their own books! Sign up for Melissa's newsletter to be notified of her next release!
http://www.MelissaFoster.com/Newsletter

Want to know more about Sky's friends Blue & Lizzie?

Please enjoy this sneak peek of their love story, SEIZED BY LOVE (The Ryders, Book 1)

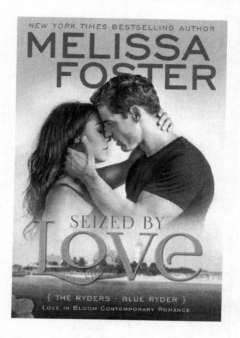

THERE WERE SOME nights when Lizzie Barber simply didn't feel like donning an apron, black-framed glasses, and high heels, covering her shiny brunette locks with a blond wig, and prancing around nearly naked. Tonight was one of those nights. Gazing at her reflection in the mirror of her basement bathroom, Lizzie tucked the last few strands of her hair beneath the wig and forced her very best smile. Thank God her elfin lips naturally curled up at the edges—even when she wasn't smiling, she looked like she was. And tonight she definitely wasn't in the mood to smile. Her oven had been acting up for the last few nights, and she prayed to the gods of all things sugary and sweet that it would behave tonight.

Tightening the apron tie around her neck and the one around her waist, to avoid wardrobe malfunctions, and tugging on the hem of the apron to ensure her skin-colored thong and all her naughty bits were covered, she went into the studio—aka the miniscule kitchen located in the basement of her cute Cape Cod cottage—and surveyed her baking accoutrements one last time before queuing the intro music for her webcast and pasting that perfectly perky smile back in place.

"Welcome back, my hot and hunky bakers," she purred into the camera. "Today we're going to bake delicious angel food cupcakes with fluffy frosting that will make your mouth water." She leaned forward, flashing the camera an eyeful of cleavage and her most seductive smile as she crooked her finger in a come-hither fashion. "And because we all know it's what's *beneath* all that delicious frosting that counts, we're going to sprinkle a few surprises inside the thick, creamy centers."

Lizzie had mastered making baking sound naughty while in college, when her father had taken ill and her parents had closed their inn for six months to focus on his medical care, leaving Lizzie without college tuition. Her part-time job at a florist shop hadn't done a darn thing for her mounting school loans, and when a friend suggested she try making videos and monetizing them to earn fast cash, she drew upon her passion for baking and secretly put on a webcast called *Cooking with Coeds*. It turned out that scantily clad baking was a real money earner. She'd paid for her books and meal plan that way, and eventually earned enough to pay for most of her college tuition. Lizzie had two passions in life—baking and flowers, and she'd hoped to open her own floral shop after college. After graduation, *Cooking with Coeds* became the *Naked Baker* webcast, and she'd made enough money to finish paying off her school loans and open a flower shop in Provincetown, Massachusetts, just like she'd always dreamed of. She hadn't intended to continue the *Naked Baker* after opening P-town Petals, but when her parents fell upon hard times again and her younger sister Maddy's educational fund disappeared, the *Naked Baker* webcast became Lizzie's contribution to Maddy's education. Their very conservative parents would have a conniption fit if they knew what their proper little girl was doing behind closed doors, but what other choice did she have? Her parents ran a small bed-and-breakfast in Brewster, Massachusetts, and with her father's health ping-ponging, they barely earned enough money to make ends meet—and affording college for a child who had come as a surprise to them seven years after Lizzie was born had proven difficult.

Lizzie narrowed her eyes seductively as she gazed into the camera and stirred the batter. She dipped her finger into the rich, creamy goodness and put that finger into her mouth, making a sensual show of sucking it off. "Mm-mm. Nothing better than *thick, creamy* batter." Her tongue swept over her lower lip as she ran through the motions of creating what she'd come to think of as *baking porn*.

During the filming of each show, she reminded herself often of why she was still doing something that she felt ashamed of and kept secret. There was no way she was going to let her sweet nineteen-year-old sister fend for herself and end up doing God knew what to earn money like she did instead of focusing on her studies. Or worse, drop out of school. Madison was about as innocent as they came, and while Lizzie might once have been that innocent, her determination to succeed, and life circumstances, had beaten it out of her. Creating the webcast was the best decision she'd ever made—even if it meant putting her nonexistent social life on hold and living a secret life after dark. The blond wig and thick-framed spectacles helped to hide her online persona, or at least they seemed to. No one had ever accused her of being the Naked Baker. Then again, her assumption was that the freaky people who got off watching her prance around in an apron and heels probably rarely left their own basements.

She was proud of helping Maddy. She felt like she was taking one for the team. Going where no girl should ever have to go. Braving the wild naked baking arena for the betterment of the sister she cherished.

A while later, as Lizzie checked the cupcakes and realized that while the oven was still warm, it had turned *off*—her stomach sank. Hiding her worries behind another forced smile and a wink, she stuck her ass out and bent over to quickly remove the tray of cupcakes from the oven, knowing the angle of the camera would give only a side view and none of her bare ass would actually be visible. Thankfully, the oven must have just died, because it was still warm and the cupcakes were firm enough to frost.

Emergency reshoot avoided!
Smile genuine!

A few minutes later she sprinkled the last of the coconut on the cupcakes, narrating as she went.

"Everyone wants a little something extra on top, and I'm going to give it to you *good*." Giving one last wink to the camera, she said, "Until next week, this is your Naked Baker signing off for a sweet, seductive night of tantalizing tasting."

She clicked the remote and turned off the camera. Eyeing the fresh daisies she'd brought home from her flower shop, she leaned her forearms on the counter, and with a heavy sigh, she let her head fall forward. It was after midnight, and she had to be up bright and early to open the shop. Tomorrow night she'd edit the webcast so it would be ready in time to air the following night—*and* she needed to get her oven fixed.

Damn thing.

Kicking off her heels, Lizzie went upstairs, stripped out of the apron, and wrapped a thick towel around herself. A warm shower was just what she needed to wash away the film of shame left on her skin after taping the webcast. Thinking of the broken oven, she texted her friend Blue Ryder to see if he could fix it. Blue was a highly sought after craftsman who worked for the Kennedys and other prominent families around the Cape. When Lizzie's pipe had burst under the sink in the bathroom above the first-floor kitchen while she was away at a floral convention for the weekend, Blue was only too happy to put aside time to handle the renovations. He was like that. Always making time to help others. He was still splitting his time between working on her kitchen renovations and working on the cottage he'd just purchased. He was working at his cottage tomorrow, but she hoped he could fit her in at some point.

Can you fix my oven tomorrow?

Blue texted back a few seconds later. He was as reliable as he was hot, a dangerous combination. She read his text—*Is that code for something sexy?*—and shook her head with a laugh.

Smirking, she replied, *Only if you're into oven grease.*

Blue had asked her out many times since they'd met last year, when she'd handled the flowers for his friends' quadruple beach wedding. Turning down his invitations wasn't easy and had led to more sexy fantasies than she cared to admit. Her double life was crazy enough without adding a sexy, rugged man who was built like Magic Mike and had eyes that could hypnotize a blind woman, but her reasons went far deeper than that. Blue was more than eye candy. He was also a genuine friend, and he always put family and friends first, which, when added to his panty-dropping good looks and gentlemanly demeanor, were enough to stop Lizzie's brain from functioning. It would be too easy to fall hard for a caring, loyal man like Blue Ryder. And *that*, she couldn't afford. Maddy was counting on her.

She read his text—*Glad you finally came to your senses. When are you free?*—and wondered if he thought *she* was being flirtatious.

Time to nip this in the bud, she thought. Her finger hovered over the screen while her mind toyed with images of Blue, six foot three, all hot, hard muscles and steel-blue eyes.

It had been way too long since she'd been with a man, and every time Blue asked her out, she was tempted, but she liked him so much as a friend, and she knew that tipping over from friendship to lovers would only draw her further in to him, making it harder to lead her double life.

That was precisely why she hightailed it out of her house on the mornings before he showed up to work on her kitchen. Leaving before he arrived was the only way she was able to keep her distance. He was *that* good-looking. *That* kind. And *that* enjoyable to be around. Not only didn't she have time for a relationship, but she was pretty sure that no guy would approve of his girlfriend doing the *Naked Baker* show. Of course, the mornings after taping her shows, she left him a sweet treat on the counter with a note thanking him for working on her kitchen.

Even though Blue couldn't see her as she drew back her shoulders and put on her most solemn face, she did it anyway to strengthen her resolve as she typed a text that she hoped would very gently set him straight. *After work, but this is REALLY to fix my oven. The one I cook with! Thank you! See you around seven?*

She set the phone down and stepped into the shower, determined not to think about his blue eyes or the way his biceps flexed every time he moved his arms. Her mind drifted to when she'd arrived home from work yesterday and found Blue bending over his toolbox, his jeans stretched tight across his hamstrings and formed to his perfect ass. Her nipples hardened with the thought. He'd been the man she'd conjured up in her late-night fantasies since last summer. What did it hurt? He'd never know. She closed her eyes and ran her hand over her breasts, down her taut stomach, and between her legs. She may not have time to date, but a little midnight fantasy could go a long way...

To continue reading, please buy <u>SEIZED BY LOVE</u>

Please enjoy a sneak peek at the first
Seaside Summers novel, SEASIDE DREAMS
(Bella & Caden)

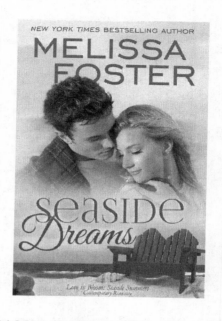

BELLA ABBASCIA STRUGGLED to keep her grip on a ceramic toilet as she crossed the gravel road in Seaside, the community where she spent her summers. It was one o'clock in the morning, and Bella had a prank in store for Theresa Ottoline, a straitlaced Seaside resident and the elected property manager for the community. Bella and two of her besties, Amy Maples and Jenna Ward, had polished off two bottles of Middle Sister wine while they waited for the other cottage owners to turn in for the night. Now, dressed in their nighties and a bit tipsy, they struggled to keep their grip on a toilet that Bella had spent two days painting bright blue, planting flowers in, and adorning with seashells. They were carrying the toilet to

Theresa's driveway to break rule number fourteen of the Community Homeowners Association's Guidelines: *No tacky displays allowed in the front of the cottages.*

"You're sure she's asleep?" Bella asked as they came to the grass in front of the cottage of their fourth bestie, Leanna Bray.

"Yes. She turned off her lights at eleven. We should have hidden it someplace other than my backyard. It's so far. Can we stop for a minute? This sucker is heavy." Amy drew her thinly manicured brows together.

"Oh, come on. Really? We only have a little ways to go." Bella nodded toward Theresa's driveway, which was across the road from her cottage, about a hundred feet away.

Amy glanced at Jenna for support. Jenna nodded, and the two lowered their end to the ground, causing Bella to nearly drop hers.

"That's so much better." Jenna tucked her stick-straight brown hair behind her ear and shook her arms out to her sides. "Not all of us lift weights for breakfast."

"Oh, please. The most exercise I get during the summer is lifting a bottle of wine," Bella said. "Carrying around those boobs of yours is more of a workout."

Jenna was just under five feet tall with breasts the size of bowling balls and a tiny waist. She could have been the model for the modern-day Barbie doll, while Bella's figure was more typical for an almost thirty-year-old woman. Although she was tall, strong, and relatively lean, she refused to give up her comfort foods, which left her a little soft in places, with a figure similar to Julia Roberts or Jennifer Lawrence.

"I don't carry them with my arms." Jenna looked down at her chest and cupped a breast in each hand. "But yeah, that would be great exercise."

Amy rolled her eyes. Pin-thin and nearly flat chested, Amy was the most modest of the group, and in her long T-shirt and underwear, she looked like a teenager next to curvy Jenna. "We only need a sec, Bella."

They turned at the sound of a passionate moan coming from Leanna's cottage.

"She forgot to close the window again," Jenna whispered as she tiptoed around the side of Leanna's cottage. "Typical Leanna. I'm just going to close it."

Leanna had fallen in love with bestselling author Kurt Remington the previous summer, and although they had a house on the bay, they often stayed in the two-bedroom cottage so Leanna could enjoy her summer friends. The Seaside cottages in Wellfleet, Massachusetts, had been in the girls' families for years, and they had spent summers together since they were kids.

"Wait, Jenna. Let's get the toilet to Theresa's first." Bella placed her hands on her hips so they knew she meant business. Jenna stopped before she reached for the window, and Bella realized it would have been a futile effort anyway. Jenna would need a stepstool to pull that window down.

"Oh...Kurt." Leanna's voice split the night air.

Amy covered her mouth to stifle a laugh. "Fine, but let's hurry. Poor Leanna will be mortified to find out she left the window open again."

"I'm the last one who wants to hear her having

sex. I'm done with men, or at least with commitments, until my life is back on track." Ever since last summer, when Leanna had met Kurt, started her own jam-making business, and moved to the Cape full-time, Bella had been thinking of making a change of her own. Leanna's success had inspired her to finally go for it. Well, that and the fact that she'd made the mistake of dating a fellow teacher, Jay Cook. It had been months since they broke up, but they'd taught at the same Connecticut high school, and until she left for the summer, she couldn't avoid running in to him on a daily basis. It was just the nudge she needed to take the plunge and finally quit her job and start over. *New job, new life, new location.* She just hadn't told her friends yet. She'd thought she would tell them the minute she arrived at Seaside and they were all together, maybe over a bottle of wine or on the beach. But Leanna had been spending a lot of time with Kurt, and every time it was just the four of them, she hadn't been ready to come clean. She knew they'd worry and ask questions, and she wanted to have some of the transition sorted out before answering them.

"Bella, you can't give up on men. Jay was just a jerk." Amy touched her arm.

She really needed to fill them in on the whole Jay and quitting her job thing. She was beyond over Jay, but they knew Bella to be the stable one of the group, and learning of her sudden change was a conversation that needed to be handled when they weren't wrestling a fifty-pound toilet.

"Fine. You're right. But I'm going to make all of my future decisions separate from any man. So...until my life is in order, no commitments for me."

"Not me. I'd give anything to have what Kurt and Leanna have," Amy said.

Bella lifted her end of the toilet easily as Jenna and Amy struggled to lift theirs. "Got it?"

"Yeah. Go quick. This damn thing is heavy," Jenna said as they shuffled along the grass.

"More..." Leanna pleaded.

Amy stumbled and lost her grip. The toilet dropped to the ground, and Jenna yelped.

"Shh. You're going to wake up the whole complex!" Bella stalked over to them.

"Oh, Kurt!" Jenna rocked her hips. "More, baby, more!"

"Really?" Bella tried to keep a straight face, but when Leanna cried out again, she doubled over with laughter.

Amy, always the voice of reason, whispered, "Come on. We *need* to close her window."

"Yes!" Leanna cried.

They fell against one another in a fit of laughter, stumbling beside Leanna's cottage.

"I could make popcorn," Jenna said, struggling to keep a straight face.

Amy scowled at her. "She got pissed the last time you did that." She grabbed Bella's hand and whispered through gritted teeth, "Take out the screen so you can shut the window, please."

"I told you we should have put a lock on the outside of her window," Jenna reminded them. Last summer, when Leanna and Kurt had first begun dating, they'd often forgotten to close the window. To save Leanna embarrassment, Jenna had offered to be on sex-noise mission control and close the window if

Leanna ever forgot to. A few drinks later, she'd mistakenly abandoned the idea for the summer.

"While you close the window, I'll get the sign for the toilet." Amy hurried back toward Bella's deck in her boy-shorts underwear and a T-shirt.

Bella tossed the screen to the side so she could reach inside and close the window. The side of Leanna's cottage was on a slight incline, and although Bella was tall, she needed to stand on her tiptoes to get a good grip on the window. The hem of the nightie caught on her underwear, exposing her ample derriere.

"Cute satin skivvies." Jenna reached out to tug Bella's shirt down and Bella swatted her.

Bella pushed as hard as she could on the top of the window, trying to ignore the sensuous moans and the creaking of bedsprings coming from inside the cottage.

"The darn thing's stuck," she whispered.

Jenna moved beside her and reached for the window. Her fingertips barely grazed the bottom edge.

Amy ran toward them, waving a long stick with a paper sign taped to the top that read, WELCOME BACK.

Leanna moaned, and Jenna laughed and lost her footing. Bella reached for her, and the window slammed shut, catching Bella's hair. Leanna's dog, Pepper, barked, sending Amy and Jenna into more fits of laughter.

With her hair caught in the window and her head plastered to the sill, Bella put a finger to her lips. "Shh!"

Headlights flashed across Leanna's cottage as a car turned up the gravel road.

"Shit!" Bella went up on her toes, struggled to lift

the window and free her hair, which felt like it was being ripped from her skull. The curtains flew open and Leanna peered through the glass. Bella lifted a hand and waved. *Crap.* She heard Leanna's front door open, and Pepper bolted around the corner, barking a blue streak and knocking Jenna to the ground just as a police car rolled up next to them and shined a spotlight on Bella's ass.

***

CADEN GRANT HAD been with the Wellfleet Police Department for only three months, having moved after his partner of nine years was killed in the line of duty. He'd relocated to the small town with his teenage son, Evan, in hopes of working in a safer location. So far, he'd found the people of Wellfleet to be respectful and thankful for the efforts of the local law enforcement officers, a welcome change after dealing with rebellion on every corner in Boston. Wellfleet had recently experienced a rash of small thefts—cars being broken into, cottages being ransacked, and the police had begun patrolling the private communities along Route 6, communities that in the past had taken care of their own security. Caden rolled up the gravel road in the Seaside community and spotted a dog running circles around a person rolling on the ground.

He flicked on the spotlight as he rolled to a stop. *Holy Christ. What is going on?* He quickly assessed the situation. A blond woman was banging on a window with both hands. Her shirt was bunched at her waist, and a pair of black satin panties barely covered the most magnificent ass he'd seen in a long time.

"Open the effing window!" she hollered.

Caden stepped from the car. "What's going on here?" He walked around the dark-haired woman, who was rolling from side to side on the ground while laughing hysterically, and the fluffy white dog, who was barking as though his life depended on it, and he quickly realized that the blond woman's hair was caught in the window. Behind him another blonde crouched on the ground, laughing so hard she kept snorting. *Why the hell aren't any of you wearing pants?*

"Leanna! I'm stuck!" the blonde by the window yelled.

"Officer, we're sorry." The blonde behind him rose to her feet, tugging her shirt down to cover her underwear; then she covered her mouth with her hand as more laughter escaped. The dog barked and clawed at Caden's shoes.

"Someone want to tell me what's going on here?" Caden didn't even want to try to guess.

"We're..." The brunette laughed again as she rose to her knees and tried to straighten her camisole, which barely contained her enormous breasts. She ran her eyes down Caden's body. "Well, *hello* there, handsome." She fell backward, laughing again.

Christ. Just what he needed, three drunk women.

The brunette inside the cottage lifted the window, freeing the blonde's hair, which sent her stumbling backward and crashing into his chest. There was no ignoring the feel of her seductive curves beneath the thin layer of fabric. Her hair was a thick, tangled mess. She looked up at him with eyes the color of rich cocoa and lips sweet enough to taste. The air around them pulsed with heat. Christ, she was beautiful.

"Whoa. You okay?" he asked. He told his arms to let her go, but there was a disconnect, and his hands remained stuck to her waist.

"It's...It's not what it looks like." She dropped her eyes to her hands, clutching his forearms, and she released him fast, as if she'd been burned. She took a step back and helped the brunette to her feet. "We were..."

"They were trying to close our window, Officer." A tall, dark-haired man came around the side of the cottage, wearing a pair of jeans and no shirt. "Kurt Remington." He held a hand out in greeting and shook his head at the women, now holding on to each other, giggling and whispering.

"Officer Caden Grant." He shook Kurt's hand. "We've had some trouble with break-ins lately. Do you know these women?" His eyes swept over the tall blonde. He followed the curve of her thighs to where they disappeared beneath her nightshirt, then drifted up to her full breasts, finally coming to rest on her beautiful dark eyes. It had been a damn long time since he'd been this attracted to a woman.

"Of course he knows us." The hot blonde stepped forward, arms crossed, eyes no longer wide and warm, but narrow and angry.

He hated men who leered at women, but he was powerless to refrain from drinking her in for one last second. The other two women were lovely in their own right, but they didn't compare to the tall blonde with fire in her eyes and a body made for loving.

Kurt nodded. "Yes, Officer. We know them."

"God, you guys. What the heck?" the dark-haired

woman asked through the open window.

"You were waking the dead," the tall blonde answered.

"Oh, gosh. I'm sorry, Officer," the brunette said through the window. Her cheeks flushed, and she slipped back inside and closed the window.

"I assure you, everything is okay here." Kurt glared at the hot blonde.

"Okay, well, if you see any suspicious activity, we're only a phone call away." He took a step toward his car.

The tall blonde hurried into his path. "Did someone from Seaside call the police?"

"No. I was just patrolling the area."

She held his gaze. "Just patrolling the area? No one *patrols* Seaside."

"Bella," the other blonde hissed.

Bella.

"Seriously. No one patrols our community. They never have." She lifted her chin in a way that he assumed was meant as a challenge, but it had the opposite effect. She looked cuter than hell.

Caden stepped closer and tried to keep a straight face. "Your name is Bella?"

"Maybe."

Feisty, too. He liked that. "Well, Maybe Bella, you're right. We haven't patrolled your community in the past, but things have changed. We'll be patrolling more often to keep you safe until we catch the people who have been burglarizing the area." He leaned in close and whispered, "But you might consider wearing pants for your window-closing evening strolls. Never know who's traipsing around out here."

370

—End of Sneak Peek—

To continue reading, BUY: SEASIDE DREAMS
(Seaside Summers, Book One)

Sign up for Melissa's Newsletter to be notified of her next release!
http://www.MelissaFoster/Newsletter

COMPLETE BOOK LIST

LOVE IN BLOOM SERIES
Characters from each family appear in future series.

SNOW SISTERS
Sisters in Love
Sisters in Bloom
Sisters in White

THE BRADENS
Lovers at Heart
Destined for Love
Friendship on Fire
Sea of Love
Bursting with Love
Hearts at Play
Taken by Love
Fated for Love
Romancing my Love
Flirting with Love
Dreaming of Love
Crashing into Love
Healed by Love
(MORE COMING SOON)

THE REMINGTONS
Game of Love
Stroke of Love
Flames of Love
Slope of Love
Read, Write, Love

SEASIDE SUMMERS
Seaside Dreams
Seaside Hearts
Seaside Sunsets
Seaside Secrets
Seaside Nights
(MORE COMING SOON)

HARBORSIDE NIGHTS SERIES
New Adult Romance, includes characters from the Love in Bloom series
Catching Cassidy
Discovering Delilah
(MORE COMING SOON)

LOVE ON ROCKWELL ISLAND
Cape Cod Kisses

Stand Alone Novels by Melissa

Chasing Amanda (mystery/suspense)
Come Back to Me (mystery/suspense)
Have No Shame (historical fiction/romance)
Love, Lies & Mystery (3-book bundle)
Megan's Way (literary fiction)
Traces of Kara (psychological thriller)
Where Petals Fall (suspense)

Moon-Shine Jelly Recipe

1 apple
1 cup water
1/3 cup powdered pectin
1 bottle of your favorite chardonnay
1 cup brown sugar
1/2 teaspoon cinnamon
1/4 teaspoon nutmeg
5 cups sugar

Cut up the apple and then chop in a blender until fine; then, in a large saucepan, combine water with pectin and bring to a boil, stirring slowly. Add the chopped apple and chardonnay and bring to a boil. Continue to stir the mixture so it doesn't burn. Add brown sugar and nutmeg, stirring slowly as you add these ingredients. Bring the mixture back to a boil and slowly stir in the sugar. Return to a boil for one minute. Remove from heat and skim off any foam from the top.

Makes between 7 and 8 eight-ounce mason jars

Acknowledgments

When I write, I'm inspired by family, friends, fans, and life in general. I'd like to thank my loyal supporters who follow me on social media and take time to email me and share my work with your friends. You inspire me on a daily basis.

If you follow me on Facebook, then you probably know how much I love writing about the Cape, and that makes writing about the Seaside gang all the more fun. You probably also know that I often turn to fans to help me come up with names of characters, shops, and even streets. I've also been known to create a story line or two based on fans, which is always incredibly fun. I'd like to thank each and every one of you, because while I might not choose your suggestion today, you never know what tomorrow will hold. I hope you continue to enjoy our fun chats, sexy photos, and quirky comments.

A special thank you goes to Nina Lane for our brainstorming sessions. I truly appreciate our hero-making chats.

I'd like to thank my editorial team for their meticulous attention to detail and patience. My work shines because they care. Kristen, Penina, Jenna, Juliette, Marlene, and Lynn, thank you for all you do for me and our readers.

As always, major gratitude goes to my own true-life hunky hero, Les, and my children, who are my fans, my friends, and often, my biggest cheerleaders. Thank you, guys. I couldn't create such wonderful worlds without your support.

Melissa Foster is a *New York Times* and *USA Today* bestselling and award-winning author. Her books have been recommended by *USA Today's* book blog, *Hagerstown* magazine, *The Patriot*, and several other print venues. She is the founder of the World Literary Café, and when she's not writing, Melissa helps authors navigate the publishing industry through her author training programs on Fostering Success. Melissa also hosts Aspiring Authors contests for children and has painted and donated several murals to the Hospital for Sick Children in Washington, DC.

Visit Melissa on her website or chat with her on social media. Melissa enjoys discussing her books with book clubs and reader groups and welcomes an invitation to your event.

Melissa's books are available through most online retailers in paperback and digital formats.

Made in the USA
Lexington, KY
03 February 2019